CERTAIN
LIBERTIES

CERTAIN LIBERTIES

A Novel

Sidney S. Stark

New York

AUTHOR'S NOTE

This book is inspired by actual events. While the main characters and plots are all fictitious, some of the secondary characters and subplots are not. It is, therefore, a true composition of historical fiction.

Certain Liberties
Copyright © 2019 by Sidney S. Stark

Published in the United States by Momentum Ink Press, New York.

PUBLISHER'S CATALOGING IN PUBLICATION DATA
Names: Stark, Sidney S., author.
Title: Certain liberties / Sidney S. Stark.
Identifiers: ISBN 978-0-9975239-3-5 (hardcover) |
ISBN 978-0-9975239-5-9 (paperback) | ISBN 978-0-9975239-4-2 (ebook)
Subjects: LCSH: Women musicians—Fiction. | Women—Social conditions—Fiction. | Underground Railroad—Fiction. | Slavery—United States—Fiction. | Nineteenth century—Fiction. | BISAC: FICTION / Historical / General. | FICTION / Women. | GSAFD: Historical fiction.
Classification: LCC PS3619.T3739 C47 2019 (print) | LCC PS3619.T3739 (ebook) | DDC 813/.6—dc23.
814'.6   QBI16-600081

https://theunblockedwriter.com
https://momentuminkpress.com

For information about special discounts available for bulk purchases, sales promotions, fund-raising, and educational needs, contact the author at sidney.s.stark@gmail.com

Book design by KSH Creative | https://kshcreative.com

For the Writers' Table

...then, now, and tomorrow

PRAISE FOR *CERTAIN LIBERTIES*

"In this historical novel set in the 19th century, a young woman of uncommon musical talent longs for the freedom that's typically reserved for men ... The author masterfully sets the historical stage—the United States as it devolves into the Civil War—and she addresses the issue of slavery with nuance and rigor ... a riveting storyline. Emily is a delightfully complex mix of defiance and prudence, as she learns early in life that "there's a very narrow line to negotiate between freedom and responsibility for women." ... Stark's prose is reliably lucid and consistently faithful to the setting ... An emotionally affecting and historically edifying tale." — ***Kirkus Reviews***

"As much a quick-paced mystery as social commentary, Stark's novel captures and keeps the reader's attention through memorable characters in historically well-researched settings, and adds her protagonist, Emily Alden, to a list of nineteenth-century literary heroines like Elizabeth Bennet and Isabel Archer."

— **Denise B. Dailey**, Author of *Listening to Pakistan*, *Riko: Seductions of an Artist*, and *Leaving Guanabara*.

"With a wealth of historical detail woven into an intriguing plot, Sidney Stark has written a wonderful novel ... with a roster of lively characters headed by Emily Alden, a young female musician fighting for many freedoms denied to women of her time, including the right to perform in public. It's a wonderful read ... not to be missed."

— **Jia Kim**, Cellist, and Artistic Director of the Central Chamber Music Series and Stowe Chamber Music Society. https://jiakimcello.com

"*Certain Liberties* is an emotional thriller ... a page-turner coming-of-age adventure and romance ... wrapped up in the social and historical context of nineteenth-century New York ... the mosaic blend of characters reach out to the reader and reveal inventive resilience to overcome weights and challenges of life ... Emily, Corey, and their sphere of family and friends remain memorable and inspiring ... The thematic melodies strike a responsive chord ... !"

— **Paul Pitcoff, JD, Professor Emeritus, Adelphi University**, Author of *Beyond the Foster Care System* and his forthcoming memoir.

TABLE OF CONTENTS

BOOK ONE

The Children

CHAPTER ONE

ROBERT HAUSSMANN slowed his stride as the imposing French Renaissance building came into view. The quarter-mile walk from his rented apartment in Yorkville to the de Koningh mansion on upper Fifth Avenue was usually a pleasant way to experience spring's overtures. But this day, anxiety about his expenses robbed him of appreciation for the natural beauty around him. He truly had no need for an apartment with four rooms. One hundred dollars was an outrageous sum of money to part with each month, and as he was still single, the extra space seemed redundant.

A musician's earnings didn't go far, and he wondered if he'd have to sell his grandfather's beautiful Guarneri violin to cover a year's rent in advance. Worry was taking much of the pleasure from a profession he loved. Robert knew arriving on foot might be attributed to his lack of funds for a hansom cab, but he was still a vigorous young man in his twenties. If Alexander Hamilton's ancient widow could arrive at dinner parties on foot, climbing over hill and dale for the pleasure of it, he hoped he could walk the short distance to his best pupil's lessons for whatever reason he chose without public censure.

Pausing at Ninety-Second Street, his spirits rose as his musician's ear picked up the harmonies of birdsong coming from the woods across the avenue. New York was beautiful in spring, and the de

Koningh mansion, modeled after the late Gothic Hôtel de Cluny in Paris, was one of his favorite buildings. It nourished his foreign sensibilities in ways he'd hungered for since coming from Vienna ten years ago. He'd told people he was escaping the loneliness of a home with no mother, but in truth, the exhausting European wars springing up like poisonous mushrooms every season of his life had repelled him. Now, piano lessons for the twelve-year-old Corey de Koningh were a weekly pleasure he'd looked forward to over the last two of those years. The boy had a good nature, if a bit rowdy at times, but he was more than competent at the keyboard. Robert had taught much worse. And it was a joy to play music in the de Koninghs' graceful, sunny home on a modern pianoforte, instead of the dilapidated Chickering upright that came with the rental of his narrow, dark town house.

Arriving at the front portico of the de Koningh mansion on Ninety-Fourth Street at precisely ten, as always, he was greeted at the door by the footman and ushered into the front hall. After parting with his hat and gloves at the footman's request, Robert walked through the marble foyer and down the hall to the library, where he stopped, straightening his waistcoat and savoring the room in expectation. He knew the room's oak paneling glowed in the morning light and added to the depth and weight of the library's importance. Along the opposite wall, three large French doors arched toward the garden outside. They framed daylight from the southwest, and a graceful limestone staircase to a lower terrace could be seen inviting those inside to the outside. Pink buds were poised to burst on bushes clustered around the steps, and Bradford pear trees exploded with white puffs along the perimeter outlined by an ornamental wrought-iron gate. Was he not lucky to have such a place to visit each week?

This time, however, Robert was surprised to find the door to the library nearly shut, and the change in routine put him on guard. The massive oak portal didn't invite a gentle tap, so he pushed it open just as his young student came barreling through at full speed, almost knocking Robert over. Instinctively, the music teacher grabbed for the back of the child's jacket, causing Corey de Koningh to lose his footing. Robert held on to be sure his pupil regained his balance, as well as to prevent him from escaping. Something about the boy's demeanor suggested he'd been up to no good, and Robert Haussmann considered it his responsibility to discover what it was.

"Where do you think you're going in such a hurry, Master de Koningh?" he asked. Holding fast to the back of the boy's collar, he noted it was rather a nice weave for a child of twelve, evidence of the rage for silk since the Americans had opened their own Chinese trade routes. Britain's restriction of goods from Asia to the colonies had obviously increased the appetite for them, highlighted by the horrors of the Americans' Revolutionary War. He wondered if the child's father's cotton export to China had secured the goods his family now displayed so comfortably on their own backs. Regaining his footing with arms spinning like a pinwheel and jacket flapping, the boy couldn't hide some papers gripped in his right hand. "And what have you there?" Robert asked.

"It's music . . . just a . . . a score, that's all," the boy stammered, presumably breathless from the surprise of his discovery and the suddenness of capture. He tossed back his long, blond forelock to meet his teacher's eyes, and gave Robert Haussmann not a rude or challenging gaze, but more one of well-bred confidence.

"Are you not going in the wrong direction then, Master de Koningh? I believe music is played on the instrument in the music room, as there are no other pianos in the house." Robert watched his young pupil smooth and button his jacket, running his free hand through his unruly locks to tame them behind his ears. He made no attempt to hide the score any longer.

"It's not for playing, Professor," Corey said.

"What then?" his teacher asked.

"Reading," Corey answered, without further comment.

"Reading! With no piano to work on? Have you reached that level of expertise?" Robert Haussmann was beginning to sense a much bigger story lurking behind his young charge's attempted theft, so he put his hand back on the boy's shoulder and spun him around to face the music room door. "Let's discuss this further, in private," he said, with a gentle, consistent pressure on Corey's shoulder moving him into the library. Robert closed the door behind them both, turning toward the boy again and eyeing him with curiosity. "Now, Master de Koningh, please start from the beginning."

"It's not for me, Professor; it's for our new houseguest." Robert Haussmann's red eyebrows drew together, but he said nothing. "I found her looking over the music on those shelves the first day she came. She asked if she could borrow some, just to read . . . but I think she wants to take lessons, too." Corey finally paused for breath, and Robert seized the opportunity.

"Houseguest? I had no idea . . . Who is she?" Realizing he was probably in for one of the child's long-winded accounts, Robert put his hand on the boy's shoulder to delay the onslaught. "Wait, Master de Koningh," he ordered, with a small sigh. "Let's go sit at the piano and you can tell me all about this new houseguest. I only hope we'll have time for your music lesson, as well."

Together they moved to the shiny black piano, and Corey slid easily onto the bench as Robert moved to a chair on the left side. It was equally convenient for page turners as for teachers, and so had been left permanently in position. "Now, young man, let's go back a bit. Who is this houseguest and where did she come from?"

"Her name is Emily Alden, Professor, and she came from England last week!" The boy's flare for drama flashed in his intense blue eyes, and Robert Haussmann braced himself for more to come. Accustomed though he was to the emotions of his students, he realized his young pupil was vibrating with a level of excitement he never displayed for his music lessons. "Our fathers are friends. Hers is an English lord sent here by Prince Albert to find out about American slavery, I think. He travels a great deal." Corey paused, possibly to see if the reference to Queen Victoria's consort had secured special interest.

Robert was intrigued, but tried not to show it. He didn't share Corey's enthusiasm for having the new houseguest invade their piano lessons, although it might mean more money, which would certainly be most welcome. "Your father never mentioned teaching two children, Master de Koningh," he said. "Is she family? How old is she? Your father said I was being retained to teach the family, quite specifically."

"No, not exactly family. But Emily's mother died last year," Corey burst out, "and her father told mine he was uncomfortable leaving her alone with servants in their big house in England when he came to America. He thought she needed young people around. She's only six months older than me, so she's thirteen now." He looked sideways at Robert. "It's almost as if she's an orphan with no mother, and her father away from home so much."

Robert shifted uncomfortably in his chair. He thought for a moment and then raised one eyebrow. "What does this sad story have to do with music lessons? Does the Lady Emily have any musical ability, Master de Koningh?" Corey hopped up from the piano bench as if he'd been stung, and Robert could tell the chances of getting his young pupil to focus on his own lessons were diminishing with each twist and turn of the houseguest's saga.

Corey ran over to the shelves lined with sheet music. "She's already halfway through these," he cried. "Why, Professor Haussmann, she reads music in bed at night the way most people read stories before they go to sleep!" He started to bounce with excitement.

"Stop hopping, Master de Koningh. You look like a rabbit with nowhere to go," Robert said, not unkindly. "Does she play the piano?"

"Yes, but she wants to play the violin, and they won't let her. They say it's not nice for a lady to stand in public and raise her arms to play an instrument . . ."

"Quite right," Robert nodded, "the music critics would all agree, and it's such a masculine instrument at that. Why would she want to play a violin? Where did she get it?" he asked, clearly intrigued with the surprising direction the conversation had taken.

"She doesn't have one," Corey said, shaking his prodigious head of blond hair, "but you have a violin, Professor, and you could teach her." Corey was so excited now he was sucking in on his lower lip, a habit he'd had from early childhood. Robert didn't draw attention to it, although he was arguably responsible for the boy's manners when they were together for his music lessons.

"Indeed." The professor tugged on the middle of his red beard. A small smile lifted his mouth and spread to his eyes. "Vivaldi dealt with that problem by putting his all-female string orchestra behind a tall screen. That way the audience wasn't subjected to the outrageous spectacle of women playing violins." He chuckled to himself. It was his opinion that women were too easy on the eyes and therefore a distraction from the music, and that was something to be avoided in performance. The sound always had to come first. But he knew those thoughts put him somewhere uncomfortably caught between the cultural and musical norms of the day.

"Believe me, Professor," Corey cried, "Emily is not a girl you put behind a screen. Her mother's choice of a name suits her. It means 'striving.' She told me it's from the Roman 'Aemilius.' Her mother gave it to her because she wanted her to be courageous and strong. Emily won't be governed by old-fashioned notions, and she needs help to follow her musical passion; she needs you, and your violin."

The silence that followed must have been almost unbearable for the boy. He was stretching each finger on his right hand as if preparing to play, but more likely to count in his head so he wouldn't blurt out something he'd be sorry for later. Robert Haussmann cleared his throat.

"Why don't we have her in and I'll interview her," he said, sighing as if relieved of a great weight. "I suppose your father would pay for an extra student, but I promise nothing. Do you understand? Nothing, except my willingness to talk with her. If I judge her to be acceptable, we'll see about the rest. For now, Master de Koningh, that will have to do. And by the way, I'm surprised that her mother chose that name."

"She just liked what it stood for, Emily says. It wasn't in the family before her. Isn't it wonderful not to carry around the names of a lot of dead people you never knew, the way I do? Adriaan Hindrick Klaas van Cortlandt de Koningh, the Third, doesn't say anything about who I am, just who many of my relatives were."

Robert stared at his young student, tapping the bench to indicate it was time to sit down again for his lesson. "Perhaps," Robert said, opening one of the scores on the music rack and smoothing it flat. "But most people have names connecting them to their family's past. Now please, Master de Koningh, it's time for us to get back to Clara Schumann." He nodded toward the music, imagining the larger-than-life female pianist who composed it. "I fear your houseguest's name will be difficult to live up to," he added.

"Not for her, Professor Haussmann. You'll see when you meet her." He flashed a dazzling smile that lit up his blue eyes and made them dance, leaving Robert with the feeling that the boy knew something he did not, and that he was greatly enjoying whatever it was.

"Yes, I'm sure we'll see," Robert muttered under his breath.

CHAPTER TWO

COREY BOUNDED up the marble stairs to the second-floor bedrooms two at a time with the score he'd pulled for Emily in his hand. Skipping steps was easy, even for his skinny little legs, as the risers were shallow, but the stretch still made him feel big and capable. Professor Haussmann's possible capitulation about shared music lessons gave him the extra spring he needed to reach the top landing without a pause, and he would have, had he not suddenly realized he wasn't alone and stopped short partway up.

"Jesus, Mary, and Joseph!" the young Irish parlor maid swore as she came down from the second floor. Her language surprised him, as well as the fact that she didn't care if anyone heard her. A small gold cross bounced on her chest as a silver tray supporting a plate of untouched scones and a full cup of tea rattled precariously with every step she took. Her black uniform with white apron matching her white cap perched on her short black hair gave her the appearance of a chickadee, enhanced by her quick, darting steps. She paid no attention to him, and Corey made a wide detour around her as they passed so he wouldn't be responsible for causing an accident he'd most assuredly, and possibly rightly, be blamed for.

"What's wrong, Mary?" he finally asked, stopping a few safe steps above her. "Can I help? My music lesson's over now and I have some free time."

"It's that poor girl in the guest room. Guest!" Mary huffed as though there could be no greater fiction. "It's a crime! Them heavy curtains is pulled shut, and she's all alone, poor little thing. Is that treating a guest right? A crime, I say."

"Didn't she want her tea?" Corey asked, eyeing the scones and jam artfully arranged on the tray. They made him realize he was hungry, which was often the case after practicing the piano. "Is she sick, Mary?"

"Homesick, I reckon. She didn't eat breakfast, neither." The maid turned to start down the stairs again, but Corey stopped her.

"Wait. Let me try. I'm hungry enough to eat a horse, and maybe if she sees me she'll realize she is, too." Tucking a roll of music up his sleeve so he could use both hands, he went down a step to take the tray from the maid. He was excited about delivering the news of shared music lessons, and recognized that tea, scones, and jam could make a good excuse for barging into her room. Once Emily saw what else he had with him, he was sure he'd have her eating out of his hands, both literally and figuratively. The thought brought him a smile. His plan was taking shape with Professor Haussmann's help, and now there was no time to waste.

"I've got it, Mary," he said, pulling the breakfast toward him a little too forcefully. He'd turned and gone up to the landing with the loaded tray before Mary could object, so she shrugged and moved on down toward the kitchen.

"Too familiar with grown-ups," she muttered. "Those Dutch treat 'em like adults, so no wonder they think they can run the world. Never see that with an Irish lad," she exclaimed, a little louder. "Only Dutch think they're all growed up. Fault of the parents," she added, disappearing out of sight.

Realizing he'd never get the door to the guest room open, and would probably spill the tea and jam on the carpet even if he did, Corey carefully placed the tray down in the hall so he could use both hands. As he pushed the door open slightly and put his head into the room, his soft blond hair curled into his blue eyes and brushed the silk collar of his coat. His delicate features could fool a casual observer into thinking a young girl had come to pay a visit. But the spark in his eyes and swing in his step spoke of a male entitlement to freedom certainly found wanting and inappropriate in a female, and the fine lines of his cheekbones, nose, and lips suggested aristocratic ancestors, rather than femininity. He saw the houseguest lying propped up on a pillow and staring at the ceiling. Arms crossed over each other at her waist, there was no movement to indicate a spark of life. She reminded him of a medieval sarcophagus in eternal contemplation of the heavens. Too quiet.

"Hello," he called, hanging on the edge of the massive door like a monkey wrapped around a tree. "How are you feeling, Lady Emily?" His pretty, upturned mouth lit his face as if he held the loveliest thought in the world and couldn't wait to share it. The girl's head popped up so she could look at him, but nothing else moved. He thought he saw curiosity in her huge, dark eyes, leading him to believe she was not dead yet. Skipping over to her bed, he bowed slightly, assuming it was expected when greeting an English girl. He noted the cream-colored skin of her face was framed with softly curling, sable-brown hair parted in the middle and surrounding her neck with ringlets, each perfectly arranged. "It's me again," Corey announced with a grin. "Adriaan, or Corey, whichever you like."

She looked at him for a moment, and then put her head down on the pillow to continue her ceiling vigil. "Which is it?" she asked.

Feeling challenged in some way, he put out his hand to her, as if being formally introduced. "Adriaan," he answered, surprised to find hers suddenly in his, even though she still hadn't looked at him. "But my friends call me Corey." Turning her head to eye him straight on, the girl started to smile a little, and her big dark eyes, set wide apart over even features and a small round nose, were suddenly bright with humor. He watched her smile deepen, two small dimples tugging at each cheek.

"Then I hope you'll count me as one of those friends," she said, looking at him sideways under her long, dark eyelashes. "Corey de Koningh, the rest of your name's a mouthful." He didn't want to let go of her hand, so he didn't.

"How are you feeling?" he asked. "Not so good, I guess." He eyed the pile of bedcovers around her and the dark curtains pulled shut to keep out the light. His smile faded, dancing blue eyes narrowing under ridges of worry across his forehead. "What's the matter? Are you missing England?" He hated leaving things unsaid, and saw no reason to avoid the subject the parlor maid had introduced.

The girl didn't answer, and looked down at her chest so he couldn't see her eyes. He felt as if the sun was going in behind a cloud, leaving him searching for a way to make it stay out for good; or maybe he could just get rid of the cloud. "No, I'm not missing England," she said, softly, her hand still in his. "Well, maybe. Just a little," she added, slipping a furtive look at him from beneath her lashes again. He suddenly realized she might be uncomfortable being held as she was, so he released her hand, placing it gently on the covers beside her. He was vaguely embarrassed by the intimacy he'd forced and didn't know what to do next.

"I'll bet you miss your father, and of course, your mother too. Or maybe you're over that, since she died a while ago." Again, he thought the touchy subject the de Koningh household had been avoiding needed exposure. From the sudden blank look in her eyes suggesting she'd pulled down a shade to block intrusion, he could tell he'd gone too far. This was no way to banish the cloud.

"Just a minute," he said. "I forgot, I brought you something, or rather some things." He turned and ran back out of the room, returning almost instantly on tiptoe with the tray. Putting it on the table beside her so he could go back to shut the door, he turned to look at her, and saw she'd become a lifeless corpse again in the middle of the massive old carved bed. He glanced around the stuffy room, eyeing the closed draperies. "Lord, it's so still and dark in here." He shook his head in disgust and the blond curls danced. "Would you like me to open the window a little and let in some air?" She nodded. A very small movement of her head up and down, but he saw it.

Running quickly to the heavy fabric covering the balcony doors to the left of her bed, he grabbed one side of the draperies and yanked. It took five tries with both of his small arms, but he finally moved them enough to let in some light and expose the casement door handle. Looking pleased with himself, he turned the scrolled brass knob with both hands and pushed the weighty glass-paned door open, taking a huge breath of fresh spring air at the same time. "Better!" he announced. "But maybe a little too much." He pulled it closed slightly. "Is that enough?" The girl watched his efforts with her head turned sideways on the pillow. She seemed to like his attention, but didn't say anything. "Honestly, the way they treat children you'd think they were trying to get rid of us," Corey muttered aloud. "Someone should have told me you were feeling poorly without my asking."

He lifted his chin, and buttressing his declaration with both hands on his hips, announced in a clear voice, "I won't let them leave you alone anymore now that I know what's going on." The girl looked him up and down. He hoped instead of a small boy, she saw a giant defender. "So, now that we have enough light, I'll show you what I brought." A furtive smile started across Corey's face as he pulled something from inside his jacket. He raised it high for her to see. "Ta-dah!" The book he held over his head looked new and untouched. He'd told her the first day they'd met they weren't allowed to take anything from the library, least of all new books. Even the magazines, illustrated with pictures of men's beaver hats and ladies' high-button shoes, were restricted to adults. Emily said she knew young girls and women weren't allowed to read novels. They'd shaken their heads together in disgust over such restrictions. Reading was, after all, just a means to an end, which was of course, knowledge. Apparently, there was some knowledge adults didn't want children to have.

"For you," he said. "It's for you, and me, too. It's the latest novel by Mr. Dickens! We're going to read it together!" He saw at last that he had her full attention, amazement showing on her face. He skipped across the room to her bed, clearly excited by the prospect of shared contraband. "Shall I hide it behind your pillow so you can get it when you want?" He sucked in a little on his pretty lower lip. "Sorry. Not so good behind the pillow." His eyes darted around the room. "They'll be changing your bed linens again." His eyes locked on hers, which were wide. "Don't worry. The sewing table will do just as well."

He darted over the lush carpet to the sitting area. "No one will find it here." Slipping the stolen book into the table's drum below the notions drawer, he shut it quickly. His eyes sparkled again as he pranced back to her bed. "Did you read the last installment in the *Examiner*?" She nodded slowly and smiled, making him feel as if they'd been sharing secrets a long time.

"And now," he said with a flourish, raising his chin and both arms as if conducting an unseen orchestra, "the best of all!" She watched as he pulled a long piece of paper from his sleeve. Rolled tight like a spyglass, he held it high over his head and grinned, waving his magic wand. She struggled to sit up fully on the soft bed, unable to hide her enthusiasm any longer.

"What . . . ?" she whispered.

"I'll show you. Just have patience," Corey ordered, knowing the power of anticipation. He had her now. Unrolling the score and trying to iron it flat on the bed beside her with the edge of his hand, it still curled up at the ends, but not so she couldn't see what it was: music of some kind. And on the top right-hand corner was printed *Schumann*. She saw it clearly and her big dark eyes widened.

"Robert Schumann," she said, her voice strong and sure. He hadn't heard its full tone since he'd come to her room. It had a resonance that made him wonder what kind of a singer she'd be.

"No, Lady Emily." Corey shook his head and looked like the secret he held would split him wide-open. "It's by Clara Schumann, Robert's wife. I'll bet you've never seen a published score by a woman before." He watched her look closer at the print to be sure he told the truth. "My music teacher, Professor Haussmann, gave it to me for you." He put his hand on her shoulder and squeezed. She looked down at his fingers, and then back up at him with a smile. He wondered if anyone else had touched her since she'd come, other than to brush her hair into ringlets.

"Professor Haussmann told me about Mendelssohn's sister, Fanny." Corey dropped his hand down to hers lying on the covers. It made him feel attached. She couldn't slip away behind the cloud while he was holding her. He squeezed her fingers a little tighter. "Do you realize that's two musical women who perform and publish? I told Professor Haussmann you're the first person I know who reads music like most people read bedtime stories. So, he left this sitting on the music stand and nodded to me when he left the room. He wanted you to have it, I think." Corey opened the drawer in the bedside table, lifting the paper liner to slip the sheet music underneath. "No one will find this here, and you can see it whenever you like." He closed the drawer quietly again and perched on the bed.

"You'll see it's for a piano trio. Clara and Fanny both wrote for the violin, too. I know you prefer the violin. Professor Haussmann doesn't care about women lifting their arms and playing in public. Oh, he knows it's frowned on by society and critics alike, but he doesn't feel that way."

"Why not . . . ?"

"Because it's the music that matters. I know him pretty well, and it's always the music that comes first for him. If only my father and yours felt as he does." Corey shook his head and pursed his lips in exaggerated disgust. "But I'm sure you can have lessons with me. You must show the professor how much it means to you. By the way, how shall I introduce you?" Corey felt it was time he let his guest do some of the talking. "Lady Emily Alden, right? You're the daughter of a lord, after all."

"Not in America," she answered, quickly. "Here I want to be just Emily. My mother named me Emily because she liked the sound of it. I do, too, because she gave it to me, and because it's so musical."

"How so?" Corey asked. He'd never thought of the sound of a name before—just where it came from.

"It has three syllables, so it's well-balanced rhythmically." Corey mouthed the syllables slowly, and nodded. "My mother told me Emilys are creative and courageous, but they can tend to hate authority, so I have to be careful of that." She looked away again. "I miss my mother all the time," she said. "She was so beautiful and strong, and we were friends—not like most mothers and daughters, but real friends." She swallowed hard.

"Did you mind your father bringing you with him to America?" Corey asked, trying desperately to keep the conversation going. He'd noticed how talking about Emily's mother collected storm clouds of huge proportions over and around them both.

"Not really," she answered thoughtfully. "Though I wish he'd asked first. My father and Prince Albert support freedom for every-one," she said, pushing herself halfway up and propping herself on her elbows. "So that's why he teases me, calling me 'Lady Liberty' and why he wanted me to come to America with him, I guess. Soon, I hope no one will know I'm British. I shall work at getting rid of my accent from now on. This will be my new home and family." Her dimples were deepening, and Corey noted a certain lift in himself when she smiled. It was rather nice, but he couldn't fully understand it. "You're Dutch, obviously," she said, still looking at him with her head straight and her eyes firm.

"No, I'm American," he contradicted. "My great-great-great-grand-father was Dutch. And good luck getting rid of your British accent. Anyway, I like it." Her eyes shone with a light that made him want to turn around to look for its source, but he realized it came from her.

"Where did you get all those names no one can say?" she asked. Her eyes narrowed, warning him he'd better make a lot of sense or he'd lose her again.

"Oh, both my parents are Dutch, so between the family up in Albany and the rest here in New York there were too many names needing an heir to put them on. I don't think any of them mean anything, other than that someone now long dead lived on my family tree before me. My mother chose my nickname, though. The Van Cortlandts were her relatives and she took it from there. My father thought it would disappear once I got older so he let her have her way. But it hasn't," he laughed, "disappeared, I mean."

"Koningh means 'king,' doesn't it?" Emily lifted her chin a little, her challenge now clear.

"I don't know. I never thought of it." Corey suddenly realized he hadn't bantered with someone his own age in his own home for a very long time. His cousins from Albany were all older, and besides, they only came overnight or occasionally for a weekend. This girl was going to stay indefinitely, his father had said.

"Well, it does mean 'the king.' And believe me, Corey, that didn't happen by chance. Someone in your family's past was most certainly of royal blood." She nodded for emphasis and her dark ringlets bobbed.

"Then what does Alden mean, if you know so much?"

She shrugged, looking doubtful for the first time. "I never thought of it, either." They both laughed, enjoying the shared joke. "I'm going to be here a while, you know . . ." She looked a little troubled. "So maybe you can find out for me before I leave."

"I shall make it my business to find out what Alden means," he announced, wanting to weight his friendship with a value that might matter to her. How he would do this he had no idea, but his father had connections with businessmen who spoke many languages and he knew he could go to him for advice on researching the name. His books in the library mostly contained maps, and the new novels starting to appear would be very unlikely research possibilities, but he was delighted she seemed pleased about her stay and wanted to be sure he retained her interest.

Her dimples deepened again, but she didn't exactly smile. Whatever she was feeling, he liked the way she looked. It made him feel strong. "I'm really glad you came, Lady Liberty!" Corey jumped back a few feet from the bed. "Would you like to look around the house?" he asked. "I'd be happy to be your guide. I know a lot of secrets about this place." He was pleased to see she moved quickly to push herself off the bed, ringlets bobbing. Her legs were probably longer than his, since her tiny waist was higher, and she maneuvered her long skirts as if she barely knew they were there.

"Are those ringlets of yours real?" He reached out his hand and touched the end of one, pulling it down past her shoulder and then letting it go. It bounced back to its place around her neck.

"Of course not." She didn't try to hide her disgust, but whether it was caused by his question, his handling her hair, or the ringlets themselves, he wasn't sure. "My hair is long and too thick. They have to torture it into these silly things, and I *hate* them." The way she spat out the hate left no room for doubt. She swept the ringlets back with both hands and pushed them up. How lovely she looked with her hair off her neck and piled high on her head. "But of course, straight hair left alone is not permitted at my age." She made a face that reminded him of an angry gargoyle on one of the mansion parapets.

Corey put his head back and laughed. "I'll bet you don't make it easy for them to get you to do what they want. But I'm awfully glad you've come, Lady Liberty." He grinned at her, relishing the mischief he envisioned for them both. He turned to lead her out of the room, noticing at the last minute the silver tray of cold tea and scones. "I'm starving," he announced, "and this has to go! It was my excuse for getting in to see you alone." He picked up the delicate bone china cup, draining its contents, and placed it carefully back on its matching saucer. "Done," he said, grinning at Emily. "Now, the scones. I can't eat both. You'll have to help." He picked one up in each hand and held them out. She touched the one in his right hand. He gave it to her, and they bent their heads close together over the plate so the crumbs would end up on the dish instead of the floor. Giggling, they stuffed the raisin-and-baking-powder muffins into their mouths fast. "Well done!" Corey mumbled, eyeing the empty tray with satisfaction. "Now, Lady Liberty, we're off!"

"Is your father around much?" she asked his back as he turned to go. He stopped, sensing a serious tone had crept in when he least expected it, and turned to look at her. "Mine is always traveling," she said. She sounded matter-of-fact. "It's hard for him to handle a home and his work for the queen," she added. "Now that my mother's gone, he's . . . well, I get in his way. Which isn't my fault!" she finished, angrily. He didn't want to see the darkness cover her face again and started to turn away. "I'm tired of being pushed around as if it doesn't matter what I want." She sounded quite fierce. "So, where's your mother, by the way?" She'd pulled on the back of Corey's coat, so he had to stop and turn to face her again.

"Who knows? Probably in bed. My father travels down south a lot for his textile business and Mother disappears into her room. I read her the morning paper sometimes and take care of her as best I can, but frankly I wish my father would do more of it himself. You may not like always being away from home, but I don't like being left behind. We're a fine pair!" he chuckled. "And now, Miss Emily, shall we go?" He bowed slightly at the waist over his right arm and swept the other out graciously toward the door.

"Lead the way," she said, sparkling with pleasure, full brilliant sunshine all over her face. She looked so different from the gray statue she'd been when he first entered the room. "Corey, I'm glad you came to get me today. I was feeling so bad. Would you be my permanent friend?"

"Most definitely," he answered. "But only if you'll be mine. I don't like one-sided agreements. And no mind-changing, no abandoning allowed." He grinned at her as she stood, clearly poised for whatever he had in store for her. He liked that about her.

She put her hand out. "Shake on it," she said.

"Girls don't shake hands with boys." He was intrigued, nonetheless.

"I do," she said; and so he did.

"No questions, and no talking." He raised his index finger and pressed it against his lips in explicit warning, jerking his head toward her door and turning to go out in a stealthy crouch. She followed, holding her skirts flat against her legs so they wouldn't rustle or hit the furniture. He looked back and nodded approval, and together they tiptoed through the hall toward the stairs leading up to the top of the house. He wondered if she knew that where he was taking her was somewhere neither one of them was meant to go. They climbed two more full flights, and then a strange half-flight to a door under the eaves opening into a large attic.

"Almost there," Corey whispered, steering carefully through boxes and trunks piled at haphazard angles all over the attic floor and up against its walls.

"This is a special room," she said, "but I'm not sure I could stand the mustiness of it for long." She stepped high over a child's upholstered rocking chair with the springs poking out of the seat. "Places like this can be a little sad, too," she added.

Not wanting her to slide back into her earlier dark mood, Corey turned to face her fully and shook his head. "This is not our destination, Lady Liberty. The surprise still awaits us." And with that he grabbed one of her hands, turned around, and pulled her after him. Moving around a dusty old sewing basket with disintegrating handles, Corey stopped at the back wall of the attic. Emily peered past him and saw there was a substantial door with a lock on it. He let go of her hand and reached in the old basket to pull out a brass key hidden inside, inserting it in the lock and turning it easily. Both the lock and key were bright, so he must have used them often.

"Do you come here a lot?" she asked, mesmerized by the smoothness of the opening door on its huge hinges. It seemed too important for an attic closet. Corey pushed it out away from him. Suddenly she felt cooler air and the sweet smell of freshness rushing in from beyond the opening. He walked forward through it, and Emily followed. Stepping over the metal threshold, she took a deep breath. Before her, Corey had stopped to look around, and beyond them lay the roof of the de Koningh mansion leading to the entire cerulean sky and emerald woodlands of New York.

"For the love of angels," she breathed.

"Not at all," Corey laughed. "It's for the love of adventure. This is not something I would share with angels. You are the only recipient of the secret to date. And I expect you'll keep it safe. Angels can't always be trusted."

"Can we go out on the roof?" she asked, eyes shining and breath short with excitement.

"I thought you'd never ask. Follow me!" He started to move out across a well between two dormers. "Do you have soft soles on your shoes?"

She shook her head. "I'll slip," she said, sitting down on the doorsill. He watched as she pulled off her black leather shoes and white stockings. She left them together in a pile and stood up. "Oh, the roof tiles are warm from the sun," she laughed. "They feel wonderful on bare feet." He too sat down and pulled off his buckle shoes and silk knee socks. He grinned up at her, tucking the socks inside the toes of the shoes just as she'd done.

"Okay, Emily, we go together—on equal footing, so to speak." He stood up and took her hand. Together they walked carefully across the roof, threading between gables. "Now," he warned, "comes the real challenge." Leaning in against the slanted roof between ogee-arched windows and angled dormers, Corey worked his way over the slate mansards. When he reached the edge of the roof he stopped and propped his heels into the gutter behind a projection of decorative molding. He lay back against the slanting slate roof, looking like he was lying on a tipped blackboard.

"Come on," he urged. "The tiles feel great and the view . . . well, see for yourself." She inched her way carefully over the roof, taking care to scan the shapes and angles in her path. She reached him and eased herself down to lie beside him. He turned his face sideways on the slate to look at her. She was staring out across the sky.

"Never, ever have I seen such a sight," she breathed. "Why do you come out here?" He could tell she was as impressed as he'd hoped, but she wasn't scared, as he'd feared.

"It makes me feel free . . . and I like doing something the grown-ups don't know about. How does it make you feel?" he asked, giving her a chance to say she was uncomfortable or wanted to go in, if she did. Turning her head next to his, he was shocked when she said, "I love you for bringing me up here, Corey. Thank you." Slowly they turned their faces up again and said nothing for a while, drinking in the spring sweetness.

Then Corey stirred and looked back at her. Feeling her connection still, and thinking it gave him new strength, he asked, "Is it awful without a mother?" Not wanting to push their friendship too fast too soon, he added, "You don't have to tell me if you don't want to."

"Yes," she said, "it is awful. You might not feel the same, but you're a boy. It seems like no one misses her as much as me. My father just keeps working as if nothing's happened. I hate that."

"Oh Emily," Corey sighed. "Don't hate! Adults need all the help they can get. They're always upset about something and they don't really talk about it the way we do. Look at what I have to do for my mother."

"Pretend you're her husband." Emily looked at Corey sideways.

"I take care of her for my father, because he can't," Corey corrected. "He doesn't talk to her much because she's a little silly. She's delicate and breaks easily, like a precious doll."

Emily stared at Corey with her eyes narrowed. "Taking care of your mother should be your father's job, Corey."

"I know that."

"Why doesn't he talk to her?" Emily asked.

"She hasn't got much to say. I think they're not very similar. But how should I know? I'm just grateful he takes care of his textile business so we can live as we do . . ." Corey waved his hand in an arc, taking in the house and possibly everything else.

"My father loved being around my mother when she was alive. Everyone did. We'd be together all the time if she was still here." Corey noticed the hard look coming back over Emily's face.

"Don't look so sad, Lady Liberty," Corey ordered. "You have me now, and we'll be friends forever."

"I think you're wonderfully kind . . . to treat your mother as you do, Corey. It would be different for me with my father. I couldn't spend all that time alone with him. I'm his daughter, not his wife or his nurse."

"It's not that bad. I like being treated like an adult instead of a child." Suddenly Corey whipped his head back toward Emily, exclaiming, "I almost forgot. I have something from the paper for you. I got it this morning when I read to Mother at breakfast, but all that turmoil in the library with Professor Haussmann put it right out of my mind." He pulled a ragged piece of paper out of his pocket.

"On the last page, I found this article, and I quote: 'We publish herewith a notice of . . . Mr. Dickens's first reading at Steinway Hall—the choicest of his own productions will be an event in the life of any man worthy of remembrance, and it would be a tradition for his descendants if the happier fortune of our day did not bring it within the personal experience of more persons than ever read or heard of Sir Walter Scott during his lifetime.' There! What do you say to that?"

"I want to hear about Mr. Dickens's school for unwed mothers in England!" Emily bounced up to a sitting position. "And his hospital for the poor. Mr. Dickens is a man who lives the things he cares about; he doesn't just write about them." Corey nodded agreement so hard his hair fell in his eyes.

"Although," he added, pushing his bangs back, "sometimes I think he should be more careful about what he says. People all over the world read his books and you never know who'll get the wrong ideas. Still, I suppose he doesn't write for them," Corey said. "He writes for himself."

"It's no different in music," Emily murmured. "Don't you remember Mendelssohn wrote that he'd never let other people influence how he composed his music . . . even some pretty girl telling him to do *'thus and thus.'*" They both laughed at her attempt at a German accent, quoting the composer's pronouncement. Then she looked serious again. "Mendelssohn will only compose for himself, as Mr. Dickens writes. His books influence because he believes what he says. Do you see?"

"You don't understand compromise, Emily. That's very British." Corey smiled, remembering her insistence on losing her accent.

"This is so exciting! I never got anywhere near Mr. Dickens when I lived in England; yet I come to America and now I have a chance to see him in person. I'm about to explode—everything's so wonderful!

I only wish it could stay this way forever. I just hate the way bad feelings overcome the good ones at times."

"There's that 'hate' again. Emily, we can't always have things the way we want them, my father says."

"I know. But lately I've felt like a prisoner in my own body." She looked out over the bright green canopy of the forest protecting them and keeping everyone else away. "*Take pity upon a lonely and desolate child,*" she murmured, looking out to the horizon. "Mr. Dickens is becoming my favorite author," she said.

"*Think that he may never have known a mother's love, or the comfort of a home . . . ,*" Corey quoted with her from the hugely popular *Oliver Twist*.

"*. . . that something taught my heart to love so dearly from the first!*" she finished for him. Her voice trailed off as she looked out across the roof of the de Koningh mansion, wondering if life would always be such a mystery, or if those who lived more normally with fully formed families already knew the answers.

CHAPTER THREE

As the weeks went by, Corey and Emily found they had more in common than they'd have believed possible. They even stopped asking each other's opinion as they already knew it. Not so much because their circumstances were parallel, as indeed they were not, but more that their feelings ran along an amazingly similar course for two children whose nature and nurture had delivered opposite practices. They took such joy in being with each other and learning music together that their world seemed unusually rich. No one denied them their time and they were often on their own without adult supervision, except for Professor Haussmann, whom they regarded as a friend more than a guardian.

Life seemed "almost too perfect," as Emily would say, until quite suddenly a real stomach ailment manifested itself in place of the homesickness Corey had banished with his friendship. Unfortunately, he too came down with the same intestinal malady, mistakenly diagnosed as something life-threatening, which interrupted the children's scheduled music lessons and upset the entire de Koningh household. Corey's father canceled his business trip to be home with the children, halting all homeschooling for two weeks for the safety of those who taught them. Corey's mother showed up fully dressed every morning, a very rare occurrence, to position herself at his bedside until his stomachache had subsided, and the entire staff ras on call day and night bringing the children a continuous flow of fresh water and juice to ward off dehydration.

Emily's father was in England, but Corey's parents wrote him daily of the children's progress. Cholera epidemics in crowded cities had claimed many lives over the past twenty years, arriving first in London before New York. Although the open land and clean conditions of the few existing streets on the outskirts of the city where the de Koninghs lived would suggest safety, there were pigs on the farms nearby. Nor did anybody understand how the disease was spread. A lot of wild theories and very few facts fostered hysteria and discrimination against those who caught it, exploding each time an outbreak was feared.

But at last, after a two-week hiatus, Robert Haussmann stood at the de Koninghs' front door again, his grandfather's Guarneri violin held securely by his side. The weight of the case in his hand conveyed more than the mass of old-growth wood composing one of the world's most glorious musical creations and its horsehair bow, both safely cushioned in a red velvet lining. He could sense the hundred-year span of musicians carried within the instrument, as well as the luthier who had made it. That artisan's mark—a cross clearly stamped inside—had earned him the nickname of "Del Gesù," bestowed posthumously for his work.

Yet, it was said that this instrument was the work of Guarneri's German wife, Caterina Roda, which was why a famous Italian luthier's violin had a decidedly German flare. Returning to her homeland in poverty after her husband's death in 1744, she sold this delicately engineered violin to Robert Haussmann's grandfather, who'd known her as a child. Robert appreciated the irony of subterfuge, when a violin made by a feminine hand, credited to a masculine designer, was now to be played by a young girl feigning interest in becoming a pianist to preserve her femininity. Emily knew nothing of this of course, but he couldn't wait to see her face when she realized her dream to play the violin would finally come true.

Robert knew very little of his father's family, other than this connection to an instrument none of them played. He and his father had been left alone by his mother when she'd sought a fuller life with a richer husband. Robert's father never recovered from the shock of her desertion, drinking himself to death to fill the void much as Beethoven's father had, a connection Robert had comforted himself with at the age of fourteen. He and the greatest pianist in the world bore the same burden. Robert hoped such parallel suffering might infuse his own playing with the qualities of the maestro's. His hope had not been realized, so he intended his emigration to America as a new beginning when he was barely sixteen. The violin and its provenance, tied directly to him through the men of his family, was all he brought with him from Vienna.

Waiting a moment before ringing for admittance to the mansion, Robert glanced out over the eight hundred acres of forest and farm country to the west. There was a rumor that this land at the center of Manhattan island, much of it owned by the city, would all become a public park someday, with a contest soon to pick a landscape designer. It seemed an unlikely plan.

Mary, the pert young parlor maid, opened the door for him and Robert stepped through holding out his calling card. "Robert Haussmann, Professor of Music," she read, slowly and deliberately, much as a child sounds out its first lines. "I didn't know there were so many letters in it, sir." Robert had to stop himself from saying he was surprised she could read at all.

"German spelling, Mary. It's bound to look odd to you." He smiled at her while privately chiding himself for thinking she'd be illiterate.

"But why do you want to leave a callin' card, sir? We all know who you are." She held his identification poised above the pile of cards on the silver tray.

"To inform Mr. de Koningh I wish to speak with him when he returns from his business travels, as I noted on it." He took the card and turned it over, pointing to his handwritten message. "That's what they're for, Mary: to say that someone called. Thank you," he added, hoping to spur her on to put it with the others on the tray. "Now that the children are both well again, I'll be back every week."

"Aye." She nodded, her little face puckered with worry. "We were all afraid the cholera had come, what with their stomachaches. I've known deaths in friends' families. I saw one who was barely four, a horrible sight . . ."

"It was very hard for us all, Mary." Robert noted her anxious expression was identical to his own. "But I'm sure Corey and Emily will spring back to health quickly now that we know it wasn't cholera and the worst is over." He smiled as amiably as possible without appearing too familiar, and started for the door beyond the stairs. "I'd like to set up some music in the library for our lesson today. I'll just run in early. No need to take my hat and gloves." He moved past her toward the library, realizing he'd just called both children by their given names in front of the maid. The threats to their health had brought him so much anguish and their recoveries such relief he couldn't go back to the old formalities. Anything distancing the children seemed ungrateful.

Mary nodded and curtsied as he went by, putting his card on the silver tray on the table by the stairs. He saw her instinctively glance up at the landing above. The children often took delight in dropping spitballs down on the calling cards from the second story, but there hadn't been any of that since they'd both been ill. Who'd have thought their antics would have been so sorely missed?

"Well, if you're needing anything, sir, just ring for me. I'll be in the kitchen finishing up." Mary smiled at him through half-lowered lashes, and Robert reminded himself to be on his guard. It wouldn't do to have Mr. de Koningh misinterpret and suspect him of fraternizing with the help. But then he, too, was a servant of sorts, just a different sort.

"Thank you, Mary." Civility and a kind word were always

appropriate if they weren't misunderstood. It was a tricky balance here in America, and musicians had always been caught between two worlds, with the customs of one overruling those of the other at times.

Moving silently on the carpeting in the hall, Robert paused to take a closer look to appreciate a Dutch landscape on the wall halfway down to the library. He'd noticed it often but was usually in too much of a hurry to get to his young charges' music lessons to pay much attention. Now he noticed billows of atmospheric light and space filled the top two-thirds of the canvas with white, gray, and blue clouds. Below that lay a flat countryside in various green shades created by the moving clouds. A sand dune rose unexpectedly in the foreground. There were no people, and only a vague hint of a tiny house with a red roof lost in the foliage. A river curved through the center, reflecting more moving light. The most unique thing about the painting was that the elevation suggested the viewer was a bird or a deity. The varnish was aging, and a few cracks ran across the surface, telling of a centuries-old history.

He peered closer to see if he could make out the date under the artist's signature: 1660, he thought, but he couldn't be sure. The name painted around the date was harder to read. Moving in closer still, he realized it all ran together rather than separating the letters. Spelling it out loud, he read *philipdekoninck*—Philip de Koninck, 1660. The artist must be a relative of the de Koningh family. He squeezed the handle on the violin case to reassure himself of his own ancestral ties. He'd asked Corey about the painting once and found his explanation wanting. All the boy had said was that he enjoyed it because it made him feel free, as if escaping the boundaries of his house and city. He offered nothing about its history or the artist, no context within which to appreciate it. But maybe how it made one feel was more important. Robert was always learning something from his students, and these two were exceptional in that regard.

Once inside the library, Robert carefully lifted his violin case and laid it on top of the Steinway, running his hand tenderly over the satin curves of the piano's elegant top board, closed in its confinement of the past two weeks. He took pride in the fact that Henry Engelhard Steinway, also a German immigrant, sold his lovely instruments to the elite of New York. Robert had promised himself a trip down to the new showroom on Fourteenth Street and a visit to the innovative Philharmonic Orchestra housed there as well, an excursion perhaps to include Emily and Corey.

Stepping to the music shelves with row upon row of ordered folders just behind the piano, he looked for a violin piece to take Emily through the instrument's early history. His first interview evaluating her after Corey's plea made Robert understand he'd never taught such an exceptional student before. She and Corey were truly cut of the same cloth. Flattered by Mr. de Koningh's faith in him, and delighted with the increased income Emily's addition provided, he was determined to let neither their parents nor the children themselves down in any way. It had certainly been a special day when Corey begged to have his new houseguest join his music lessons. Only a few weeks of teaching had been completed before the fear of a cholera infection descended on the house, but they could now finally begin again. He'd missed them, the children and the lessons.

Moving up closer to the shelves, Robert found the madrigal he was looking for, composed in the early sixteenth century by a woman named Francesca Caccini. It had a wonderful part for violin where the piano played only a small supporting role. He could think of no more fitting offering than this, from a young woman who'd broken all the rules centuries ago, to another young girl today who would undoubtedly do the same; to say nothing of breaking numerous hearts along the way. Robert smiled, glancing up as if he could see the children in their rooms upstairs and enjoying thoughts of Emily's undoubted conquests to come.

"Ready?" Corey launched himself over the threshold into Emily's room, his momentum carrying him past her sitting area and almost to the empty bed before he saw she wasn't in it. He spun around in place, curls flying and jacket flapping open at the waist. Emily saw something sticking out of his pocket.

"Corey de Koningh, don't you ever knock?" She was waiting for him on the settee next to the sewing table, the hiding place for the book he'd "borrowed" from his father's library, *Oliver Twist*.

"The door was open, Lady Liberty. Nothing to knock on."

"I know. I opened it," she sighed. "It's about time. Whoever thought living with an open door could be so important? It's meant to show I'm not a threat for disease any longer." She folded the book shut on her lap. "What's that you have in your pocket, Corey?"

"My recorder." He pulled a short, straight wooden instrument out. It had a high russet sheen and the look of a pitch pipe. "Listen," he said. He put the wooden mouthpiece between his lips and placed his fingers over some of the holes on the stem, closing his top lip back over the mouthpiece and blowing gently. Covering and uncovering the holes with his fingers as he blew, a wispy, romantic rendition of "Greensleeves" floated across the room.

"When did you get that? I've not seen it before." Emily realized that although she felt as if Corey had been her friend a very long time, she was still a newcomer in his life.

"A year ago or so. I picked it up again when we were sick, and I couldn't get down to the piano." He wiped the mouthpiece on his sleeve and put the recorder back in his pocket. "That way I could practice and keep on writing my music. You know I prefer composition to playing any day, don't you? I'd have gone mad without it. You should get one, Emily." He pranced across the floor like a young satyr to join her on the settee.

She shook her head. "It wouldn't work for me. I need my violin. You have all sorts of sounds in your imagination, Corey, which is why you compose. I've only one, and nothing else will do. That's the difference between us."

"Oh, there's a lot more than that difference. But you need to learn give and take." He nodded with assurance. "They'll never let you have a violin in your room."

"I know." Emily knew well how quickly a violin would be confiscated, as the little one in London had been when it was discovered in bed with her. "I'll have to do something else, but I don't know what."

"We'll ask Professor Haussmann. He'll know. What's that you've got there?" Corey pointed to the book lying on Emily's lap. "Oh, I see it's Mr. Dickens's novel. Have you started it?" He reached out and turned it up so he could look at the front better.

"Of course," she said with a grin. "I had no recorder and too much time on my hands when I was getting well. Even though you and I read the first installments in the magazine, I started over. I don't think it's going to be as humorous as his others. There are darker things in this *Oliver Twist*." She turned the book back as she'd had it, so she could start later just where she'd left off.

"Well, this is not a day for darkness!" Corey grabbed the book off her lap and tossed it back in the sewing table drawer, which he shut with a definitive shove. "Our first music lesson with the professor since our taking sick doesn't lend itself to gloom. Let's get going." He jumped up from the settee and pulled Emily up by the hand. Standing at her full height, she was almost a half head taller than he. "Corey, you're looking wan and ghastly, and perhaps a bit smaller since I saw you last."

"How very good of you to say so." He stretched up on his toes with as much regal hauteur as he could manage.

"Have you been obeying the doctor and resting all you should?" She ran her hand over his forehead, pushing his unruly hair out of his eyes and considering him with concern.

"Stop, Nurse Emily," he huffed, brushing her hand off. Pulling away from his rebuff, she turned to march out the open door. He watched her walking fast down the hall toward the stairs. There'd been times during their stomach trouble he'd thought he might not see her again. The doctor had filled everyone full of threats, which hadn't done a thing to help them get well. But he and Emily had fooled them all and survived anyway.

"You've shrunk," she flung over her shoulder. "At this rate, I believe you'll be entering a second childhood any day now." She made sure to toss her long, dark hair, straight without its former ringlets, as she started to run toward the library on the first floor.

"That's my Lady Liberty," Corey laughed, pushing himself to keep up with her. They scampered down the stairs. Careening around the newel post at the bottom, chasing each other through the hall and tumbling into the library. They arrived laughing and out of breath. Emily stopped short just inside when she saw Professor Haussmann sitting at the piano already. Corey crashed into her from behind and almost fell, giggling over his own clumsiness.

"Children!" Professor Haussmann called out. They both froze. The professor shot up from the piano bench with both arms outstretched. "Children!" he cried again, this time starting toward them with a huge smile on his face. All three of them ended up in a tangle together in the middle of the room, the professor rocking them back and forth, and all of them grinning. "I'm happier to see you both than you can imagine," he said, with a catch in his voice.

"No happier than we are to see you," Corey laughed, and Emily nodded. The rough wool of the professor's sleeve rubbed her cheek and she realized that no man had ever embraced her that way before. The unfamiliar sensation stiffened her.

"We've been too long apart," he said, "and the anxious wait for your recovery was most difficult." Professor Haussmann pulled back to look at them both. Emily could see his eyes were moist, which made her even more uncomfortable.

"It was horrible for us as well, Professor, believe me," Corey said.

"And unlike you, we had no music," Emily chimed in, with a look as grim as the thought deserved. "Except Corey, of course, because he had his pocket recorder." She untangled herself from their knotted embrace.

"We need to find something for Emily to play in her room that will help her practice, too, Professor. She wants something like a violin, but something that wouldn't be seized if they found it." Robert looked from Corey to Emily, who frowned, but Robert smiled and nodded slowly, his eyes lighting up with a pleasanter thought than hers.

"Why not a tenor guitar? It has only four strings and can be tuned to the violin perfectly. It looks like a lute, so no one would object to such a classic instrument in your room, Emily. I'll rent one for you and we'll see what happens. You'll be missing a bow, but everything else will be there musically, and later on, we'll get you lessons on my violin, perhaps at my house where you won't be under scrutiny." The professor smiled at her gently, and Corey grinned back, obviously relieved to have Emily's problem so quickly solved. But Emily's frown deepened.

"Maybe," she muttered. "But it's a shame to waste time on an instrument without a bow." She took another step back with an agitated glance at the professor's Guarneri violin in its case. She felt odd and wondered if her stomach was acting up again. "I think I need some air," she said, glancing toward the garden. "Could we open the doors for a while, Professor Haussmann?"

"I'd just been thinking that myself," he said. "Corey, give me a hand." Corey jumped up, obviously delighted to have something specific to do that might cure whatever was bothering Emily. The doors were excruciatingly heavy, with double-height glass panes and lead mullions, but once started, they swung smoothly out of the way to the right and left of each opening. Corey felt as if they were preparing a stage set. The heft of the doors slowed the process down, adding to the solemnity of it. Once open, they could hear birds singing in the garden, and smell magnolia and jasmine through the archways. Securing the last of the three doors, Corey turned to look at Emily, delighted to see she'd calmed down. It must have been the lack of air after all. He walked over and stood right in front of her, studying her face. "Is that better? You were looking pretty strange."

"I've been locked up too long," she admitted. "I think I've forgotten how to breathe."

"Not likely," Professor Haussmann laughed. "Anyone who glows as you do, Emily, hasn't forgotten how to breathe." He patted her shoulder gently and she flinched stiffly. Thinking she might loosen up with the pull of his lovely Guarneri, he decided it was time to break the news.

"Emily, I've decided to instruct you on my grandfather's beautiful old violin while Corey can work simultaneously on the piano. If you're uncomfortable doing it here, we can move to my study, but for now . . ." He watched to see if she understood the true import of what he was saying, but couldn't read her expression. "You must always treat this instrument, and the bow as well, with the utmost respect. Maybe I shouldn't provide you with something so valuable, but I think it's important to satisfy your perfect pitch with the kind of sonority this beautiful old instrument provides. You'll surprise yourself when you hear it under your left ear. You must work very hard to live up to it." He pulled the top back, so she could see the prize waiting for her on red velvet in its slightly battered old case. "I cringe at the way people think the beginners in any discipline don't need good tools to work with. They actually need the best, to encourage and motivate them." He smiled to encourage her, thinking she might be in awe of such a gift.

Moving to the piano bench and sitting down with his familiar air of serenity and authority, he suggested it was time to start their lesson. Emily still stood next to the violin without picking it up. She looked strained, so Corey again asked her what was wrong. "Nothing!" she snapped, still glowering at the violin. Robert could see Corey was disturbed when he looked up from his place at the piano. Feeling it best for the children to settle down a bit, he started speaking to give them time.

"Before we begin, children, I have something wonderful to discuss with you." Corey instantly redirected his attention, but Emily still set her pretty little jaw and narrowed her eyes. In fact, Robert could almost believe she was scowling at him. "I've been barely able to contain myself until now, I wanted so much to tell you about my surprise," he went on.

"Please, Professor." Corey's eyes danced. "We don't use torture here, so you shouldn't taunt us. What's the surprise?" He walked over behind Emily, and Robert took one quick glance at the lovely portrait the two of them made, with their shining faces reflecting the sun from the open doors to the garden.

"I recently heard from a friend of mine, a musician who formed a small group to play orchestral music in public a few years ago." He looked at the two young students watching him expectantly and saw they hadn't absorbed the implications of what he'd said. "They call themselves the New York Philharmonic," he went on, "and it's the first orchestra of its kind in this country, or indeed in the entire world, I believe." Robert glowed with a pride as if the orchestra was his own. "Although of course the whole world is a very big place," he added, as if to allay any objections they might have to such an outrageous statement. "News from abroad travels slowly, so it's possible I'm not informed on the subject, but I do think it was the first one anywhere!" He finished with such obvious smugness that the children glanced at each other.

"Haven't there been plenty of musicians who've come together to play chamber music in the past, Professor?" Corey asked.

"Indeed, yes." Robert nodded. "But this is a larger ensemble with a bigger purpose. In the past, as you said, the music's always been for someone's personal pleasure, a private audience, or possibly a king. Salons and royal courts in Europe are the perfect examples of those."

"And how is this different?" Corey blurted out.

"They perform strictly for the public at large. Their mission is to introduce a taste for concertizing the most glorious music on earth for those who have perhaps never heard it before."

"Who hires and pays them?" Emily chimed in. "I'm sure they're not playing for nothing. They have to live, too, and concerts are expensive." Robert noted how quickly she went to the heart of the matter: no money, no Philharmonic.

"Their audiences are their patrons, Emily. If people don't go to hear them, the Philharmonic will cease to exist."

"Could we go to one?" Corey asked. "Would you take us?"

"You anticipate me!" Robert was delighted to have one of the children already supporting his plan. "The tickets are very expensive—two dollars apiece—and the venue is on Fourteenth Street, so it's quite a trip."

"I'm sure my father would be delighted to pay for the tickets and give us the carriage for a day if you would take us, Professor."

"I would enjoy that no end, Corey. I know both your fathers would expose you to such important events themselves, but since they're both traveling, I consider it my responsibility to suggest these occasions in their absences. Your father and mother suggested these educational ventures should be part of my mission at all times."

Emily had been listening and watching, and apparently thinking deeply, but she suddenly asked, "Will Mr. Paganini be invited to perform with this Philharmonic?" Robert was surprised she'd heard of the great Paganini, but then remembered she'd been exposed to the European concert stage.

"Who is he?" Corey asked, turning to focus on Emily as if Robert were no longer there.

"Definitely not, Emily." Robert ignored his question, fascinated that Emily's second thought was for the world's most famous violinist. "The group is entirely self-governing, Emily, and I know they make their own decisions about who plays. They'll even rotate the conducting between them as the year progresses. And besides," he chuckled, "the great Paganini died over a decade ago."

"Truly?" Corey's voice lifted. He looked at Emily defiantly, seemingly pleased there was something she didn't know. "A democratic orchestra. Now that's something I'd like to compose for and lead," he added, obviously indifferent about the passing of the world-famous violinist.

"Someday, maybe you will." Robert nodded at him at last. "Have you both some formal attire appropriate for a concert?" He smiled at his foolishness, realizing that was probably the only kind they did have.

"What would I need, Professor? Just silk waistcoat and dark trousers?" Corey bounced with excitement.

"That would be fine, Corey." Robert nodded. "And Emily, perhaps you could get a new dress. Even something cut down off the shoulders would be pretty this time of year." He smiled to himself again and looked up, expecting to see delight on Emily's face, but was greeted instead by an intensifying storm cloud.

Slamming down the top of the violin case and glaring from him to Corey and back again, Emily stamped her foot and cried out, "What a complete waste of time this is, talking about nothing but clothes and entertainment. I won't listen to it anymore!" She looked as if she'd burst into tears at any moment, and as Robert and Corey watched in shock, she spun around and ran out of the room.

Corey stared after her for a moment before recovering his voice. "Professor, I'm terribly afraid she's not well! Don't you think we should call the doctor?"

"Heavens, no," Robert chuckled. "The female of the species is always unpredictable and volatile, Corey, and never more so than in its transition from girl to woman."

"Then you don't think Emily's ill?"

"Absolutely not." Robert shook his head and frowned. "The shame of it is that she's alone and has no older female companion to turn to for friendship and advice."

"She's not alone!" Corey cried out. "She has me, Professor. Would you mind if we canceled our lesson for today? I want to go make sure she's not getting sick again." Corey stood balancing on one foot in preparation for immediate flight.

"She's fine, Corey. There's nothing wrong; nothing a little growing up won't cure, anyway. I fear we have a bit more of this behavior to endure."

"Really?" Corey's eyes were wide. "How can we survive it?"

"We have no choice." Robert reached out from the piano, tousled Corey's blond hair, and looked him in the eye. "I guarantee the results will be worth the wait."

"Are you sure?" Corey held his teacher's eyes before he turned and ran after Emily. He'd forgotten permission to leave had not been granted.

"Sure," Robert called after the boy, as he disappeared down the hall. "You have my word on it," he added softly to himself.

✦━❧ ❦ ❧━✦

The panic Corey felt at the thought of losing Emily again to some unknown malady made him realize his whole life had started to revolve around his new friend. No matter what he considered doing, no matter how outrageous the adventure seemed to be, he knew she'd never turn him down. Sometimes she would even encourage him to punishable and dangerous feats of daring—smoking his father's cigars on the roof of the mansion shortly after her arrival came instantly to mind. They'd both been banished with solitary confinement for that infraction, which had driven Corey almost mad, while Emily just continued to read her violin scores Professor Haussmann had given her.

The things Corey imagined, places he wanted to explore, music he wanted to play, all would not only be possible, but vastly more pleasurable with Emily by his side. They'd read the same books (novels meant to be off-limits to children), enjoy the same music (Corey wanted to play accompaniment for her now), and they could even give performances in the library someday. He realized he would not be himself anymore without her.

BOOK TWO

The Adults

CHAPTER FOUR

ROBERT HAUSSMANN paused in the lobby, hat and gloves in hand, watching the crowd milling about before the concert started. It had been many years since his planned visit to the Philharmonic Society of New York with his young charges in the de Koningh household and much had changed. He stood alone, smiling to himself. The Apollo Rooms on lower Broadway seated an audience of six hundred, and the box office manager had told him it was a sellout crowd today. The eager crowd moved toward the orchestra seats, and he knew he'd enjoy describing the palpable atmosphere of anticipation to the musicians afterward. He'd accepted their invitation for dinner to catch up on their careers and assure them of their popularity here at home. He was proud of what these men, his colleagues, had accomplished for New York and for America: the advancement of instrumental music, which had always been their mission. Soloists had a less altruistic agenda, although the few women joining that rarified group were expected to have the same unselfish goals that male ensembles championed. Some thought bringing culture to those who had little was the only excuse for allowing women to perform in public.

Watching the expectant throng awaiting the all-Mozart offering, Robert was pleased to be on his own. He took guilty pleasure in the solitary enjoyment of music. No polite commentary with a friend would be necessary, no notes for future study jotted down on the playbill for his students. Tonight would be just for him. Some of the ladies in the crowd looked at him as they passed, and assuming his smile was for them, nodded back. But he looked through and beyond them. Some might suggest he'd gotten lazy living by himself, yet he wasn't unhappy. When he'd moved to New York from Vienna, he made up his mind to remain a bachelor, just as his father had after his mother moved out. He'd seen the entrapment of marriage firsthand and knew he was too sensitive to survive it. No indeed, he needed certain liberties, so remaining single was his priority even though the intentions of the ladies and conventions of the day would have it otherwise. After the de Koningh children stopped their homeschooling four years ago, it had taken a while to be rid of that old feeling of abandonment, but he was fine now.

Shifting his position to get out of the traffic streaming from the box office, Robert suddenly paused, catching sight of a shiny, dark brown head of hair swept up off a long, graceful neck. Something about the way it was carried was immediately recognizable: straight and sure, without effort. A pulse jumped in his temple and he gripped the brim of his own hat. Daring neither to breathe nor move, he watched as the young woman turned to speak with a tall, older male companion. He was right. A mature Emily Alden was certainly on her way into the concert hall. He'd often wondered what the full-grown version of the young Emily would look like, living with the imaginary pictures these past few years. Yet here she most certainly was, moving as only a live woman could. He let out his breath slowly as she was carried by the tide of people from sight.

Once inside the hall, he scanned the audience from behind as he moved down the center aisle to his third-row seat, but couldn't spot Emily's proud head. He spent most of the first movement of Mozart's Sinfonia Concertante fighting the impulse to twist around to look for her, so he missed much of the music entirely. The audience also seemed restless, and he used the commotion to adjust his own position. He sat forward a bit and then turned around, ostensibly to stretch and review the spectators and seating capacity of the hall behind him. But in truth, he was prepared to search every face, if necessary, for Emily's. It wouldn't be necessary, because he finally spotted her a few rows back. He turned forward again for the next movement, the presto, but couldn't resist reassuring himself of her presence numerous times, so often that her handsome companion noted his attentions.

The serious expression on Emily's face as she listened to the conversing instruments convinced him he must listen too, until a noise from behind gave him another excuse to turn. The unusually bareheaded Emily was trying to lean sideways on her companion to see better past a woman seated directly in front of her with a huge-brimmed hat. The mature Emily's big dark eyes met Robert's for an instant before the offending hat and brim repositioned itself. Emily's male companion, whom Robert had developed a vicarious dislike for, was questioning her. The rest of the concert was lost to Robert, and his usual resentment at interruptions was replaced by a numbness he couldn't explain.

⊱•━ ❦ ━•⊰

Sinfonia Concertante in E-flat, K. 364, Emily read from the Philharmonic's playbill. She felt the presence of her father beside her and looked at him as he studied the program. He attracted appreciative glances from both men and women. It occurred to her how much they looked alike, but it worried her to think her mother's fair, delicate features were lost to the world. She seldom heard from her father now that she was away at school, and saw him even less. She didn't know if he spent all his time in America or returned to England more often than when they'd first come to New York. She assumed he'd marry again someday, but that would of course be to an Englishwoman, and so less time in the States would follow. She feared he intended her to be his occasional hostess until he found a replacement, and she knew she must disappoint him when he realized her heart was in New York, not London. Lord Alden noticed his daughter watching him and leaned over to whisper, "Is Alfred Boucher leading tonight?"

"I think so, but I'm not sure. They may still rotate conductors," Emily whispered back, ruffling through her playbill to find the listing of performers. Now that she was away at Miss Carter's Finishing School in Connecticut, she didn't come to the Philharmonic often enough to recognize the players.

Mozart's double concerto for violin and viola caused flashbacks for Emily. Corey had lightheartedly sung the viola's part while she played the violin and Professor Haussmann the piano. Those days of homeschooling in the de Koninghs' library held some of her favorite childhood memories, all coming together after her arrival in New York from the lonely, motherless home she'd shared with her aunt and her father in London. The woman with the oversized feathered hat in front of her now reminded her of Mademoiselle Piquet, the prissy French teacher she and Corey had purposely tortured with feigned horrible accents. The literal translation of the woman's name—a needle, or a sting or bite—had seemed apt as she looked down at them over her sharp nose, nostrils pinched tight as if to ward off bad smells. Who else had come to teach them? Mr. Bone for math and science; for history and English, Mrs. . . . . She couldn't remember. She and Corey had often taken over that class themselves to discuss their latest favorite author, leaving Mrs. Something-or-other lost behind them.

Three years of homeschooling, then she and Corey were off to finishing and preparatory school, respectively. They were nearly the same age, so why was she assumed to need "finishing" before she'd even begun, while Corey was being "prepared," but for what? Corey had headed for college, and she'd gone nowhere. It would be the recognizably bleak picture for women of her day, unless she could talk her father into different music lessons, perhaps somewhere near Corey's school. It was interesting how the only teacher they'd enjoyed together was Professor Haussmann. Music had joined them then. She knew nothing about Corey since he'd stopped writing to her from Boston. Had all this been brought back a few moments ago by that fleeting glimpse of their former teacher whom she'd rudely refused to acknowledge?

Turning to watch the violinist start his part of Mozart's virtuosic presto movement, Emily noticed he was hunched around his instrument, his defensive stance detracting from Mozart's intended lightness of the piece. To prepare himself for the quick, athletic fingering of the measures to come, the lithe young man with a black shock of hair falling in his eyes had adopted the pose of an elderly gnome. How often her own lessons had led to Robert's outcry: *Lift! Lift! Lift your chest!* Her initial hesitancy to strike such a stance, even in the privacy of the de Koninghs' home, had produced an outpouring of proof from the professor, much of it gathered around the opening of the Guarneri violin's sound. He'd often demonstrated the difference between an open and closed stance, leaving neither she nor Corey in any doubt that open sounded better.

What a cruel irony. Her stomach muscles clenched, tolerable since no one could see them, but she felt the expression on her face must give her away. She could feel her angry, tight jaw and narrowed eyes surely telling anyone glancing at her that the green-eyed monster of jealousy ruled her heart. Here she would give anything to command center stage, with no question in her mind she could do it so much better; but this man, who took his right to be there for granted, crouched over as if to hide himself and his violin from view. Emily was not unsympathetic. She knew the tension came from nerves and caring too much. *Practice with focus, but perform with abandon,* Professor Haussmann had always said. But there were few female violinists to match herself with and only one she could think of who apparently played with "abandon." She'd read of her, the French

49

violinist Camilla Urso, described by critics as "a statue on fire" and "ethereal." But she'd never seen her perform in person, so she had to use men like this unexceptional musician before her now for particular inspiration.

"Queen Violinist of the World," Urso was called in print, "with an intonation as nearly perfect as the human ear will allow." One unsubstantiated story claimed that three hundred timber wolves were slaughtered to raise money to bring her to the frontier of the Northwest United States. She was described as having an "inscrutable face" and "dark lustrous melancholy eyes," but the lack of promotional photographs suggested to Emily that Camilla's protests for equal pay and opportunities for women musicians where "now men alone profit" kept her in the background, where the men wanted her. The critics had often presented a narrative of her as a child prodigy, however, the public being more likely to find children precocious than outrageous when they outdid society's expectations. But Camilla's encouragement and promotion by her Italian flautist father, all of which gained her acceptance to the Paris Conservatory as its first female student, bore no relationship to Emily's own upbringing, and so no connection of experience as an example she could draw from.

There'd been no support from parents in her own childhood to encourage her passion for the violin. She'd had only an inattentive father, and the welcome consideration from the de Koninghs had lacked the thrust she'd needed to excel. Even Corey's cheerful, humorous musical collaboration had been more fun than fire. But she knew she was, at the very least, fortunate to have a father who appreciated music somewhat and allowed her to continue with lessons at finishing school. He'd even accepted her occasional performances for friends and faculty at Miss Carter's, believing as he often repeated that she'd never play professionally and would soon lose interest. Her father didn't know she had every intention of continuing to seek opportunities to play in public now that she was almost an adult in her own right. Though in fact, she really had no rights; at least, not yet.

What would it be like to see a *statue on fire* performing on the violin as Clara Schumann did on the piano? Could she ever catch up to the lead these women had on her? Could she still learn something from them by absorbing their live performances now? Ultimately, all the greatest musicians came to New York without having to kill wolves to get them there. She'd have her chance to see Mrs. Schumann or some other woman in the spotlight, eventually. Change was in the air, if not yet on the stage. She shook herself imperceptibly to clear her thoughts and concentrate on the man playing before her now, as she felt all performers deserved her respect and attention even if she knew they were lacking. Robert Haussmann had taught them that, too.

The viola came in next at its lower register, answering the violin like a young suitor, repeating its refrain. Back and forth, the two matched instruments exchanged the playful talk of friends enjoying a good conversation. Neither took offense nor did they dominate this perfect partnering of similar sympathies, just as she and Corey had done once. The young man with the violin was clearly loosening up with the flow of Mozart's sublime music and the warmth of a collaborator to share the musical discussion and the open stage. There was so much more to music than a steady technique and beneficent birthright. Perhaps she'd had an unbeatable advantage through her early partnership with Corey. They'd both gained so much confidence playing together, learning to listen to each other and be supportive. No wonder memories were flooding her now. Mozart's youthful Sinfonia Concertante would remind anyone of the dialogue of friendship. Two soloists stood prominently center stage, yet they were obviously a part of the total orchestra and not singularly important. The composer's form that was so new a hundred years ago was already birthing the double and triple concerti of its modern nineteenth-century descendants. She and Corey had always felt they were a part of a continuum of music, too. Professor Haussmann had been that kind of inclusive mentor.

But in many ways, that time was receding into a dream. Growing up had come between them, and with both away from the house that had seemed like a benevolent grandparent, she felt untethered. Was Corey still working on his music and composing during his time at university? She'd decided not to ask again in letters that didn't get answered. Did his pieces sound like those of a playful Wolfgang Mozart or a romantic Felix Mendelssohn? Apparently, he was too busy to share those thoughts. Someday, this very orchestra might perform Corey's work as they were already renowned for commissioning and presenting new compositions. She'd like to share a musical life with Corey, but couldn't figure out how to make that happen, or how she could get there from where she was now—where the world would have her stay.

She thought of the Philharmonic performance she and Corey had planned to hear with Professor Haussmann years ago, but the rally for the war against Mexico had prevented them from traveling downtown in the end. The orchestra had chosen the astonishing Ninth Symphony of Beethoven to raise funds for the new and struggling Philharmonic. How astounded they'd been that journalists, not politicians, had whipped public opinion into a frenzy. The new telegraph had, for the first time, brought news of war into their drawing rooms, frightening people into mobs that clogged the city and forced transportation to a halt. It was a devastating blow for the young Philharmonic. No money had been raised for a new hall that day, nor had she and Corey ever attended the live performance Professor Haussmann had hoped for them.

"Do you know that man?" her father muttered. "He's turned often to look at you. See there, three rows down." He nodded, pointing with his playbill. Emily shifted in her seat to try to look around the woman in front of her with the wide-brimmed hat. Emily was of average height, but the woman's hat was not. It was insensitive of her to wear the huge bonnet at a concert with close seating. At least men removed their hats, but witlessly controlled by fashion dictates of the day, women seemed to defy the logic of care for others in the audience. Emily shook her own bare head and held it a little higher.

"I can't see the man you mean," she whispered. "Can you describe him?"

"Quite young, a slight red tint to his hair and beard . . ." Her father's voice trailed off and he shrugged, as if there was nothing else of note. "He's no longer turned our way. It's not important."

An undeniable prick of recognition pierced Emily for the second time, tingling down her back as she struggled to look around the voluminous hat just as the woman leaned closer to her companion to whisper behind her hand. Now Emily could see the man perfectly. She'd recognized him earlier in the lobby before they were seated. Seeing Robert Haussmann in the flesh had somehow disturbed her in a way her memories couldn't, although at the age of thirteen she'd felt much the same: profoundly unsettled by him. She couldn't allow the past to hold her hostage now.

"He's hardly young, Father," she said, more forcefully than she intended. "That's the music professor from the de Koningh home. His name is Robert Haussmann. He must be in his early thirties by now. I haven't seen him in years."

"S-h-h-h!" hissed the woman with the hat in front, spinning around to glower at Emily, her brim nearly decapitating the people on either side. Emily hoped they were friends, lest the shock of her assault have repercussions. "Pardon," Emily said to the hat lady, but the man to the woman's right growled, "Remove that hat, please!" and much to Emily's amazement, the huge feathered nest on the head in front of her was unpinned and placed in its owner's lap.

Her view now cleared, she looked to the man three rows down, who had turned to see what the noise was about. His eyes met hers, and there was no denying the connection. He lowered his head slightly, and then looked at her father. Lord Alden leaned over to

Emily and whispered, "You'll introduce me when the concert is over." She nodded, taking a deep breath and forcing her attention back to Mozart's Sinfonia Concertante, unimpeded by eccentric hats or former teachers. The violinist was more relaxed now, too, and finally seemed to be enjoying himself. She wondered if it had something to do with his breathing, which now seemed to come more slowly and from deep in his body. He stood straighter, like a singer opening as much space as possible for his lungs to expand. She would pay attention to her breathing in practice this week and see if it made a difference. The music came to an end, and the polite applause seemed short and perfunctory. Emily suddenly wanted it to go on to delay introducing her father to Robert Haussmann, though she didn't know why. She leapt from her seat, hoping to be swallowed up by the swell of audience members rising to exit for their carriages. Some memories were better left in the past like fossils frozen in time.

❦ ❦ ❦

"Ex-*cuse* me, sir." A woman on Robert's right prepared to leave his row of seats by squeezing her wide skirts past him. "Are you leaving now?" He looked around through his daze and realized the concert was over. The seats to his left were entirely empty. He struggled to his feet to make more space for her. "After you, then." She nodded, impatiently. He moved as fast as his deadened legs would allow. Through the row of seats at last and out into the aisle, he was driven forward with the flow of bodies. But panic rose in his throat as he realized he couldn't see either Emily or her companion anymore. Feeling the pressure in his forehead and eyes, he rounded the back divider behind the last seats and turned to watch the rest of the audience file past him. Without Emily.

"Is it Professor Robert Haussmann?" a female voice asked from behind. It resonated with many subtle nuances, but he recognized it immediately. Low, sultry notes modulated with bright, sparkling ones, suggesting allure, surprise, humor, and even a bit of reserve all at once. He turned. "Yes, it is," she continued, reaching toward him with her hand outstretched. After shaking Robert's hand, somewhat to his surprise, she turned to her companion. "Father, this is my music teacher from the de Koningh household, just as I thought." Robert still had his hand extended, so her father took it as Emily introduced him. Feeling sheepish about his earlier jealousy, Robert considered the masculine face above the hand he shook, recognizing much of Emily's in it.

"Pleased to meet you, Professor," Lord Alden said, with the same challenging gaze Robert knew so well in his daughter. "Emily's told me much about you and her fortuitous music lessons with the de Koningh boy. Ironic you should meet again here at the Philharmonic."

"Not so, Lord Alden," Robert said, finding his voice at last. "Running into her here with Mozart is what I'd expect. She was my most gifted and dedicated student. But it has been a long time," he added, turning to Emily, "and she has certainly grown from the child she was then. She's quite changed, and the British accent has all but disappeared."

"I can imagine," her father replied, assessing Robert carefully up and down.

"How have you been, Professor?" Emily asked. "Still offering musical inspiration and guidance to those in need of it? I used to have private violin lessons at the professor's house when Corey was busy," she explained to her father. "He knew I'd learn the violin faster without the fear of discovery, so we worked on the piano at the de Koninghs' and the violin at his place."

Robert stared at her, fully aware that his responses were delayed, but unable to speed them up. She was exactly the woman he'd envisioned she'd become, but she stood before him instead of in his imagination. It was like watching himself wake up in a dream. The dark hair was no longer forced into bouncing ringlets to her shoulders, but piled onto her head in soft, slightly disobedient waves surrounding her face. And that face was a little longer, more angular and intelligent, but those huge dark eyes were still speaking a language all their own and the small dimples still punctuated the corners of her delicate mouth as if she was perpetually amused. Looking from her to her father, he noted the similarity in their coloring and posture—who could not?—but her increased femininity must surely have come by inheritance from the mother he'd never met. "I am still teaching, of course," he said, recovering himself at last. "Although I perform more often now here," he waved his hand to take in the concert hall, "and other local venues."

"Do you see Corey de Koningh and his family anymore, Professor?" Emily asked. "Do you know if he's still writing his music now that he's at university?"

"I have no idea," Robert answered, surprised that he hadn't asked himself the same question. "I don't see any of the de Koningh family now that Corey's away. And you," he added, "do you still play your viol—the piano seriously?" His comfort level rose as the subject turned to music.

"No, Professor, because my accommodating father has permitted me to continue with the violin," she said, her dimples deepening with her smile. "There are limitations, of course, but not as many," she added. "By the way, what did you think of the violinist this evening?"

"Not much," Robert replied, because he hadn't really been listening, though he didn't want Emily and her father to know that. "So, you have your own violin now?" He looked at her father, assuming the investment in such an instrument would have been his decision.

"Unfortunately, no." Emily's dimples deepened with consternation rather than pleasure. "Things have changed, but not that much." She looked at Robert, but he had the impression she was talking to her father.

"Emily . . . Lady Alden," he corrected himself, as a daring thought suddenly occurred to him. "I have two instruments now. I have a modern one for my students, but still have the Guarneri as well. I would consider selling it, but only to someone I know will care for it properly. Would you consider such a purchase?" He was tempted to look at her father for guidance, but the inner voice that knew Emily quite well warned him not to.

"What an intriguing idea, Professor. Perhaps I could borrow it, so we could become reacquainted. And I'd like my father to hear it as well." Emily finally turned slightly to include Lord Alden, who bowed to Robert and thanked him for his offer, but shook his head. Announcing he had a carriage waiting, Lord Alden pulled Emily's arm through his and offered Robert a ride uptown. Robert felt the opportunities of his chance encounter starting to slip through his fingers as he explained his prior dinner engagement with the musicians. He was desperate to extend his time with the Aldens but couldn't think how. They started to move away.

Suddenly, as her father continued toward the exit and his waiting carriage, Emily slipped her arm free and turned back. "I'm intrigued by your offer, Professor Haussmann. Could I try the violin out at your home while I'm here? I knew it in the past, but I've changed, as has my playing." There were a few feet between them now, but Robert felt them dissolve as they talked.

"I have no students the rest of this week. They're all on Thanksgiving holiday. You were the only one who ever worked between lessons," he added, with a small smile. "I guess some things haven't changed. When would you like to come?"

"I could be there tomorrow by midafternoon," she said, just before her father reappeared at her elbow. Placing his hand at the back of her waist, Lord Alden turned his daughter around and started steering her toward the exit. "And now it appears I must be going," she said to Robert over her shoulder. She lifted her chin and smiled in defiance, and he remembered the same flashing eye and firm jaw in a much smaller, rounder face. He felt sudden empathy for a single parent bringing up a daughter alone. Robert gave Lord Alden a glance of apology, for Emily's behavior and his own part in it, if indeed he regarded Robert as responsible in any way.

"I'll tell my housekeeper to expect you around three o'clock then," Robert said, raising his voice, both to bridge the gap between them and to notify her father. No secret collaborations here. "Do you remember how to get there? It's very near your rental home. Please, take my card as a reminder," he said, holding out his calling card, reaching toward her and bowing slightly in her direction as she left. He added under his breath, "I'll tell the Guarneri to expect you, too." He was almost sure he saw her smile back at him. The dimples gave her away.

CHAPTER FIVE

ROBERT WATCHED EMILY turning slowly in place, taking in his front parlor as a smile started at the corners of her mouth. She pulled off her gray kid gloves, releasing each finger from its cocoon one at a time. Gently enfolding them both in one hand, she raised them to her hat's brim and removed a hat pin from her small straw bowler. He watched mesmerized as she gracefully lifted the hat off her dark hair piled beneath without the aid of a mirror. She turned to lay the hat, with its pin neatly reinserted in the crown, and gloves now draped over its brim on the hall demilune table against the wall. Mild Thanksgiving weather required less outer clothing, and he realized his apartment seemed a little too warm to be comfortable. As if reading his mind, she removed her short wool jacket trimmed with small embroidered flowers. It was not as ornate as many of the waistcoats worn by fashionable ladies, but it was well tailored and emphasized her tiny waist most becomingly. He jumped to take the jacket from her and noticed the slight discoloration on her neck under her left jawbone. It had been hidden by the high collar of her jacket when she'd come in, but he knew the bruise verified the many hours she'd put into practicing the violin.

Her brown eyes had the same snap they'd always had, but her face was a little longer and the bones more pronounced, as he'd noted the other evening at the concert. Her skin had an even luminosity without the heightened color he'd come to expect when she'd raced around the de Koningh mansion all day like a whirlwind. "Is my apartment as you remembered it?" he asked.

"Yes . . . and no," she said. "It's smaller."

"And you are taller." Her thick hair looked darker now, perhaps a trick of the light, since he was no longer able to look down on her head.

She stopped turning to look at him. "It's not just our size that makes us feel places are smaller than remembered. Something happens to the inner eye as well." A mischievous smile broke out from a private thought. "I don't miss irritable old Mrs. Miller meeting me at the front door. She used to scare me."

Robert laughed under his breath. He was sure Mrs. Miller had done her best to make her disapproval of Emily clear. She'd always complained "the wild one never sits still," and that Emily's gaze was too direct for a child. "Hard to believe you feared anything in those days, Emily, though sometimes you were very standoffish with me if Corey wasn't around. Mrs. Miller retired two years ago, and I now have a sweet, round little housekeeper who refuses any contact with my guests or students. She prefers only to cook and clean."

"Perfect for you." Emily laughed and resumed her review of the room. "I never saw these pocket doors fully open between the front and rear parlor." She turned to face the southwest room, where music lessons always took place. "I remember sitting here in the front room waiting for the earlier student to finish before the doors slid back. I hated to wait for anything then. I was so happy to be studying the violin I wanted to push the doors apart and get rid of whoever was in here. With these doors open you have a huge entertaining space." She flung her arms wide now, finally able to do what she hadn't then. "It must be wonderful for parties." She walked into the rear parlor to look out its corner windows to the small garden.

Robert enjoyed watching her review the house, taking in the full thirty-foot expanse of hardwood parquet floors and twelve-foot ceilings trimmed with plaster moldings. It was certainly more space than he needed, but he was just too used to it to move to something smaller, and both his former tutoring at the de Koningh mansion and current increase in performance and teaching jobs had relieved his worries about the rent. Still, financial anxiety always had a way of lurking in the back of his mind. It was not a grand house, but appropriately proportioned as a wedding gift for the daughter of one of the German beer barons. He'd felt immediately at home in this part of the city when he'd first arrived, where immigrants from Bavaria had chosen to settle together. The materials throughout the house had all found passage on ships from Germany coming to supply the many taverns in the city; a reminder for the brewmaster's daughter of her European legacy in a new world.

"Have you many new friends . . . gentlemen callers?" He could feel the pressure in his chest, and tried to keep his voice light.

"Some," she answered, denying him clarity about her personal life, "but it's surprising how alone one can be in a crowd of people with dissimilar interests," she continued, watching him carefully. He feared she'd detect his discomfort. "I don't have much in common with the other students at Miss Carter's Finishing School for Young Ladies." Her voice sounded a derogatory note Robert hadn't heard before. Then she looked away again into the east parlor.

"Some of them are at the school to enhance their hostessing skills, and others to gain expertise in attracting men of means; both are of little interest to me." She took a few steps away from him into the parlor for a better perspective of the whole room. "The classics are considered essential, not to expand a lady's intellect, but to ensure her ability to hold a man's attention in conversation." Emily's attention seemed riveted on the floor-to-ceiling windows and the ornate tracery surrounding them, which diffused what light filtered in from the avenue. Robert wondered if she'd ever let her imagination wander through the molding's shells and leaves as a child, just for the fun of it. Probably not. Corey had always been the more romantic of the two.

"And so," Robert said, "the 'finishing' Miss Carter's school offers includes academic subjects as well as housekeeping and deportment? That's truly a better outcome than I'd have expected of such a place." Robert watched Emily's eyes move over the room, seemingly engaged in both the past and present, here and away, all at once. "Miss Carter is the daughter of a Congregationalist minister from Connecticut, am I not right? I wonder how she started a school of such unique qualities."

"Miss Carter was well-educated at home by the best tutors from Yale . . ." Emily's voice trailed off as she turned in place again. "She speaks four languages," she added, looking back now at Robert directly. "But then, so do many marginally educated Europeans. Not so unique, after all."

"But it sounds like an excellent opportunity for you," Robert interjected. "I don't understand why you're so . . . indifferent." He could see Emily was growing impatient as she turned her attention to the piano on the west wall between the windows.

She sighed, suggesting it was all too obvious. "There's no serious classical art training and only rudimentary music, with no opportunity to learn the protocol of performance, of course, unless it's part of some evening dinner entertainment at home. A paying audience is not acceptable for 'young ladies' of my class, I've been told. Again and again."

"Oh, Emily." Robert shook his head almost imperceptibly. "Can you not accept it?"

"I cannot. Remember wealthy Fanny Mendelssohn? No performing for her! But Clara Schumann, wife and daughter of lowly music teachers, she was encouraged, exploited might be a better word, to perform and earn her living by it." Emily stopped abruptly to glance at Robert, possibly aware that her tirade might have been insensitive and insulting. But seeing no change in his expression, she continued. "Thus, Professor Haussmann, I have no one to talk with of the things I care most about. I have no interest in decorating parties with effervescent chatter, or ironing a linen napkin three times to excel at training future servants—" She broke off abruptly. "I've always liked this parlor," she announced, changing the subject so fast he felt as if a seat had been snatched out from under him. She ran her hand across the back of one of the worn side chairs, a small smile lighting her face, as if she'd encountered an old, familiar friend.

None of the furniture in the music parlor of Robert's apartment had changed, and even the massive partners' desk between the windows sat with the same double-faced clock quietly chiming the hour. None of it was his, of course, including the piano in this rear parlor. His landlady was responsible for the home's décor. But remembering that Emily and her father also lived in a rented town house, Robert let go of the discomfort his borrowed status gave him. It was common, of course, for diplomats like Emily's father to rent homes for the duration of their assignments. And just as common for immigrants like Robert to be unable to afford their own for years after coming to this new country. Maybe someday.

"I don't give parties," he said, surprising himself by discussing his social life, which she knew nothing of, instead of his teaching with which she was so familiar. "I'm a bachelor, still."

"More reason to give parties," she countered, cheerfully. "Unless, of course, you intend to remain a bachelor forever." Her voice was steady and matter-of-fact. There was no judgment or tease he could detect. He walked over to the unassuming Chickering piano in the corner to settle himself. It was only an upright, without the high back many had. But though it might look and sound inferior to the larger pianos, he could spread sheet music out within easy reach, and keep the violin at hand without having to leave the bench. He touched the violin case now resting on top of the piano. This was a sure way to distract Emily from commenting on his thoughtlessly blurted-out marital status.

"Why don't you come and have a look at your old friend, the Guarneri," he suggested. "I wonder if the two of you will remember each other. You may recall I brought it with me from Europe, though I never really played it. It was my grandfather's, and the only good thing that came from my mother's side of the family." He ran his hand slowly over the stiff wooden box covered with black painted canvas. "I always regretted that it lacked an owner who could live up to it." He opened the three clasps on the violin case slowly and deliberately, and then lifted the top and laid it back on the piano. Red velvet was the only thing visible from where Emily stood. He looked back at her and nodded toward the case, sliding quietly onto the piano bench. He folded his hands in his lap and settled down to watch.

Emily reached toward the violin after hesitating slightly, and looked down into the case. She lifted both halves of the rose silk shroud covering and laid it back with the reverence of an archeologist discovering ancient treasure. A small gasp caught in her throat. "Good Lord," she finally breathed. "Just look at how the honey varnish glows." She touched the violin with her index finger, tracing the shape of its hundred-year-old maple body down its ribs. "I had no idea it was so beautiful," she murmured. "Where was I when I used to play it? On the moon? It must have cost a fortune."

"You were much younger and very new to the instrument then," Robert answered, watching her stare at it. "Even when it was new, it was worth a king's ransom. Luckily my grandfather was a Guarneri family friend, which lowered the price considerably, but that's another story. I've always felt this violin had a hypnotic effect, but whether that's intrinsic to the instrument alone or its reputation, or both, I could never say."

"Is it a Del Gesù?" Emily asked, never taking her eyes from it. "They're certainly acoustic perfection, but also probably part of that Cremonese mystique that makes musicians feel they're under the influence of something magical."

"True. Have you made a study of the Guarneri instruments, or been to Cremona?"

"No," she answered. "But I'm fascinated by Niccolò Paganini's virtuosity as described in the newspapers, and my current teacher, Maestro Adina, told me it was Paganini's favorite violin of the four or five he owned."

"How is it you're working with a music teacher if there is no music at the school?" Robert asked, eyeing her with a suspicion and vague jealousy he'd been unaware he felt before.

"I employed him to work with me privately," Emily explained, with no more interest in the subject than she'd displayed before. "I noticed one of the other students hired some professors to teach her about architecture, so I asked around in the village and luckily enough, found a maestro who'd lived and worked in Italy. He's talked with me a lot about the importance of the right bow and violin for a particular concert hall, something Paganini has written extensively on. The maestro has even heard his favorite violin in person!" Her eyes snapped with either the excitement of the thought or the challenge to those who hadn't yet heard him, most definitely including Robert.

"Ah yes, the Del Gesù he calls Il Cannone." Robert nodded, and watched Emily with even more interest. "Has Maestro . . ."

"Adina."

". . . Adina discussed the differences between the Stradivari and Guarneri?"

"Not beyond the particulars of the luthiers' families. I don't play either one now. I borrow a modern instrument from my school." Emily pulled her eyes away from the violin with some difficulty and looked at Robert. "I suppose practicing on the equivalent of a cigar box with strings gives me a new appreciation for this one."

"You know, Emily, I've always wondered if the spirits of the luthiers—Stradivari and Guarneri, to say nothing of Amati and Bergonsi, who started it all—have permeated the instruments as they do the air of Cremona. It's a lovely place, with the mist undulating in off the Po River. Yet you know as well as I do these instruments don't show their beauty on the outside, and are even a little worn in some cases, the dye in the varnish gone from repeated handling over the last hundred years. I'm sure it's the magic of their stories that makes musicians covet them so, but the first glance can be a letdown."

"Supply and demand," Emily added, with a smile. "Their creators are dead and there will be no more offspring. But, Professor, I think if the musician believes he will play better on one of these, he will. Perhaps that's the magic."

"Well, I wouldn't be at all surprised to find that you and the Guarneri have a natural affinity for each other," Robert said. "I remember how we found you asleep in bed with the little tenor guitar I gave you after you were sick." He watched Emily's dark eyes tracing the flow of the violin's body, convinced she was playing it in her head. "The Strads are in many ways more popular with their higher, lighter tone," he continued, to give Emily time to commune with the violin's fluid curves. "Perhaps perfect for mimicking the human vocal qualities of the violin. But the Guarneri has a warmer, richer, more complex tone. Like a Burgundy wine. It's definitely a more powerful sound, hence Paganini's reference to the cannon." Robert stopped, not knowing whether she was listening or not.

"And you think I might identify more with a *cannone* than a *pistole*?" Emily laughed. "I don't know quite how to take that, Professor." She looked down at the violin lying quietly in its case. "Were there no pictures or postcards pasted in the lid, no mementos of the musician's travels? It looks lonely and a bit sad." He thought it best not to distract her with the fact that it had never been used in performance, just enjoyed in the privacy of his grandfather's home. He understood a musician's thoughts might be of the shared public life of the instrument rather than of its former owners.

"Why don't you play it?" Robert suggested, gently. "That's the only way to appreciate the quality you have in your hands and, more importantly, under your left ear." Emily smiled at the reference to the unique position of the sound that only the performer can hear.

"Could I? Perhaps just a little Bach," she breathed. "Something sweet and low, like the Guarneri itself." She took the bow out of the case and adjusted it. Then she reached for the violin. Not daring to breathe for fear it would break the spell, Robert stayed on the bench and watched, hands still resting in his lap. He noted her back straighten and chest rise, as if she was supported by an unseen arm just below her shoulder blades. She tucked the violin under her chin and ran the bow lightly back and forth over each string to check its tuning, making slight adjustments to the pegs where needed. Then she lowered her bow to her side and considered the space in front of her before shutting her eyes for a few seconds. Taking a slow, deep breath, she raised the bow, holding it delicately but firmly with her fingertips, right hand poised above the violin. Nodding slightly to her exquisite instrument partner tucked under her chin, she touched the bow to the strings.

What followed was an experience Robert would never forget and would describe often to students and friends throughout his musical life. It was Bach's first concerto in A minor, the Allegro Moderato movement. Emily started from the violin solo part, seemingly becoming one with the gentle optimism of Robert's favorite piece. Had she chosen it for him? Did she remember it, drawn to it because they'd worked on it together in this very room? How different it sounded now with a few more years of training and practice. The tempo was so right, neither too fast nor too slow, always the temptation with Bach. Surely this was just what the composer had intended. And those five notes chasing each other in thirds always set off an ecstasy in him of unknown origin. He felt the sound through every pore of his body and fiber of his soul, just as Emily did, it appeared.

But her experience, as the intermediary for the composer and the instrument, was exclusive, while his came from her skill and intonation in concert with the Guarneri. The graceful fingers of her left hand seemed barely to touch the strings, yet the truest sound came from the instrument, as if each note was born from her delicate connection to it. Was this the result of a woman's lighter touch and her technical expertise? He thought not. This was the consequence of creativity freed from any restraint. She was a true artist, not just a great musician. The fact that her playing surpassed his expectation heightened it for him, just as her unusual and unexpected loveliness held his attention without effort. He couldn't tell if the Bach and her beauty amplified each other, but the power to resist either one was not his to command. If she could inflict such unearthly joy in his music room without preparation or direct intent, imagine what she would do to an audience of committed concertgoers in a great space. Her performance career was assured with the right violin for the bigger halls, and he felt this would be the one she'd want to call hers. He would never forget the day he was there to see the old violin and the young woman choose each other.

"Love at first touch," she said quietly, after finishing a phrase and laying the instrument gently back on its velvet bed at last. She closed the case and fastened the clasps. Her hand rested a moment on the last one, reluctant to let go; then her eyes met Robert's with a frank, even gaze. "Now that was an experience to remember," she said.

"Indeed, it was," he breathed. "You should own this violin, as it appears to own you."

A low cough and rattle jarred the space around them and Robert looked up for its source with no attempt to hide his irritation. The sight of his housekeeper, white wisps of hair escaping from the bun on top of her head and apron powdered with flour and sugar, surprised him more than the sounds announcing her entrance had. "I couldn'a help hearin' the music from the kitchen," Margaret O'Brien said over the tray of teacups and saucers. She put them down on the table in front of Robert and dropped her eyes in apology. "The door was open," she added, in her defense.

"And what did you think of it, Margaret?" he asked. It was the first time she'd ever made a reference to his teaching or the life going on above the kitchen. They were in an odd position, musicians and teachers. Even Mozart had recognized he was more servant than master, though he was often better educated and poised than most of those he served.

"Heavenly," Margaret said, straightening up and smoothing her apron over her rounded middle. "I never heard nothin' like it before," she added, both hands resting together on the white apron like a nun in prayer.

"I'm sure that's true," Robert said with a smile. "Miss Alden's musical gift is special and certainly heaven-sent."

"Mother of God! It was the young lady playin'?" She stared at Emily.

"I used to be a student here with Professor Haussmann a while ago," Emily answered from her wing chair next to the table.

"I'm glad you enjoyed the music," Robert said. "I'll call you when we need the tea cleared away. Thank you." He nodded to encourage his housekeeper's departure. "That exchange was positively verbose for her," he whispered to Emily as Margaret's little round figure rocked from side to side on its way down the hall toward the stairs to the kitchen. "It appears your performance freed her tongue as well as her spirit."

"Music has a way of doing that." Emily smiled back.

"Well, yours certainly does, anyway. Have you considered pur-chasing a violin worthy of your talent?" Robert handed Emily a cup of tea.

"Often, but never seriously," she answered, with a small nod.

"Milk?" he asked, lifting the silver pitcher in her direction. "Why not seriously?"

"Because I'm a pragmatist," she answered.

"Since when?" Robert put the pitcher carefully down on the tray as if it took all his concentration. "I remember your stubbornness easily overcame rationality when you were a little girl, Emily." He watched her take a thoughtful sip from her cup.

"Some things seem easy when you don't know how hard they are," Emily said. "And of course, you and Corey supported my dreams when I was a child." She smiled at him over her cup.

"And now?" he asked, barely moving as he watched her put the cup down.

"Now I have neither one of you for support, Professor. Perhaps if I did, my aspirations would be different." Robert shifted in his chair, uncomfortable with a discussion that had moved from the general power of music to diminished personal expectations. Emily glanced across the room to the violin in its case on the piano, and Robert couldn't help remarking how like her father's face her strong, perfectly balanced profile was, a smaller but no less impressive version of British aristocracy.

"Your father has always seemed unusually . . . enlightened, especially for a member of the British aristocracy; and he's enormously proud of you. Don't you think he would want you to have the Guarneri?"

"No, Professor, I do not," she answered. "I've learned there's a very narrow line to negotiate between freedom and responsibility for women. My father may be enlightened, as you put it, but he is not revolutionary. There are certain liberties reserved only for men and he is still a firm believer in the rules." Emily took another sip of her tea. "After all," she went on, "there wouldn't be an aristocracy without those rules."

Robert couldn't believe he was sitting across from an Emily who appeared to accept the parameters of her new adult world. The silence extended further than he was comfortable, but she seemed to sit easily without the need to fill it with talk. Finally, he stirred in his chair and met Emily's eyes directly for the first time since they'd sat down. "If you feel a bend in his rules would be impossible with the suggestion coming from you, perhaps he would be more pliant if I introduced the idea. Would you be comfortable with me approaching him on the purchase of the Guarneri for you?"

"Oh, Professor," she said, sighing and putting her cup down. "Of course, I'd be comfortable with anything you want to do on your own, but I must warn you that it will have no impact. An instrument like that one represents a huge financial investment, and my father would not consider it appropriate for a woman's pleasure." She hadn't suggested her father had any inkling she dreamed of becoming a paid performer with the violin.

"Are you sure?" he asked, leaning forward with a resolve he hadn't shown before.

"Certain," she replied. Robert took a long sip of his tea. The time had come to put his plan into action.

"Then I shall loan it to you," he said definitively over his cup. "You can consider it my support for your intention to become a concert musician."

"You can't do that." Her expression was so severe he half-expected corporal punishment to follow.

"Indeed, I can," he said, just as sternly. Emily stared at him with shock and disbelief. "All I ask is that you stay in touch about your progress and play for me occasionally when you are in the city, if it's convenient. Does that sound reasonable?" He drained his cup and replaced it with the saucer on the tray. Emily watched him in silence. "Well, does it?" he asked her again with a little smile.

"Of course, Professor. Your offer humbles me beyond words." She turned to place her cup and saucer on the table beside her.

"Are you quite done? Another cup, perhaps?" Robert asked, as she gently shook her head. He stood to pull the bell chord, signaling Margaret in the kitchen that they were finished with their tea. Slowly Emily rose from her chair as well and moved toward the piano. "Are you absolutely sure?" she asked him.

"Absolutely."

"It's against the rules, you know," she said, with a familiar, daring little spark in her eye. It relieved him to see the child Emily still lived inside the grown woman.

"Not my rules," he answered. "It's absolutely in support of the laws of music and nature. The world will thank me for it someday," he added, smiling.

"Well I already thank you for it," she cried out, grabbing both of his hands. "But how can I—properly? There's no way." Robert found himself looking down into soft brown eyes with the depth and beauty of a Schumann fantasy.

"Just keep playing it the way you did today. That will be thanks enough," he said. "And you'll stay in touch, so I know how you're doing . . . with it, I mean?"

"You are a dear," she said, standing on tiptoe and lightly brushing his cheekbone above his beard in a kiss. She was still holding on to his hands with her eyes shining into his when Margaret appeared in the doorway.

"It's decided then. The Guarneri is yours," Robert said, slipping his hands hurriedly out of Emily's. It did not escape him that she would leave his house that day with something of his that was far more important than his violin.

CHAPTER SIX

"You've really done it this time, de Koningh," Charlie Hancock muttered under his breath, hovering at the foot of Corey's hospital bed like a lingering nightmare. But there was nothing spectral about Charlie. Long, wavy brown hair almost to his shoulders, and what was probably a fine bone structure beneath his still baby-fat face, Charlie's two-hundred-pound bulk made a very solid impression on anyone who saw it. "You look ghastly, Corey! Doesn't he?" His tone dripped with acid as he sought the corroboration of his classmate, little Bill Henry, who stood at the head of Corey's bed. The only member of their quartet missing was Jock Mitchell, probably because football practice had started.

"Thanks, Charlie," Corey groaned through his bandages. "If I look half as bad as you do looming over me, then I must be pretty frightful." He grimaced and tried to push himself up on his cot. "Can you stick a pillow under my head, Bill? I can't sit up on my own steam yet."

"Don't say steam anywhere anyone can hear you," Bill cried, grabbing the pillow and wedging it under Corey's shoulders. "I know you're a veteran rule-breaker, but what caused you to take on the university administration and your father at the same time? Driving one of those murderous steam engine carriages was the worst idea you've ever had." Bill tried to settle the pillow low enough to prop his friend higher.

"You can't break the rules if you don't know them, Billy," Corey sighed. "How did I know there was a ban on students driving the new steam engines? No one said anything about it until I'd gone off the road and turned over."

"Not exactly, de Koningh." Charlie shrugged the collar of his camel hair coat up higher as if to protect against his friend's foolishness. His hands thrust in his pockets, he looked like he was enjoying a casual get-together in the quad instead of enduring the college infirmary with his classmates. "Meeting that inventor, Mr. Roper, in Boston was one thing, but joining him on a test drive was quite another! And your father was certainly not amused. I think he's despairing of you ever taking over the family business."

"Oh, I do hope he's despairing," Corey muttered. "Nothing would please me more."

"He has such high expectations for you," Bill sighed. He was the only friend of Corey's who seemed to think his father offered him a viable alternative to bad behavior.

"The wrong expectations." Corey closed his eyes. "High or low is of no consequence," he groaned.

"Come now," Bill begged, bending down over Corey with a worried expression. "Don't go unconscious on us again. We have important business to discuss."

"I say, de Koningh, is this another one of your bright ideas to get closer to the female form?" Charlie dropped his voice when he saw a young nurse pass by on her way down the hall. "If so, I'd say you've gone too far this time."

"Yes, you've both said that already, Charlie. Now just help me drink a little of that water, Billy, and then leave me alone to wallow in my misery in peace." Corey moaned as he tried to shift his position to ease his cramped legs, the bed being too short for his six-foot-plus frame.

"None of that," Bill scolded, supporting his friend's head with one hand and holding the glass straw in the water glass to his lips. He took to his volunteer role as Corey's nurse with obvious pleasure. "Feeling sorry for yourself will do neither you nor us any good."

"What 'us'? Why should I be worrying about anyone other than myself right now? I'm the one who was almost killed in Roper's newfangled contraption, and I'm the one with the concussion and enough bandages to do an Egyptian mummy proud."

Bill hovered by Corey's head, concern for his friend clear in the furrows on his forehead. "I have some great news for you," Bill said, heralding an announcement clearly designed to raise Corey's spirits. "Our recently formed singing group has an engagement to perform at the Artists' Club in New York! That's the 'us.' The University Glee Club, as I believe we agreed we should call ourselves, is to do a half-hour of glees and four-part songs for the club's new members at the artists' mansion downtown. What do you think of that news, Corey?"

"How did that happen?" he asked. Their four-man choral group had never performed outside the university and he couldn't imagine how word spread from Boston to New York in a matter of the three days he'd been hospitalized. Seeing his friend standing by his bed with a chest so full and smile so broad, Corey thought Bill might explode at any minute. What an odd group they made. Somehow, they'd all known they were cut from much the same cloth— although every cloth had different characteristics depending on where its thread had been grown. Bill, from his big family and solid middle-class background in Philadelphia, Charlie and Jock, from their New England rural aristocracy that only a "new" England could have produced, while he . . . only his Dutch ancestry gave his family its position of elite power in New York. Music, or specifically sing- ing, had brought them all together.

"A university alumnus is on the Artists' Club board," Bill explained. "He heard us sing at the alumni dinner and called the chorus master to ask if we would perform for the opening of their new building in New York. The master told him we're a private student group and not promoted by the university, so that's how he got to me. I am the business manager, after all," he added, pulling over a chair by the bed and perching on it like a proud blue jay staking a claim.

"Indeed, you are, Billy," Corey agreed, careful not to smile because it would pull the stitches in his face. "But we don't have the repertoire to perform for a half-hour. We've sung 'Turn, Amaryllis' and a few madrigals, but they're not enough for a longer concert."

"Precisely!" Charlie looked as discontented as Corey.

"What am I missing, Billy?" Corey asked. "Should this make me happy?"

"You're missing the fact that you'll compose new songs for us," Bill announced with satisfaction. "That should make you happy. You can do it, Corey, if you stay out of trouble. No more rule-breaking for at least a fortnight. Agreed?"

"You must be mad," Corey groaned beneath his bandages. "I write music. I can't write lyrics. Are we going to hum for half an hour?"

"Jock can write the lyrics," Bill said. "He can't play football all day, and we all know he avoids his homework. He should have plenty of time to come up with something new for us. If you can keep your nose clean, we can get this done. Corey, we must be the first glee club anywhere. We can get some attention for ourselves and your music. What say you put your fertile brain to the task of composing instead of misbehaving for a while? It could be the start of a whole new career, one that's more acceptable to the university administration as well as your father!"

"Sounds boring," Corey sighed, closing his eyes. But in truth, he could already hear a four-part a cappella song dancing through him in teasing counterpoint.

Three weeks later, and already sporting their Thanksgiving holiday moods, Charlie Hancock, Bill Henry, and Jock Mitchell stood together across from the Artists' Club mansion on the edge of a private park in Manhattan. They gazed at the building as carriages rolled by, occasionally interrupting their view.

"Rather vulgar, don't you think?" Charlie had an expression of disgust on his face. "What do they call that style? It looks like it can't make up its mind what it wants to be. Victorian? Greek Revival? Architecture in transition is a redundancy."

"Oh, come now, Charlie. All new buildings offer a kind of transition between styles. I think they call this movement aestheticism." Jock sounded pretty sure of himself, either due to his actual knowledge or because he didn't want to let Charlie get away with his air of superiority. "They say it's a very middle-class style, offering nice things for everyone instead of just the wealthy."

"What's wrong with that?" Bill muttered.

"Not a thing, Billy," Jock crowed, cheerfully. "Some people just don't like change, even in art." The three young men seemed hesitant to move from their side of the street, where they could view the Artists' Club at a distance. Pre-performance jitters likely kept them there rather than an appreciation for the aesthetic style of the building. They were more than an hour early for their performance, as requested, but nerves and curiosity had assured their premature arrival. They watched as cabs began to roll up, horses' hooves echoing on the cobblestones sporadically. The light had already faded from a gray layer of dusk to the eventual darkness of an early winter evening, making their performance loom closer than they were perhaps prepared for.

"Where the hell is Corey?" Jock asked.

"Walking," muttered Bill.

"All the way from his house on upper Fifth Avenue? He'll never get here in time, if at all." Jock shoved his hands in his pockets and kicked the granite paver in front of him. He had a way of getting his feet involved when he was uncomfortable, the athlete in him attempting to control the situation as he would a ball. "I knew we never should have taken this concert, Bill. Didn't I tell you that from the beginning?"

"Oh, cheer up, Jock. He's not coming from home. I left him at the Astor Free Library just south of here. He said the walk would quiet the jitters. He'll be here." Jock and Charlie looked somewhat relieved, knowing Bill could read Corey better than they could. Streetlights started to go on around the park and all three young men sighed in unison, which made them look up at each other and laugh.

"Nothing better to banish nerves than a good deep breath, boys," Jock intoned, just as their chorus master would. The old-fashioned advice followed them whether they liked it or not.

"Look, fellows," Bill said. "Don't those streetlamps turn the park into something magic? But I never noticed the lamplighter going around."

"There isn't a lamplighter anymore, Bill. What rock have you been living under? Maybe that's why you're so short," Jock teased, pushing Bill's cap down over his eyes. "They're all on automatic starters. Even in a backwater town like Boston we have those. You're just new to gaslight, coming as you do from the swamps of Philly, Billy."

"Not exactly. We already have gas in our house, big man." Bill pushed his cap back off his forehead. He was used to the teasing from his friends and took no offense, since he knew none was intended. He had a temper, but few ever saw it. It seemed easier to deal with teasing by relying on his empathy for others. Their tension was palpable.

"Fellows, we can't wait any longer," Charlie said, grimly. "People are arriving now, and we need a little warm-up before we perform even though we've already rehearsed. Too bad the club wouldn't let us in this afternoon to warm up here. Corey can find us inside on his own, damn him!" Whether it was just Charlie's performance nerves, or he was really angry, none of his friends could tell, but they all started to cross the street behind Charlie's huge bulk to the front door of the mansion.

A private carriage driven by a man in elegant livery pulled up just as they got to the stoop. The doorman came out from the club to assist the passengers. All three glee club members watched in silence as a tall, handsome older man ascended from the coach. A younger man with red hair and beard followed, and then turned to help the last passenger out. A young woman with a head of rich, dark hair and an intelligent face dominated by lively brown eyes straightened up as she reached for his hand, stepping easily down to the street. She attracted attention effortlessly, emerging from the carriage bareheaded, which was a surprising fashion choice, making her even more noticeable. Her glossy auburn hair swept up off her neck and wrapped around itself, glowing in the early evening streetlamps. She appeared to be traveling in her own personal spotlight. She wasn't tall, yet somehow gave an impression of command. Holding her head and eyes level, she looked out without reserve.

They were so close they could hear her say to her red-haired companion, "That's quite a façade. Designed by one of the famous architects of the day, I'll warrant." Her companion nodded to her and they followed the older man in the lead. Just as they'd almost reached the door, a human missile streaked from the side to grab the door handle, almost knocking them down. His lengthy frame would have attracted notice even if his actions hadn't.

"Corey!" Bill cried, forgetting he was no longer standing apart at a distance in the park. "Finally, you're here!" His face lit up with relief.

The carriage passengers froze with the shock of the assault, and all the classmates, save Bill, stood speechless staring at Corey, but none of them showed the effects of the impact as profoundly as Corey himself. The red-bearded man was the first to recover his voice. "Well, my goodness, I do believe we've been attacked by a grown-up Corey de Koningh. Is it possible?" He stretched his free hand toward Corey. "Robert Haussmann, Corey. Your old music teacher." Corey looked from the face to the gloved hand and back before he met the offered greeting. He still couldn't seem to speak. "Well, indeed I was right!" the music teacher laughed. "I noticed that the glee club performing tonight was from Harvard, and wondered if we might get a chance to see you in action at last! It seems we won't be disappointed."

The young woman held both her gloved hands out as if to grasp both of Corey's, seemingly a reaction to the fact that he was staring at her without any pretense of reserve or politeness, but he didn't react to her reach. She folded her hands in on each other again as if to protect her small leather purse. Bill guessed it was more likely she was covering up her embarrassment at Corey's refusal to respond. She nodded her head slightly at him and smiled, two dimples punctuating what was clearly meant to be a friendly greeting.

"Right." Bill looked hard at Corey. "And we are his fellow musicians performing here tonight. We call ourselves the University Glee Club. Delighted to meet you, Mr. Haussmann and Miss . . . ? This is Jock Mitchell, and Charlie Hancock, and I'm Bill Henry."

"Delighted, Mr. Henry." The young woman stepped in front of the teacher and took Bill's hand. "And this is my father, Lord Alden." None of them could have missed that her attention was riveted on Corey still. But she was indeed worth noticing for other reasons. Bill noticed the way her confident, dark eyes rested on each one of them before settling on Corey. Her slow laugh stimulated them all unexpectedly. "Corey," she exclaimed, eyes dancing, "it is you. Emily Alden, in case you've forgotten." She slipped her right arm out of her companion's, and rose on her toes to kiss Corey's cheek. He bent forward to receive it in a trance. The entire University Glee Club looked stunned, but no one so much as Corey.

She turned to the older man and led Corey toward him. "Corey," the young beauty said with a faint trace of a British accent, "this is my father, Lord Alden. I'm not at all sure you've ever been formally introduced. Father, you probably remember Corey . . . my precocious twelve-year-old friend who played the piano at the de Koninghs' when you visited from London." She leaned away to get a better look up at Corey. "He's grown—a great deal!"

When Lord Alden turned to meet Corey with the same open, pleasant expression his daughter had mastered, Corey suddenly found his elusive voice. But instead of reaching out to Lord Alden, he shook off the young woman's hand and dashed past them both, muttering, "I'm terribly late . . ." With that, he disappeared through the Artists' Club door to the vestibule, leaving the scattered group gaping at the spot where he'd been standing moments before. Bill was the first to apologize.

"I beg you," he said, "please forgive Corey. He's been terribly ill . . . had a concussion . . . still suffers effects . . . If you'll excuse us, we should prepare. I hope you enjoy the performance." He pushed Jock and Charlie through the door in front of him with a scowl.

He couldn't meet Lord Alden's eyes, and ignored the girl and the red-haired man so he could stop apologizing. At their first encounter with audience members and possible supporters, they were running away instead of courting them. Not exactly the best way to build a base of admirers. "Jock, get him and find out what's happening," Bill muttered under his breath. "Settle him down somehow. We'll meet you in the bar. They've closed it off for our warm-up. Bring him along when you can."

"I write his lyrics; I'm not his keeper. I don't know how to settle him down. That's your department. I've never seen him like this before," Jock whispered. The look on Jock's face told Bill they were all shocked by Corey's bizarre behavior.

"Nor have I," Charlie agreed. "We're used to his habitual

shenanigans—a bit of innocent skirt chasing, occasional immature pranks for fun—but he's always been thoughtful and never outright rude. That's not Corey."

"Well, it is tonight," Jock stated, flatly. The three young men circled together, trying to keep their backs to the Artists' Club members arriving in a steady stream.

"I'll find him and talk to him," Bill said. "Our goal is to get him to perform. A four-part glee with three voices fails miserably before we open our mouths." Bill rushed off toward two huge oak doors at the back of the hall.

"Where are you going?" Charlie called after him.

"We were all supposed to warm up in the closed bar, and this looks like a bar to me," Bill called back over his shoulder. Jock and Charlie followed, pulling up short when they reached the door. The oak-paneled room with a stained-glass ceiling had a long counter, polished to mirror sheen. Red leather upholstered stools lined the front and side of the bar, and they were relieved to see Corey settled on one of the stools, staring into the mirror behind the glasses displayed on the wall. But they could tell by his glazed expression that he was focused on something only he could see. Big Charlie was the first to move. He sprang forward with his huge frame, nearly knocking Bill over, and grabbed Corey by the lapels of his jacket. "What are you doing? Have you lost your mind?" he hissed. Corey just looked at him.

"Let him go." Bill forced his short, compact frame between Corey and Charlie. "I'll handle this. It's time you two started your warm-up, Jock . . . Charlie. Come on, Corey," he ordered in a quiet voice. "Let's find the gentlemen's lounge." Pulling Corey off the stool and putting his arm through his friend's, he steered the way out of the bar. Charlie and Jock watched as if they were seeing a theater act leave the stage. They were used to seeing the unmatched pair linked arm in arm. "Vaudeville's best material if I ever saw it," Charlie chuckled. "Five-foot minus and six-foot plus make for strange bedfellows indeed."

"There's no hope," Jock moaned. "We'll be the laughingstock of the university when word gets out about our debacle at the Artists' Club."

"Give Bill a chance." Charlie moved over to close the massive oak door they'd left ajar, watching his classmates' backs disappearing around a corner in the distance. "He and Corey have an uncanny way of communicating," Charlie said. "Can you locate middle C on that piano over there?" he asked, turning back to the room as he pushed the door shut. "If so, strike it for me so we can find our pitch. We need to vocalize and be ready in case Bill works a miracle." Together they moved over to the piano, their discomfort more acute with the absence of Corey to support their voices and spirits. No one played the piano the way Corey did, and no one could ignite that spark in them before a concert as he could. They looked at one another anxiously.

On the other side of the door and down the hall a waiter indicated there was a lounge attached to the men's room, and Bill steered Corey toward it. Once over the threshold, he turned to pull his friend after him. Anyone watching would have assumed from the tall young man's pallor that he was ill, and so the rush to the lounge only produced a few sympathetic stares.

Inside the room, Bill spotted a chaise longue in the corner next to a table with a huge brass ashtray, presumably meant to balance large Cuban cigars. Thankfully there was no one present, and Bill grabbed the ashtray, dashing off to a sink to fill it with cold water. He returned with it and a towel, ordering Corey to lie down on the chaise and putting the bowl on the table. Soaking the towel and wringing it out with forceful determination, he ordered Corey to loosen his collar while he started to wipe his face. Then he told Corey to rest his head on the back cushion of the chaise while he placed the washcloth across his forehead. "Better?" he asked, watching Corey close his eyes for a minute and take a deep breath. "Headache again?" Bill asked.

"Not really."

"What then? Performance jitters?"

"No."

"Then could it have been those people we ran into outside the club?" He tried to sneak the question past Corey almost unnoticed.

"Yes, I suppose." Corey's face was suddenly grim.

"Should we talk about it?" Bill asked, suspecting he'd uncovered more than he'd intended.

"Not now," Corey answered, turning the washcloth over on his forehead and closing his eyes. Bill watched him with a pain of sympathy rising in his chest along with a panic for the work that lay ahead of them all.

"Can you pull yourself together enough to help us through this performance?" There was no time to avoid the point of it.

"I don't think so, Bill," Corey said, weakly. Bill had never seen his friend's beautiful face so pained.

"This isn't the concussion, is that what you're saying? It's emotional?"

"What's the difference, Billy?"

"Don't get cagey with me, de Koningh," Bill snapped, suddenly losing the patience that had seemed boundless a few moments ago. "You have a responsibility to your fellow glee club members, and you know that perfectly well. I suspect something important is attached to those people you met . . ." His voice dropped to a lower pitch and slower cadence. ". . . but, whatever it is can't take precedence over our first public performance and your music." Corey opened his eyes and reached up to pull the towel off his forehead. He slipped it back in the bowl and turned his head slowly to look at Bill.

"I'm not without compassion, Corey," Bill continued, looking his prostrate friend in the eye. "I see you've had a shock. But you must find a way to put it behind you for the next hour or so and help us get through this concert. You owe it to us and to yourself, even if that seems far-fetched in light of whatever is bothering you right now."

"Impossible." Corey closed his eyes again for a second. Bill couldn't help staring at his insensible friend, appreciating what a handsome man Corey was. The grace of those long fingers placed on the piano always caught Bill's breath before the first tones from the instrument ever could. He knew he wasn't alone in that. You could hear the hush in the audience as it took stock of the willowy blond pianist at the keyboard. Then of course the music that seemed to flow from his body instead of the piano overcame all other impressions. Corey truly was stunning to look at as well as listen to.

Bill often enjoyed watching other people watch Corey play as much as he enjoyed the music. He'd volunteered to be Corey's assistant, do all the business administration for his performances just to stay close and follow him. But he knew they all needed a leader tonight. They had no one as engaging as Corey, no reputation to go on, and no preparation to perform three-part harmonies. They were nothing without Corey. With him, they could do almost anything. That made Corey the linchpin. Bill wasn't sure it was good for one glee member to have that kind of impact on the group, or on him, for that matter, but it was reality. "It's impossible without you, Corey." He could think of nothing else to say but the truth.

Corey looked just over his friend's head and beyond the room. "You're right, Bill," he sighed, starting to push himself up off the chaise. "There's no choice in this, even if I'd rather disappear into a big hole and pull it in behind me." He looked as if the blood had drained completely from his face and left it a gray mask. "Let's go back to the bar. Maybe a little vocalizing will bring us all together for long enough to get it over with."

"I know you can do it," Bill said, grabbing Corey's arm and turning him toward the door, as if pointing him in the right direction could ensure success. "Let's go. The fellows will probably be out of their minds with worry by now." Corey nodded, and forced himself up straighter, looking far away again. Bill wondered if he was seeing those people on the street again.

That threesome coming out of the carriage outside the club

hadn't been overly remarkable. But what was notable was that they'd known Corey almost instantly. Bill had never heard him mention them before. The nobleman was dark, graceful, and attractive with a pleasant expression; the redheaded man interesting and friendly, and the girl . . . odd he'd never mentioned that girl, who was so obviously an old and very good friend. Bill suddenly knew he was angry about and jealous of the intensity of Corey's reaction. There was a thread connecting Corey and the girl. He watched as the University Glee Club's pianist and composer buttoned his collar and tied his tie before leaving the gentlemen's lounge. Bill wished he'd made a mistake diagnosing Corey's affliction, but knew he hadn't. His heart fell.

CHAPTER SEVEN

THE EXPLOSION in Corey's head had detonated with more force than when he'd hit the road after his steam-powered automobile turned over in a ditch. He didn't know if the shock had come from the sight of Emily emerging from the carriage, or of Professor Haussmann reaching up to take her hand. There was something smooth and familiar about them together, as if their lives had swept forward, altering and re-forming along the way without Corey being aware it had happened. Then, suddenly, he'd been let in on the changes without warning.

He realized he'd assumed Emily would never grow up. It was easier to leave her in clear amber, a fossil beautifully frozen in his memory. Moving at the age of fifteen to preparatory boarding school in New England and then university had been a big adjustment in Corey's life. He'd worked hard to replace home, family, and Emily with classmates, friends, and teachers. Yet he'd surely changed, too. All the outrageous growth, yearning, learning, and hard-won independence was accomplished by leaving everything from childhood behind, or so he'd thought. He hadn't wanted to admit how totally Emily had filled the emptiness he'd been forced to grow up in. Obviously, he hadn't left Emily since the first day they'd met, and she'd raced down the hall ahead of him; always ahead of him. She'd been hard to follow.

What a relief it had been for Corey to have someone his own age to play with, offering an escape from taking care of his supposedly invalid mother. After Emily arrived he had less time and inclination to be drawn into his mother's need for attention. Even living a life totally circumscribed by the de Koningh mansion, with Emily living there, too, Corey had found a freedom he'd never dreamed of. She seemed to ignore the boundaries of its massive limestone walls, moving with a lightness and ease through them to the outside world with all its fascinations. At the same time, she'd helped Corey see how lucky he was to have such a lovely, cheerful home with a father who returned regularly from his business trips to listen to the children's tales of adventure and music. Occasionally Emily's father stopped by on his way to somewhere, but neither Corey nor Emily had paid much attention to those visits. Lord Alden hadn't seemed to fulfill Emily's need for a father as well as Corey's father had. Nor had Corey's mother qualified as a replacement for Emily's own mother, who Corey believed had taken on heroic proportions in Emily's memory. Not that his real mother lived up to his own idea of a desirable parent, either.

He wondered what Professor Haussmann had to do with it. He'd been Corey's childhood music teacher—their music teacher—his and Emily's link to each other and the adult world. Professor Haussmann hadn't changed a bit, except perhaps he wasn't as big or as old as Corey remembered. They'd all caught up with each other, yet apparently Emily had gotten ahead of him again and somehow it appeared the professor was her collaborator now. That was the worst thing of all. Corey had been left out of their threesome. Always before, he and Emily had stuck together with the professor's help, to negotiate the necessities of the adult world.

The constriction in his throat said he wanted to leave Professor Haussmann out now, permanently. He concentrated on the task of fastening his collar and knotting his tie, aware that Bill was moving him forward toward the lounge door. His thoughts had to coalesce around the music. His focus needed to be on the harmony, not the discord. A small gathering like this tended to bring musicians and audience together. Surely tonight would be no different. Corey had two instruments to deal with, the piano and his voice, as well as leading the others in the new music he'd so recently composed. With so much to concentrate on, he could keep specific members of the audience out of his mind.

He, Bill, Charlie, and Jock all wanted to be heard. They needed the public exposure to ensure a future for their glee club. The chance of their college lifetimes mustn't be squandered. He had to put blinders on his imagination and forget about Emily sitting up straight and compelling somewhere in the audience. He could almost see that little half-smile on her face with the dimples at the corners of her mouth giving away the laugh inside, always sharing her private joke with life. He remembered the zest of that smile.

Corey and Bill sped down the carpeted hall to the bar behind the oak doors. "Ten minutes, just give us ten minutes," Bill kept saying every time he passed someone looking like Artists' Club staff. Twenty minutes later they all left the bar together and marched, heads held high with frozen smiles on their faces, toward the chamber music room at the rear of the building. Looking greatly relieved, the club manager smiled back at them and opened the doors to the room. He nodded slightly, and together they strode down the aisle between chairs arranged in front of the piano. A huge Steinway concert grand stood waiting to be brought to life. It was turned parallel to the audience with its lid fully extended, satin black finish gleaming in the light from wall sconces and a multifaceted crystal chandelier in the center of the coffered ceiling.

"Oh, my God!" Corey moaned under his breath. "We could be heard across Niagara Falls the way that's set up. Charlie, keep them busy with your patter. Jock and Bill, I need you to help me push it back angled away from the audience."

He raised the massive lid and removed the prop so he could close the piano completely. Then he crouched over to loosen the brakes on the shiny brass wheels at the base of the legs. They moved easily. Bill dropped down to loosen the one at the far end as he'd seen Corey do. Corey signaled Jock and Bill to push the piano back as far as possible and turn it on an angle to reduce the resonance a little. They could hear Charlie, his tongue loosened by relief and necessity, entertaining everyone with his signature charm and wit.

"You thought we were musicians," Charlie quipped. "Wrong! We're just the movers." A unanimous chuckle arose in the room. "We're good at this, aren't we?" Charlie went on, obviously delighted to find the audience with him. "Well, just wait till you hear us sing if you like this." He laughed with the audience and shoved his hands in his pockets while he watched the others working on the piano. "Why aren't I helping them?" he asked. "Because my agent doesn't allow any piano moving," he answered himself. "Too delicate," he sighed, patting his large stomach. A few guffaws broke out. "But I can sing, and so can they. Come on, fellows, let's show them!" The audience started to applaud encouragement, which was all Charlie needed.

"Time for introductions," he said, "in case you need to call us to move something for you later. The little fellow at the end there is Bill Henry. Don't worry. He won't take offense. He knows we love him. He's only little compared to the wide, heavy, and tall rest of us. And in front there is Jock Mitchell. He's the strong one, as you can see, but he mostly lives in his head making up his wonderful lyrics." Jock faked a glowered warning at Charlie to go no further.

Charlie backed off. "At the keyboard is Adriaan de Koningh. Adriaan writes the music for us, and plays it too, and I'm Charlie Hancock. So, Adriaan's the tall one, Jock's the strong one, and Bill's the little one. I guess that makes me the heavy one." A round of laughter indicated everyone was enjoying Charlie's self-deprecation. "We've been together so long I can only tell who I am in comparison with them." He chuckled, and the audience applauded their welcome again.

"Let's get going, men," Charlie cried. He watched the others straighten up and come back to the keyboard at the end of the piano, then turned back to the audience. "Glees, as you may know, are four-part a cappella songs, which means we don't have to learn to play an instrument because there aren't any." He looked around to be sure he had everyone's attention. Satisfied, he turned back to look at his friends again. "We'll start with an old seventeenth-century glee by Thomas Brewer called 'Turn, Amaryllis, to Thy Swain,' and end with some nineteenth-century ones written by our own Adriaan de Koningh." He bowed slightly in Corey's direction. "In between, we'll sing some intricate part-songs by John Travers and William Haves from the eighteenth century. You have those marked on your pro- grams." He held up a copy of the brochures the audience had on their laps. "Why the piano, you're asking yourselves, if we're singing a cappella? Good question! We just like to move furniture! No, the last songs by Adriaan are composed with and sung to piano accompani- ment. He makes up his own rules. Always has."

The other glee club members formed a semicircle upstage, behind Corey at the piano, so that he could see them, and they could watch his directions. He looked at all three while he sat very still on the piano bench, his hands resting in his lap. Waiting for the singers and audience to settle, he was reminded of the taut silence filled with expectation surrounding him and Emily years ago when they hid behind the door in the library waiting to surprise Professor Haussmann.

"Don't breathe," twelve-year-old Corey had whispered as they watched and listened.

"You just did," she'd whispered back.

He couldn't suppress a smile now, recalling her sparkling eyes and upturned lips behind the warning index finger pressed against them. Forehead to forehead, they'd waited to spring out of their hiding place just as the professor walked into the room. She'd almost exploded with pent-up excitement, but Corey always pushed the door slowly away as the professor walked in, and with a quiet, formal voice said, "Good morning, Professor. We've been waiting for you."

"Why don't you ever let me jump out and really frighten him?" Emily had asked when they sat up on the roof together one day. "I hate when people tell me I can't do something without giving me a reason."

"Silence can be more affecting than noise," he'd said, while she pouted next to him. "Even Mozart said that the space between can mean more than the notes themselves, Lady Liberty." They'd looked out over the tops of the trees across Fifth Avenue where the park might someday be. He could still remember the canopy of red and gold leaves packed tight below them, a fall crazy quilt of incomparable richness. Sitting next to each other, they breathed in the spice of earth and wet leaves, saying nothing, until Emily could stay silent no longer.

"You think people will listen to you because you're a boy. So was Mozart," she'd added, though it was clear she knew that wasn't the point. "You start out believing people will pay attention to you no matter what. It's really not fair."

He'd frowned, knowing it takes a lot of confidence to realize you can be quiet and noticed at the same time. He'd tried to help her with that. He remembered how she'd looked at him then so seriously. He wished she would look at him that way right now. He felt as if he was on the wrong side of the door tonight with her father and the professor watching him instead. A hiss from Bill followed by an order to *Wake up!* brought him back to the piano.

Corey sighed and played four notes of a chord separately and together. Each of the singers, including him, sounded out their tone as he rose to join them in their semicircle, until all four were humming the chord together. Corey nodded, looked at each one of them individually, and started to mouth the count silently with his back to the audience, and then lifted his head. The University Glee Club, first collegiate group of its kind in the country, was about to perform in public. Emily, his young friend from England, had introduced him to the songs that set his interest in them at first. He'd thought of her when his friends had suggested they form a club of choristers to celebrate the vocal specialty known as glees. He just didn't admit it to anyone, including himself.

He could feel the melody resonate in his head and listened carefully for the others' voices. They all watched him and each other with the same intent. Jock needed to push his big bass voice up a little and Bill had to cap his enthusiasm. His countertenor soared with such purity it could carry them all away. Corey turned his head from the audience for a minute and put his finger to his lips when he looked at Bill, who got the point and adjusted. Then Corey smiled at Jock and lifted his head a little. Jock also understood. His bass moved up to fill the space Bill had left for him. Now they were all blended together like one glorious voice. The last notes of "Turn, Amaryllis" died away and the audience applauded with what sounded like true enthusiasm, though none of the singers could be sure—the moment existed for them in another dimension.

Charlie announced the next songs in turn and each one was offered from the performers to the listeners to transport them; some of the audience members seemed to be lifted in their seats to the lilt of the music. There was nothing as wonderful, even the fun they had singing together, as when the audience connected with them and they could see and feel their partnership. After each song, the listeners were extremely generous with their applause. It didn't surprise Corey, knowing there were musicians out there, including the professor and Emily. He looked out now to connect with them as he'd always done in the library at home when he played during their lessons. Before he could stop himself, he realized he'd made a mistake allowing her back in his head. He couldn't resist connecting with the faces in front of him instead of looking out over them. And there she was, smiling broadly with those dimples so deep they looked permanently molded in her cheeks. There the professor was too, right beside her, clapping enthusiastically. He was leaning in toward Emily to say something only she could appreciate.

Corey heard Charlie announce he was handing his job over to the composer of the next four glees. That should be him, but he couldn't move. Charlie picked up on his distress before anyone in the audience could, reached out for Jock's hand and pulled him forward.

"Unfortunately, the composer of the music and the lyricist can't talk at the same time, so we've decided Jock will tell you about the songs. Adriaan's the quiet type, like most composers," Charlie added as an afterthought, with a wink at the audience. They seemed to be with him, as he heard a few low chuckles. He'd gambled that Corey's height and blond good looks would deny the assumption of a shy persona.

Corey took his place at the piano, thankful to have something so familiar to do, and the next four songs floated past him in perfect tempo and tone. The applause gained energy. The last song was a rousing combination of a sea shanty and madrigal, and the audience started to call out *Bravi* as the clapping grew louder and louder. When it ended, Corey joined his friends and the young singers linked arms and all bowed together as one, flushed with excitement and pleasure. All but Corey. He couldn't get rid of the chill in his chest and was glad for the physical support the fellows gave him as they held on to each other in bow after bow. The room swam every time he lifted his head. Finally, they stood still, and the Artists' Club manager darted through the audience and came to stand in front of them. He seemed very pleased with himself, and took full credit for inviting the new glee club to perform for the members that night.

Corey was relieved to find they were ushered out ahead of everyone else and taken to the manager's private office where he was already seated waiting for them. Corey was even happier to see the door closed behind them, as some of the audience would soon leave the music chamber and move down the hall past the office. He began to relax a little.

"Is your music in print yet, Mr. de Koningh?" the manager asked. "If not, I hope you'll allow me to introduce you to the best publisher in New York."

"Adriaan, please sir," Corey answered, "and no, I haven't pursued publishing yet, but I'm flattered you think my songs worthy."

"Oh, I do, I do, young man. Am I wrong, Mr. Clarke?" The manager seemed to suggest it inconceivable he could be mistaken, as he turned to the club president for corroboration.

Corey rose to his full height, smiled his thanks with all the graciousness his friends had come to expect but seen little of that evening, and thanked the manager for his offer to arrange a meeting for him with the publisher. Looking from one to the other, he suggested perhaps they might choose another performance date for the glee club, at which time he could present more new work. Both the manager and president beamed and each shook Corey's hand in succession, sealing the deal right on the spot. At that moment, a knock came on the door and it opened just enough to allow Professor Haussmann's copper head to appear around it.

"Any objections to allowing one of your founding members to congratulate these young men on their fine performances?" the professor asked. "My guests would also like to greet an old friend," he went on, opening the door wider to reveal Emily and her father standing behind him.

"Oh, by all means, come in, Professor Haussmann," the manager called. "Mr. de Koningh has just been telling me all about the glee club's plans and his desire to publish his songs." The professor smiled and stepped back to usher Emily and her father through the door before him. Emily passed him with her hand already reaching out to Corey.

"You're still composing, Corey," she said. "Wonderful. But when and why did you change your name?" Corey suddenly felt very hot, wishing he could fall through the floor instead of taking up so much space in the already overcrowded office.

Emily looked at him, amusement and delight lighting her eyes, as he struggled to find his voice. He took her hand and said, "It's still Corey to my friends, but I use my given name in public. It makes my father happy," he added, noticing she still held his hand, but it was now grasped in both of hers.

"I understand." She nodded. "You'll notice I gave in and no longer wear my hair loose. That makes my father happy. But we compromise to keep hats off my head when I deem them significantly inappropriate, as at a concert where they can block views to the stage for anyone behind them." They stood smiling at each other as the professor and Lord Alden stepped around them to shake hands with the Artists' Club officials and other members of the glee club. Corey was aware of sound and movement but saw nothing other than Emily standing with him in the middle of the room. Moving themselves off to one side, he heard Emily say, "We lost touch with each other, Corey, why? I've continued with my music, too."

Why, indeed! Corey wondered now with the same acute sting he'd felt often before how it could be that his father hadn't urged Lord Alden to visit the de Koningh mansion in Manhattan whenever he'd returned from England. And why had Lord Alden been "somewhat resistant," as Klaas de Koningh had put it, when Corey asked occasionally about the possibility of having Emily return to the de Koningh home during school vacations? It seemed to him now that their frustrating separation had been almost purposeful, although of course that was undoubtedly his imagination rather than reality.

"Do you play the piano?" he asked, wondering where her musical life had taken her in their years apart.

"Oh Corey, you should know better!" She pulled back looking dubiously at him. "Violin. Though I get no chance to perform, and little opportunity to play with others."

Suddenly his words rushed and tumbled over one another to get out of the way of the thoughts he hadn't been aware he'd had. "We need a second violin to fill out a quartet I play with here in the city. Would you consider joining us?"

"I'd love to!" she answered, her voice ringing with genuine delight.

"We don't meet often, only when I can get back from Boston," he told her. Eyes filled with light, he raised his other hand to cover hers and they stood knotted together.

"Write to me, Corey," she said, gripping both his hands more firmly. "Let me know when we can see each other again. It would be wonderful to catch up with all you've been doing and to play chamber music with you."

"I will," he answered.

"Soon, I hope," she urged.

"Very soon." He smiled down at her as if he hadn't a care in the world.

"I hate to break up this reunion, but we must be on our way." Lord Alden appeared at Emily's elbow, easing her hand out of Corey's. "Thank you for your cheerful performance," he added, bowing stiffly to Corey. "Remember me to your father, please. I've missed him. And now, we must be off to dinner." He nodded at the club manager, who rushed to hold the door. Corey felt as if he'd been thrust to the middle of a hurricane. The room was swirling around him while he stood alone in a vacuum at the center of it all.

Emily and Lord Alden left the room first and Robert Haussmann followed, hesitating to look back at Corey almost quizzically, then turning slowly to leave. He blocked Corey's last sight of Emily completely as the door shut behind him. Corey struggled for breath. All the air had been drawn out of the room with them as they left it.

CHAPTER EIGHT

Rushing to get indoors on an unnaturally cold day for the middle of April, Robert paused for a moment at the bottom of the marble staircase leading up to the exclusive New York men's club. His hesitancy was understandable, trepidation on this first visit to such a place to be expected. He'd settled in America and developed his life as a music teacher with a complete dedication. Now at the age of thirty-three, he'd begun to sense an alteration, the pull of a life with someone else. Starting up the steps toward the wrought-iron gates, he wondered if places like this might become a part of his world if he settled down.

A smartly uniformed attendant stood inside the entry at the top of the stairs watching Robert climb, one white gloved hand resting on the huge iron doorknob. The doorman's dark fitted jacket with gold trim and epaulets announced his role as guardian of the royal portal, although the royalty he protected drew its power from the flow of commerce rather than the blood of some European monarch's lineage. The long ascent to the entrance was clever, and Robert smiled a little approaching the gate at the top of the steps. Those within had plenty of time to assess whether he was friend or foe before that final door opened. And even then, his acceptance was far from assured.

"Professor Haussmann to see Lord Alden." He slipped his card onto the extended silver tray. The look of direct appraisal he got back was neither welcoming nor unfriendly. Robert wondered if the doorman's manner came naturally to him or had to be learned on the job. A look of benign reserve stayed on his face while he placed Robert's calling card on the tray of another attendant, who vanished with it behind a huge, carved oak door.

Standing just inside the gates, holding his hat in his gloved hands, Robert waited for the climate to change with one word from Lord Alden. It gave him time to take in the imposing architecture this adolescent American royalty had chosen to represent it. The ceiling rose at least twelve feet and met the walls of the entrance foyer in a rounded dome. He could tell the amplification of the butler's footsteps across the thirty-foot interior from the perimeter was a direct result of the unique acoustics.

Although the entrance floor shone with the mirror polish of fine marble, the inner sanctum would probably be decorated with native woods of the continent's prolific forests, as the marble and granite around him were from Vermont and Indiana rather than Europe. America's natural resources were finer than those abroad, though most Europeans didn't admit it. The sensibility of the building suggested a European aesthetic, but there was something fresher about it. The men who'd planned it honored this new world they'd won rather than inherited from generations no one alive today had ever known.

"This way please, sir." The attendant who'd disappeared a few minutes before reappeared now at Robert's elbow with a smile and a bow. "May I take your hat and coat before you enter?" Slipping them off into the outstretched hands, Robert adjusted his shirt cuffs and nodded back with his thanks. "I hope we didn't keep you waiting too long," the attendant said, with a deference entirely missing when Robert first entered.

"Not at all," Robert assured him. "I enjoyed the time to appreciate this impressive architecture. I've never been here before."

"I know, sir." One of his small bows would have been easier on

Robert's ego. "This way, please," the doorman added, gliding through a partly opened deep-paneled door into a huge carpeted space with fireplaces at each end. Groupings of chairs and small sofas were positioned around the room and next to the floor-to-ceiling casement windows in welcoming patterns encouraging easy conversation. The room was almost empty of visitors, so Robert easily spotted his host seated in a large wing chair by one of the far windows. The attendant's feet whispered across the carpeted floor with Robert close behind.

Sensing their approach, Lord Alden looked up from his reading. He quickly folded the paper and rose to meet Robert with an outstretched hand. No one could ever doubt that Sir William Alden was perfectly suited to his life as a diplomat. His easy grace and charm seemed totally natural, but probably weren't. Robert knew all about the acquisition of manners from his life in Europe. He'd seen the hours of instruction and rigorous, belabored repetition of mannered conversation practiced to a point of perfection. The governesses and tutors he'd watched at work in the houses where his father had taught music made him grateful he'd been left on his own. To have been the sole target of their attention, as so many of the young boys and girls he'd watched were, would have crushed his artistic soul completely. He understood the conventions perfectly, but wanted a little discretion as to where and when they were employed.

"Professor Haussmann, what a pleasure to see you so soon again. Thank you for coming. I hope you take no offense to my inviting you here instead of to my home."

"None at all, Lord Alden. I'm delighted to have a chance to see the interior of this lovely building. I've often wondered what was inside." Robert returned the hearty handshake.

"It is a necessary escape from both work and domesticity for many men. Although I have neither excuse for being here. Privacy is my only motivation. My daughter is at home and I wanted to meet you without her inclusion." Lord Alden missed Robert's startled expression at that disclosure, motioning for him to be seated in the chair next to his. "Would you join me in a drink before lunch? I took the liberty of ordering some whiskey for myself before your arrival."

"Certainly, sir. My teaching schedule is sporadic during the school holidays, so I have no other appointments this afternoon." Robert forced his worried forehead to relax.

"Good. Harry, another whiskey, please." He motioned to the attendant still hovering nearby in hopes of being useful. The drink arrived in an identical cut-crystal tumbler and was carefully lowered in front of Robert onto the small table between the two men. "Thank you." Lord Alden nodded, in polite dismissal rather than appreciation.

He raised his glass to Robert in a toast and said, "*Aux absents.*" His expression was serious but not morose, so Robert was unable to assess how personal the toast might be. Was it a remembrance of loved ones long dead, or merely friends not enjoying his hospitality? Or even his own daughter? He raised his glass to meet Lord Alden's and took a sip, letting the whiskey glide slowly down his throat in a warming flow of what was most likely the best Scotch money could buy. His host did the same.

"Oh my, that certainly is fine." Lord Alden held the tumbler in his fingers and swirled its contents around in a smoky topaz whirl. "Did you know it's made in this country?" Robert raised his eyebrows. "Very appropriate in a gentlemen's club filled with the aristocracy of American ingenuity, don't you think?" He smiled at Robert and started to talk about something, but Robert had suddenly lost his place. He could see Emily's father sitting in his huge wing chair with a glass of "something fine" in his hand, the best whiskey money could buy. But Robert was still focused on the crystal tumbler and not what was in it. Light from the stained glass of the lamp shade on the table behind Lord Alden's chair sent colored rays across his hand, sparkling and refracting in the crystal from one deeply cut geometric prism to another. Magic. How was so much brilliance concentrated in an object of no significance? America was supposed to have set him free from everything that came before, everything in Germany and everything at home—in fact, everything—but ap- parently, he was still held hostage, then just as now, by beauty. He thought perhaps the whiskey was already working its wiles on him. He was unused to its strength. ". . . and Emily's future is the topic I want to discuss with you today, Professor," Lord Alden was saying. "You've known her since her childhood, and you must admit she has strength of spirit and determination, unusual, and perhaps even unseemly, in a woman." Robert smiled to himself, watching the thirteen-year-old Emily in his head hiding sheet music in her bed when violin lessons had originally been denied. "But she is bright," her father continued, "and that brain was given to her by nature. I'm a firm believer in supporting and enhancing what is natural rather than stifling it. Although, of course, there are rules of conduct that must be adhered to for the good of civilization. I'm sure you agree."

Robert nodded. But what rules? He was suddenly aware of the uniformed attendants moving silently around the room, seen and unseen yet always accessible, never truly existing in the world of the civilized gentlemen they were there to care for.

"You do agree, Professor?" The increased urgency in his host's voice showed he was eager to hear Robert's philosophy on discipline. Robert sat up straighter in his chair to focus, leaning forward to place his glass on the table. He took a deep, sobering breath. "Music is my civilization, Lord Alden. Without the structure, there would be no communication. I teach my students to make the rules an intrinsic part of their lives as well. I don't find guidelines confining. It's the early discipline that sets you free eventually, and the real work for me as a teacher is convincing them of that truth before they can know it from experience."

"Just so, Professor. We do think alike." Lord Alden shifted in his seat, although he'd seemed settled just a moment before. "Perhaps our shared European background, emphasizing culture, history, and especially the importance of music, puts us in a different place from most Americans." He glanced pointedly around the room, then continued. "My daughter is my sole responsibility, as I have no wife to share the burden of her upbringing." Lord Alden stared down into his glass. "I feel she is so close to the kind of polish and integrity I want for her, yet just as close to tipping into a morass she'd never extract herself from. There are certain liberties Emily would have for herself that are not hers to take."

Robert nodded. "As a child, Emily was always one for pushing against conventions, Lord Alden. But, I haven't seen her over these last three years after she left the de Koningh household, until recently."

"It is her recent thoughts that disturb me, Professor. Surely you saw her reaction to that young de Koningh boy at the Artists' Club the other evening. She was demonstrative in the extreme, and I would say he was no less beguiled." He raised one dark eyebrow and stared at Robert.

Robert sat up straighter in his chair. "Lord Alden," he started, quietly, "Corey and Emily have been fast friends since childhood. They always had an unusually strong bond, almost akin to sibling devotion. They hadn't seen each other for some time, what with both being sent away to school. The surprise of finally running across each other the other night was understandably unsettling. I wouldn't read anything more into the encounter." His voice dropped uncertainly at the end, though he hoped the obvious truth of his statement would speak for itself.

"Then you don't know my daughter as I do, Professor. I found Master de Koningh's behavior toward Emily overtly emotional, and I heard her encouraging their correspondence to arrange meetings in the future. That is something I cannot condone."

"Why not, Lord Alden? Surely you have every confidence in the son of your dear friend, Mr. de Koningh."

"It's not young Adriaan's lineage I object to, it's his nationality and upbringing. He's American, Professor, and you know as well as I do that assures a tendency to wildness and lack of traditional values. He's also more immature than Emily, and I want her exposed to the sophistication of European men worthy of her grace and skill. It's high time she prepared for marriage, Professor, and the de Koningh boy will only get in her way."

Robert stared at his host, slipping into an inexplicable numbness at the sudden turn the discussion had taken. There seemed no way to unseat Lord Alden's logic on such short notice, but every instinct told him to try. He owed loyalty to the two children he'd nurtured musically for so long, and felt he owed their friendship his protection. He understood better than Emily's father how important Corey had been to Emily's happiness. Theirs had been a perfect collaboration of childhood wills and imaginations. But of course, they'd both undoubtedly changed and moved on into completely different worlds now. He cleared his throat. "There's a chance your disapproval of their friendship will have an adverse effect and push them closer together, Lord Alden. From the child's perspective, a parent's motivation is always suspect. We all know that from our personal experience, and I see it every day with my pupils and their families. Would it not be better to keep your worries private and let them work out their own solution to youthful nostalgia?"

"I understand the danger, Professor, and that's where your contribution becomes important. In Emily's childhood, you were almost like a surrogate parent to her, and I know how she admires you and trusts your judgment." Robert stiffened visibly, remembering the obvious discomfort Emily had often displayed toward him when they'd first met. "It's a rare position of honor to hold a child's trust," he heard Lord Alden say, ignoring the change in his guest's manner. "That is why I've come to you for help now. Indeed, you could be her mentor again." Lord Alden swirled the whiskey in his glass, watching his own thoughts in its vortex.

"How can I help, Lord Alden?" Instantly, Robert realized his mistake, but it was too late. The words were out. His host took a final swallow of the whiskey, draining the glass and placing it down on the table in front of him. Leaning back in his wing chair with both hands resting on its arms, Lord Alden scrutinized his guest. Robert knew his only hope for hiding his turmoil inside lay in a calm appearance. Maintaining his equanimity during the silence took a massive effort.

"I want to send Emily back to England to attend the Royal Academy in London," Lord Alden said, at last. "It's a fairly new music school and so may be more amenable to accepting female students than the Paris Conservatory. She has none of the professional attachments that little Camilla Urso woman had when she became the first female at the Conservatory, but with Emily's intellect and my political connections, that rare acceptance of a female student to the Academy in London should be assured. I know she would recognize the opportunity as a golden one for her."

"I'm certain she would," Robert said, hesitating. The full design of Emily's father's plan seemed clear, but Robert's role in it remained stubbornly opaque. He awaited clarity.

"But I worry about her using her time to its best advantage if she's alone in my house in London," Lord Alden continued. "I'm seldom there now, and her aunt is rather frail and sickly."

Sighing deeply and signaling to one of the attendants, Lord Alden waved his hand over their glasses on the table, using a sign language instantly understood to mean they were through and he wanted the glasses removed. It was neither rude nor demanding, but directly expressive of his wishes without words. Robert realized he was experiencing, from the inside, a world he'd never witnessed close up in America before. Who could not admire the speed with which this burgeoning society had acquired its polish? Robert knew he should get out of his music room and into society more often. As the waiter moved off with the glasses, Lord Alden continued in a normal voice, clearly unconcerned with his guest's possible need for another drink or about being overheard.

"With Mr. Lincoln's ascent to the presidency, and nine states seceding from the Union, war is assured. I not only worry that I might be away from England even more, but am also uncomfortable with my daughter's presence in a northern city of New York's prominence. There's no accounting for what will happen next, or what chaos might follow."

Robert drew in his breath sharply. "I had no idea . . . people say it will be over before it's begun . . . maybe I'm too isolated in my work. I did see that Mr. Lincoln issued a blockade against Southern ports, and I wondered about Mr. de Koningh's business when I read of it. Do you think it will be harmful?"

"Of course. I travel a great deal in the South, as I believe you know, and Klaas de Koningh has his textile business firmly entrenched there. We discuss what we see and feel in the winds of Southern life these days, and there are terrifying signs that things are about to change for the worse. Such lovely people, Southerners are. But, I want to remove my daughter from the threat of both social unrest and young de Koningh's attentions. I want to send her to Europe."

"Europe! But sending her abroad alone now?"

"Not sending her abroad, Professor, sending her home," Lord Alden interrupted, holding up his hand. "She's European by birth, and returning her to England now might well be viewed as the first sane move I've made in her upbringing." He laughed ruefully under his breath, possibly reliving some of the criticism leveled at him by friends and family when he'd first brought his daughter to America.

"She comes by her progressive streak honestly, Professor. I admit to one of my own in the way I run my personal life, though it's far more acceptable in the male of the species." He smiled, an expression meant to be charming and inclusive, but Robert understood it was more than Lord Alden's maleness that gave him privilege. "I'm sure you can imagine the hue and cry from my European friends," Lord

Alden was saying, "when I sent Emily to America after my wife died; turned her loose in the wilderness, in their eyes. Returning her to Europe would be like bringing her back to the bosom of civilization."

Robert shook his head. "Life on the European continent is far from civilized," he said.

"Oh, I agree! I was simply describing the predictable prejudices we know so well."

Robert looked back up at his host and forced himself to meet his eyes. "To send Emily home alone now, knowing her impatience with protocol . . . is that wise?" The men stayed fixed on each other. They were more equal than Robert had realized; both surrogate parents of sorts, and both resisting a culture they were products of but no longer tightly tied to.

"I want to send her away to be safe, but not alone. I want you to go with her."

The directness of Lord Alden's message took Robert completely by surprise, though it shouldn't have. It showed his host's professional skill at its best. No distractions or change of topic would deter a good diplomat from his mission. Robert braced himself against the back of his chair, rigid with the blow. "Me! But I couldn't possibly . . . Everything of mine . . . is here in New York."

William Alden leaned forward toward Robert. One might suddenly have thought him an old acquaintance. "I know. And I know I'm asking a great deal. But I could guarantee you a year or two of every advantage, every luxury, exposure to every great composer and musician in Europe today. I'd want you to take Emily to all the cultural capitals. She wants to perform in public someday. I fear that's going to be impossible. You know better than I what the hurdles are. No matter how well she plays, she'll be stamped as a 'painted woman of the stage' if she's not careful. She needs to be presented in the right places as an artistic phenomenon. You could mentor her in a way no one else could. You're the only person I know and can trust who has both a European background and the connections to the continent's society of musicians."

"But surely a woman, her aunt perhaps, or some female friend of yours would be a more appropriate choice than I."

"No, Professor. Emily is beyond those conventions already. I'm always delighted when she hosts a dinner for diplomats with me or accompanies me to an evening out with friends. In fact, I'll miss her as my hostess when I have to entertain without her."

"Entertain? It's not the conventions of entertainment but of propriety I fear. A woman can't even stay in a hotel on her own. How can one ignore those dictates of decency?" Apparently, Emily's father was willing to dismiss many of the requirements of bringing up a young woman properly in Victorian society. Had he somehow terminated his role as her father in favor of promoting her role as his hostess? Lord Alden smiled gently to himself, pleased, Robert supposed, with his personal remembrance of his daughter at his side in a theater or at a grand dining table lined with dignitaries decorated with ribbons and medals. Then he focused on Robert again with a new determination that forced Robert farther back against his chair, whose wings closed in on either side of his head like blinders, holding him captive. Lord Alden's change of mood put Robert instantly on the defensive.

"You've often said, in fact you were the first to recognize, that Emily has unusual musical talent, which you alone brought out." Before Robert could protest, Lord Alden continued, "Undoubtedly, it's my own aristocratic background that makes music a priority, but I think Clara Schumann has broken through the performance barriers for women musicians today, and although the piano is not the violin, and there are still strong objections to women performing on that masculine instrument in public in a compromising position, I'd like to see Emily be the violinist to break down those hurdles." *You can't want that kind of pressure for your daughter*, Robert wanted to scream. "It makes every bit of sense to have her teacher be the one to start her on a career in Europe. You, Professor, are the mentor who can do that. She is your protégée." Robert shook his head distractedly, but his host pretended not to notice. Pinned to his wing chair, feeling the leather upholstery from the base of his spine to the back of his head, Robert was paralyzed by the boldness of the plan.

A look of disquiet crossed Lord Alden's eyes, telling Robert his reaction was producing some doubt in his host. He could feel Lord Alden starting the final phase of his argument as he leaned forward again, suggesting a kind of intimacy they certainly did not enjoy. "I know this is a valuable period in your own life, Professor Haussmann. But Emily's study at the Academy would give you some private time for yourself, and when you travel to the musical capitals of Europe, you'd find my daughter a pleasant companion, lively and lovely in every way. Time spent with her is never a hardship."

Robert realized that if he could still hope for personal integrity, this was the moment to be honest with his host. "Lord Alden . . ." Robert shifted awkwardly in his chair. It was clear his thoughts were giving him trouble, and not the rich upholstery. "I'm flattered by your confidence in me—more than flattered, privileged. But have you considered that the very people you want to accept your daughter might condemn her when they saw her escorted by a man?"

"Impossible, Professor. My judgment for Emily has always been acute, and I'll make sure people know you are my personal choice for her companion. Her musical career must be our priority. There will be no misunderstanding." But in truth there was a misunderstanding, and Robert knew he should attempt to clear it up. "If you decide to assist me in furthering Emily's performance career and removing her from harm's way at the same time, I would be grateful to you beyond measure. Consider it."

"Of course, Lord Alden. I'll . . . think it over. I certainly owe you and Emily that." Robert stared down at his hands, feeling detached from his body. He couldn't look at his host's eyes or explain, as he surely should have, that this father might well be exposing his daughter to a different kind of danger. It did not occur to Robert Haussmann that Lord Alden might be aware of it, and using Robert's attachment to his daughter to his own advantage. He was no match for the diplomat's skills, a fact he felt keenly but tried to ignore.

CHAPTER NINE

A COLD WIND hinting of snow had suddenly sprung up as Robert Haussmann returned home, struggling up the stoop to his brownstone with an overstuffed parcel full of cheese, bread, sausage, and bottles of Yorkville lager. He wasn't fond of last-minute preparations, but playing the accompaniment for an opera singer performing at a private Christmas lunch had delayed him. Focused on his purchases for his proper German celebration, Robert didn't hear the carriage wheels and horse's hooves coming down the street and stopping in front of his house. As he pushed his door wide, he realized someone was calling to him from the sidewalk.

"I hope I'm not disturbing you, Professor," Lord Alden said with a smile striding up the stairs, "but I saw you as I was going by. Could we speak for a moment?" Robert looked surprised, but stepped aside warily as Lord Alden moved past him into the front hall. His visitor glanced into the adjoining front parlor and stopped, silk top hat in hand, gazing at a large spruce tree standing in the front bay window. "Why, Professor, how charming. A Christmas tree in your home."

"Naturally, sir. Prince Albert brought the tradition with him from Germany, and here in Yorkville, nothing could be easier to purchase this time of year."

"Prince Albert will be delighted to hear that," Lord Alden said. "He wrote recently to remind me to find one for my own rented house. I'm glad to know where to get one now."

"Happy to be of service." Robert dropped his head in a small bow. "But I doubt that's why you stopped in, and I'm afraid I must prepare for my friends' momentary arrival. What else can I help you with?"

"Oh, I apologize, Professor . . . holiday guests?"

"Not guests, sir," Robert corrected him, "instrumentalists; friends who come to read and play music together."

"Read?" Lord Alden looked completely baffled. He ignored the housekeeper waiting to take his shiny black hat, so Robert shook his head at her and she disappeared.

"Read music. It's an adventure we all enjoy, playing chamber music we don't know but want to explore. But they'll be here any minute, so . . ."

"I won't keep you then. I just wanted to check and see if you'd given my offer further thought. I'm hoping to present it to Emily to celebrate the New Year . . ." Robert looked down. He'd known the minute he turned to see Lord Alden behind him this was coming.

"Lord Alden, I don't think . . . I'm sorry, but I can't possibly decide so fast . . . There is much at stake . . ." Robert's fair skin was turning a deep shade of pink above his beard as he stammered his apology. He'd hoped that if he just ignored Emily's father's proposal, Lord Alden would drop it, but wishful thinking had no chance of success.

"Oh, indeed I know what's at stake," Robert's uninvited guest said, slowly adjusting his top hat and tipping it slightly forward on his forehead. "England is preparing for the inevitability of war on the American continent and is more than ready to jump into the conflict. There's nothing the Crown would prefer than to break up the union of their former colonies." Robert felt a sharp intake of breath, not having heard before such a blatant statement of intervention from one in a position to know. "But there's also a potentially brilliant music career at stake," Lord Alden continued, pretending to be unaware of Robert's distress.

A threadbare young man carrying a cello in a case on his back started up the steps. "I hope you'll think of Emily when you make your decision," Lord Alden finished. Tapping the brim of his hat with two gloved fingers, he bid Robert goodbye and moved down the front stoop, nodding as he passed the young cellist. Robert stood inside the open door finding it hard to breathe. "Who's the gentleman?" the musician asked. "A wealthy patron, I hope."

As Robert closed the door to his Yorkville apartment behind his friend, a small group was chatting in the de Koninghs' oak-paneled library less than a mile away. Invited for drinks after a matinee, they were celebrating the season, enjoying each other's company and conversation. A large spruce tree stood behind the piano in front of the French doors to the garden, and rows of attractively hand-painted Christmas cards decorated the mantel over the fireplace. Braided evergreen garlands wound through shiny brass wall sconces on the paneling every few feet around the room. It was an unusually decorative display, but modern New Yorkers' appetites for celebrating Christmas had increased, and this year the effort was more enthusiastic. With a civil war imminent, they were championing the sense of community that still structured people's lives.

The fear and anxiety New Yorkers felt made conversation flow easily, and quick inclusion was assured as guests moved from one discussion group to another around the room.

"Secession is assured now that Mr. Lincoln is our president," intoned a tall, middle-aged man trussed up in many festive layers of silk and embroidery. His starched, high white collar made him seem virtually paralyzed, unable to move other than with small jerks of his head. Too hampered in his movements for easy directional changes, he spoke to no one in particular, allowing his proclamations to float on the air between them all.

"Thank you, my dear," his haughty wife replied. "I think we can all read." Her dark eyes flashed a warning to be still if he couldn't offer a comment of greater value. Standing between the two, their unassuming son darted a glance from his overdressed father to his overbearing mother. The conversation seemed to have stopped after the mother's judgment of diminishing returns with her husband's participation. "I fear trade with the South will be cut off completely," said the young man, almost apologetically. "Our host Mr. de Koningh may not be able to afford these lavish parties if his cotton trade runs dry." He downed what was left of his Christmas cream sherry in one swift, appreciative swallow.

Turning her visual daggers on him, his mother pulled herself up and lifted her chin. "You don't know what you're talking about, young man," she snapped. "And so what if cotton trade with the North is stopped? Mr. de Koningh will find a ready market overseas in England. Anyway, we all know profiteers do particularly well during times of war!" Her voice had risen a couple of notes, and her son turned slightly to see if their host was close enough to have heard his mother's derogatory comment.

"Now, now, I think we're all on edge these days, and anxiety has a way of putting strange words in our mouths. Don't you mean 'businessmen,' rather than 'profiteers'?" A handsome elderly dowager in gray silk draped with ropes of fresh-water pearls put her hand on the young man's arm, offering him support instead of the other way around. "We who have known Klaas de Koningh all our lives can certainly attest to his integrity. I hardly think he would be involved in any illegal activity, and trading with the South during a time of war will most certainly be considered one of those." She smiled reassuringly at the young man and squeezed his arm to say *we'll muzzle your mother together if necessary.* "And besides," she went on, returning to his original thought before his mother had intervened, "these de Koningh Christmas parties are becoming a mainstay of our New York holidays. I can't imagine his ever denying his friends and family the warmth of their camaraderie." Her shy young mentee smiled and nodded, letting out a sigh of relief as he reached for a vanishing tray of sherry sweeping by on its way to the other side of the room.

"The de Koninghs feel it their duty, as do other wealthy

Americans, to remind us of simpler times before steam and manufacturing stole the quiet," continued the lady in gray. "I think industry today is threatening the integrity of the family." She looked at the lavish middle-aged couple quite pointedly.

"In what way, Granny?" interrupted a bell-like young female voice, its owner only just coming into view from behind another group of guests standing near the fireplace.

"Why Louise, my dear, don't you look lovely. I didn't see you before at the matinee." The *lovely* Louise smiled and rose on tiptoe to place a kiss on the soft, crepe-paper cheek of the group's elderly conscience in gray silk and pearls. "You all know my granddaughter, Louise, don't you? Oh, of course you do!" her grandmother exclaimed, as everyone nodded in Louise's direction. "You young people were in dancing school together," she laughed.

"So, as I was explaining when you arrived, Louise," the still angry mother said, raising her voice again, "industry is becoming a danger to family living in our country, with employed people drawn from home to work in factories."

"Yes," nodded the grandmother emphatically, attempting to calm the rhetoric with agreement. "The intrusion of so much machinery in our lives is supposed to streamline the irritating challenges, but I fear we are becoming more isolated and losing personal connections as we rush from place to place in trains." The young people caught each other's eyes, rolling them at the familiar stance of their elders against progress.

"It's said to be so in England, too," the quiet young man finally offered, daring to speak up with the added support of someone his age and the ever-replenished tray of sherry nearby. "In London, tensions caused by growth and engineering have caused even the queen to call for a slower pace and return to peace and goodwill." He looked around the group, and aided by the warmth of the sherry, wondered why he'd been reluctant to speak out in front of his mother before. The group seemed to reassemble itself in the lull and prepared to move on to form other alliances, when the young man, whose soft glow from the Christmas cheer had taken away his sense as well as his inhibitions, raised his own voice to prolong his time in the spotlight and stall the departure of his family members.

"Of course," he said with the sudden authority of the fortified wine, "the threat that relatives in America might be separated by the pending civil war cannot be ignored." Stunned into momentary silence, his parents eventually regained their composure, nodding at grandmother and granddaughter as they left.

"You're right," the girl said to him where they stood, alone now except for her grandmother. "So, celebrating Christmas with one's family has become the rejoinder." He nodded, inclining his head to both the ladies and withdrawing as well.

"Not for the less fortunate, perhaps," her grandmother said, watching the butler and maid circle the room for the hundredth time.

"But the de Koninghs make time for their servants to celebrate, I'm sure," her lovely granddaughter answered. Arm in arm, they moved off across the room together, each looking as if they felt lucky to have the other by her side.

"She's still going," Klaas de Koningh muttered in his son's ear as he passed behind him.

"You couldn't change her mind?" Corey looked unperturbed. He'd never considered his father's mission to convince his mother to stay in New York for Christmas to have a high probability of success. "I tried, too, but it's her relatives upstate. You know," he added, before taking a long, slow sip of his sherry. "She said she feels more comfortable the closer she gets to the Canadian border."

"More like the farther away she gets from here. You'd think she'd seen enough of that family for one lifetime," Klaas muttered. "I certainly have. She never made the transition from her father's house to mine." He turned to take a demitasse cup of coffee off the tray offered by the butler. "Thank you," he said with a nod, and then turned sideways so as not to be overheard, and whispered, "Do I know him?"

"Probably not. Mother told me she hired two new servants while I'd been away. I think she thought we'd need more help for the festivities, though why I don't know, when she's never been to one of our parties this time of year." Corey sat down on the piano bench, his back to the keys, looking over the guests spread out across the room. "Sit with me a minute, Father," he said, tapping the seat beside him. "You've been on your feet all morning at the docks. Can't you find someone else to handle the warehouses?"

"I like to have personal relationships with the people I do business with." His father put his coffee cup and saucer on the piano and sat down with a sigh. "Especially as the election of Mr. Lincoln has fomented such unrest in the Southern states that supply me," he added, dropping his voice. "Could you accompany your mother to Schenectady? You could stay with the Schuylers for Christmas and go back to school from there. My, you've gotten awfully tall away at Harvard," he exclaimed, sitting up straight and barely reaching his son's shoulder.

"Will parents never stop saying things like that?" Corey chuckled, downing the rest of his sherry in one swallow.

"You're supposed to sip that," his father said. "That's another thing that never changes: young people in a hurry. How did you find your mother when you visited with her?"

"Fine," Corey answered, with a shrug. "Why not? There's nothing physically wrong with her, but her emotional strength . . . that, too, never changes. And yes, I could take her upstate. There's nothing much for me here, anyway."

"Oh Corey, you make your trips home sound a terrible bother. Do you take no pleasure in returning to New York and this house?"

"I love New York, but this house is pretty big and empty without any other young people around. I suppose I could bring my friends from school home with me, but I'd gotten used to having Emily . . . By the way . . . will the Aldens be here this afternoon?" He quietly congratulated himself on keeping his voice steady but light. It reminded him of how often Emily had told him of the challenges presented by high, ephemeral notes on the violin played with little pressure but much control. She'd taught him a great deal.

"Oh no, this group is all business," Klaas de Koningh answered, letting his eyes drift around the room. "Speaking of which, I want to discuss the new warehouse space Peter Schermerhorn's offered me. Stay away from the sherry," he added, winking at Corey as he struggled to stand. Corey slipped his hand under his father's elbow to steady him, sending him off with a quiet "thank you" and a small nod.

"Home from school, at last!" Mrs. Van Hoorn blared in Corey's ear. Her rotundity was unforgettable. He'd always felt she'd been blown up like a balloon years ago and no one had ever let her air out. As a child, he was sure she clutched her husband's arm to prevent herself from floating up to the ceiling. Sure enough, here was Mr. Van Hoorn, the inventor of dye processing for cloth and yarn, still anchoring her to the ground. Though judging from her increased weight and his decrease in height since Corey had seen them last, she might float up to the ceiling and take Mr. Van Hoorn with her at any minute. "Perfect timing," she announced, before Corey could respond. "Would you play us a little something, seeing as you're already at the piano?" She turned around and crooned, "Wouldn't that be wonderful?" but no one else was listening.

"Not today, Mrs. Van Hoorn," Corey said, rising to his full height so that he towered above her. "I think people have had enough entertainment already at the theater but thank you for asking. Another time, perhaps." He bowed slightly as if to take his leave with his empty glass, but she put her sausage of an arm on his long, slim one to stop him.

"Such a gentleman, always," she hummed to her husband. "Isn't that so? Didn't I always say that? And the way he takes care of his poor, sick mother and dear father! What a perfect family it is." Mr. Van Hoorn continued to nod no matter what she said, so, thinking he wouldn't be noticed, Corey tried to back off slowly. But she grabbed his hand with her puffy, bejeweled fingers, exclaiming, "I'm so happy you have your family to yourself again."

"To myself?" asked Corey, obviously perplexed.

"Yes, just the *real* family. I never understood why your father put up with the intrusion of that little orphan from England a few years ago. Your parents showed their charity when they took her in." She sighed, eyebrows arched in sympathy. "Imagine taking care of a foreigner's child dumped on your doorstep—an immigrant with no mother—welcoming her as if she were your own when she didn't belong at all, not at all! But now, you have your own home back just for yourselves. You must be delighted!" she warbled, loud enough to cause two nearby groups of guests to stop talking and look to see what the fuss was about.

Corey could feel his temperature rising from his collar to his hairline. It made his head pound, as it often did since his concussion, even with much less provocation than Mrs. Van Hoorn offered. He was afraid of what was going to come out of his mouth when he found his voice. He took a deep breath, and just as he started to let it out, his father moved between him and the human dirigible with diamonds, removing her hand from Corey's arm so he could take it in his.

"The Van Hoorns!" Klaas uttered happily, as if they'd been the only people he'd wanted to see all afternoon. "It's been too long. I was just saying I hoped you'd be here to see my new Thomas Cole painting. I want your opinion, since you are truly experts on the Hudson River artists and own some of his work yourselves." Somehow, Klaas moved her away with her husband still attached to her other side, giving Corey an eye roll along with a nod as he went.

Of course, he was right. Nothing would have been gained by telling Mrs. Van Hoorn his heart had been broken when Emily left to rejoin her father. Klaas also understood how shattered the family had become without her, or even just the expectation of her. He'd missed that connection almost as much as Corey. Now Corey felt he was the one who didn't belong. The house, the servants, the music room, nothing felt familiar or comfortable anymore, and it wasn't just being away at school. It was the lack of Emily. Having seen her recently at the Artists' Club, he realized how futile all his efforts to forget her had been. What a joyful shock it had been running into her by chance. Like a memory he hadn't known he had, the thrill of excitement and hope that shot through him that day reminded him of the first day they'd met here in this house when they were children. Anything had seemed possible then. He wanted that feeling back.

"Can we talk?" His father reappeared at his side. "Get your coat. We'll go for a walk." Klaas put his finger to his lips as he and Corey slipped out of the room past the new butler. "Not a word," Klaas said to the man. "We'll be right back. My son and I need some time alone."

The butler watched them disappear into the cold dusk. He shut the door quietly behind them, while just a few blocks away, Emily Alden sat in a warm window seat in the front parlor of her father's rented house near Andrew Carnegie's hill. She did not enjoy reading poetry alone as much as she had with Corey.

Oh, there is blessing in this gentle breeze.... She'd read the lines often. Though Wordsworth's full poem hadn't been published until 1850, just after his death, Corey's father's library had once owned an early, incomplete volume, and she'd bought herself the complete edition as soon as she saw it in a bookstore. Now, every time she revisited the verse, she found something new to consider in the poet's thoughts. His embrace of nature reminded her of Beethoven and so many other Romantic composers. Wordsworth's optimism spoke of hope for humanity, something often missing in a cynical world. Perhaps it was more Brahms than Beethoven.

While the sweet breath of heaven was blowing on my body . . . She moved uncomfortably on the window seat, unable to concentrate fully on the lines moving before her eyes . . . *felt within a correspondent breeze, that gently moved* . . . she stretched her back and tried to reposition the pillows stacked across the windowsill . . . *but is now become a tempest, a redundant energy* . . . she sat up straight with a sigh of exasperation. "Vexing its own creation," she recited aloud. Yes, the flow of life outside was repeated inside, and yes, in her soul it was more often a tempest than a breeze, and indeed yes, it was extremely vexing at times.

"What are you reading?" She'd been so engrossed in the poetry she hadn't heard her father come into the parlor. Startled, she gave a small, embarrassed laugh, stammering apologies for her complete engrossment in a book that once had been deemed inappropriate. Realizing she was no longer in Corey's library at the age of thirteen, she raised her head to meet her father's gaze with a smile.

"*The Prelude*," she said. "Wordsworth. Although the introduction contains a letter from his friend Coleridge who got all tangled up in the horrors of the French Revolution—"

"Understandably," her father interrupted. "What a perfect 'prelude' that is to the American Civil War boiling up in the South. One bloodbath looks much like another. Some things will never change," her father said, as Emily frowned. "And my Emily is ever exploring the outer and inner reaches of her universe." He smiled with something like admiration, she thought.

"Where are you going?" She felt particularly blessed by his unusual attention, Wordsworth already closed and forgotten in her lap, and talk of war dissipating on the air. "I thought you were on your way out somewhere, but heard the carriage return almost immediately."

"It's getting cold. I came back for a warmer overcoat. I'm going down to Fulton Street to inspect a new boardinghouse there on Schermerhorn Row. I want to see if it would be adequate for some British dignitaries who are coming. I hear it's the first of its kind in New York—not a tavern or inn, but quite luxurious living rooms in a row of converted brick warehouses."

"It sounds a bit like Brown's Hotel in London. Do you remember when you and I went to inspect it together for much the same reason?"

"Indeed, I do," her father exclaimed, starting to shrug his wool overcoat up over his broad shoulders. "We often went scouting around town together before . . . well, often. Even when you were a child I felt your opinions could be relied upon, and I enjoyed our talks enormously! Why don't you come with me this time? We could pick out a Christmas tree together on our way home. It would be a good opportunity for us to catch up, something we seldom do now that we're both so busy."

"A Christmas tree! Are you trying to mimic the royal family? Where would we get one?"

"I'm told they're easy to come by here in Yorkville. Decorations as well. I think it might make us feel more . . . familial and remind us of home." He smiled with a considered, winning grin Emily recognized uncomfortably as almost her own.

"I'd hardly call myself busy," she said, laughing at the thought of her days, weeks, and months of napkin-ironing and table-setting classes at Miss Carter's. "But yes, why not? I do remember what a pleasant surprise Brown's in London was, those Georgian town houses all strung together. Although I suppose with Lord and Lady Byron's former valet and maid running it, we had little to worry about. Who owns . . . ?"

"Peter Schermerhorn, a wealthy merchant and friend to Klaas de Koningh. That's how I heard about it. Let's go have a look. I ordered a hansom carriage, so it will fit on those narrow streets downtown.

We can bundle up in it together and be quite cozy . . . like old times."

"Why not? Any friend of the de Koninghs is a friend of ours." Emily jumped up as she put her book on the table beside the love seat. "It isn't often I can ride in one of those sporty little cabs. I'll get my warm cape and meet you in the courtyard." She ran out of the room, brushing past her father's large frame as if she hardly saw it.

"Do you ever *walk* anywhere? Slowly?" he called, as she dashed by. She turned to flash him one of her smiles punctuated by dimples, because she knew he liked them and because she knew her headlong sprint, unacceptable at Miss Carter's school, would be happily sanctioned at home when her father was in such a good mood. It had been too long since they'd had any time together and she knew the spring in her step was in response to the fact that he wanted to be with her. Only a few minutes later, she was reaching for his gloved hand as she climbed into the carriage next to him, their arms touching in the closeness of the small, easily maneuvered cab.

"Comfortable?" he asked. "No gloves?"

"Very," she answered, slipping her arm through his and resting her head just below his shoulder. "I forgot gloves in my haste and I'm too lazy to go back for them." He smiled down at her and patted her hand before tapping on the cab's window behind them to alert the driver they were ready. The little carriage started to move forward, and Emily felt a complete peace within its tiny universe and herself.

"So, tell me about your school." Her father's voice broke the serenity. The spell he'd cast over her with warm reminiscences of her early years in London with him when her mother was alive vanished with just one change of conversational direction.

"Nothing to tell," she said, sitting up straight and focusing on the changing landscape out front. "You know what those places are like. All table settings and polite conversation; and rules. Lots of rules."

"They've never been your strong suit, Lady Liberty," Lord Alden said with a chuckle, ignoring her change of mood. "But I'm not happy with the education at your finishing school, and particularly with the lack of a more sophisticated music curriculum. I'm very sorry for that. It seemed the best this country had to offer a young lady like you, but I sense it's been inadequate."

"I understand," she said with a deep sigh, although she knew she didn't. "You've had a lot of distractions with your work, which in truth, I know nothing about. Can you explain to me what you've been doing?" She was tired of the formality layering their relationship ever since her mother died. Why could she not simply say, "Why are you always away? Are you a spy?" instead of dancing around the subject. By the look of surprise on her father's face, she suddenly realized she'd indeed voiced her question out loud without meaning to. There was a momentary silence before he answered.

"I fear the United States will soon be at war with itself," he said, a small frown furrowing his brow. She thought him upset by her directness. "The Crown wants me to learn all I can about the current health of America. That's just good business." Emily still looked confused. "We count on trade with this country, and as an ally, promise to help finance her wars when it's in our interests to do so," her father went on, seemingly comfortable talking in the cab's total privacy. "Though which side we'd support when the war is domestic isn't entirely clear. The political currents are very important to our sovereign. She believes in getting out among people to experience them. Obviously, though, there's only so much 'getting out' she can do herself, so . . ."

"Obviously. She's always with child!" Emily laughed, watching her father intently.

"So, she and Prince Albert ask others to be their eyes and ears for them," her father continued, ignoring his daughter's indelicate comment. "But you've known I did this since you were a child," he said, looking perplexed as he pulled back to see her face better. "They trust me with matters of life in America."

"Ah, trust," she said, and looked out the window again at nothing. "Trust is the key to everything, isn't it?"

"Of course," he answered, quickly. "And because I trust your judgment when you relate your experiences at Miss Carter's school, I feel you have every right to a better education." Emily stared at him. "I want you to go to the new Royal Academy of Music in London," he said. "Would you like that?" No wonder he had to prompt her. She didn't dare move in her seat or say a word for fear it would be the wrong one, breaking their spellbinding rapport already fraying around the edges.

"London!" She had to force the word out. "I live *here* now," she whispered, as if he didn't know. He said nothing, blocking any expression. "I don't want to leave New York, or Corey . . . the de Koninghs . . . to the possible catastrophe of war," she added. "I belong here, I think." Her voice sounded very small.

"This is only about your music and building on your education. It's your chance, Emily." She had the impression he wanted to say, "your only chance."

"But Father . . ." She wasn't sure what register of resistance she should use. "I don't think these are the best circumstances for me. I don't know anyone in London anymore. Not even any of the musicians who work there. I've started to build friendships, join a group of performers here . . . You saw how Corey de Koningh offered me a spot in his chamber music quartet. . . . I don't want to give it all up and begin again . . . somewhere I don't . . . belong," she finished, looking at her father as if begging for help.

"Don't worry, Lady Liberty," he said, putting his arm around her and giving her shoulder a squeeze. "I'll get you into the music academy with the help of the Crown, and I have an idea for furthering your performance career, too. I can't say I understand why you want it, but I do understand it's the most important thing in the world to you, so I want to help."

"How?" she asked, staring at him now in open skepticism, and then out the window again. They'd only had time to move along Third Avenue about a mile to begin the trip down to the bottom of the East River, and although the carriage driver clearly knew where he was going, Emily suddenly felt lost.

"By hiring your former music tutor to go with you. Professor Haussmann can introduce you to the music community in Europe and expose you to many of the finest orchestras. He can enrich the Academy education with what would amount to a grand tour of Europe. Why should young men be the only ones to benefit from that exposure? Surely my daughter deserves as much!"

His daughter pulled away a little and stared at him. "But the professor has his own life, Father, his work is here."

Her father's eyes shone as he grabbed her small, bare hands in her lap, covering them with his large, gloved ones. "Trust me," he said, "I'm sure Robert Haussmann will recognize the opportunity and seize it."

CHAPTER TEN

KLAAS STOOD on the bottom step of the kitchen staircase, unannounced and momentarily unnoticed. He wasn't sure what tide had pulled him there, but knowing he might find Corey in easy conversation with the staff was probably a contributing factor. A family's most basic needs were satisfied in a kitchen, so if one wanted to return to one's core, this was a good place to do it.

The scene in front of him had a well-choreographed flow. Everyone went about their individual tasks without speaking but never bumping into each other, seemingly joined by filaments of understanding. An occasional cheerful word, having nothing to do with the work at hand, was all he could hear; other than the movement of pots and pans, chairs and eating utensils. The warm welcome emanating from the two cooking stoves reminded him of another home he'd grown up in long ago. Much smaller in its brick Dutch frugality and thus easier to heat than this limestone French monstrosity, he was aware of the mistake he might have made in purchasing a huge "chateau" on upper Fifth Avenue. Despite the continuing generational financial success, earlier de Koninghs had avoided all display of wealth. You could say that his wife had wanted this big house without the need for it connected to a large family, but in truth he'd been seduced in his youth by its physical beauty, rather than its practicality. He'd made the same mistake with his wife.

He realized he didn't know this kitchen, hadn't spent any time in it at all, while his boyhood had found him camped out in that other cozy pantry, with the elderly laundress ironing and telling tales of life in the old country. He noticed an evergreen bough, probably fallen from the Christmas tree up in the library when it was carried in, now set in the middle of the kitchen table with a big red ribbon tied around its base. It added to the cheer in this room.

The parlor maid Mary's back suddenly straightened as she sensed his presence and turned to stare at him in surprise. "May I help you, sir?"

"Where is everyone?" Klaas murmured, as if in a dream.

"Mrs. de Koningh is in her room," Mary said, still looking a bit stunned herself by his kitchen intrusion.

"What a surprise," Klaas muttered.

Adroitly dodging his sarcasm, Mary turned to face him in female solidarity. "She has the seamstress with her and they're taking lunch in her sitting room. Lots to be done before leaving for the family upstate."

"She has her family here," Klaas replied with a dismissive shrug. "And my son. Where is he?"

"We let the piano tuner in a while ago. I think Master Corey is in the library with him. He pays so much attention to that instrument, don't he? They're like relatives or something."

"Indeed," Klaas nodded. "But his father would like some attention, too." He slowly turned and started up the stairs to the entry level, noticing with each step a creak from his knees echoing the complaint of the old floorboards. Near the top, the sound of piano keys being singled out for sonority came floating across the foyer, a relentless, repetitive pressure signifying a piano tuner already hard at work.

Klaas paused on the threshold of the library music room, again unnoticed. Corey sat in a small armchair pulled over to face the piano, his long legs stretched out straight. He looked as relaxed as anyone could while still concentrating with full attention. A smile played on his lips as he listened and occasionally nodded or raised his eyebrows. The tuner, a little, round, partially bald man, seemed to respond intuitively to each of Corey's expressions with a delicate twist of a tool. Klaas didn't like to interfere, but he needed to be a part of this scene, too. Walking silently across the library carpet until he stood between the piano bench and his son's outstretched legs, he looked down at a white cloth covering the seat next to the tuner. An intimidating array of shiny silver instruments, pieces of rubber and wheels of felt tape were lined up in neat rows within the tuner's easy reach.

"What are all those for?" Klaas asked. "They look highly reminiscent of a doctor's surgery." Corey chuckled and started to stand, but Klaas shook his head, indicating he should stay where he was.

"They're not all necessary here," the tuner answered, with a smile. "I bring them just in case, but this piano is always kept in the best condition, so I only need a few—the tuning lever and the fork and mutes, for the most part," he added, pointing to a few items nearest him on the bench.

"Father, have you ever met Mr. Becker? Professor Haussmann recommended his services ages ago and he's been coming ever since. Max, this is my father, Klaas de Koningh." The two men shook hands as the tuner started to struggle to his feet, but the task was impossible from behind the piano.

Klaas shook his head again. "No, please, I didn't mean to interrupt. I just heard the voices and piano from the hall, and Mary told me you were in here, Corey. I'm sorry I never spent time learning how the piano worked," he added, turning back to the tuner. "I didn't join my son enough in his fascination with it as a boy. I regret my omission; I'm a negligent father, I fear. I know most parents wouldn't have cared, but that's not how Dutch children are raised, and my conscience worries me. But I can see there's a powerful partnership here keeping our pianoforte in great voice." He still looked doubtfully at the implements on the bench.

Max bowed his head slightly with a gentle smile. "I was always impressed with your choice of Robert Haussmann as a teacher and musical mentor to guide your son. Many would not have chosen a teacher so carefully."

Klaas shared a small smile with Max as he looked at Corey. "It was my attempt at the Dutch method, treating children as if they have the right to an independent way of their own. If the piano was his calling, then the answer had to be the right one at that time."

"It's never too late," Corey interjected. "Would you like to learn about the piano now, Father?" Corey rose and pulled another chair over next to his and directly behind the tuner on the bench. "Max won't mind since he's done the important work already. If you're interested, we can easily satisfy your curiosity." Klaas smiled and nodded, seating himself quite upright and looking expectantly from one to the other.

"Max has just finished tuning all the keys in the middle octave, which is from middle C, up," Corey explained, pointing to the center of the keyboard and gesturing with a sweep of his hand above the keys. "That's called *setting the temperament*."

"Temperament, as in personality?" Klaas interrupted, looking at the tuner for guidance.

"Sort of." Max laughed, softly. "It sets all the musical characteristics by which we'll judge the other octaves. Then we move up and down the keyboard from high to low and back again, so we have even tension on the board."

"Balancing, always balancing," Klaas murmured, nodding slowly as if in full agreement. "And these little wedges? What are they for?" he asked, fingering one of the rubber pieces lying with the tools.

"They're mutes," Corey said. "They fit between the strings you're not working on. There's a little-known secret about these new pianos, that each note is produced by three strings together. It sounds like one, but that's what gives it depth. You tune each of the strings to the first one you've done, so the others must be silenced when you're working. Everything is adjusted by ear after the original tuning with the fork." He pointed at the tuning fork sitting next to the mutes on the bench.

"Why use the ear if you have the tuning fork?" Klaas asked.

Max smiled. "Because the human ear appreciates what it hears so much more if the piano has been basically tuned to it," he said, looking directly at Klaas. "No mathematical equation could satisfy the heart. This is an art form," he added. "And your son has perfect natural pitch and an incredible ear. He and I have worked together tuning the temperament of this piano for years." Max and Corey beamed at each other.

"What's natural is best," Klaas murmured. "Yes, I agree. But now what's natural is a growling stomach reminding me of lunch. Will you excuse us, Mr. Becker? I have an indoor picnic planned in my study so I can share thoughts with my son before he leaves on a trip with his mother."

"Of course." Max dipped his head to Klaas. "I'm almost done here. Have a good trip, Corey, and a successful semester back at school. All the best to you," Max added. "I look forward to hearing about your adventures in music when you return."

Corey rose and raised his hand as if to wave his goodbye to Max, but Klaas had an odd feeling as he watched his son. There seemed a reluctance to leave the room and the piano tuner in far greater proportion to what Corey showed at parting from his home and family.

"You have time to join me for a sandwich in my room," Klaas said to his son. It was not a question.

They both started up the curved marble staircase to the second floor and Klaas's sitting room. Father and son seemed vaguely uncomfortable, climbing in silence with none of their casual rhythm of conversation on the way up. Arriving at the top of the stairs behind his son, whose long legs made short work of the shallow risers, Klaas couldn't help thinking how quickly Corey had taken the lead in many ways, all unexpected and not entirely welcome in their over-whelming speed and surreptitiousness. But perhaps all fathers of sons felt that way.

"Why, look," Corey called out. "The picnic beat us here as if by magic!"

"Humph!" Mary muttered. "The magic of hands in the kitchen."

"Indeed," Klaas said, smiling gently at her as she started to leave with her empty tray. "Milk, sandwiches, and coffee—a very Dutch lunch if ever there was one—and the helpful hands in this house are most certainly magical and extremely hardworking. Thank you, Mary." Entering his sitting room, Klaas was more comfortable where he was fully in charge. He enjoyed the feeling more than usual, but wondered if he might be getting too sensitive about his shifting role in the family, and worried about changes in the larger world outside as well. Perhaps he was less contented with alteration of any kind now. Corey waited to sit, presumably out of respect for his father, but also with an air of hesitancy, suggesting he wasn't completely sure of why he was there.

"It's been so good having you home for the Christmas holiday," Klaas said, brushing past Corey, to sit at his desk by the window. He gestured to one of the side chairs and Corey pulled it up so he could easily reach the picnic laid out. "This house is teeming with guests this time of year, but you'll be gone with your mother tomorrow and it will all change back to a different routine. Have you ever noticed how the subtraction of just one person from a home alters the energy of the family entirely?" Klaas started to pour himself a cup of coffee, continuing with Corey's cup without asking. He stopped himself, pausing above it to raise a questioning eyebrow to his son. Corey smiled and nodded, and the cup was filled to the brim to match his father's.

"I've also noticed that the *addition* of just one person can also change the dynamic of a family," Corey said, taking the filled cup carefully from Klaas. "I well remember how different this house felt when Emily arrived." And as if the thought had just struck him, he added, "You may be sensitive to her absence, as am I." Klaas was fully aware that the loss had been ongoing for Corey, even if the rest of the house had settled into a different pattern.

"When Mother leaves with me—or I with her—and her servants, I suppose things get very quiet for you around here." Corey smiled with his eyes over his raised cup, trying to convey full empathy for Klaas's potential loneliness.

"Your mother's presence has never been a contributory asset to this family," Klaas answered testily, taking a large white damask napkin from the tray and laying it deliberately across his lap, smoothing it out with more care than it needed, delaying to be sure his thoughts were in order. This was an important discussion to have before his son returned to college and he didn't want to set the wrong tempo or waste his chance to communicate difficult truths while he had the resolve to do so. He knew silences between family members could cause permanent misunderstandings and damage, and where relationships were concerned, the harm could be irreparable if the source was hidden for too long. Klaas's marriage with Corey's mother was just such a threat.

"I mean no slight to your mother, Corey. I know my tone may have indicated otherwise, but that was a result of frustration more than anything else." Klaas reached across his desk for his chicken sandwich with the crusts cut off. He was very precise about arranging the plate so it was directly under the half he was preparing to eat. All this was done without meeting Corey's eyes. "Please, please feel free to eat," he said, gesturing at Corey's plate with his sandwich before he took a careful bite off the pointed end.

"I know better than most how difficult it can be around Mother when she's irritated, which is much of the time," Corey added, keeping his tone light.

Surprised by the carefree manner of his son, Klaas looked up at him, a deep frown darkening his usually placid expression. "Sadly, anger—sometimes vaguely veiled, but often overtly menacing—has been the driving force in your mother's life for as long as I've known her," he said, quietly. "I was aware she wanted to escape the boundaries of her family home, and with the shining ego of a very young man, I was convinced I could rescue her from the world that had fostered that exasperation. I thought I could save her from what I judged to be a boring life with her large family stuck up in Schenectady. I didn't see I was just trading one family for another, and that might not solve the problem." Klaas's partially eaten sandwich, poised in his right hand and momentarily forgotten, was repositioned carefully on the plate as if he'd decided to start lunch over again. He reached out to organize a small pile of letters, lining the edges up neatly and positioning the silver letter opener next to them. The unnecessary task gave him more time to think. He glanced briefly at Corey, and then back at the desk.

"She wanted a new life," Klaas went on, "but never separated from the old one, and she held me accountable for her failed transition to wedded bliss. However, I hold her entirely responsible for that failure. She punished me from then on in many subtle and not-so-subtle ways, and her frequent trips home to the Schuyler relatives rank high among the most obvious ones." He looked into space, his long, graceful hands in his lap and his lunch barely touched.

Corey nodded slowly. "Father, I've always felt Mother was her own worst enemy, right from my earliest days of reading the morning newspapers to her in her room. I often wonder if those times set my own preference for optimism. Her view was the most negative and bleak imaginable, and I had to work very hard to keep from slipping into that dark hole with her, but I think the continuous effort taught me how to resist the pull. Music was my secret weapon," he chuckled, picking up his own sandwich. Almost devouring it in one large bite, a murmur of appreciation for its texture and taste interrupted his words.

Then he looked at Klaas with an even gaze and smiled. "I know she thought I was being diligent when I ran off to practice, but really,

I was lifting the pall of her moods. I knew what you had to endure, and knew you did your best to ease the cloud of despair she spread over the family. Much like the mutes in the piano, I often felt it was as if you'd put protection between us and her, not wanting her to spoil the sound a happy family makes." He reached for the second half of his sandwich, still looking easily and directly at Klaas, who glanced away for a moment to study his own barely touched food on his plate.

"How did you figure all of that out when you were so young?" Klaas asked, finally raising his eyes to his son's. "Your mother never figured out that you'd be the greatest gift she could give me, and I tried to share you with her, but like most people, you just became her caretaker rather than her simple joy. I knew you needed someone your own age to interact with. Your mother was doing you more harm than good, and that's why I jumped at the chance to help my friend William Alden and have Emily come stay with us. I think I understood then that the extra 'string' in this family needed to be muted so the balance could be maintained." The eyes of father and son met with a small shared light, and both smiled, Corey pleased to have contributed to his father's understanding.

"You did well with Emily, Father," he said. "Pitch perfect." He reached for his water glass to follow his pleasurable picnic lunch.

"I agree," Klaas replied, "and I know what Emily's friendship means to you, but I do hope you'll spend some time meeting other women and studying hard in college so you can have a fuller view of life's possibilities than your father had." He made a determined effort to finish his half of the chicken sandwich, and reached for the coffee cup with his right hand.

Finally fully engaged with his meal, Klaas felt the shock and relief of realizing he'd completed what he wanted to say, seemingly with no discomfort or real surprise on Corey's part. He saw Corey had angled his legs sideways to find a more relaxed position now that he'd finished eating. "This must just sound like the usual father-son advice," Klaas continued with his first real smile in a while, "but your unusually strong attachments, your friendship with Emily and fascination with the piano, both could get in the way of your education. I hope you won't let that happen."

"Father," Corey said, sounding even lighter than when they'd begun their talk, "I've had many opportunities for that 'fuller' life, as you put it, in Boston, and have never lacked for feminine company and entertainment if I want it. Those New Englanders know how to stay warm through long, cold winters," he said, an easy smile on his face making Klaas feel a little foolish for his fatherly concern. "But Emily is unique," Corey continued, a new seriousness taking over his face and voice. "Our shared passion for music is at the heart of our relationship and always has been."

Fine, white eyebrows drawn together, Klaas looked doubtful as he took a last drink from his cup. "Please, continue," he said, putting the cup down and patting his mouth with his napkin. He looked steadily at Corey, paying the closest attention to his son's description of his and Emily's relationship. It was Corey's turn to explain the private truths of his own world. "I'm listening," Klaas said.

Corey sat relaxed, just as he had attending to Klaas when he spoke. "Once," Corey was about to say, "up on the roof" but thought better of it, "when we were talking about music, Emily described the exquisite pain she felt hearing certain phrases in violin sonatas. She told me they made her want to live forever and die instantly at the same time. I'll admit, the sound of the violin doesn't resonate in my soul that way, but her description made me appreciate my own instrument so much more."

Klaas stared at Corey in wonder tinged with jealousy. He'd never experienced such a feeling, nor would he have understood the thoughts that went along with it at Corey's age. He shook his head slightly, more in wonder than doubt, but Corey seemed to feel he had to explain further.

"Emily and I used to talk all the time about all aspects of music, some of them ethereal, but many of them specific and technical. She told me about playing on two strings at once on the violin. It's called double-stopping, and she explained what that extended sound had done to her the first time she'd ever heard it. I told her I understood the impact that could have because the piano now has three strings for every note. I told her how I love to sit and strike just one key, listening to the resonance until it dies away completely. She said that made her listen differently to the piano, and that finally she could hear the notes between the notes, and especially in the silences."

Corey leaned forward toward Klaas, supporting himself with one hand on his thigh. "I can tell you, Father, that none of the women I've met outside this home appreciate the notes in the silence." He sat back in his chair, spine straight and hands resting on his knees, and Klaas was aware that Corey had just disclosed one of the big secrets in his life, as Klaas had too, only moments before.

"I see," Klaas said, "and I wouldn't have you spend your life, as I have, with someone who couldn't appreciate the silences as well as the notes." He smiled a little, hoping he'd convinced Corey that he understood even before he'd said so. "But all I'm asking is that you take advantage of this unique time in your life, and of the chance to be educated better than most of the citizens in our country, and experience all that means; including all the people and friends you can meet only there. And I know—or am sure—that Emily's father feels the same about this time in her early adulthood."

Corey collected his napkin from one leg and tossed it lightly on the desk near the scraps of his picnic lunch. "I promise I'll use the time away to learn, make friends, and work, although not necessarily in that order," he grinned, pushing himself up from his chair. "And now, Father, I'd like to say goodbye to Max, who's undoubtedly about to finish some of Mary's biscuits in the kitchen, and then check on Mother before packing to leave tomorrow. You know," he added, turning back for a moment, "she's never angry with me; just very needy."

"Ah yes," Klaas nodded, "but the neediness is part of the anger, and it manifests as concern for the caretaker and an expressed desire 'not to be a burden'—all the while becoming more of one. Emotional neediness is the most exhausting of all, Corey."

"That's another thing music is good for."

"Relieving neediness?"

"No. Releasing stress on the caregiver," Corey said, grinning at his father. "I shall put in a few hours at the piano before leaving for Schenectady," he added, with a wink.

Klaas smiled back at him. "Would that I had your skill," Klaas said. "But I'm most grateful that you have it. To be able to tune a relationship by ear is a wonderful thing."

CHAPTER ELEVEN

"Turn, Amaryllis, to thy swain," COREY SANG the familiar part-song under his breath, prancing at the start of each phrase. Passersby couldn't help but notice. Unusually balmy weather for New England in April flushed him with spring fever, and a cerulean blue sky with no clouds to soften the hue made him feel life even more keenly. Still, he knew the strength in his legs had more to do with Emily than the balmy weather. He could still appreciate her spirit, so clear in the way she held her head, feel the challenge in her comment, *in case you've forgotten me,* see the glow in her warm skin, dark hair and eyes, the surprise of her dimples, and most of all, the way his life felt changed forever, just as it had the first day she'd come to live with them. He knew he tended to romanticize. She'd always told him so. But that's because it's how she'd always made him feel: alive and full of hope.

What a shame it had been to miss her again over the holidays in New York. Delivering his mother by carriage up to Schenectady had deprived him of any chance of being with Emily over the school vacation. He'd finally understood that Klaas wanted to remove both him and his mother from the political tension after South Carolina's move to secede from the Union five days before Christmas. Rightly so, as the state made it official on December 26, and the rest of what was now called the Confederacy not long after. His father had quietly made it clear he needed Corey to care for his mother, which was usual, but the foaming stew of emotion had boiled over after Mr. Lincoln's election, and seemed the more likely impetus for their departure. Even the meeting of his chamber music quartet had to wait. But he was sure, just from seeing Emily at the Artists' Club concert, that she was as eager as he to renew their friendship, war be damned.

"Where're you going, and why so cheery?" Bill called out, coming up behind Corey unexpectedly. His small, compact frame supported a stack of newspapers extending from hip to chin. Both arms swayed, their hammock support strained by the unwieldy weight. He staggered like a drunken sailor to get in front of Corey and face him.

"I'm off to the practice rooms, Billy." Corey put his hand on Bill's head and steadied him at arm's length. "Want to come? I'm trying out two new songs for the glee club and could use your voice for the parts."

"Keep your hand on my head, honorable sir, and then maybe I'll consider it." Bill grinned back up at Corey from behind the tower of papers, tilting his head back under Corey's palm.

"Speaking of cheery," Corey laughed, "why are you, a lowly student not yet released to the heaven of summer vacation, grinning as if you hadn't a care in the world, when the world itself is coming apart all around us? And by the way, aren't those newspapers supposed to stay at the library?" He slipped his hand off Bill's head and rested it on his shoulder, helping to steady the foundation for the leaning tower of papers. Bill didn't move, considering Corey's eyes for a few moments and saying nothing.

"Yes, indeed they are," he finally laughed from behind the stack. "Unless you're the new editor of the university review, which I am! And you would know that, Corey de Koningh, if you ever read any of the campus newspapers." He peered over the stack to gauge his friend's reaction.

"How did that happen? Did you get straight A's again on your exams to impress Professor Stuart?" Corey grinned and then waved a hand in front of himself. "No, don't tell me."

"Okay, I won't, but I don't understand why you have no curiosity about what's happening in the world. You never read a paper, Corey, so this tabloid is meant for you. It compiles all the big stories reported in the most popular papers and reviews them in one place."

"I call it gossipmongering, not curiosity," Corey countered. "And why should I waste my precious time and energy reading all that gloom and doom?"

"Okay, be obtuse. But you'll miss all sorts of important happenings in society and around the country, de Koningh. You have heard of Fort Sumter, haven't you?"

Together the two friends slowly maneuvered the stairs. Bill took the lead, swaying with his load, and Corey guarded his back just in case of a slip along the way. He knew better than to offer Bill any help. Short though he was, Bill was extremely strong, and exceptionally testy about being presumed disadvantaged because of his height. It did enter Bill's mind, occasionally, that his attachment to Corey was weakening him in some way; robbing him of his ability to care for himself. But never having had a male sibling, he assumed his connection might well be like that of a younger brother. Surely there was nothing wrong with that, even if it made him a little uncomfortable at times.

Corey bounded up the remaining stairs to hold the door open for Bill to stagger through with his load. Just then other students came careening out with books and jokes, threatening Bill with annihilation, but somehow just missing him at the last second. Corey's benevolent protection had the desired effect. He paused, hailing the students by name and briefly asking how exams had gone. His height and good looks always made him a lightning rod for attention, and the stunning smile he wore today as he chatted made everyone feel singled out for something special. Bill watched from partway up the stairs, an odd expression on his face. The photograph he'd discovered in the copy of the *New York Daily Mirror* still electrified him.

"Hold on a second while I unlock it," Corey called. One big stride swept him to the door to his practice room just in time. Bill staggered through without a pause. "Put them down on the table," Corey said, laughing, "before they all end up with you on the floor in a heap." He moved around Bill to collect some scattered sheet music into a neat pile and scoop it up in one move.

"You can leave your music there, for heaven's sake," Bill said, breathlessly. "Say, that's a lot of sheet music, Corey. How long did it take you to write all of that?"

"Too long, if you ask my father," Corey said. "Anything that detracts from my going into the textile business is too long." He put the last piece of sheet music neatly on the pile.

"So, he hasn't told you outright he wants you to join him?" Bill started pulling his pages together. "Sometimes I assume things about my own father that couldn't be further from the truth. Of course, it would help if he told me what he wanted, too. I don't think parents are good at expressing their feelings."

"Mine doesn't have to. Four generations of de Koninghs have worked with the finest cloth in the world from the start of the first manufacturing business in Bruges in the 1400s. And I can tell by the way his eyes dance when he tells me specific things about his work, he's always planned we'd be a team carrying on the tradition." Corey started over to the piano with his collection of sheet music. "We had a talk when I was home and in his quiet way, he urged me to pay better attention to my schoolwork and less to . . . distractions; but that won't bring me back."

"Please don't move those away to make space for me," Bill said, again. "This is your practice room and I'm interrupting your work."

"I'm finished with all of it, Billy. It's ready for airing. That's why I'm glad you came by when you did. I'll start playing while you read your papers."

"Very well . . . but has your father heard your music lately? Does he know how serious you are about composing?" Bill spread one of the newspapers open in front of him and ran his eyes up and down the columns. "I'm not sure you've really shared your music with your family, as you do with us. Maybe he'd understand better if you included him in your life."

"He has no idea what I'm doing, Bill, and I want to keep it that way for the time being. Three of the four songs we did for the Artists' Club concert are with a music publisher right now. I'm going to move along until I'm too far into it for an argument from anyone to stop me."

"Are you sure you don't actually want to consider going into the family business? There are loads of men who'd be thrilled to have a successful career ready and waiting for them after school, Corey."

"That's their dream, Bill, not mine. As painful as it will be, I'm sure my father will see that in the end, even if my mother can't. He's a fair man. I just must prove my commitment. I can hear him now: *men don't make careers playing music—unless they're a Wolfgang Mozart or Felix Mendelssohn, perhaps. Which you are not, my boy.*" Bill couldn't help chuckling along with Corey, as the slight bow at the waist and soft-spoken phrases reminded him so much of Corey's father. "Get to work there, Billy. I'll tinker around with some arrangements here before I ask you to join me."

Bill turned his attention back to his papers, and Corey started playing from his first piece of new music. "Toss me that pencil, will you? I think I see a way out of this dissonant chord. Don't know how I missed it the first time," Corey said, shaking his head in bewilderment and bending in over the music. He tried the new chord out twice and smiled. "Better," he said, and went on playing.

Bill nodded. "I'll take that pencil back now if you don't mind, maestro." He started taking notes on a pad he'd pulled out of the middle of the stack of papers. "I'm going to stick mostly with the *Ledger*. I see this edition has chapters from Dickens's *Hard Times*," he said, starting to write on his pad.

"Why don't you look at the *Philadelphia Dollar Weekly*?" Corey suggested. "Do you have the most recent one there? When I was in the library, I noticed it has an installment of George Eliot's *Adam Bede* on the front page." He started humming lightly along with one of his songs.

"Nice, very nice, Corey," Bill said, looking up and smiling. "Nice counterpoint in that new piece, and it's not too complex. Even someone with a tin ear will pick up on it." Corey rolled his eyes at Bill and kept on playing.

"So now, to the *New York Observer*," Bill said. "Say, did you know it's published by Sidney Morse? It says here he's working on a pump design with Samuel—that Morse clan—here's another story on Robert E. Lee declining the offer to command the Union army."

"Hardly news, Bill. He's a Virginian. Likely Virginia will be next to secede. And how long do you think it will be before he resigns his commission in the United States Army?" Corey pushed a new piece of sheet music on top of the one he'd just finished playing.

"Enough of all this heavy reportage," Bill said. "I need some of the fine arts to lighten the mood. Maybe the *New York Mirror*—a weekly journal devoted to literature and the fine arts. Here's something on the opening of a new Academy of Music in Philadelphia, and wait a minute, here's a story on a new ocean liner making transatlantic crossings in spring."

"I thought that was too dangerous," Corey said.

"Not anymore. You'd know that if you kept up with the news, Corey. Don't you remember how the *Great Britain* was the first iron-hulled ship to cross the Atlantic? It says here it set a new standard for ocean travel by having first-class cabins amidships, oversized portholes, electricity, and running water! There's a list of the first-class travelers; very chic. Vanderbilts and such . . ." Then he went silent.

"What happened, Bill? Can't find anything more on the arts? That's depressing." Bill still didn't answer. "Did you end up with more stories on thunderstorms, canal tolls, and letters on the education of immigrants instead of music?" Corey tried to pretend he'd been listening all along. He stopped playing and looked over at Bill. His friend's stunned expression had finally gotten his attention. "What, Bill? What is it?"

"A picture—a portrait really, like an engagement or wedding photograph. It's your former piano teacher, that professor we met at the Artists' Club concert last December. Did you know he was engaged to be married?"

"No, of course not. I hadn't seen him in years until then," Corey said. "Are you sure about the picture? What does it say about him?"

"It says, quote, 'Leaving for London. Professor R. Haussmann, one of New York's premier proponents of the pianoforte, and Lady Emily Alden, grace the passenger list.'" Bill paused, turning the paper so he could see it better. "That's the young woman we met with him, isn't it? Did she tell you she was getting married?"

Corey stared at his hands in his lap, his long torso rigid. "No," he whispered. "No, she didn't say. But maybe I didn't give her a chance. So many things were happening at once."

"They look happy," Bill chattered on. "You know how photographers don't want their subjects to smile, but the professor looks very pleased, and the young woman is leaning slightly in. They'll be nice additions to the social scene on board. They're a handsome couple." Corey made an odd little choking sound and his whole body collapsed like a mountain of melting sand. Bill seemed to pay no attention and continued to look at the paper.

"Funny she didn't write you about it, Corey," he said. "Maybe she thought you wouldn't care after all this time. Or maybe she was embarrassed. He's a lot older, I think. Are you sure you don't want to see the picture?" He started to separate the page from the others.

"No," Corey said, "I don't."

Bill watched as Corey pushed himself slowly up from the bench. Then, leaning heavily on the top of the piano, he pressed himself up straight enough to stand. The progress of a very elderly man could not have been more tortured. The weight of what Bill had done suddenly came crashing in on him just as it had on Corey, the only person in the world Bill truly loved. They could have been a family had others not interfered. Corey had all but discarded his own family and Bill would gladly have taken their place. That big house of Corey's would never have seemed empty if they'd shared it together, instead of with that young woman. She was the catalyst for everything going wrong now.

Bill watched as Corey drifted out of the room and headed to the staircase, every step seeming to cause him pain. The staircase swam, a mirage of shifting light and form making it difficult to balance, until Bill wiped the tears from his eyes, realizing they had been the cause of the hallucination. Corey's tall form started to descend the stairs, deliberately but relentlessly, one at a time. He never looked back at Bill or said a word to him.

"Corey!" Bill called after him. "Corey, where are you going? I love you, you know," he whispered under his breath. He looked down at the picture again, trying to ease his own pain. After all, he'd told a half-truth—the picture was there, but he'd purposely misrepresented it in his description. Still, Corey could have looked for himself, but chose not to. It wasn't all Bill's fault, but now he realized that his contorted lie had only focused more attention on the girl and convinced him of her prominence in Corey's life. He may have helped keep them apart for the present, but there seemed an inevitability about Corey and Emily's relationship that sickened him.

"I'm coming, Corey," Bill called out, suddenly springing into action. "Everything will be all right. Wait for me!"

CHAPTER TWELVE

KLAAS DE KONINGH eyed the pile of newspapers as he stood behind his desk in the library. "Too many to read in one day," he said, his remark meant for both him and the parlor maid in the doorway. He'd always liked getting to know the servants personally, avoiding both being overly familiar and ignoring them as if they didn't exist. He felt a basic level of politeness toward another human served as the best standard. He looked up at her and smiled. "All these powerful papers help shape political opinion in the city, Mary, and if we're to keep up with things we have to read as many as we can." Starting to slip the top paper off the stack, he suddenly realized she was still perched in the library's entrance. "Is there something else?" He peered over the top of his reading glasses, his eyebrows rising gently in a welcoming gesture, not a glare of irritation at the interruption. The parlor maid saw the signal and stepped across the threshold into the room.

"It's only . . . I don't know what to do with that boy in the kitchen. Don't know why he came here in the first place," she sniffed, and then muttered, "Not sure why beggars are welcome in this house."

Klaas let the paper drop to the desktop and pulled his glasses off. "Tom? He's not a beggar, Mary! I brought him up from Virginia with me. I had a great deal of trouble convincing both him and his parents he should come."

"Why in the name of Jesus, Mary, and Joseph did you do that?" The maid's blue eyes were round as robins' eggs. "We don't need any more of his kind in this city."

"Why Mary, whatever do you mean?" The parlor maid had suddenly transformed into an irate bird, her frilly apron-clad chest puffed up with indignity. It was all Klaas could do not to laugh, but her obvious distress silenced him.

"I mean those Africans. They should stay down on their plantations and leave the jobs up here for the Irish." The small gold cross at her neck rose and fell with her faster, shallow breath.

Klaas stared at the parlor maid in silence before he put his glasses down. "Is it the job or the African you object to?" Buttressing his tall, thin frame against the desk, he leaned toward her. Dropping his head for a moment to compose his thoughts, he looked up again, eyes holding hers, with the desk lamp shining in them and on the tight skin of his high cheekbones. Everything about the silence called for attention and made Mary more agitated, so Klaas continued.

"I met Tom at his family's vegetable stand in Virginia in March. They're free sharecroppers who sell their produce to pay their landlord's rent." Klaas lifted one of his gray eyebrows, clearly suggesting the life they were living was one Mary could sympathize with, but she showed no appreciation. "Tom was studying mathematics on his own and writing music when he wasn't selling or helping out with the chores. I was so impressed that I had to . . ." Klaas paused to find just the right words. ". . . that I offered to help him get an education. His parents didn't want to let him go for many reasons, but they all knew it was for the best, especially since Mr. Jefferson Davis's election as president of the Confederacy. It was time to get Tom out of the South." Klaas's pale blue eyes were taking on an intensity that bored into the parlor maid. "He's a wonderful young man, Mary, and there are plenty of jobs in this big city. But, if it's his color you don't like, you must get over that." He stood up, straightening his back to indicate his speech was over, as was the discussion. He wanted to leave no room for confusion about his expectations.

Mary bobbed her head and smoothed her apron with a nervous brush. She dropped into a small curtsy, leaving the room as silently as she'd first entered it, giving no sign of acceptance. Klaas sighed and shook his head at her retreating back. He slipped his glasses up the narrow bridge of his nose and settled down at his desk with the *New-York Tribune*. "Yes, Mr. Greeley," he muttered to the publisher of the city's most influential newspaper. "'Anti-slavery migration stirs up Irish immigrants—makes more trouble for the city,'" he read out loud. "What happened to the paper's mission to report the unbiased truth? Why don't you make more of the slaves moving to the wide-open West instead of overcrowded cities?" Klaas muttered. He was still buried in a mound of newsprint when the library door slid silently open and his dinner guest stepped into the room, covering the distance from door to desk in four long strides.

"Klaas! So good to see you again at last." William Alden beamed with pleasure and grasped his host's long, elegant hand. He cradled it like a precious bird: firm enough to keep it safe, yet gentle enough not to hurt. This was both the instinctive and practiced greeting of a diplomat, but the two old friends smiled at each other with the communication of many years of work and friendship between them. "I appreciate your understanding my need to see you in private instead of at the club," Lord Alden added.

Klaas glanced over at his porter, who stood behind their guest. "I'm not sure I do understand," he said. "But it's been too long since we shared a meal. It was an excellent idea on your part. Thank you, McBride, I'll handle the drinks. Please leave us alone until dinner." Klaas smiled at the porter, who nodded, a combination of affirmation and leave-taking, slipping off to close the door behind him.

"What a comforting room," Lord Alden said, taking in the

paneling, high ceilings, plaster moldings, and French doors to the Fifth Avenue garden. His eyes lingered on the piano in the corner. "I'd forgotten what an important addition a pianoforte is in a room like this. Do you think it's the grace of the cabinet, or the promise of pleasure and culture it delivers that makes it so?"

"Both!" Klaas nodded. "I wish I could play it, but I'm very blessed to have a son who's so accomplished. When he's home from school I can hear him practicing every day for hours. It gives me no end of enjoyment and makes up for my own inadequacies—both good reasons to have children in the first place, wouldn't you say? Music has never been my strong point."

"You have many others, Klaas," Lord Alden said. "I'm sorry I never heard your son play before his performance at the Artists' Club downtown. He was clearly very facile, but the part-song genre doesn't show off a musician's talent to best advantage, do you think?"

"He loves his composing for the University Glee Club, though it's hardly serious," Klaas laughed, moving toward the bar tray set in one of the bookcases along the wall. "But boys that age need to have some fun, so I don't begrudge him such an innocent pastime. He's had a few others that stood my hair on end, but those, too, must be expected at his age."

"I suppose . . ." Lord Alden looked doubtful. But he nodded confirmation to the raised tumbler of whiskey in his friend's hand.

Once settled in front of the hearth with their drinks, the men let the heat of the blaze from both the fire and their cocktails take effect before talking. Lord Alden broke the amiable silence first. "Is your son enjoying his time at university, Klaas?"

"I believe so, at least as much as any young man enjoys doing things his elders require of him." He laughed softly to himself, his long, elegant body fitting the high-backed wing chair perfectly. The sparkle in his eyes gave away a relaxed humor more frequently found in a younger man with fewer responsibilities. "And your lovely daughter, William; she is also in school, I believe. Is she doing well? I don't think I've ever been as impressed with a child as I was with Emily when she lived with us. She was a delight to have around, and I must say I miss those days now. We all do," he said, circling his long, graceful hand at the wrist to take in the imaginary universe of the de Koningh mansion. He watched the flames dancing in the fireplace as if seeing the antics of the two young children who'd grown up together in his house.

"She's very well indeed, Klaas, thank you for asking. In fact, she instructed me to deliver her warmest regards to you when she heard we'd be dining together tonight." Lord Alden swirled the whiskey in his glass, seeming to compare its weight in his hand with the thoughts in his head. He took a deep breath. "But she's no longer in school here," he said, looking up at his host, who frowned slightly. "She leaves soon for London, hopefully to attend the Royal Academy." Klaas de Koningh's raised eyebrow asked all his questions for him. "She'll live at my home there while she studies music, as well as a few other subjects. I'm not sure what classes they'll open to a woman. I know there are limits, but the music will be very fine, and she'll have private lessons with your son's former teacher, Professor Haussmann, as well."

Klaas shifted forward in the wing chair. "Really? I had no idea Professor Haussmann had moved to London. When did that happen?" His eyes narrowed. "This is the first I've heard of it," he added, "though of course, we're no longer in touch."

"It hasn't happened yet," Lord Alden said. His host leaned farther forward as if to catch every nuance of his guest's news. "He leaves with Emily next week and will be living in my house in London for the duration of her education. I'll cover all his expenses both here and in Europe and pay him a fee commensurate with the income he'll forgo here. I believe he looks forward to returning to his European roots and feels that promoting Emily's talent will benefit him as much as her."

Klaas leaned back in his chair and rested his head between its wings, studying his guest's face as if it could tell things his voice hadn't. Finally, he took another sip from his glass, allowing the smoky liquid to slip down his throat on its own. "I suppose it's a logical time to send her away," he said. His friend looked up at him and then back down at his own glass, discomfort growing in the space between them.

"I'm not sending her away. I'm sending her home. And yes, I'm very worried about the war here, Klaas. I know the North thinks it will be over quickly, but the Southerners are extraordinarily firm in their decision," Lord Alden said, nodding toward the desk still strewn with newspapers and periodicals. "Emily's a British subject. There's no reason why she should be caught up in a war that doesn't concern her. I want her back in England where she'll be safe, and I believe her former mentor and teacher can assist in the start of her performance career. Why do you look so stern, my friend?" Lord Alden asked.

An oversized log collapsed in a shower of sparks, rolling to the edge of the fire grate and threatening to topple out on the hearth. Klaas jumped to his feet and grabbed the fire tongs, saying nothing while he worked quickly to return the recalcitrant log to the top of the burning stack. Then he swept the ashes it left behind back under the logs obediently burning in place, using long, careful strokes that cleaned the marble hearth without fanning the flames. Still he said nothing. Finally, he sat back down in his chair and looked at Lord Alden with his eyes narrowed. He drained his glass and put it down on the table next to him. "There's nothing more incendiary right now than this country, except perhaps that log on the fire," he said, so low William Alden could barely hear him. "Will you stay here in America during the conflict?"

"We've always been honest with each other, at least in so much as our lives and careers would allow," Lord Alden answered. "I look forward to working with you even more closely than ever before," he said, leveling a gaze of grim determination at his friend. "Even with Queen Victoria's recently stated neutrality, there are many in Britain with strong sympathies for the Confederate cause . . ."

"And even stronger ties to cotton," Klaas said, finishing Lord Alden's sentence. "So, this is why you requested privacy for our dinner tonight. I mistakenly thought it might have something to do with our children. Very well, I shall try to be as direct as you have been."

"Of course, I expected nothing less, but I'm sure with the constriction of trade for your textiles in this country, you'll be relieved to find a ready market in England for cotton, as your Southern plantation owners will be buoyed by the arms and warships offered in exchange." Both men watched each other in silence as the fire hissed quietly on the hearth, apparently not yet comfortable in its new configuration.

"I love my Southern friends and much about their culture," Klaas finally said quietly, without moving in his chair. "But I am not naïve enough to reduce this coming conflict to a turf war over self-determination. I think many of the aristocracy in your country are seduced by the charm of the South and equate the way of life to their own in Britain, and the anger over our separation from the Revolutionary War persists, but this is a war about the right to determine the lives of their African slaves as much as anything else, and I am separating myself completely from any domestic commerce for the duration of the war to avoid aiding the continuation of that evil." Klaas's eyes never left his guest's. "I'd advise you and your countrymen to adopt your sovereign's position of total neutrality as well, unless you want to prolong the agonies."

"The abstention of a couple of businessmen will affect nothing in the long run," Lord Alden said, shaking his head gently, and almost apologetically, as if he felt for his friend's predicament but judged his naivete to be the greater. "There are many in Parliament who align themselves and their money with the Confederacy. But I won't press you further, my friend, except perhaps to ask your help in explaining my daughter Emily's departure for England to your son." Lord Alden smiled. It was a calm, relaxed expression that seemed to signal many things at once: the end to an interrogation, the beginning of a paternal plan, and the continuation of a friendship no matter how uncomfortable the occasional bumps in its trajectory might be.

Klaas de Koningh, offspring of as many generations of practiced negotiators as his guest, relaxed the muscles in his jaw, allowing a softening around his eyes to herald his acceptance of his friend's change in mood and conversation. "Should we not have your daughter explain to my son in person?" he asked lightly. His guest sat up very straight, tightening the grip on his glass until his fingers grew pale.

"Absolutely not!" Lord Alden cried, his dark eyes flashing with what seemed at first like anger but then widening to a mix of fury and fear. "Please, Klaas, you must forbid him to contact her at any time." Klaas's querulous eyebrow shot up when he heard the word *forbid*. "You know how hard it is for them to stay focused on a goal. It's imperative that my daughter have no distractions, no temptations, while she begins this most important time of her life and career." Lord Alden held his friend's gaze. "You mustn't allow your son to try to see her or write her before she leaves. She has to stay totally engrossed in her work if she's to succeed." He closed his eyes briefly, opening them again with a new look of a man who knows how to get what he wants, no matter what it is. But Klaas could feel the tension in the air around them, understanding he'd get no more information under the kind of stress now openly affecting his usually cool and equable friend.

"I had no idea you felt so . . . strongly . . . about Emily's musical career, William. You understand, of course, that I cannot watch my son every moment. But I'd agree with you that there can be no doubt

Emily's unusually gifted and deserves a chance to follow that talent wherever it leads, if she wants to."

Lord Alden collapsed a bit against the back of his chair with an almost imperceptible sigh. "I'm grateful to you, Klaas. I see you understand perfectly. I'm sure your son has shown signs of being easily distracted at this age as well." Klaas nodded gently and smiled a little. "Just help me keep them apart until she's well ensconced at the music academy and on her grand tour of Europe with the professor, please." William Alden sighed worriedly, clearly still feeling some tremors in his paternal footing despite Klaas' efforts to restore his balance.

"I'll discuss it with Corey, if necessary. Can I get you another whiskey?" Klaas asked his guest. "We have time for another drink before dinner, and this discussion definitely amplifies the need." He rose, unfolding his long legs with the grace of a dancer. At the shake of his guest's head indicating he was satisfied with the drink he had, Klaas moved to the bar tray to help himself. Grateful for the chance to stand, he turned halfway to his guest and began to talk as he poured. "I don't believe any parent, especially the father of a boy, could watch the world's political developments without fear and foreboding for the safety of his child." Now driving the conversation from a superior physical vantage point, he felt the need to remind his guest that he was not the only one with a child to protect.

Lord Alden's face had reassembled with the expression of attentive care and concern his acquaintance had come to expect. "Do you see it in your travels, Klaas?" he asked. "I can imagine the amount of time you spend with cotton plantation owners must bring it even closer."

It did not escape Klaas that his guest had returned them to their original subjects, the sale of cotton and impending war, with little more than a brief disappearance behind an emotional shadow and the blink of an eye. He was secretly relieved, feeling duplicitous discussing his son's affairs behind his back, so he leaped willingly back into talk of war. "Yes, of course." Klaas nodded agreement, hoping to keep his friend focused only on this theme. "But in many ways, that only makes the issues more complex." He moved back to his chair beside the fire, but sat instead on one of the arms, bringing himself closer to and still a little above his friend. His jaw was set in a firmer line, his eyes pained.

"Why does your work in cotton complicate the issues?" William Alden asked.

"Because I can see the duality of it all," Klaas answered. "I have many friends in the South from my business and I understand their way of life and the pressures they live with. I love their land, their grace, and their commitment to family and tradition." He took a long sip of his drink, clearly putting the liquid between his thoughts and his words. "At the same time," he continued, "though I'm no aboli-tionist, there can be no doubt that the freedom of every human being is an undeniable right. My forefathers in the Netherlands assured me that the right to work for one's own place in the world is paramount. I speak more metaphorically than literally, but the mind-set prevails. So, you see, in an odd way, I have a leg in both camps."

"That stance could prove very uncomfortable," Lord Alden said. "Has the blood of the slaves those ancestors of yours traded for animal hides not shrieked accusations at you all along?"

"We all reform the lives of those who came before us," Klaas said without a pause. "I reject the mistakes and embrace the successes to build on them. When the rest of Europe still lived with the shackles of royalty around its neck, Holland had thrown them off and moved to a society where a man's—or woman's—hard work and ingenuity ruled. It isn't a perfect system, but I find it more acceptable than the land-grabbing ambitions most nations would go to war for today, though perhaps that's because the Dutch are happier at sea."

"So do you also believe this struggle to be about preserving the South from the insatiable appetite of the North, in some way?" Lord Alden asked.

Klaas shook his head. "Although many private citizens in the South are trying to preserve their economy and way of life, collectively the South is going to fight to preserve its right to burn slaves alive if it wants to."

William Alden's head snapped back, and his eyes widened. "Just so?" he whispered, almost under his breath. He stared in disbelief at his ordinarily quiet, gentlemanly host whose invective on Southern slavery had come virtually without warning.

"Yes, which is chilling if you believe in the rights of humanity," Klaas shot back at his friend. His words had started to spill out over one another. "All men should be free, not just those in the North or the South of this country." He looked at his friend with grim determination. "Every human being must fight to protect certain liberties: the right to a home, a job, a family, an education . . . a life," he said. "And neither sympathy for those I know in the South nor the realization that war will decimate their economy and much of my business with it can convince me otherwise."

Both men considered the fire together, each lost in his own thoughts as the embers started to glow with the special heat that comes before their end. "Can you afford such personal economic losses?" Lord Alden asked.

"I believe so." Klaas nodded. "I'm fortunate to have trade all over the world. That was another lesson my forefathers taught me and a reality I thank them for daily. But I fear for the human loss of life rather than my fortune if this war is prolonged."

William Alden nodded, draining his glass. "I'm selfishly glad my daughter will be removed from it all."

"Understandably," Klaas returned. "We protect our children any way we can, even when they perhaps no longer require it. They will be children to us forever." He shuddered a little, as if the dying embers left him suddenly chilled.

"Dinner is served, sir," Mary announced. She'd knocked gently on the closed door, but hearing no response, opened it silently, waiting for a pause in the conversation to make her announcement. Both men started and looked up at her, neither one comfortable with an open discussion of war yet, as if keeping it quiet would somehow postpone its inevitability.

"Shall we go in, William?" Klaas rose and gestured toward the dining room to his friend. Lord Alden stood as well, nodding and starting to move ahead of his host toward the doorway. "We can't keep our children safe forever, William." Klaas spoke to his friend's back. "Nor can we determine their lives for them. They, too, have the right to certain liberties."

William Alden stopped and turned to look at his host. "They're not fully grown, Klaas."

"Maybe not but they're very close, and even children have the right to be treated with respect and given the responsibility of self-governance. Isn't that how we teach them to govern others fairly, after all?"

William Alden, born to privileges he'd never questioned and responsibilities for others' lives he'd learned to fulfill as a part of his heritage, halted in place. "I don't know," he answered quietly. "I've never considered it. There are fewer governance issues with a daughter."

"Really?" Klaas studied his friend from behind. "I would have thought there might, in fact, have been more. Especially with your daughter," he added.

CHAPTER THIRTEEN

STRIVE AS YOU WILL to elevate woman, nevertheless the disabilities and degradation of her dress, together with that large group of false views of the uses of her being and of her relations to man, symbolized and perpetuated by her dress, will make your striving vain.

Emily chuckled at the coincidence of finding the quotation from Mr. Smith's lecture hidden away with her petticoats in her steamer trunk, just where she'd left off reading his article while she packed. His talk to her school about ladies' fashion reform, and his criticism of the idiotic and unhealthy rituals in women's clothing styles resonated with the power of truth. She'd cut out the summary article, keeping it to remind herself she was not alone in her hatred of the crippling encumbrance of female fashions of the day.

Now facing three steamer trunks in her stateroom aboard ship, she sighed at the task ahead, unpacking and organizing her clothes for the weeks of travel across the ocean. The undergarments alone filled one trunk, even though she'd always tried to simplify her wardrobe to the point of sparseness. Her first Atlantic crossing bore no resemblance to this one in her memory, although memory could be deceiving, she knew. Still, at thirteen she'd not been asked about what was to be packed for New York and what left behind, and no corsets, either. She remembered a certain numbness about the transatlantic crossing coupled with hopelessness and fear about surviving the new life ahead without her mother or family from England. Her first memory of any return of feeling had been after she was deposited at the de Koningh mansion on Fifth Avenue. Rage at her father's seeming rejection of her still seethed someplace deep inside, although she made a point of avoiding that wound.

"Petticoats and corsets." She moaned in disgust, unhooking the hangers from the first standing trunk. A knock interrupted her. "Yes?" she called, unable to disguise annoyance.

"Professor Haussmann." The reply was muffled by the solid oak stateroom door. "I notice we're just about to leave New York harbor," he called out louder. "I thought you might want a last glimpse of America. Would you join me on deck?"

Emily looked up and saw the horizon and water meeting in a shimmering line through her porthole. She hadn't noticed the ship moving away from land and out into open water. Suddenly the anger at being forced to leave what was dear to her returned with the same intensity it had when she was so much younger. Her home was America and New York now, her family the de Koninghs, and her heart with Corey. There was nothing she thought she wanted waiting for her ahead. Had she taken a deep breath, she might have remembered how fortuitous the trip had been the first time, but blinded by the injustice of her current impasse, she saw nothing but darkness as the ship moved forward.

The steamer trunk was listing a little, a clumsy pendulum marking the rhythm of the sea. She steadied herself, planting her feet wide against the stateroom's deck. "Just a second, Professor," she called out crossly, stuffing her armload of undergarments into the top of the chest. She shoved the two halves of the standing trunks together but couldn't get them closed. Her frustration escaped in a shove at the top lock, which popped open again under the strain. Maneuvering to the stateroom door, she pulled it open abruptly. "Just in time. I need to get some air," she announced. "But I wish you'd accept your given name after all these years we've known each other." Her dimples deepened as she saw his cheeks redden. It was unkind of her, she knew, but she couldn't resist striking out at him since he was so handy.

"I wouldn't object to you calling me by my given name," he said, still poised at the door.

"Perhaps . . . when you start to think of yourself less formally." She watched the realization spread across his face that she was right.

"Come on then," he said. "Get a coat. It may be unseasonably mild for this time of year but the wind up on deck drops the temperature another fifteen degrees."

Emily turned back to the room with an eye on the clothes sticking out of her steamer trunk. "I think my jacket's in there." She pushed the trunk open with an exaggerated shove and peered inside. Mr. Smith's article floated past her to the deck at Robert's feet.

"What's this?" he asked. "Won't the ink print get all over your clothes?"

"Hasn't yet," she said, taking it from him and reaching under a loose petticoat. Trying to keep everything from slipping out again, she handed it back to him so both her hands would be free. "Read it and see what you think," she added, still searching for the wayward jacket. "Finally!" She pulled a short woolen coat out and slipped it on over her dress. It was embroidered at the collar and cuffs with black thread, a compromise she'd negotiated with the dressmaker who'd initially insisted on jet beads. They would have added more weight to the twenty pounds her outfit already forced on her, which was a compromise over the thirty pounds most fashionable women her age dealt with. Fastening the long line of buttons from waist to collar, she watched Robert's expression as he stood reading the Smith quotation. He looked up at her, giving nothing away. She'd come to expect that from him over the years.

"Who wrote this and where did you get it?" he asked.

"A man by the name of Gerrit Smith," she told him. "He's a well-known abolitionist who lives in upstate New York." Robert looked doubtful. "He came to speak to us at school, ostensibly about slavery, but we found out it was a different kind of repression he was addressing that night. As you can imagine from that quotation, I took to his cause instantly."

"I had no idea you viewed fashion so unfavorably, Emily." Robert tilted his head a little to one side as if to see her in a different light.

"You probably have no idea what women's fashionable dressing entails, either." She wasn't quite sure how the intensity of her anger at him had been fueled. "I particularly appreciate the fact that he isn't focused only on the rights of men of color. There are many kinds of slavery, and women have been part of that oppressed mass without recognition for much too long." She could tell by his quizzical expression that Robert had very little idea what she was talking about, which made her even madder.

"Perhaps you're overdoing it," Robert rebutted, becoming the unwitting catalyst to her fermenting explosion.

"How can you say that, Robert? You, who always try to see the view from both sides? Surely you can't have looked upon the multiple layers of weighted undergarments women carry around every day with anything but sympathy for the wearer."

"I've never looked on them at all, Emily. With no mother or sister in my childhood upbringing and no wife in my life now, that's a perspective I lack." His tone of growing impatience, as if spending too long reviewing scales with a lazy student, betrayed his annoyance.

"What? No concern for the health of a mistress then?" She held her face straight with only the tiniest twitch of her dimples to give away the irritation inside. A telltale glow rose from Robert's collar and spread up the only part of his cheeks showing above his red beard. He ran the back of a gloved hand over his forehead, returning it beside the other to clutch his hat's brim.

"Emily, please keep some semblance of civility. Your attempt at humor is offensive," he muttered, realizing he might have overreacted to the mockery she'd flung at him.

"Oh, for heaven's sake, Robert. If you won't let me tease you a little, we'll have a difficult year of travel ahead of us." She glanced around the stateroom, then nodded and picked up her wool-lined gloves draped over the middle steamer trunk. "Good Lord . . . a whole year," she muttered. "I wonder what will have become of America in that time. Will the war already be over, as so many predict?" Starting to pull gloves on, she paused for a moment to look directly at Robert. "Are you not afraid for this country, Robert? Do you not feel cowardly running away just as the war is beginning?"

"I'm sure it won't amount to much, Emily, and in truth, I pay little attention to it. There are so many wars in Europe, they all begin to feel the same after a while." He gestured for her to pass ahead of him, which she attempted to do after closing her door, but the bulk of her skirts filled the remaining space in the narrow hallway, and she had to hold them back, venting a sigh of frustration as she wrestled with them.

"It's time all you men paid more attention to the entrapments of women's clothing, Robert," she muttered. "Men like Gerrit Smith draw much needed attention to the problem because they're wealthy, powerful, and vocal. Eliminating half the undergarments, including the horrid corset with whalebone stays, as well as these long skirts . . . ," she continued, teeth gritted as she tugged on them, ". . . that sweep vermin off the streets and into our homes . . . ," she'd finally reached the end of the hall, ". . . would be both humane and liberating." She had to pause at last for breath, a little chagrined by the strength of her assault. Robert looked stunned.

"All right, Emily, I'll take your word for it," he said, frozen to his spot. Her lavender scent, enhanced by the heat of her tirade, had enveloped them both as she'd swept by. It hung in the hall between them, a waft of tranquility softening the tension in the air.

"Don't take my word," she snapped, as she reached for the door handle to the deck. "Read Elizabeth Cady Stanton. I quote: 'A woman's tight waist and long trailing skirts deprive her of all freedom,' unquote." Emily started to move through the next narrow door while Robert stared after her before following at a safe distance. Looking up the staircase as she disappeared above him, he watched her yank her skirt through the portal like a prisoner pulling a ball and chain. He stepped easily over the riser to the deck, unaware that his trousers allowed him the freedom of movement she was denied.

Emily struggled with the yards of billowing fabric as it caught the wind when they came out on the main deck, suddenly finding herself assaulted from all directions by swirling gusts. She was glad she'd left her hat in the stateroom, and just as happy for her wool jacket buttoned up around her neck. Threatening weather lay ahead on the open water. Few passengers had braved the cold air, most undoubtedly still settling comfortably into their cabins with afternoon tea or already celebrating their departure with others in the bar. The ship seemed smaller than the one she'd been on, but now she was bigger, after all. The ship had seemed threatening when it took her from London and the only home she'd known, and now, ironically, its menace was the power to leave New York to return to London again. Emily stared at the white foam wake churning behind the stern, its relentless drive bringing a sense of panic she'd not experienced for many years.

"Look!" Robert called, clearly hoping to turn her attention elsewhere. "That little rock in the water is the last piece of America we'll see until we return." He moved over beside her at the railing and pointed to a tiny island in the middle of the harbor. She could feel his closeness, as if there wasn't enough room for them both, which angered her. "I remember seeing that when I first came to this country," Robert said, "but I thought then it was an ignominious introduction to such a famous port of entry." An older couple moved past them to the portal, shivering together in the wind and clearly heading for a more comfortable venue. They nodded as they passed, taking a long, curious look at Robert and Emily.

Emily nodded back. "What do you suppose they're staring at?" she muttered under her breath. Drinking in a last look at the country she'd come to call home, she added, "There should be something to mark this spot in the harbor for people entering and leaving the port." She tried not to let the nostalgia rising in her throat take over and choke her with unwanted tears. She suddenly knew how deeply she didn't want to go. She cleared her throat with a small cough. "Can I ask you something, Robert?"

"Of course," he said, warily. She couldn't blame his reluctance to engage easily with her now after all the trouble she'd been giving him ever since they'd arrived on board. Weighing the likelihood of an honest answer from him, she decided it was worth the chance. She turned to look out at the faster moving water and took a breath.

"Why did my father make the decision to send me to England so quickly, and without asking me if I wanted to go? Did you have any part in it?" she added, refusing to look at him as she spoke. She knew he could hear the tightness in her throat, but didn't care. He seemed to take forever to answer, but whether because of her bitterness or his difficulty with her question, she couldn't tell. Finally, he shifted his attention to the moving water and started to speak quietly.

"Your father is afraid of this war in America. He didn't want you caught in it, and saw a way to get you both safety and the best musical education available in England." He stopped, and Emily assumed he was waiting for her to react. But she'd never have been satisfied, no matter what he'd said, and so she let the force of her discontent gather momentum.

"Why didn't I hear from Corey de Koningh before I left?" she asked. "He promised." She hadn't expected what came out of her own mouth. She'd thought of nothing else as she'd unpacked in her stateroom, yet never intended to admit to the disappointment and hurt. Now she'd given herself away, to of all people Robert Hauss- mann, who had sometimes come between her and Corey even when they were children. Or so it had seemed to her.

Robert made a start of surprise and cleared his throat. "Corey is still a child, Emily, not much more than a boy, while you have become a woman. His judgment is limited by his youthful self-ab- sorption. He probably didn't consider the impact his omission would have." She stared at him in disbelief, turning slowly back to watch the bare little island in the harbor recede into the setting sun while the wind whipped her ever loosening hair around her face in a frenzy.

An elegant couple strolled by on their way back down to the cabins, and as they were the only other people on deck now, Robert nodded and bowed to them, politely. Emily turned away as she struggled to swallow, staring into the wind. She hoped to use the steadily increasing gusts as an excuse for the tears she was blinking back. The man offered his companion a hand over the raised sill of the portal, watching Emily and the professor as he did so. Their attire labeled them as over fifty, the woman in a dark shapeless dress to the floor with an ugly black hat with a brim too large for the windy weather, and the man in a nondescript waistcoat and gray trousers with a low top hat pulled down over his forehead.

"Scandalous," the woman whispered to her companion, her exclamation unexpectedly carried on the wind to Emily's ear as well as Robert's. "An older man like him with a pretty, young woman. A Casanova if ever there was one."

"None of your business," her husband hissed, giving her a light shove through the portal. "But I agree with you, for what it's worth."

CHAPTER FOURTEEN

E-A-D-G. Corey repeated the four notes on the piano with his right hand over and over again, slowing them down one minute, then speeding up and changing the emphasis giving weight to different ones. He looked over the top of his father's piano to the garden outside the library. Spring weather was exploding all around him, just as Mr. Lincoln's inauguration as sixteenth president of the United States had lit the cannons in the South. Buds were bursting open on trees along the Fifth Avenue gate where the sun warmed them directly. Corey added a chord with his left hand to fill out the right-hand melody. He tried it again and sang, "*You* can't do that, you *can't* do that, you can't *do* that, you can't do *that*." Over and over, he repeated the four notes, putting emphasis on different parts of the phrase.

Looking out to the sky with a few cotton clouds stuck here and there, he remembered a less tranquil scene in his small practice room at college.

"You can't do that!" Bill had cried, reeling as if he'd been hit.

"I have to tell you, I think Bill's right this time," Charlie chimed in.

"Corey, you'll ruin everything. You'll wreck your life!" Bill's shout ricocheted around the tiny closet-like space and he seemed to want to jump over the piano and tie Corey to it. He looked for help from rotund Charlie, to their lyricist with a wrestling physique, Jock, and back to Corey. Packed with the members of their glee club, the tiny practice room had the air of a cage for crazed animals. All except Corey, who appeared to be unnaturally tranquil.

"I've made up my mind," he'd told them all quietly. He'd finally felt exceedingly calm. Leaving school would bring about change for the glee club, and that would upset him more than if his family was separating, as it had done so often. But Emily's departure for London had caused this tidal wave in him, something far more earth-shattering than the breakup of his singing group, although he did not share that reason with his classmates.

Now he had to face his father with the same resolve. That would not be nearly as easy nor the outcome as sure. But he'd thought his way around each facet of the argument and was positive he'd found a winner: the momentum of the war gaining on them all. His father was deeply committed to ending slavery in the South, even though its demise might ruin his business there, and Corey was confident that his father's conviction would accept the reason from his son.

"You can't do that" suddenly switched to "You must do that." He could feel the smooth, hard connection of one ivory piano key to another under his fingers and hear the responsive impact of the felt hammers on strings under the piano cover. The familiar percussion coming from the instrument was the voice of an old friend, one he'd known since he was a child. They belonged together, he and this piano, and he would miss it, too, when he left. He set his jaw, pulling himself up with a back as firm as his decision, and started to add some counterpoint to his chords. The contrasting notes reminded him of the relationship between him and his glee club friends, interdependent in their love of music yet independent in the momentum and direction of their lives: the perfect family dynamic.

Enveloped in his music, he didn't hear his father close the big oak door. Corey looked up suddenly to see Klaas de Koningh standing silently, watching with his hands folded in front of him, a posture that said he had all the patience and time in the world to wait. "Father, I didn't hear you come in." Corey jumped up from the piano bench. "I hope you haven't been here long."

"Long enough to be curious about what it is you can't and must do," Klaas answered with a spark in his eyes. His sense of humor never left him; an enviable trait. Corey was struck by how much he loved and respected this man. Gripping the piano top tightly and praying to spare them both misunderstanding and pain, he pushed the bench away and said, "I need to talk to you about why I'm leaving college and what I want to do next." He knew his announcement in a letter home had been too spare.

"I appreciate that, Corey," his father said without moving. "I need to hear and understand your reasons just as much as you need to talk about them, so it seems we're both blessed with like motivation." He smiled at his son, grown so tall in his youthful legacy to outdo his father.

The two of them moved to the wing chairs by the cold hearth where they could face each other, but not be so close they'd lose the chance to weigh their words before delivery. Corey felt once he'd figured out how to start he could mask the feelings of a small boy who'd fallen in love with a little girl many years ago. "I can't go on in school, Father, knowing other men my age are signing up to fight for the Union. I want to be part of the stand against slavery." He was afraid to look at his father, so he stared at his own hands, something he was comfortable doing after so many years of playing the piano.

"With only a small professional fighting force," Corey continued, "the president's going to need every soldier he can get. I want to join the army, too." The grandfather clock in the corner swung its pendulum back and forth relentlessly. There was no other sound but the marking of time. "I have to be involved. I can't sit the war out behind books and music. Many of us in college don't find it important now that war's been declared."

"I see," Klaas said quietly. "And you want to fight instead of study?" He watched his son.

"I certainly do," Corey answered. "My friends tease me about my lack of interest in newspapers, but there are better ways to be involved with what's happening." Klaas said nothing, so Corey went on, struggling to fill the silence. "Do you remember Alan Wood from Albany?" he asked. Klaas nodded. "I saw him in Boston last week. He was on leave from West Point visiting his aunt for her birthday. Alan told me many graduates of the Point have resigned their commissions to fight for the South, especially in the cavalry, if you can believe it."

Klaas raised his eyebrows and let out a deep sigh. He nodded almost imperceptibly, but it was enough. Corey saw it. He waited for his father to talk now. "The South knew of the resupplies on their way to the federal garrison at Fort Sumter," Klaas said. "Everyone did. I've often met ships with my cargos in Charleston harbor, and I know how strategic South Carolina is. The fort's commander, Major Robert Anderson, is a friend of mine. I was always afraid he'd be exposed to symbolic attack." Deep worry lines cut across his forehead for the first time.

"The administration will have to rely . . . on large numbers . . . of volunteers," Corey said, in a short, breathless burst.

"But you, Corey, cannot be one of those volunteers; not in uniform, anyhow."

"Why, Father?" Corey exploded. "You've always taught me to do my part. Are you in favor of paying off my conscription? That doesn't sound like you."

"No. I can't imagine compensating someone else to fight in your place, though I know plenty of men have done and will do just that." Klaas shook his head and gave a wry smile. "No, Corey, it's because the uniform won't fit. It's just that simple."

Incredulous, the son stared at his father. "What are you saying?"

"The administration has asked me to supply the army with cloth for uniforms," Klaas explained, putting his head back on the chair and watching his son's face. "There's a standard range for height and weight in the army because there's no way to clothe or house men way over or under the norm, and they're not considered capable of long sieges and marching, I believe. No uniform, boots, or cot for that matter would work for you. Beyond that, you tower so far above everyone else you'd make an easy target on the ground, endangering everyone around you. In short, you're just too tall."

Klaas rested his long, graceful fingers, so like his son's, loosely on the arms of his wing chair. Corey noticed how thin the skin looked now that his father had aged; like fine porcelain, well used, but equally well cared for. The fingers were alert yet relaxed, the mark of a man sure of his facts. Corey had no reason to doubt his father's word. The lengths and expense he'd been driven to having clothes fitted and shoes handmade, to say nothing of the special bed designed just for his length, convinced him his father was right. He was not built for the public army.

"Don't look so stricken, Corey," his father said with a smile. "There are many ways to fight. You can do something to support the Union even without a rifle. From this point on, though, our talk must remain in this room, between you and me. No one can ever hear what I'm telling you now. Do you understand?"

Not knowing what he was agreeing to, Corey nonetheless nodded. He glanced up instinctively at the library door to be sure it was shut. Just then a muffled knock reverberated through the dense wood, making them both jump. Corey leaped to his feet to answer it. He opened the door just enough to see the porter standing in the hall with a beige envelope in his white gloved hand.

"This just came for Mr. de Koningh by messenger," Tom said, holding it out. There was no crest or identifying mark on it and no return address. Corey took it to his father, who raised it to the light to check the seal. Apparently satisfied, Klaas forced the flap on the envelope open neatly with one of his long fingers. He read what was inside and looked up at Tom, still standing in the doorway. "Tell him yes, please. Oh, and Tom, I'll need the big carriage ready for tomorrow."

"How early, sir?"

"Before breakfast. Thank you, Tom." The porter moved off down the hall and disappeared through the door to the dining room. Ordering Corey to check that the hall and staircase were both empty, Klaas indicated he should shut the library door. "Where to begin?" he said, watching Corey sit down again slowly in his chair, balancing almost on the edge of his seat so as not to miss a word. "I'll begin at the beginning. We were talking about fighting a war without guns," he said, "so we'll start there." A slightly pained expression darted across his face.

"Father," Corey said very low, "you don't have to tell me anything if you don't want to."

"But I do, Corey," Klaas answered. "You should know about the army I've joined and the men and women I've been fighting along-side for years now." Corey looked stunned and sat with both hands on his knees, bracing himself for whatever was coming. "You know I'm not an abolitionist," Klaas said quietly. Corey nodded. "But there has been another war raging over freedom without the benefit of an official sanction from the administration. That battle for the right of a human being to life, liberty, and the pursuit of happiness was one I decided to join a long time ago." Corey, looking confused, sat silent and tense. "My travels through the South to cotton plantations and all ports of entry, as well as along major roads and across rivers, have given me unique access. I've used my business connections to help ᴏ and participate in what we are calling an Underground ᴅ to take slaves to freedom all the way to Canada. I don't ʰat will surprise you. You may have had suspicions about my trips." Corey looked puzzled, so Klaas explained, "It's not a real railroad, of course, but a series of safe places for runaway slaves and people who will help them from one such dwelling to another."

"In truth, I did wonder about your work," Corey said. "But whatever you were doing didn't seem to affect me or Mother." Corey hesitated, then plunged ahead. "And I also feared you wanted me to join the textile business." Klaas laughed ruefully, but let Corey continue. "So I stayed clear of whatever you were doing. I wanted to focus on my music rather than the buying and selling of cloth. I was afraid if I gave you any encouragement you'd snatch me off my piano stool." Corey looked down at his long, strong fingers spread out over each knee as he leaned on them. Then he looked up to see his father's smile: soft, comfortable, and full of wisdom and affection. He had a brief, agonized yearning to describe the pain in his heart that Emily had caused, but then, just as suddenly, he hardened his resolve not to think about her again.

"I know," his father said, "and I knew then. But now with the war on, the other side of my role, gathering information, must be expanded. It's more important than ever to provide the president with dependable facts about the South. I'm going to give you the chance to join me. Not in the textile business, but in the business of learning and delivering the truth."

"That's a different assignment," Corey said. "It's certainly an important one . . . but in a way, it sounds like what Lord Alden's always done for the queen of England."

"They are pieces of the same puzzle," Klaas said, nodding emphatically. "Our president has told us the government can't survive half-free and half-slave. I strongly agree." He watched his son's face, trying to judge the impact of what he was saying. "The very things that give me access to move supplies up the coast," he went on, "now give me an advantage to move information for the president. The problem is that what was work for freedom alone will become intelligence work; spying, to put it bluntly. With war declared, engaging in the movement of information about the opposing side is a hanging offense. Yet that is what I intend to be involved in. If you want to help me, I know how you can do it."

"You would allow me to join you in a . . . a . . . spy ring of some kind?" Corey said in a hoarse whisper. A visible shiver ran down his spine, making his skin crawl with the sudden realization that his father undoubtedly was in a great deal more danger than he'd originally believed.

Klaas nodded, a grave look on his face. "I know there's risk in it. But not so much as on the battle lines, and I'd rather have you involved in something where the peril is more removed. Taking an incompetent commanding officer or the fog of war out of the equation would go a long way to ease my mind about you. Naturally, I can't protect you from the unpredictable risks . . . but the people I work with are honest, brave, and well-trained. That alone is enough to give you a safer experience, if war can ever be considered so."

"But Father, no one will trust me as they do you. They'll know I'm a novice in the textile business." Corey sounded both fearful and disappointed.

"Oh, you won't be going into my business, Corey. If I've learned anything about intelligence gathering it's that your supposed work must be something you know well. Your cover must fit comfortably. My thought is for you to assist in the music department at a university. That position should give you access to wealthy families in the South and it will be your task to make sure you take advantage of it. What do you say, Corey? Is this the way you'd like to make your contribution?"

Corey stared at his father. He was trying to weigh so much new nation it threatened to overwhelm him. Finally, after a long he looked back up from his hands to his father's face. He saw it a quiet gravity in the older de Koningh's expression—no impatience, no tension, and, most of all, no fear. "If you think I can do it, and you're willing to teach me what I need to know, then yes," Corey said.

His father sat forward and reached out his hand. "Good," he said. "Then we'll contribute together." Corey took his father's hand and held it in his. They sat that way for a time, reaching across the open space and holding on to each other. Finally, letting go of his son and sitting back, Klaas said, "Corey, will you tell me honestly how much of your decision to leave school was caused by Emily Alden's departure?"

Corey started and sat up straight with another shiver, as if he'd suddenly been hit by an icy draft. He didn't like the shock of hearing Emily's name when he wasn't prepared for it. He glanced over at the piano, searching for something, and took a breath. "I was very upset at first," he said. "But she's become someone I don't know anymore, and she made up her own mind. My leaving school has nothing to do with Emily." His heart jumped inside his chest in protest, but he had to stick to his resolve. He was starting his new life with an anger that would give him purpose. The trust he and his father shared didn't extend to his relationship with Emily; she had no right to his family or his soul anymore.

CHAPTER FIFTEEN

"DON'T LEAN out so far!" Robert shouted. He wondered if Emily's rational judgment had been affected by her change to modern trousers. "For God's sake, Emily, have a care!" He grabbed her forearm, dropping his climbing stick in his haste. But either by chance or her design, Robert's hand just missed Emily's and she stepped farther out on the rock ledge. As he couldn't envision himself hanging off an outcrop to save her, he profoundly wished for someone to save them both. In his panic, he waved his arms frantically as if grasping for unseen aid.

"Calm down!" she called back, giving him a mischievous smile. "This granite's been here for centuries defying the elements. It's not going to slip away just because I'm standing on it." Emily herself looked elemental. Wind, clouds, sun, and rocks all included her as one of their own. Her long dark hair spilled around her shoulders from a small wool cap and whipped back and forth around her face as if caught in a riptide. *Mountaineering!* she'd exclaimed gleefully, when he first mentioned the stopover in Switzerland. *Alpinism,* he'd corrected. He never envisioned their walks involving demanding terrain, but she had, and her vision won, as usual. So here they were, ing on a pinnacle in Switzerland with nothing to save them but memory he'd had of his childhood in Bavaria came close to ures Emily sought now.

He'd felt out of place ever since setting foot in London. He'd thought the stares and whispers on the boat would be the worst of it, gossip clearly running rampant about "the lord's daughter" and "that pretty girl and her theoretical tutor." He'd overheard more comments on the decks passing lounge chairs in the sun, and in the bar and dining room, about the impropriety of an older man and young woman traveling together. Traveling? They were standing on deck or dining together, but never alone. There was always assigned seating by the captain, probably prompted by the unseen hand of Emily's father. Attractive young men accompanying their mothers, unattached American businessmen filling the seats on either side of her at the table, and even—twice—male friends of her father on their way home to London, reinforcing the assumption that William Alden's planning was always prevalent during their crossing.

Emily had made her disdain for the gossip all too clear, and even went to the captain to complain about the lack of privacy due to the ship's newsletter printing biographies and table numbers in the dining room. Supposed to be a stimulus for the "who's who" of the elite, it seemed more of a gossip rag aimed at entertaining some of the passengers at the expense of others. Scaling that social ladder unscathed had seemed the most challenging thing Robert had ever done. Lord Alden, it was said, was the kind of man who followed all the rules in society, but in this case, Robert had been left holding the ladder steady for both him, and to some extent, for Emily as well. She had shown no awareness of his discomfort or his efforts to shield her from gossip, and as they moved from London to the Scottish Highlands to Germany and finally to the mountains of Switzerland, Robert had the uncomfortable feeling that his exhaustion at keeping up with Emily's pace of involvement with the world around her was bringing on a complete breakdown of his nervous system.

She'd leapt at the chance to buy the new athletic clothes offered for women in Berlin. "Don't be ridiculous," she'd scolded when he suggested she was going too far. "Even in school we wore loose pantaloons for gymnastics. Trousers are becoming acceptable for women in sports."

He translated "die Normalkleidung" for her as "rational clothing" when she saw the phrase in a German magazine, and she instantly adopted the rationale as her own. "Europeans are ahead of Americans, so I'm going to buy new mountaineering pants while I'm here in Switzerland," she'd exclaimed. He'd pointed out there were no men present when she'd worn trousers at her gym classes, but she stared at him as if he was speaking Greek instead of English.

Emily looked very fetching in her climbing outfit, but Robert doubted her father would approve, and naturally he continued to suggest she practice discretion in her choices. Her agility tested the clothes to limits they might not have been designed for. Robert particularly liked watching her legs, unencumbered by long skirts, stretching out to climb the steep terrain. Opponents of the ladies' fashion reform movement most likely wouldn't, but he had to admit to himself it was a pleasure to see her body less restrained and concealed.

Her father had warned Robert of Emily's ongoing battle with propriety, as if he hadn't seen it himself often enough in her teenage years. Though her father seemed unaware of that closeness Corey and Emily had developed with Robert, he wondered what Emily's mother would have said if she'd lived. Too bad he'd had no experience with women in his own upbringing. In any case, a mother and a father to Emily he could not be. Somehow, he'd allowed himself to be put in this wretched bind. Her father should just come and take over her care, he fumed, whatever urgent work for the Crown he had. Even Klaas de Koningh had delivered an evenhanded, calming influence on Emily in her youth, to say nothing of Corey. For some reason, Corey had been able to talk reason into her head that ordinarily heard no voice but her own.

"Emily! Where are you going now?" Robert called, as she started to climb again.

Dimples deepening at each corner of her mouth, she flung her voice back over her shoulder. "I want to get to the top of that next outcrop. People coming down are raving about the glacier lake up there."

Robert's blood pressure dropped so fast he thought he might faint. "I need to rest," he gasped. "Why don't you go on without me. But please come back soon. I doubt I could explain your solo climb to your father." He struggled to smile but it looked more like a grimace.

"Do you feel all right?" she asked him, seemingly concerned for the first time. "Your eyes have dark circles around them, and you look pale."

"I must admit to a bit of vertigo," he said sheepishly. "I've never liked the mountains. That's one of the reasons I moved to New York and never came back to Austria." He lied. Escaping the mountainous regions he'd come from played very little role in his decision to leave at the age of seventeen. The breakup of his family happened when his mother left home, which had loosened the ties that bound him. Avoiding conscription in the endless European wars had also played a role, but above all, finding a more productive and creative life had led him to America.

"Why don't I help you to the deck at the octagon," Emily offered. "You could order us lunch and by the time it arrives, I'll be back." The idea appealed to him more than climbing another thousand feet, so he happily agreed, keeping his back to the cliff and looking only at her abundant, shining dark hair as they moved away from the edge.

She left him on a wooden bench at a corner table, relieved to sit watching the climbers arrive for lunch, rather than being over-whelmed by the view. They'd seen entirely too much scenery for one day. He needed some time to regain his equilibrium. He realized now that he'd experienced galloping blood pressure ever since he'd accepted Emily's father's offer. Though in truth, it had never felt like an offer, but more of an order. Still, he knew he could have said no, and he didn't, because . . . he wasn't sure why. The money had been enticing, but not the deciding factor. He was doing well now with his teaching and performing, his reputation in both growing stronger with every year. He hadn't realized how acutely he felt his responsibility to spend as much time with Emily as possible to ripen her technique and, yes, her passion for the music. No matter how remote the possibility of success might be, he was resolved to spare no effort working with her. He might have also wanted the time alone with Emily, but for some reason her father had discounted that possibility, and so made it easier for him to do the same.

He waited for Emily, confident she would return. She was a musician after all, used to discipline and precision. She'd be back within minutes of the arrival of the cheese fondue, crusty bread, and white wine he'd ordered. He waited several minutes longer. Of course, if she fell in a glacial crevasse or was kidnapped by an Italian national crossing the border, which they were sitting almost on top of . . . He inched forward, forcing himself to look out at the mountain. Not seeing her, he felt quite nauseated. Maybe she wouldn't come back after all. He couldn't imagine why he'd let her go, when all he'd wanted for so long was to be with her. It wasn't the same feeling he'd had for the Italian opera singer. She'd had much of Emily's fire but none of her refinement. Perhaps that's why he'd never questioned the propriety of that Latin romance. Livia was a member of his own class and had never been his student. And of course, there had been no violin with Livia and no ongoing and unfolding relationship. Nothing could equal the joy and agony he felt listening to Emily play. He wanted to live every day of his life hearing that sound.

He wondered if Emily knew she was a woman now. As they sailed out of New York harbor, she'd been agitated over Corey's silence, totally unaware that he was still a child, but she was not. She hadn't seemed to accept that at the time. Perhaps her father sent her away to give her more time to grow up. Was he pushing her too fast, or not fast enough? Suddenly a sick assurance hit Robert that Lord Alden understood everything: Emily's commitment to her childhood friend to the exclusion of others; Robert's weakness for his former pupil and willingness to be drawn in as an accomplice to Lord Alden's plan: to break Corey and Emily apart using Robert's attachment to her to do it.

He must have been crazy to let her out of his sight. It must have been the vertigo that robbed him of his reason. Fear was a sensibility thief and anxiety even more destructive. He'd often been afraid in his life, but never of his instant, visceral reaction to a woman. All he wanted to do now was escape. But he had to fulfill his responsibility to Emily's father and go find her quickly before something terrible happened. He tried to stand up by pushing the wooden table away but found it immovable. That was because two young men had just stepped up to it, and one leaned over, holding out his hand to Robert. "Anders," the young man said with a smile, "Richard and Arnold Anders. We're staying at the same hotel in the valley. My brother and I saw you checking in yesterday. You're here with your wife?" Robert looked from one to the other in a daze. The one who spoke was taller and obviously older, but not by much. They were young, handsome, blond Adonis specimens of male perfection.

"Haussmann," he said, shaking the younger man's hand. "Robert Haussmann. Professor . . ." He knew he was doing everything backward but couldn't seem to stop. He needed to end the discussion immediately and find Emily.

"Delighted, Professor Haussmann," the tall one said, "but where are you going?" His bemused look questioned Robert's wild-eyed distraction. He realized he was still struggling to get out from under the table and had shoved his chair over in the effort.

"Miss Alden is my student, not my wife," he said, still pushing himself up. He noted, or possibly imagined, a heightened look of interest on the young man's face, perhaps relief at finding Emily was single. Robert had been dealing with those looks, too, ever since the start of their trip on the ship, and all through their various stops, including London. They infuriated him even more than the disapproval. Whether it was the parents of young hopefuls or the gentlemen themselves, he'd started to feel like a butcher offering his best meat to the public—a treasure he'd rather keep for himself. "She's been gone too long, and I have to find her. Please excuse me." He started to push past the gregarious pair toward the edge of the deck, but the bigger of the two held his arm, motioning to his brother to right the chair and place it behind Robert again.

"You seem very upset, Professor Haussmann," the younger one said, gently, looking concerned. "Please, let us be of some assistance. Where has your student gone, and why is she alone?"

Robert began to look wildly from one to the other but allowed himself to be helped back down in the chair. "She wanted to climb farther than I was capable of today," he said, feeling both relief at sitting down again and guilty for not being already on his way to find Emily. He felt a very poor excuse for a protector and hoped to hide that fact from his new acquaintances. "I wanted her to have some time in the fresh air. Too much work indoors isn't good for anyone. She's been practicing as much as six hours a day. It's too much." He glanced from one brother to the other, neither one following what he was saying with ease.

"Six hours of what?" the older one asked. He looked as if he thought Robert was perhaps a little mad.

"The violin," Robert answered. "She's a musician. I just wanted— her father would be out of his mind if he knew she'd gone off on her own," he finished, gripping the arm of the chair and looking as if he might faint. The fact that Robert was already out of his mind at the thought of losing Emily had suddenly closed in on him to the point of suffocation.

The other brother reached for a glass of water on the table and moved to hand it to Robert. "Your meal will be coming soon," he said, motioning to a waiter in a wool coat and scarf approaching one of the tables with a pot of hot cheese and a small coal stove.

"And so will your young student," the other brother said, his voice rising with anticipation. "Here she is now." As if coming out of a frustration nightmare, Robert saw Emily approaching at last at the far side of the deck and the young gods pulled themselves up to attention as if he no longer existed.

"Robert, whatever is wrong? You look absolutely terrible!" Breathless, her dark eyes shining with a light even his anxiety couldn't dull, Emily moved quickly to his side.

"I was coming to look for you, Emily. I was worried when you didn't return," he announced testily. She shook her head, as if assessing the level of anxiety she could see on his face and judging her part in it.

"Well I'm here now," she said softly, much as a mother would to soothe a small child, "so let's settle down and have some lunch while I tell you all about what I saw." She put her hand on his arm to comfort him as well as halt his panic. "Who are these gentlemen, Robert?" she asked, smiling pleasantly at the Anders brothers. "Do we know each other?"

"Oh no, we've just met," one of them assured her when Robert didn't answer. "We were trying to assist Professor Haussmann. He looked quite upset, almost ill, in fact. Richard and Arnold Anders," he said, tipping his felt hat with a feather in its band to Emily. She looked at Robert, but as he was still frozen in place and silent, she put out her kid-gloved hand, which was eagerly grasped by both young men in succession.

"Emily Alden, gentlemen," she said, looking each one in the eye. "I thank you for the assistance you gave the professor. The altitude proved to be too much for him today. I probably shouldn't have abandoned him to do that last climb."

"Happy we could help," said the taller one in the Tyrolean hat, his younger brother smiling his silent appreciation of Emily. "And now that all is well, we'll be on our way. Enjoy your lunch, and perhaps we'll meet again." They bowed slightly to Emily with a little more attention than necessary before they disappeared.

"Oh dear," she murmured. "I get so tired of the eligible young men springing up all over Europe. Where in heaven's name do you suppose they plan to see us again?"

"In the hotel," Robert answered under his breath. "Apparently they're staying in the same one we are. Though to be honest, I don't remember them at all. You may have much better recall. After all, they are more your age than mine."

Emily shook her head. "I've grown allergic to the steady parade of potential beaux, and my father's unending introduction to 'Lord this' and 'Lady that,' to say nothing of their gangly young offspring with the brains of gnats. I'm sure they all have vast fortunes and lands aplenty, but I'm supposed to be here for an education, not a husband. If that's what my father had in mind, he should have had the courage to say so. Not that those two were part of his entourage, but still . . . ," her voice trailed off in a sigh.

"Well, thank heaven they've gone," Robert said. "I was afraid they'd want to sit with us for lunch. Tourists who think you're 'from home' because you speak their language always want to talk you to death. I find them far more difficult to put up with than your father's acquaintances." He motioned to the waiter, who was standing by with the fondue pot while the Anderses said their goodbyes. A little coal heater was on the table waiting to be lit. "Come, Emily." Robert struggled to regain his composure after the strain and embarrassment of his obvious nervous collapse. "Let's try to enjoy our meal. You can sit there across from me, so you can see out over the valley. I've had enough of wide-open spaces," he said, trying to confirm his return to sanity by referring to his vertigo. The seating arrangement would also place him so he could look at Emily rather than the mountain.

"I guess I don't give you vertigo then." Her laugh hung in the mountain air. Exhausted by his morning's exercise, Robert found himself profoundly grateful for the waiter's arrival. The placements of the cheese pot, bread, wine, napkins, glasses, forks, and spoons were welcome distractions. He feigned involvement with the lighting of the flame under the Swiss pot, thanking the waiter as if his actions went beyond the requirements of his job. The familiar formality of manners gave Robert time to settle his nerves and calm his thoughts. By the time the wine had been poured, he was ready to raise his glass with a steady hand and offer a toast to continued inspiration along their musical tour through Europe.

"It has been truly wonderful," Emily agreed, holding her glass and looking out over the scene behind Robert. "When the Royal Academy in London refused my application, I thought our trip was ruined." She took a large sip of wine before putting the glass down. "But you were right, Robert. There's all the education one needs in experiencing the natural world and the many vibrant cultures around us." She kept her hand on the base of the glass, running her tapered index finger along the edge in a slow, rhythmic circle.

Robert frowned. "That's not exactly what I said, Emily." His voice took on a professorial tone. "It was John Locke who argued that knowledge comes entirely from the senses. It's a very British notion that foreign travel completes the education of a gentleman. I never said travel was all anyone needed to be educated."

"Of course, you didn't, Robert." Emily pursed her lips and then let out a breath. "Forgive me. I guess it was my father's idea, as he told me that I should complete my education the way any young man would, with travel. I was only trying to make the best of a disappointing situation for me with the Royal Academy."

"I'm still angry about that, too." Robert stared morosely into the pot of foaming cheese, hoping to regain his rhythm with her. He reached over to turn the flame down under it without thinking and noticed her watching with interest as if she'd not seen it done before, which he realized she probably hadn't. He smiled at her as if to say,

This I can do. "There are many things I can't teach you, and even more I'd never know to show you on this trip that you deserve to learn," he added, as if to distract her attention from the cheese pot. "If there was ever a mind with aptitude, it's yours, Emily." He stretched out his long hand and pressed it on the table, palm down and fingers spread wide, as if to steady himself. "But there's no doubt European training is a must for any musician today with a desire to perform on the world stage, as well as to teach, eventually."

Emily let go of her glass and rested her hand on the table as well. He could tell she was barely aware she'd done it, but watching her fingers almost stopped his breathing. "You're so supportive of me," she said. "You always have been. When I was little, you were the first adult to believe in my passion for the violin, as if it was the most normal thing in the world, which of course it wasn't; I've never forgotten that." She closed her fist as if to hold the memory tight. Robert felt a shiver ripple through him. "But I don't care anymore about the Academy," she said, opening her fist and putting her hand down in her lap. "I've never liked living in London, and thank heaven I haven't had to for very long. And I don't want to give the Academy a second chance to turn me down." She lifted her glass of wine and took a decisive swallow.

"Be careful," Robert warned. "At this altitude the wine could have a morbid effect." He was upset about her taking her hand away, so he added, "Your father would be very disappointed to hear you've given up on the Academy. What would you like to do instead of going back to London?" He concentrated hard on spearing a crusty piece of bread on his wooden fork, lifting it to twirl in the rich, melted mountain Emmenthaler cheese. The seesaw of his emotions left him struggling with a floating sense of unfocused anger.

"I don't know yet," Emily said, taking another swallow from her glass. "It will depend on how long it takes us to finish our tour and what I feel I still need to learn," she admitted, seemingly oblivious to his irritation. "But I'll be ready to return to America when our travels are over. I should like to celebrate my birthday there." Robert felt his stomach clench, and he frantically tried to calculate how old she would be. He realized he didn't even know when her birthday was. There were many small, but important personal details about her he'd never been privy to. He'd always been hovering at the door to her life without being invited in.

Emily reached for her fork and skewered a piece of bread. "Like this?" she asked him, concentrating hard on her dipping and twirling technique. Robert felt her silence, sure she was testing his reaction to her last comment. He might as well satisfy her unspoken question.

"Your father would never sanction you going back to America now that war has started. And who could blame him? I hear it gets worse every day." Robert noticed the waiter hovering closer to their table, like a bee looking for a place to land. He waved him off, with the expectation that, much like any curious insect, he'd undoubtedly be back again in no time.

Emily sat up taller in her chair, suddenly focused directly on what Robert was saying for the first time during their meal. "It was only weeks after the taking of Fort Sumter that we left the country by boat," she said. "I felt as if we were abandoning our people as I watched New York slip away on the horizon."

Robert felt oddly threatened by the look of grim determination on her face, knowing it had nothing whatsoever to do with him. "Tell me what you saw on that exploratory climb you thankfully survived to the glacier lake. You promised me a full account." He forced himself to listen in hopes of diverting her from talk of returning to America. Her face softened and she sat back in her chair, looking far away at nothing in particular.

"Heaven," she breathed. "I saw heaven in the mountains. Do you know what it reminded me of?" He shook his head. "All I could think of was *Lohengrin*," she sighed.

"The Wagner opera? You thought of an opera up on the glacier?"

"I did. That prelude to act one floated all through the atmosphere, with an intense blue sky reflected in the lake, and the mountain doubled in a perfect reverse image."

"I had no idea you were so affected by that production in Munich. It's still fairly new, but I agree it's already a hit for all the right reasons."

"It's gorgeous," she said. "But that man Wagner sounds dreadful. Did you read what a conductor said of him?" Robert shook his head. Emily was forever buried in newspapers, so he'd begun to count on her awareness of current events. "Mr. Alkan attended all Wagner's performances in Paris last year, and he wrote, 'Wagner is not a musician, he is a disease,' . . . or something to that effect." She laughed merrily, possibly feeling the effects of too much wine drunk too fast as Robert had warned.

"There will always be detractors of his music," Robert announced, finally at ease in the conversation. "Those who prefer the more conservative Brahms will object to the musical innovations of Wagner. But I do agree his behavior has created a bad taste in everyone's mouth. You know that he was recently banished from Germany to live in Italy and France?" He shook his head. "My friends from home write often of his disreputable lifestyle and growing debts."

"Yes, I've read of them all," Emily chuckled. "The wives and mistresses, financial bankruptcies and odd writings about other races. If he continues to make news like that, it will affect the music critics, I think."

"Indeed so," Robert said, leaning toward her a bit over the table. "And you should take note of how important an unsullied reputation is for a performer of renown. As an ambassador of the finest music in the world, you must be the finest person as well, something Mr. Wagner has surely ignored, almost purposefully one might think . . ."

"Even if his opera is sublime," Emily finished his sentence for him with a teasing snap in her eye. "And the way the golden colors of the mountain grasses in the tundra up there blended with the blue and white of the snowcaps made me hear every strain of *Lohengrin's* prelude. I wish you'd seen it," she added, suddenly looking back at Robert. "Only a musician could appreciate that . . ."

"Or a painter, perhaps, or one with an artistic soul. I'm glad *Lohengrin* meant so much to you." Robert looked away, uncomfortable under her gaze.

"How could it not? I see how close the human voice is to the violin with every production we go to. Even the singer's breathing mimics the phrasing with a bow. And there's nothing on earth like being there in person when these incredible pieces are performed. All those little black notes on the page spring to life and sing in a whole new way."

"Yes! Wasn't it a thrill to be in Bonn at Beethoven's monument and hear his chamber music in his birthplace?" Robert said, his own blue eyes sparkling above his red mustache. "I knew that would have a profound impact on you. I've been thinking you might consider tackling the Brahms violin concerto soon. I'm sure the thought must have occurred to you." Reaching for another piece of bread and putting it on his fork with more care than necessary, he knew Emily was paying attention to his movements, but couldn't define her expression. He could describe how she looked when she talked about music, but he'd not studied her everyday looks in the same way.

"Brahms is known, perhaps more than any other composer today, for his attraction to nature," Robert continued, as he toyed with his bread. "Although every composer tends to have links to the natural world, Brahms above all fills almost everything he does with it. You and he should do well together."

"Do you think I'm ready for the Brahms?" she asked. "I don't know that I could do it justice. Everything he does is so . . . big." Her hand swept through the air, taking in the entire panorama around

them. "I doubt audiences are ready for a woman playing Brahms."
She was looking out over the alpine valley beyond the restaurant
deck and through the rare mountain air to somewhere else.

"But you are ready," he said. "And that's all you should be concerned
with. Music knows no gender. Isn't that why it's made you feel so free?
Should Robert Schumann not have composed his fantasies because
they're too romantic for a man? Think what we'd all have lost."

"But the Brahms is so powerful, Robert. I don't know if I'm good
enough."

"Look there!" he ordered, frowning and dipping his head toward a
waiter just passing with a fiddle. He was playing requests from diners
at the tables on the deck, stopping now in front of a young couple
holding hands. They smiled at each other and then back up at the
waiter, who was starting a favorite modern love song of Franz Liszt's.

"I think it's supposed to be 'Liebesleid,'" Emily said, with a smile
and a little shrug.

"Of course, but look at his body language. You see the curve
around the violin, the lean toward the couple, the short bow strokes,
the light pressure? All meant to convey intimacy. You see?" Robert
was leaning halfway across the table now, lowering his voice to a
point of surprising intensity. Emily stared back at him.

"Yes, I see. The piece is just meant for them."

"And he is not feminine. Quite a large, dark, almost Latin-looking
man." Robert finished in a hoarse whisper, as the player had moved
near the next table. "But we accept his right to play like that without
question because the music requires it."

"I don't see your *point*," Emily said, a note of exasperation making
her last word emphatic. Robert jumped to his feet and snatched the
fiddle from the waiter, whose eyes opened as wide as his mouth.
Emily gasped and the group at the next table all pulled back, away
from Robert, who now stood with the violin under his chin, bow
poised above the strings, both arms supported high, with his back
lifting him as if to gain two or three inches.

"Big, Emily. The music isn't intimate and confined, it's big and open, just as you said. That's the point," he said, waving the bow in a huge arc encompassing the same vista Emily's hand had described a few minutes before. "Big, like the sky, the clouds, and the mountains. So, you hold yourself, your instrument, your bow in a big way. Open. Proud. Encompassing!" He lifted the bow and his body at the same time. "Could the waiter play an intimate, romantic, almost schmaltzy piece even though he looks like a boxer? Yes, like this," he said, crouching into a semicircle with the violin and bow. "Could a small woman play a big, powerful piece even though she looks like a pretty china doll? Of course, like this!" He lifted the violin and bow high with his back and chest opened wide again. "The music dictates the language, tone, and intensity, not the gender of the musician."

He lowered the instrument and handed it back to the waiter with care, but never took his eyes from Emily. The waiter moved off quickly, clearly relieved no harm had come to his instrument or himself. Robert sat back down directly in front of Emily with his elbows on the table and both hands clasped together in a decisive wedge pointing at her where she sat in stunned silence. "You're more than good enough," he assured her. "Emily, when you used to spend all those hours practicing as a child, who were you doing it for?"

She blinked a few times, then answered, "My teachers, I suppose—you and Maestro Adina in school, my father, Corey, Mr. de Koningh, everyone I wanted to please . . ." Her voice trailed off, but he wouldn't let her go.

"Really? I wonder. But if so, now that you've grown up, how has that changed? Who do you practice for now?" He still held her with a steady gaze, and she couldn't break away, but a small indent at the corners of her mouth told him she already understood. She was still silent, but the dimples started to deepen.

"Me," she said, finally. "I play for myself. I'm my own audience."

"Indeed. And I'd say you were always your toughest critic, as I

191

recall. But then who should decide if you can perform Mr. Brahms's violin concerto, or anything else for that matter? Who should you listen to? Let the music be your guide."

Emily finally looked away with a sigh. "Thank you, Robert," she said in a small voice.

He watched her looking out over the horizon. He could suddenly see the piece of heaven she'd described. They sat quietly, until she said, "Are you going to retrieve that bread you dropped in the cheese pot, or just let it drown?" He jumped with the shock of her teasing voice.

"You've lost your bread, have you?" The waiter leaned over from behind Emily's chair. "You know what that means?" Robert stared at him with as much hostility as he could muster. "You have to kiss the lady to your right, or endure a lifetime of bad luck," the waiter smirked. Robert could feel his skin starting to tingle.

"There's no one to my right," Robert announced, with more force than necessary.

"Then you must kiss the only lady at your table!" The waiter's voice seemed to gain cheer and strength with his delivery of the time-worn tradition. Robert glowered at him.

"Oh, come now, Robert." Emily rose a little in her seat. "My feelings will be hurt if you don't let me assure your good luck." She leaned across the table and offered her face for the requisite kiss.

"Emily! I'm your tutor and guardian." Jumping up from the table, Robert demanded that the waiter give him the check.

"Good Lord, Robert. Don't be so outraged!" Emily fell back in her seat, seemingly as upset with him as he was with himself. "It was all in fun," she muttered, rising again and starting to leave the table.

The waiter looked from one to the other and then handed Robert the bill. "Will you be taking the wine with you?" he asked.

"Carrying it how . . . on our backs, perhaps?" Robert slapped a pile of Swiss francs down on the table and moved off after Emily, wishing there was someone else to be furious with.

"You'd never know he was German," the waiter said to no one. "That's what happens when they go to America." He shook his head and started to clear the table.

"What do you suppose that was all about, a lovers' quarrel?" asked one of the busboys helping him clear away the food. They watched the young woman and her red-bearded companion disappear over the horizon.

"I'm in a difficult situation," Robert called after Emily's retreat. She stopped her descent for a moment to balance on a small rock.

"Difficult how?" she snapped. Her childish intensity surprised him. He realized instantly that for all her athleticism and artistic mastery, she was still at an age where she needed guidance. Her mature beauty was possibly as confusing to her as it was to him. He certainly knew how hard it was not to judge her an adult and expect commensurate conduct. Yet, in fact he could see her do battle with the child inside, quite often. He must remember and be sympathetic, but always supply the discipline she needed when she couldn't find it in herself. She was obviously adrift in a sea of possibilities without a compass to set her course. He felt relief flood over him because he'd finally figured her out. Now he could be that guide.

"I meant though we're far from home, we still need to observe the rules of polite society . . . and I need to get you home to England alive," he added, as he slid clumsily down a gravel pitch.

"England isn't home. America is . . ." she called over her shoulder as she waited for him to catch up. ". . . and I miss it more each day I'm away," she added, when he'd reached her side. "New York, the de Koninghs, and Corey." She looked him firmly in the eye as he paused there out of breath, as if to say, "Let there be no mistake!"

CHAPTER SIXTEEN

DESCENDING FROM her hotel room for breakfast, Emily was suddenly grateful for her long skirt hiding her aches and stiffness. Mountain hiking was wonderful fun until you had to pay the price. She'd done so little exercise of any real substance on this trip she'd promised herself to stay active every day from now on. Her shoulders, too, were becoming stiff with the extra hours of violin practice, and too much repetition and tension in muscles caused the need for more circulation. Better physical conditioning would also help her withstand the rigors of performing.

Reaching the ground floor, she glanced around the hotel lobby, which doubled as dining area and lounge. She inhaled the scent of beeswax on wood surfaces glowing from years of hand-polishing. The mellow sheen of mahogany and aged Swiss pine was softened by print fabrics on stuffed furniture. Small round tables littered with the remains of Alpine breakfasts dotted the perimeter of the room. Toast, jellies and jams, yogurt, freshly squeezed orange juice loaded with pulp, and carafes of coffee nestled together in various states of consumption, detritus of food consumed before the rush to climb the mountain with the rising sun. Filled mostly with men dressed for gentler morning pursuits, the front parlor was calming with its dark wood and cozy cushions. Pristine, high-altitude air and bright sunlight outside were balanced by the solid, shady interior, a relief from the bright energy of the natural Swiss spectacle. It was a masculine décor Emily found appealing in its quiet solidity. Occasionally, a morning reading by the window instead of a climb up the piste was a welcome respite.

She was relieved to have arrived first, before Robert Haussmann's scrutiny had to be faced head-on. It was a familiar feeling from long ago. She'd been aware of the magnetic pull toward her music teacher when she was only thirteen years old, admittedly an overly sensitive adolescent who hadn't fully understood what physical attraction was—or wasn't. But it became more difficult as the poles reversed between them, pushing them apart with age and her advancing musical maturity. She felt the force now repelling them, but knew he was denying that truth. The connection no longer upset her as it had at thirteen, and the years away from him at school had helped, but she still sometimes found it enervating to be around the professor when past feelings got confused with present ones. She'd wanted a father, not a lover.

But she still wasn't sure if Robert knew what he'd wanted then, or now, and that felt like a snare to be avoided. Her twenty-first birthday would soon be upon her, and with its arrival, the concomitant legacy of her mother's bequest, making her a financially free woman. Emily knew her mother's intent for her autonomy was purposeful, not because there had been an early revelation about her motivation, but because she'd known her mother's temperament and oft-stated wishes for her daughter's independence. Once she had the legal power to be truly free, she could put her plan to return to her war-torn adopted home into action. Until that moment, she would bide her time and study her options.

"Professor Haussmann asks that you have breakfast without him," the clerk announced, yanking Emily from her thoughts as she stepped up to the front desk. "He says he still suffers from yesterday's climb."

"He's not alone in that!" She laughed at the thought of her clumsy stagger downstairs. The muscles controlling her knees had been particularly unresponsive. "I'd like to sit at that last free table in the window," she said, though it was a table for two. "And I wonder if you could bring me some newspapers, especially the American ones." She smiled at the clerk with all the charm and confidence she could muster, knowing there might be an objection to a woman monopolizing both a larger table and the broadsheets with so many men present. She wanted to read the war news but knew what they'd be thinking: a woman was only interested in the society page and its fashion ads, or possibly the arts and entertainment columns. Giving her a newspaper reporting on current events and battles in America was a ridiculous waste.

The clerk pulled two papers off the desk and handed them to her. "I am sorry, but there's only one from America at this time, and that is being read by the gentleman over at the window. Fighting there makes small the number arriving here, also."

His announcement only sharpened Emily's appetite for updates of the war, and she turned to look at the man by the window. Reading her face accurately, the clerk added, "I could seat you at that single table next to his and as soon as he finishes, you could have the paper." Guests were coming and going, beginning to appear from upstairs and move into the parlor without waiting for help to be seated, so she seized on the clerk's suggestion. Deciding more swiftly than she might have if she'd had time to consider the issue of being purposely seated next to a single man, she answered, "Yes, thank you, that would be perfect." She nodded to him and strode over to claim her seat before someone else did.

A twinge reminded her of her beleaguered muscles. Even lowering herself gracefully would be hard after her approximation of a mountain goat yesterday, so she silently blessed the high, formal seat she could get down to and up from with the minimum effort. Actually, this life with Robert was hard on her emotional strength as well. She needed more variety of every sort. Of course, society would prefer she remain a weak, passive observer of life, perhaps another reason people didn't approve of women on the public stage, but society's preferences were seldom hers. She craved some excitement—traveling with a male companion thirteen years her senior was often boring.

Finishing her breakfast slowly, taking time to appreciate textures and tastes, Emily motioned to the waiter circulating through the lobby carrying a small carafe of coffee. She knew it might not be meant for her, but hoped her presumption would affect his decision. The waiter paused for a second, and then, no doubt responding to both her poise and her smile, came to her table and put down the carafe with a cup and saucer.

"My pleasure, Fräulein," he said, bowing slightly. Then turning to go, he suddenly stopped and raised his voice, nodding toward the gentleman at the table next to hers. "Mr. Barnes reads the newspaper from America, Fräulein Alden. I'm sure he won't mind giving it to you when he is done. Mr. Barnes, Miss Alden." He smiled and bowed, first to her neighbor who looked up, and then to her. Emily couldn't help admiring the efficiency and cleverness of everything Swiss.

"I apologize if I've been selfish with the paper," her neighbor said, looking at her with frank curiosity. Then leaning over, he put out his hand to shake hers, an unusual gesture she appreciated as more American than European. "Usually I'm the only one with interest in news from America when I travel abroad," he said, still holding the opened copy of *Harper's Weekly*.

She nodded. "I'd hoped for the *New York Times*, but I guess a weekly is the best one can expect overseas, and they're all so old it probably doesn't matter anyway."

"*Harper's* is the most popular newspaper in the country right now," Mr. Barnes informed her. "It's got the best reporters and illustrations." He was studying her intently, so she leveled her gaze back at him. He looked so relaxed she expected he'd somehow secured one of the soft loungers that flanked the fireplace in the corner, but found his square, stocky frame was balanced on a small upholstered side chair placed around the café tables. His sandy-colored hair, pushed back slightly from his forehead, revealed a gray streak, suggesting more years than his sunburned face showed at first glance. Other than his air of relaxed assurance, there were no obviously distinguishing features about him.

"How lovely to meet an American!" she exclaimed with delight. "Do I hear a bit of the deep South in your accent?"

"Only a very little bit," he answered, with a laugh. "Born in Virginia, brought up in Vermont. A life of contrasts, you might say." Emily forgot the newspaper he'd offered and looked at him more carefully, as if to see the inner conflict between the North and the South he must harbor inside. She would work to figure out which geography had won his allegiance without asking directly; at least at first. "And I detect a slight British accent in you, with a decidedly American inflection, I think," her new American acquaintance announced.

"Decidedly!" she agreed. "Born in London, raised in New York. Both cultures and locations are far apart. Although, if I've learned anything during this trip, it's that all worlds are coming much closer together. And which world are you most comfortable in, the North or the South?" She couldn't resist rushing her question but found no overt reaction on his face or in his manner. He folded the paper and handed it to her before reaching for his coffee cup to empty it with a final sip.

"Is there anything you were looking for in the paper?" he asked. "There's an amazing story about the youngest soldier in the Union army. He's twelve and a sergeant. He attained that rank by killing a Confederate colonel in action."

"How horrid!" She shivered, looking down warily at the front page as if something bad might jump out to bite her. "No twelve-year-old boy should be fighting a man's war."

"Then the personal interest stories will hold no appeal for you. I agree. For the most part they're all written to sell more papers, and you just want . . ." Mr. Barnes cocked his head to one side and raised his eyebrows. He clearly wanted to know more about her allegiances, just as she did his. She was flattered at the implication that her opinion was of interest.

"I just want news. It doesn't feel right," she muttered. An engraving of Fort Sumter and the Union officers who were defending it when the war broke out made her breath catch. "When I saw the pictures of the rebel Stars and Bars flying over the fort after its capture I felt as if America was attacking herself from the inside. Other countries watch from the outside with curiosity or ulterior motives of greed and profit. But I knew I'd become American when England's interest in the war filled me with suspicion, and I found the attack on Fort Sumter an act of treason."

"What doesn't feel right?" Mr. Barnes asked, leaning forward to hear her better.

"It doesn't feel right being here in Europe, with the war wreaking such havoc in America . . . It's like being in some sort of dream where I can't feel what's real and what isn't. I have . . . friends in the cotton trade who may be harshly affected, and it's important to support the people we love through hard times. I wish I were back there," she added quietly. "Is New York much changed since it all started?"

"Not to look at," Mr. Barnes answered. "But just below the surface, nothing's the same. There are many Southern sympathizers in New York. The city's economy is tied to the South, you know. Nearly half of its exports are cotton shipments, now illegal as you noted, and of course the slave trade has also halted. The business connections are so strong, Miss Alden, that the mayor has called for secession from the Union; unsuccessfully, I might add. But that kind of sentiment fueled draft riots, which have swiftly become race riots, and President Lincoln had to call out the militia to control them. Much has changed."

Emily gripped her hands together tightly in her lap, her dimples deepened by her mouth pressed tight in a line of worry. She started to bite her lower lip, suddenly surprised by how Corey's childhood habit had somehow imprinted on her. Mr. Barnes took a deep breath and tried to change the subject. "What brought you to Europe, Miss Alden?" he asked in a conversational tone, but his straighter posture informed her he was unusually attentive to her answers. One had to be a bit circumspect about the war, she knew. It was best to talk more of England, although that was not what she wanted to discuss.

"My education brought me back to England. When war was declared my father wanted me out of the country, though he claimed to be primarily focused on my studies. But the Royal Academy in London turned me down as a full-time student. Now I have no chance for a formal education . . ." and I've abandoned America when it's in turmoil, she wanted to add, but didn't. She stared out the window at the main street down the center of the small Swiss town. It looked so clean, untouched, and utterly removed from conflict of any kind. It made her feel miserable.

"Well, Miss Alden, it's not uncommon for fathers to want to protect their children," said Mr. Barnes, following her gaze out the window. His face was easy and relaxed again, although he still sat at attention. "But it's hard not to be where major events are happening when you're young," he added. She could feel him studying her. "Still, what is uncommon is your intense interest in education. Few fathers today would expect their daughters to be taught past finishing school, and few young women would want that, either. You impress me!" Mr. Barnes finished.

"Thank you, sir," Emily said, pulling herself back from the simple scene of the village outside. "However, few would agree with you. I often wonder why New England has been such a center for women's rights and assume it must have something to do with education." She smiled at Mr. Barnes and added, "But then I realize all that . . . transcendence might require a level of personal perfection I could never aspire to." Her dimples deepened, and her new acquaintance smiled, too.

"New England women are strong believers in human rights, you know," Mr. Barnes said. "We have suffragettes, abolitionists, and one of the first female social workers in the country." Wiping his hands on his napkin and folding it, he tucked it under his cup and saucer.

Emily shifted uncomfortably on her seat, but whether from the stiffness in her body or the pointed conversation, she couldn't tell. "Women who strike out on their own against the injustice they see around them, as do suffragettes and abolitionists, are much to be admired, and I do, but they pay a heavy price in society. I don't know what a social worker does, but I assume like the other women you mentioned, it's a difficult, often selfless stance against the prejudices of our culture." Mr. Barnes's emphatic nod indicated complete accord with her point of view.

Emboldened by his approval, Emily continued with the small flash in her eye that meant she was feeling challenged and enjoying it. "Until women are educated equally with men, there can be no social equality for them," she said, with the same snap in her dark eyes. "But there are still so many ways a life can be threatened by assumptions and limitations. I think men also lead restricted lives sometimes because of cultural mores, don't you?" She stared at him directly. "Why should men be the only ones to fight?" Emily looked back down at the picture on the front of the newspaper and the officers depicted there. "Nine men," she murmured, almost under her breath. "Where are they now? All dead, no doubt." The men's names were written under their pictures, making them seem more real. Her eyes had lost their gleam and were covered again by the haze of a faraway focus.

William Barnes watched his new acquaintance in silence. "Miss Alden..." he said, softly. Nonetheless his voice surprised her, and she jumped.

"Excuse me, sir," she breathed, embarrassed she'd left their talk so completely and that he'd noticed. "There's much to imagine, most of it unpleasant, when you know so little." She slipped back into her attentive role, holding his eyes with hers.

"Miss Alden, have you ever heard of an abolitionist philanthropist by the name of Gerrit Smith?" he asked, clearly changing the subject with specific intent. Emily noted again his seemingly relaxed expression while his posture was on point.

"Indeed, I have, Mr. Barnes." She was delighted to feel well informed at last. "Mr. Smith came to speak at my school last year, and I've been following his writings ever since. Are you an admirer of his, too?"

"You could say that," Mr. Barnes nodded. "We're old friends and business colleagues. And I'm recruiting women students to attend the University of Virginia for him."

"I don't understand, Mr. Barnes."

"The war has decimated the male population of college age, Miss Alden. As you've noted, it pulls them away from school and into battle." He looked past her. "I'm sure you know the university's reputation for academic excellence," he continued, "but it's also a campus and facility of unparalleled beauty. This country's founders were its first benefactors. It's become a treasured landmark as well as a seat of higher learning."

"I know it in pictures and by reputation only, sir, but it looks to be very beautiful and sounds like an almost rarified atmosphere." Emily watched him carefully, unable to figure out where his conversation was leading. She didn't have long to wait.

"Without students to teach and tuition to cover costs the university will close, maybe forever," he said, now watching Emily pointedly.

Suddenly her eyes began to widen, and she sat up very straight in her chair. "Do you mean Mr. Smith is recruiting female students of means to attend the university to save it financially?" she asked.

Mr. Barnes didn't react at first, and then nodded, slowly. "Those who can pay their own way will, of course, be most welcome. But he's also looking for women who can't afford tuition but want the education. He will pay for any woman capable of benefiting from the opportunity. However, they must live at the southern campus, which is a serious challenge for a woman from the North."

"But not such a challenge for one from Britain," she said, with a spark of understanding.

"Precisely, Miss Alden. That's why I'm touring Europe this summer."

"Is there a college of music at the university, Mr. Barnes?"

"A very fine one," he said. "Are you interested in music? Let me guess . . ." He cocked his head to one side and narrowed his gaze. "You're studying to be an opera singer. Is that right?" Emily smiled, or meant to, but the little twitch of her lips as she shook her head gave away her distaste.

"A pianist, then!" he guessed again. "Following Clara Schumann's example."

She shook her head once more. "I want to complete my education very much, Mr. Barnes, but don't follow the examples of others. Although it never garnered praise, my passion is for playing the violin." She watched for his reaction to her instrument, which clearly had not been a possibility in his mind. "If the music faculty is still intact, it sounds like the ideal situation for me." She could see from his raised eyebrows he was surprised, but too polite to say so. She was grateful to be spared from making the usual explanations of how she came to play and perform with an instrument considered unbecoming for a polite, upper-class woman.

"There has certainly been some faculty diminution since the war broke out and the students were siphoned off," Mr. Barnes continued, in a serious tone. "But the performance facility is very impressive, and revered among musicians," he added with a small smile.

Emily's enthusiasm grew with every enticement he offered. "And female graduates will have full baccalaureate degrees?" She moved to the edge of her chair, as if she might spring up and take flight at any moment.

"Absolutely, Miss Alden. We have the dean's word on it in writing."

Her excitement sharpened, concentrating in her dark eyes. "I don't know how I'll talk my father into this, but I must be a student at the university somehow, Mr. Barnes." Her breakfast partner relaxed and seemed to settle deeper in his chair at last, as if he'd been waiting for her declaration. He pressed his tented index fingers to his lips, as if considering a thought of enormous weight. Then he dropped his hands, sat up straight, and looked at Emily. "Perhaps we could help, if your father is resistant at first."

Emily looked at Mr. Barnes sitting across from her, hands clenching the *Harper's Weekly* folded in her lap. Maybe it was precisely because they were strangers that there'd been no prohibitions to overcome. She could feel her future opening around her like a cape unfurling, revealing a lining of rich beauty. She looked at the window framing the lovely little street with shops and pedestrians but saw only herself this time.

"Miss Alden, I'm afraid I must excuse myself," Mr. Barnes announced. "But I hope you'll continue your interest, and I will extend myself to help." He reached into his vest pocket. "Please allow me to offer you my card. I would be grateful for any reaction from you."

"Of course, Mr. Barnes. You may count on it." Emily smiled as her companion rose to go. He bowed slightly and wished her a good day.

Watching Mr. Barnes disappearing up the stairs to his room, Emily couldn't resist pulling the letter she'd received yesterday from her father out of her skirt pocket. He hadn't written before, a fact that had both dismayed and relieved her. Emily slid the letter's thick, cream-colored paper smoothly out of its envelope with the embossed diplomatic seal that so impressed the clerk at the Swiss hotel. He'd misunderstood her expression of surprise when she saw it. "We're used to royalty in Europe," the clerk had assured her.

The thought that she might now have a collaborator to help her return to the States and thwart her father's plans for her in Europe gave her a hopefulness she hadn't felt since leaving New York harbor. She unfolded the letter, all thoughts of reading the newspaper now forgotten.

My dearest Emily:

What joy it gives me to hear of the success of your European tour. From all accounts, it could not have been a greater triumph.

All accounts? Last month's letter from England was the first Emily had written her father describing the specific events of the trip. She'd realized the import of making him feel comfortable about her travels and connected to her letdown over the Royal Academy's rejection. Could he possibly mean letters from Robert? Of course, Robert must be staying in touch with his employer. If so, had he painted an inaccurately rosy picture of their crossing and time in England, surrounded by the transparent men her father had foisted on them? Was the "greater triumph" her avoidance of Robert's uncomfortable obsession with the woman she had become? Yes, it was a triumph for her, but her father knew nothing of it, so labeling the trip with such hyperbole seemed odd for a man as particular as her father.

You wrote of the disappointment you felt when the Royal Academy denied you admission, and in fact, I myself had much the same reaction.

Disappointment? Apparently, he'd found a way to soften the blow for himself. But it had crushed the breath out of her. Yes, she'd wanted her father to feel the rejection personally. She'd wanted him to experience what it felt like to be denied something others took for granted solely because of your gender, reveling in the fact that it would hurt him even more because it happened to his daughter, and so reflected on him, too.

However, the pleasure you have experienced abroad in the concert houses of the world's greatest cities is all the sweeter . . .

She was glad she'd embellished her letter to convince him of the success of his plan to keep her busy in Europe while civil war raged in America. His assumption of her lift in spirits kept him less attentive, his mind presumably on more important things. It was easy to distract men, she was finding, if you engaged them in whatever they seemed most inclined toward. It had certainly worked well with Robert in the Alps. She'd known he had no interest in trekking but was intrigued with her athleticism and trousers, therefore overcoming all his misgivings about his own fears for himself and her father's possible disapproval of the dangerous excursions.

. . . for you have acquired the finest finishing a young lady could aspire to, and I am confident Professor Haussmann's expert guidance has enhanced your trip even more. Indeed, you have been on the "Grand Tour" that only young gentlemen could avail themselves of in the past.

Men! How could her father be so naïve? Grand tours didn't "finish" anybody because most "young gentlemen" who went on them hadn't even started to live, and probably never would. Visions of the translucent-skinned youths gathered around her on board ship and in London turned her stomach. They'd all been finished before they'd begun as far as she was concerned. Even worse were the older ones, almost her father's age, so imperious in their entitlements they made her skin crawl. And speaking of older, how could her father have been so blind to Robert's true feelings? Both he and her father were examples of what emotional suppression could do to people.

Her father had never recovered from the loss of his wife, but wouldn't say so, nor would he reject the guilt he felt over abandoning his daughter at that time. And Robert felt guilty over the feelings he'd always had for her but wouldn't even admit that to himself. Neither their guilt nor their willful ignorance left room for her freedom. She looked down at her father's letter in her lap again, hesitant to let his thoughts intrude on the conversation alive in her head.

I am delighted to hear of your plan to return to London to attend the concerts of Mrs. Clara Schumann. Her reputation as one of the finest pianists of today precedes her, and the fact that her performance partner in England will be the astounding violinist Joseph Joachim makes the experience more valuable for an accomplished musician such as you, dearest Emily.

That was true. Emily could feel her pulse quicken just thinking about sitting in the audience in front of Joachim. She could only hope her timing worked out, so she would actually be in London for that concert. The logistics of her plan were very bold and untried. Perhaps her father had forgotten he'd told her of the special bequest left by her mother, of which he'd approved only to bring his wife peace in her final days. He'd informed the thirteen-year-old Emily that it was very unusual to pass a large portion of an estate to a daughter, though he himself admittedly had no need for it. Or perhaps he'd thought it would have no meaning for Emily, as she was already well cared for. But he hadn't known then of her overwhelming desire to care for herself, though she had not forgotten, and she knew what it meant.

Of course, you may use the house in London while you are there. It has not been closed since your departure for Paris six months ago. I am only sorry I cannot join you and the professor for your birthday celebration, but perhaps next year things will be quieter in America, and I will be back in England for another of Mrs. Schumann's concerts and another birthday. Mrs. Schumann returns annually, so I'm told, and you will have many more birthdays.

Would she still be around to attend a concert next year? Not likely; at least not in London anyway. Emily shivered at the thought of her father's plans for her future. Whatever they were, she could easily guess they included a husband to take care of her and a house in England she could take care of in return. But those were his plans and not hers. How could he never have discussed them with her?

Please write to me again when you have the time, as I do so love to hear your literary voice. And give the professor my warm regards. I send you my love, as always, your Dear Papa.

It was time now to put her daring plan in motion. What had she to lose? Robert Haussmann would be shocked and unlikely to remain the devoted mentor he'd formerly been. But that was what she wanted. They both needed to originate new roles for themselves in each other's lives, and she wanted Robert's to be less familial so that she could enjoy the new freedoms her independent wealth offered. Her father would most likely be furious, as men can be when their formerly unquestioned control is overthrown. He'd get over the rage eventually, or maybe he never would. But she'd had to live with her outrage over the way he'd treated her after her mother died, so he could do the same over her treatment of him now; or not. Either way, she would be no worse off in her relationship with him.

And so, the next stop on their tour would actually be the last, where she'd launch her plan to return to America on her own without her father's consent. Vienna would offer a final connection to her favorite composers, as well as the entrance to the rest of her life.

CHAPTER SEVENTEEN

The manager's chest swelled like a pigeon puffing up in the cold as he announced, "We are the oldest hotel in Vienna. Hungarian diplomats live here on a permanent basis."

Aristocratic ghosts gave Emily no thrill, but during this trip to Vienna, when she'd walked through the rooms where Mozart lived for several years, she'd felt a tingle. He'd composed *The Marriage of Figaro* there, and she could sense it. Mozart the maverick. Thank heaven he'd never been schooled at a music conservatory, or the world might never have had his daring and beautiful music. Modern dissonance, chords that don't resolve, multiple voices talking at once just as they do in the human brain, none of these would have been allowed if he'd been forced to conform. *I pay no attention whatever to anybody's praise or blame. I simply follow my own feelings*, he'd said. And Emily had taken his maxim as her own.

But even stronger than the power of the Austro-Hungarian Empire flowing through the buildings for the past three hundred years was the thrill she got from the hotel's name, König von Ungarn. In all these many months away from New York, Corey never fully left her thoughts, and the memory of her first meeting with him at age thirteen had suddenly flashed into view when she'd seen the sign for the hotel named for the king of Hungary. *Koningh means king, doesn't it?* she'd asked Corey, so long ago. *I don't know. I never thought of it*, he'd answered.

Well, it does, she'd assured him. What a little know-it-all she'd been then, and what she'd give to have those vibrant, innocent days back now, when she often felt she knew nothing. But there was no way to hold on to the past, and if she didn't act fast she'd miss out on the present, too. Returning to London would cut her stay in Vienna very short, and there wouldn't even be time for her daily walk down the Kärntner Strasse to the opera house.

If the hotel hadn't been right across from St. Stephen's Cathedral, she'd have missed every sight in Vienna with her secretly planned early departure. Walking through the Gothic cathedral just to get a feel for Mozart's wedding almost one hundred years ago, followed all too soon by his funeral, would have to be the end of her grand tour, though no one else knew it yet.

As Emily left the hotel for St. Stephen's Square, she looked across the street and saw two children playing with a hoop. The young boy and girl reminded her of the agility and ease of childhood, tumbling over each other as if they didn't care who might be watching. Suddenly the hoop started to gyrate out of control, heading away from the children and out toward oncoming traffic. Without a thought, Emily took off across the street, just as a young man looked up from his walk. He saw a beautiful young woman with shiny dark hair run after an errant children's toy as if she, too, had been caught by a gust of wind.

⊱⋆⋅☆⋅⋆⊰

Johnny Dunne, out of his office at the newspaper for lunch, fresh air, and a midday stroll, watched the dark-haired young woman dive down the curb after the rebellious hoop to catch it before one of the carriages crushed it. She was down on it so fast its careening trajectory came to an abrupt halt under her delicate boot. Lit with the flush of victory, she turned in the direction of the children and waved the hoop over her head. They ran toward her as if she held a magnet. Johnny could see the pleasure she got from the youngsters, as she tousled the boy's blond curls and brushed the girl's dress off where the Vienna streets had left their mark. He couldn't resist walking behind the three of them in the square. The children moved on together, disappearing down the block, while the young woman with the shiny hair started into the cathedral.

Johnny decided to follow her. She was so pretty he needed a few more minutes in her company to satisfy his appetite. Suddenly, he noticed a group of older students leaving the cathedral, pushing and shoving each other in seemingly good-natured play as they came out onto the street. Two of them bumped the dark-haired beauty off balance and ran for the line of carriages. In an instant, she was careening sideways, and Johnny was next to her with his arm around her waist. She fell with the full force of surprise. "What happened?" she gasped, clinging to his arm. Her dark eyes were wide with shock, and he could see gold flecks in them that seemed lit from behind the pupils.

"You were the victim of someone's high spirits," he said, tossing his thick, light brown hair back while holding on to her small, unconstricted waist as if she might sink. "I saw you from a distance with those children and could tell you were distracted," he said. "You couldn't have seen the students coming out of the cathedral. I thought you were all together, you and the children," he added, noting the curls clinging to her damp temples. Her hair looked almost black so close-up, but he'd seen its sable sheen in the sun from a distance.

"You were so swift retrieving the toy for them, I couldn't help noticing you wore modern clothes because you bent down so easily!" He realized he was rambling while he held on to her, and she was still staring at him. "Are you sure you're not hurt?" he asked. "Can you put weight on your ankle?" He slowly righted her and let go, hoping she'd assume his familiarity was born of concern.

She tested her ankle, pushing her hair off her face. "I've just come from a hiking trip in the Alps," she said, a slow smile starting to join two dimples at each end of her mouth. "I'm feeling pretty strong from the climb." She put weight on her foot with increasing levels of pressure. "But modern clothes certainly do aid one's flexibility. However, I'm not in the habit of discussing my wardrobe on the street with men I don't know; even ones who've saved me from catastrophe." He could see those gold flecks in her eyes again, alight now with a challenge. My lord, she was pretty in too many ways to list at first sight.

"Johnny Dunne," he said, putting out his hand. "Now you know him." He assumed a young woman who didn't wear corsets and could fly like the wind over cobblestones would be comfortable shaking hands. "I'm a writer with *Harper's Weekly*, in the Vienna office." She still stood looking at him. He kept his hand extended through the awkward moment, and then she took it in a grasp as firm as his own.

"Emily Alden, Mr. Dunne," she said, with the dimples deepening in her cheeks. "Thank you for saving me from something unpleasant. I'm a music student, in Vienna for all the obvious reasons." What was her odd sense of propriety and modernity? He couldn't place how someone who looked and sounded like a lady, with all the natural ease and bearing of the upper classes, had come to be leaning on his arm in the middle of the street in a casual skirt with no corset.

"A music student . . . let me guess. An opera singer here for the season." His piercing blue eyes were now fully focused on her huge brown ones.

"Wrong," she announced, with an edge. "Try again," she challenged. "I'll bet you can't guess right this time, either."

What a lovely, unusual accent she had, redolent of aristocracy, but with the cadence of a confident working woman. Johnny backed off as if to see her in a new light. "A concert pianist," he offered. "A young Clara Schumann," he added. "How long will you be here? Might we have dinner sometime?" he heard himself say, surprising even his own ear.

"No, Mr. Dunne. I'm a solo violinist," she said, obviously watching for his reaction. "And no, I cannot have dinner as I'm leaving tomorrow, Mr. Dunne. But if you're ever in New York . . ." She smiled at him with no evidence of discomfort or judgment.

"Really? You, *a painted woman of the stage*? How intriguing . . . I'll be returning to the States very soon," he said. "I've been here three years already and it's time I went home. There's a war on."

"My sentiments exactly, Mr. Dunne." She looked at him, as if she'd just recognized him for the first time. "It doesn't feel right to hide away in Europe while our country's torn down the middle." He could hear that faintly cultured tone again, probably British, and was surprised she claimed America as her own.

"Well, my incentive is a bit more financial, Miss Alden. War is a journalist's richest fodder. But I understand and applaud your motivation. Here's my calling card. If you need anything or want to contact me when you're back and settled in New York, please do." He returned both hands to his pockets, for fear he'd grab onto her again. "You've made an otherwise predictably dull day shine." He smiled and backed off a little before he finally turned to go. If he didn't keep moving he'd make more of a fool of himself. He'd already clarified his objective too well, and he wasn't used to showing his hand with so little restraint. He turned to leave, feeling her watch him until he was lost in the crowd milling about St. Stephen's Square. He stopped for a moment and turned back, just for a last look, and saw her reading his card before putting it in her jacket pocket. She turned to start toward her hotel with a slight limp and a smile, apparently willingly accepting the discomfort in exchange for the morning's excitement.

As Emily moved toward the hotel to collect herself in her room after her chaotic chance encounter on the street, Robert Haussmann was enjoying a quiet, orderly morning in his suite. He liked the Hotel König von Ungarn. Everything about it spoke of the old charm that was elegant and agreeable, rather than tired and unimaginative. It reminded him of a world he'd hungered for in his youth, but never gotten close enough to touch. It seemed ironic he'd had to move to America before the luxuries of a European lifestyle came within his grasp. The hotel management seemed convinced that Emily's father had something to do with British royalty, as he did in a way, which helped to secure many advantages, including the upright piano in the suite for Robert's daily practice. Emily had seemed pleased they could practice together again, unperturbed by the time spent alone with him in his rooms. The walls were thick in the old building, so he didn't worry about disturbing other guests as he usually did while traveling, and Emily never seemed to worry about much of anything.

Slipping a housecoat on over his trousers after breakfast, Robert had practiced his Bach in peace for two hours while Emily went out for one of her walks to feed the birds. He liked to start with Bach because it made everything that came after sound better and feel easier. He'd given up advising Emily not to go out alone after her surprise attendance at the suffragette meeting in London. It had discouraged her about the progress of women's rights, she'd said, so she wasn't going again. But nonetheless, she was truly beyond his capacity to control in any way. She sometimes apologized for the extra stress she was putting on him, and he appreciated her aware-ness, however unsure he was of her contrition. Young people were often self-centered, but Emily, the only daughter of a proud father, might finally be showing signs of growing out of that.

It was time Robert got outdoors, too. Perhaps he could surprise Emily, sitting alone on a bench in St. Stephen's Square while she fed the birds. A clean shirt, collar, waistcoat, tie, and frock coat would be appropriate for a stroll around Vienna with her this afternoon, and the pin-striped trousers he already wore. His clothes were laid out on the bed. The sheen of the dove-gray silk vest was a happy reminder of the changes in his wardrobe since the opening of trade with China. He ran his hand down the lapel of his silk bathrobe, delighting in the texture and flow of the fabric under his fingers, grateful even a music teacher could now afford the beautiful cloth. Silk waistcoats for daytime had become very popular, but so had Bach, after all. He wasn't usually affected by men's fashion trends, but there was nothing wrong with appreciating quality. He took pleasure in the discipline of dress and what it said about him—not his status, but his values.

His top hat already waited for him on the hall table, so he untied the sash of his maroon silk robe and started toward the bed just as a furious pounding came on his door. His heart jumped with the assumption of crisis. Running to deal with the emergency, he forgot to fasten the short robe. Yanking open his door, he found Emily standing outside in the hall. Too late for retreat, she was past him and inside the room before he could stop her.

"Good God, Emily, don't you know how to enter a private chamber? I'm not dressed!" He stood staring at her in horror. Frozen with shock, he made no attempt to close and retie his robe.

"I'm sorry, Robert," she gasped, her eyes dancing. "Oh, if you could only see your face. You couldn't look more horrified if I were the Frankenstein monster!" She covered her mouth with her hand. "Truly, I'm sorry. But I'm sure the silkworm that gave its thread for your dressing gown would be sad to hear you discount it so. You seem quite dressed to me." She smiled calmly at him. "I'm on the worm's side," she added, with her dimpled grin. "You look splendid."

"Emily!" Robert cried out. "Why are you here?" He couldn't move his feet, other than to turn in place to watch her walk to the piano bench. His short silk robe hung open, brushing his skin in the breeze she made as she moved past him. He pulled it closed and tied it with two sharp tugs of the sash and an emphatic double knot. "What could possibly be so important?" His tone was more frenzied than necessary and he tried to compose himself. She seemed to be struggling not to smile. He tried to ignore her effort.

"I got a letter from my father," she announced, slipping a large cream-colored envelope from her jacket pocket. He could see the diplomatic seals and Lord Alden's assertive hand in Emily's name at the top. "He left a very special birthday present in London," she continued. "But I had to think about it a few days before telling you. I didn't want you to be disappointed. But we're going to have to cut our stay in Vienna short." She slid the letter back in her pocket and sat down on the piano bench. Robert continued to stare at her without moving.

"Birthday present? Whose birthday is it?" he asked.

"Mine. I'm going to be twenty-one in two weeks, Robert. How could you forget?" Emily flashed her dimples at him to show she was teasing as much as informing.

"Yours . . ." Robert looked at her, searching for a clue he'd missed. "You never mentioned it before." It must not have been a significant goal, but he could see all sorts of advantages for her, and for him. She was no longer a child. "What did he leave for you, Emily?"

"Tickets! To Clara Schumann's concerts with Joseph Joachim in London. He knew both you and I would be thrilled with such an opportunity and asked my aunt to buy them."

"Thrilled?" Robert dropped the sash of his robe as his hands fell at his sides, still waiting for some final disclosure he could feel in the room and hear in her voice.

"That means we must leave Vienna immediately, Robert. We can attend the opera tonight as planned, but tomorrow I have seats on the train. Father says the London house is open and ready for us. I have only to telegraph my aunt and tell her what day we'll arrive."

"And will your father be joining us?" Robert whispered, finally realizing that the whole tour was suddenly ending for her birthday celebration.

"He planned to," she said, stirring uncomfortably on the bench, "but now he finds the war in the States will keep him there. So, we must carry out his plans for my birthday without him." She shifted again, seeming to Robert hurt by her father's choice of duty to his queen over the one to his daughter. He wanted to distract her from the thought and considered his quick acquiescence essential to changing the subject. He couldn't bear the thought that Emily would notice her father's preference for his job as a diplomat over the one as a father.

"Well, back to London then," Robert said weakly, a sudden suspicion he'd possibly been manipulated by both father and daughter rising painfully in his chest. "But you must give me more warning before your next arrival in my room," he muttered angrily. He could feel a hot flush rising from his face to his hairline.

"Oh, for heaven's sake, Robert. Do you think I've never seen the male anatomy outside of a biology book or Italian sculpture? You of all people should remember I grew up with a best friend of the opposite gender." She stood, and walking to the door, pulled it open with a small tug. "I'm grateful I had such an authentic homeschooling. There are no surprises left for me. Or was that not the shock you were referring to?" She stepped through the door and started off down the hall. "I'll see you for tea before the opera," she called back over her shoulder.

Robert watched her turn the corner down the richly carpeted hotel corridor. He knew she'd been purposely goading him, having lived exactly the protected life she pretended to disdain, but rather than turning him away, her teasing gave him a new determination. It was time to call her bluff. Ever since their mountain climb, as well as at the private little hotel in Switzerland, to say nothing of the crossing from the States, he'd been aware of how much more complete each day was with her in it. There was a reason she'd been thrown in his path eight years ago. He was supposed to be with her, and he knew it. He had no interest in the women he'd met since his arrival in New York, at least not for a permanent relationship. They were fine on a casual basis, but Emily was different. He was in love with her, no doubt, and with her violin. There was no sense in denying her intonation and vibrato were part of her allure. He wanted to call her back to his room, but his door was already shut, and she was gone.

"Young women today think they're free to do as they please," he muttered, scowling. How foolish she was. She'd find her flaunting of propriety the quickest way to lose her freedom when she was forced to marry someone her father chose, or she'd end up living with public censure. He could save her from all that. Suddenly Robert realized her father's considerations no longer mattered. He'd alienate Emily completely if he asked Lord Alden for her hand in marriage before he asked her, which he'd do before they left Vienna—before another day went by. The only other question of importance was . . . how.

CHAPTER EIGHTEEN

My Dearest Papa,
By the time you read this I will be on my way back to America. Your
solicitor in London, Mr. Sellwood, has explained the distribution of my
mother's trust upon my twenty-first birthday, and I have borrowed a
modest amount against the anticipated allocation to purchase passage
for our return to New York by early fall.

She felt her new coming-of-age status required that she act
responsibly and inform her father of her intentions. No longer would
she be asking his permission. She would take charge of her own life.

. . . I have told Professor Haussmann he is no longer to consider
himself my teacher or chaperone.

She'd made it clear to Robert that he could stay in Europe or
return to America, but he was no longer her tutor in her father's
employ. Her announcement had been poorly timed and she'd felt
embarrassed for Robert that he'd chosen just that moment to
propose marriage. He'd spoken of her musical voice, her vibrato, her
intonation, and how he wanted to hear her play for him every day of
his life. Initially she'd assumed he was urging her to practice harder,
something she'd announced she'd find impossible as she was already
giving at least six hours a day to it. He'd stuttered that he wasn't
talking about practice. Then he'd told her he wanted to spend the
rest of his life with her, and she'd assumed he wanted to be her
permanent music mentor, a difficult thing to respond to when she

was about to inform him that he wasn't going to be her teacher anymore at all. It was only after she'd noticed his extreme distress, marked as always by the scarlet flush of his fair skin, that she told him her rejection was not personal, and he'd announced that it certainly was, because he'd asked her to marry him.

It was all she could do not to laugh out of shame and remorse for his predicament, as well as her own. She'd not handled it well, reminding herself of the thirteen-year-old Emily running out of the music room when Professor Haussmann had shown her the first kindness she'd had from anyone since her mother died. At twenty-one, the fault was her own, but the complexity of feelings on both sides overwhelmed her. Still, she knew taking charge of her own life meant starting and ending with Robert Haussmann, and she knew her father had promised him passage home in their original agreement. She wanted to complete the bargain. It was best to keep things clean and simple if she could.

Robert's numbed silence hadn't been easy for her. He was unable to handle her rejection once he'd finally expressed his feelings for her. Odd that she'd wanted him to express them earlier to get rid of the pressure she'd felt, but once he had, she wanted only to get rid of them and run away. There were too many responsibilities she had to take on now. Robert had been born with the freedoms she was only just acquiring. Was he aware he'd never had to fight for them? But how did she know he'd never had to struggle for his independence? She knew nothing of his childhood in Germany or of his early years in America, nor had she asked. She'd assumed he lacked empathy for her predicament because he was a man. She posted her letter from London with the thrill only the launch of a daring plan can bring.

❦ 〜 ❦

"Oh, my darling Emily, what have you done?" William Alden moaned as he dropped the letter from his daughter onto his lap. This

is what came of having no mother to influence a daughter's upbringing. But Emily was bright, brighter than most people he knew, male
or female. She should have known better, used some judgment, and
controlled herself. That boldness in her spirit had always been a
problem. She'd never been good at following the accepted pathways
to polite womanhood. Now it was too late. And the professor—how
could he have betrayed a trust so completely? Why had William
ignored the warnings he'd received from friends in London? How
could he not have seen the danger? Now it was too late.

He lifted the letter slowly to read it again. It was impossible to tell
if they were married yet, or simply taking liberties. Rage rose in his
throat until he could barely breathe. His sweet Emily—how could
any man ruin her life so? A father had a right to reprisal, and in fact,
there was undoubtedly legal action he could bring against the
professor, as Emily had been a minor when her grand tour began. But
how would that help her in the end? The more negative attention
brought to her situation the more public the censure. She would
always hold his heart in her hand, just as she had since the day she
was born. Even later in life, that same bondage would be in place. He
would never be free of it.

So, nothing to be done about it now. He'd have to wait until she
and the professor were back in America, which would be any minute
now, to plan the next steps in his daughter's life. He let the letter sink
to the floor and lie there, dead at his feet. He felt like weeping at the
bitter irony in his choice of the man to protect Emily from the
attentions of the de Koningh boy. What a fool he'd been. More than
anyone in the world, he wanted the advice of his old friend Klaas, but
in his current predicament, Klaas was the last person who could
help. In all honesty, he'd had no contact with the de Koninghs since
Emily's departure for Europe. Klaas had made it clear he had no
intention of participating in the sale of Southern cotton to England
when it was banned at the start of the war, so Lord Alden had moved
quietly off to pursue discreet sales with less scrupulous exporters in

the South. He'd ignored the illegality of helping the South to a stronger financial position, as most British subjects championed, and had put the de Koninghs out of his mind, especially Corey, where he belonged.

⊷⊷❧ ⅋ ☙⊶⊶

Le Havre to New York! Brochures selling America as the "Land of Opportunity and Unlimited Employment" beckoned to travelers from every ticket window. Some offered travel deals, including transport for immigrants by rail from their homes in Europe to the steamship taking them to America. Le Havre was a teeming, confusing place with the mass exodus from Europe in hopes of finding work, and the opportunity to live a better life. Emily's conscience had pricked her more than once on the crossing, starting with the departure from Le Havre. She'd had to spend only a few hours there before leaving, but she'd seen the immigrants arriving, more than a day early, to endure medical examinations, antiseptic baths, haircuts, and vaccinations, to say nothing of having their luggage fumigated with steam, which ruined the contents. One father wept silently as he looked at the pile of debris mounded in his open bag containing all his family's possessions.

She'd imagined what it must have been like for young men like Robert Haussmann little more than a decade ago, struggling through that port on their way out of the huge Austro-Hungarian Empire. But she'd never asked him, since he seemed uncomfortable talking about himself, and she wasn't talking with him at all since their painful standoff in London. Sitting on one of her steamer trunks now in New York, Emily felt that stab of enlightenment again as she wondered if Robert had always known more than she had about fighting for personal freedom. How was that possible when he'd started so far ahead just by virtue of his gender? Apparently, there were many ways a human being could be robbed of self-determination, even in the 1800s.

The intense activity crashing around her now in New York was arresting. Noises and cries from drays with no sides, along with wagons, carriages, and fruit vendors all mixed together in a cacophony of commerce. It could have been upsetting, but it wasn't, not to Emily. She loved it all. The hum of energy excited her with the awareness of possibility. She knew the harbor had long been one of the busiest in the world. Many talks with Corey's father had ingrained the picture in her mind of the United States exporting raw materials, like his cotton, and importing finished products. She'd never had direct contact with that world other than these two recent trips of hers, but she liked thinking about Klaas de Koningh's familiarity with the docks and their commerce. It made her feel connected to the de Koninghs in a vicarious way.

"Miss Alden!" A deep male voice pulled her out of her inner world.

"Mr. Barnes, over here," she called out, waving to Gerrit Smith's agent. Making sure he'd be on the same steamship bound for America had been a difficult complication for her, but in the end, well worth the struggle. With Robert as communicative as a stone and Emily eager for any information she could get about her future education at the university in Virginia, she'd spent a week drinking in descriptions of the quality of the teaching, to say nothing of the women on campus and the greatly subdued life there now that the whole state was under siege from her Northern compatriots.

She'd never lived solely with women other than her two years of high school, and she hadn't participated in female friendships there enough to give her an awareness of what to expect. She had to remember, though, Mr. Barnes's assertion that a young woman from England could travel more easily between the North and the South than an American. "I don't think of myself as being from England anymore," she'd protested, while he assured her it was an advantage. Best to leave her Northern connections behind for a while, he'd advised, emphasizing that her concern was for her education and that her British heritage made her supposedly neutral in the war. None of it was true, but all still useful and necessary.

"Your father hasn't arrived?" Mr. Barnes asked, bringing her out of her daydream. "I had hoped to meet him personally, but I'm afraid I'll miss my train connection if I wait any longer. I still have the long miles to New England ahead of me."

"Oh, please don't run that risk, Mr. Barnes. My father may be quite late. He's often delayed by his work, and I don't want you to miss your train."

"I don't feel comfortable leaving you alone here with your luggage, Miss Alden. Would you allow me to arrange for a carriage to deliver most of your steamer trunks later so that I could take you with me and drop you at your house once I'm on my train?"

"How would my father know where I'd gone?" Emily asked. She looked at the chaos roiling around her and had to admit she didn't really want to stay in the middle of its rapids alone. Why was she always dependent on the men she knew to carry her home?

"I'll go arrange for your luggage transport and be sure the manifest lists that you left with me for delivery to your house. I also have a letter of introduction I want you to give your father, explaining your educational opportunity." He reached out and handed her an envelope.

"That was thoughtful of you, Mr. Barnes. But I hate to have you take on so much of this responsibility for my welfare. I am not a child, you know." The protest felt childish, nonetheless.

"Oh, I do indeed, Miss Alden. But if you were my daughter, these are things I would want to know. Putting myself in your father's shoes is my own point of reference."

"Well, thank you then, Mr. Barnes. I would appreciate the ride home, and I'll see to it my father receives and reads your letter in my presence."

"Let's be off, then," Mr. Smith's agent urged, marking the start of her new life.

"Yes, let's," she agreed, thrilled to be back in New York, which felt like home, and looking forward to engaging her father in a discussion about her new life plan. A small voice within her suggested he might not be as supportive as she'd like, but she was buoyed by Mr. Barnes's reaction to her desire for more education and somehow convinced that her father would reside in the same camp.

❦ ❦ ❦

An hour after Emily and Mr. Barnes had left, a tall, broad-shouldered man in a wool coat and silk top hat raced from his carriage through the passenger gate up to a shipping clerk.

"Gone?" William Alden's voice broke slightly. "Gone where?" He spun the manifest around, so he could read it himself before the clerk could stop him.

"Sir, please," the clerk begged, "the public is not allowed access . . ." but the withering glance the aristocrat sent his way quieted the protest. Lord Alden ran his gloved finger down the list of passengers, staring at the names as if to lift them off the page for closer study.

"This says that Professor Haussmann and Miss Alden left at different times, and to different locations. Is that correct?" He turned the manifest back, so the clerk could see it himself.

"Yes, that is correct, Lord Alden. Your daughter left with Mr. Barnes, a philanthropist's associate, I believe. Yes, that's right," he said, reassuring himself with another reading of the entry. "Miss Alden's luggage will be delivered to your home, as will the young lady herself. Mr. Barnes was headed for the train station and his home in New England. We facilitated the reservations for him ourselves." The clerk's voice gained strength and confidence with every additional piece of information he delivered.

William Alden clenched and unclenched a muscle in his jaw while he balanced his hat in his hand, juggling it in time with his heartbeat. "Really," he said, his eyes narrowing. "You don't say. Will wonders never cease?" He clutched his hat in his hand and thrust it back on his head with a determination that made the young shipping clerk flinch. Suddenly William Alden wasn't sure he wanted to confront his daughter and her fiancé, new husband, or whatever he was, at home or anywhere else. He was afraid of what he might do to them.

❧ W ☙

The breakfast room at the Aldens' rented house had already started to fill with early morning light. It wasn't exactly sun, but a promise of it lapping into the corners. Emily looked around at the soft yellow wallpaper with outlines in white of birds sitting on hints of branches here and there. It was bordered with a yellow-and-white horizontal stripe at the bottom before it met the warm, polished, brown oak floor. From where she sat at the mahogany table in front of the window, she could see through to the south-facing garden. It was a lovely house, and although her father had only rented it for the duration of his term in America, it gave her a solid feeling of familiarity. But this morning the warmth of the house's welcome was in sharp contrast to the restriction in Emily's chest, reminding her of how cold she felt.

Her father's rage when he'd returned from the docks yesterday had been a shock. She'd had no hint of it in advance and no way to prepare. Expecting only his usual joyful welcome, he'd stormed into the house right after Mr. Barnes dropped Emily off. Two hours of diatribe followed, two hours she'd lived through without once joining in the argument. Her father had never shouted at her before in her life, nor had he ever been so angry about anything in her presence, least of all something he thought she was responsible for. The time she'd played her violin for his guests in London when he was late for dinner came immediately to mind. She'd led them to believe he'd asked her to, when of course he'd never have sanctioned his twelve-year-old daughter making a spectacle of herself. He'd given her a look of shock and disapproval when he'd arrived to find her holding forth in the drawing room, arms raised high above her chest, but he'd never lashed out at her, neither in public that night nor to her face later.

After Emily's repeated denials yesterday, and her father's final acceptance of the falseness of his accusations, his anger intensified instead of diminishing. His fear and embarrassment seemed to join in an explosive force. But Emily knew he was a reasonable man both by nature and profession, and she understood his care for her had taken him someplace emotionally he would not have gone under any other circumstance. When he fully accepted his mistake and moved on, he would recover, but she wasn't sure she would.

Far more frightening than her father's reaction to his misconceptions was her own fury at his distrust and betrayal. Could he not have simply said he wanted her to have some time on her own away from Corey to see things and meet people outside her current milieu? He could have told her of his fear that she'd close herself off from opportunities she wasn't even aware of. Did he have to use the professor as a foil, counting on her passion for music to sell his plan without objection? How could he not have sensed Robert's interest in her? Was his jealousy of the de Koninghs so intense that it overwhelmed his scruples about throwing her in Robert's path and using the professor's vulnerability for his own ends? It served him right for trying to use both Emily and Robert against each other without the other's knowledge. Worst of all, the level of mistrust of his own daughter and of a man with a formerly impeccable reputation was totally abhorrent after he was the one who had thrown them both in harm's way.

She'd kept all her anger buried last night in her father's presence, and then when she was alone, she felt it so profoundly she couldn't handle it. Expressing his rage was undoubtedly healthier for him than hiding it was for her. His anger was probably over by now, while hers was only beginning to simmer before it reached a racing, foaming boil. She'd had no sleep and knew this day might be lost, too, unless she found a way to calm down. Her father was the only close family she had, and she'd thought they'd be friends forever, but perhaps they'd never been friends at all and that was the problem.

She picked up the bone china teacup next to her plate and took a long sip of the warm amber brew. It wasn't sweet enough, so she spun a teaspoon of golden honey into it, mesmerized by the shiny whirl-pool of spoon and liquid swirling around together. The sound of silver on porcelain soothed her. She remembered how she'd delighted as a child to music played on half-empty glasses and cups at breakfast even though the housekeeper had feared she'd break them. She smiled, not only at the thought of that small rebellion so long ago, but also appreciating how music could pacify her.

It was still very early. She'd have time for at least two hours of practice on her violin this morning. Maybe that would be where her release would come. Nothing could stay locked inside long when her violin opened her up. Or at least, that had always been her experience in the past. She would also visit the de Koninghs today, as well as Robert Haussmann. She wanted to say goodbye to the people who mattered before she left for university. She needed to explain her father's accusations in case Robert heard of them through some other source. She had to convince Robert she'd put them all to rest. She hoped his return to his own home, his students, and his music would also ease his distress. Nonetheless, it would undoubtedly be just as hard as her meeting with her father had been.

All this must come first to make her last stop possible: a visit to the offices of *Harper's Weekly*, and the irrepressible Johnny Dunne, whose calling card still lay in her violin case along with postcards from Austria, Switzerland, Italy, and France. The instrument case was her own private treasure trove of remembrances, as it was for most violinists who traveled to perform. The opened lid was a jumbled scrapbook of pictures, notes, and keepsakes, such as the silk flower Corey had given her when he'd left for college and the journalist's card resting there ever since her chance meeting with Johnny in Vienna. Now she would put it to good use.

She drained the last swallow of tea from her cup, and realized she was hungry. Picking up a crumbly corn muffin, she broke it in half, happy to find her appetite had not been stifled by insomnia. Somehow the list of assignments for the day made her feel better. She was not a person who could stay depressed for long, and she knew the plans helped her keep a hopeful outlook. Was freedom all in the power of discipline? She started to brush some crumbs off her skirt to the floor, then put down the cup to catch them in her other hand and return them to the saucer. Their cook, Emma, peered around the swinging door from the kitchen pantry.

"Will your father be with you soon or are you on your own this morning, miss?" She balanced a cup in her left hand and held the door open partway with her ample hip.

"He didn't say, Emma. I may be on my own." Emma nodded, and the door to the pantry swung closed on its hinges with a swish and two clicks, resettling in its frame. "We're all on our own," Emily muttered to herself, low enough not to halt the cook's departure to the kitchen. She stood up and took a last look at the room before she left. It was flooded with sunlight now, the southeast bay windows letting in streams of brilliance. Everything shimmered, possibly from the reflection of light in her own tears of frustration.

CHAPTER NINETEEN

𝄞 BUILT OF common New Jersey brownstone, the modest office
building was only two stories high, a testament to its owner's
limited budget. Five signs at the front door identified other busi-
nesses in residence. Coming through the wrought-iron gate and
down the steps from street level to the *Harper's Weekly* entrance,
Emily was reminded of accompanying her father to print and news
shops in London as a child, always feeling important and privileged.
She vaguely remembered tensions around taxes paid by British
publishers producing much unrest, and her father had been charged
with relaying their anger in unofficial communications to the
Crown. It hadn't occurred to her then that the attention the staff
paid her had everything to do with her father, a peer of the realm,
and nothing to do with her, his little daughter. Her father had told
her newspapers brought the citizens of the world together, and since
she was one of them, she'd always assumed she was just as important
as anyone else. Now that she knew she was not so important after all,
it had become clear she'd have to carve out her own place in the
world without her father's help.

Emily walked up to the reception desk and held out Johnny
Dunne's calling card for the clerk to read. "I'm here to see Mr.
Dunne," she announced evenly, as if she was expected.

"Doesn't work here anymore." Head tilted down to assist his view over reading glasses, the clerk's narrowed eyes and tightly drawn lips told her he was irritated by her interruption. His clean-shaven appearance added to his air of insolence. It had been a long time since she'd seen any professional gentleman without either a beard or mustache, but then, perhaps he wasn't a gentleman.

"Are you sure?" She turned the card over and checked that the print was right side up. "J. R. Dunne. *Harper's Weekly.* You see?" Her pleading tone surprised her.

"I do, but he is *no longer here.*" The tight-lipped young man looked back down at the book he was reading, an armor of disdain wrapped around him.

"Mr. Dunne was away in Europe for a long time, but now he's back."

"Yes, but not here. Doesn't work here anymore, see?" He slowed his words as if speaking to an imbecile or foreigner. Picking up his open book and propping it on his desk with a thump, the clerk erected a defensive wall more effective than any facial expression or words. Huge type on the cover announced: T. R. Dawley's *Incidents of American Camp Life,* a book she'd heard sold fifty thousand copies in one week. Why anyone would want to read "true adventure stories" about the war, she couldn't imagine, unless it helped those who knew they'd be stuck behind a desk forever feel more involved. She'd craved news herself, but only because she'd felt so removed from America while traveling in Europe. Maybe that was almost the same thing. They were all removed in one way or another, yet each of their lives was affected by the outcome of the fighting.

Johnny's card went into Emily's handbag. She tried to cover her confusion with a sharp snap of the clasp. She was unprepared for her mistake, and her regret was untimely. Why she'd assumed the handsome young reporter she'd fallen into in Vienna would be waiting for her, exactly where he'd said he'd be, was becoming a mystery to her. She felt the anger she'd begun to recognize daily since she'd been back, rising again. Even that made her mad—to be so beyond control—and the clerk and missing reporter added fuel fanned to a blaze by her realization that she was most certainly and suddenly alone in the world. In fact, maybe trying to revive the connection she'd made with a stranger had been the biggest stupidity of all.

She was still obliquely sorry to have missed out on her travels through the rest of the musical culture of Europe, still regretted the opportunity missed, although she'd had no choice. She'd been afraid she'd lose her nerve to complete such a daring upheaval if she didn't keep moving fast. Johnny Dunne's unexpected appearance had not been timed well, but she'd been intrigued by his spirit and confidence and, to be honest, maybe his looks as well. It had all happened so fast, yet she'd thought of him often since then and wondered if he was as free as he'd seemed.

Now, Johnny Dunne was the perfect person to help her, just as he had when he broke her fall in St. Stephen's Square. "I suppose you know nothing of where he might be working now?" What began as a question flung the young clerk's way ended as a sarcastic prod that must have sounded as impolite to him as it did to her. She certainly had no intention of matching the clerk's insolence.

"Why didn't you ask me that in the first place?" he sneered. "Pretty things like you always think everything comes easy." He muttered the last sentence almost under his breath, but not quite.

Emily took a deep breath and let it out slowly. Her first instinct was to fight back against *pretty things*, but taking up arms wouldn't find Johnny Dunne and would most certainly provoke her antagonist. She looked down at her closed purse with the calling card, and then raised her eyes to the clerk's, satisfied with her self-control. "Would you please tell me where Mr. Dunne is working now?" she asked. She hoped her informal clothes would help her with her adversary behind the desk, make her appear to be more of a working girl than a privileged aristocrat. "I'd be grateful for your help," she said. "I met Mr. Dunne in Europe. I need his expertise to find someone. It's so hard to get information these days during the war. Not knowing people's fate is the most difficult thing of all."

The clerk raised his eyes to look at her over his half-moon lenses, lifting his head a fraction to see her better. The gesture was barely visible, but it had a responsiveness lacking at the start of their clash. "That's why he went over to the *New York Times*," the recalcitrant young man announced. "They've started a Sunday edition called 'The War Between the States,' you know. I think Dunne was hired to run that page. He should be able to help you. Horrible war," he growled under his breath. He closed his book and put it down, slipping his glasses off and folding them on its cover. His reading material gave his vulnerability away. He was human after all.

Emily wished her motives were purer. She'd known mentioning the war, offering a connection with the shared emotional pain, would probably gain the attention she needed. It was the means to her end, and she was not proud of it, but glad nonetheless that it had worked. The war was quickly becoming a passkey to many things for those not directly involved: economic gain, jobs requiring new and unusual skills, and opportunities to take over the roles men had filled at home, such as studying at universities formerly open only to men. It was odd how something so hideous and destructive could offer new prospects.

"Thank you," she said, trying to hold the clerk's eyes with hers and reaching out to shake his hand. She knew it was still a surprise for women to use the straightforward grip that only men of a lower class had shared until very recently. She could see it on his face. But it felt right to her. "People experience the pain of this war all over the world, not just here," she added, letting go of his hand only after she'd made her grip felt.

The clerk looked at her with his eyes narrowed again. "Don't think anyone else gives a damn about us," he grumbled.

"You can rest assured they do," she contradicted. "I've just returned from a concert tour in Europe, and the war is on everyone's mind over there." He looked back up at her quizzically. She realized too late she'd given away a part of her privileged identity she'd meant to hide, but thought she'd push on as if it was the most natural thing in the world for a young woman to be on a grand tour of Europe. "The greatest composers are writing the most stirring music in memoriam, Johannes Brahms and Franz Liszt among them. Clearly neither man has been on our battlefields nor heard our cannons." She thought of the waves of harmony Brahms was so well known for, soaring, rising and falling, sweeping all emotion with them like the sand on a beach, pulling you along until you cried for release. The clerk stared at her. She wanted to tell him how that music made you happy to be able to cry, but she couldn't. She knew it wasn't the time.

"War's no topic for a woman. You don't know anything about it." The clerk flexed his jaw muscle and narrowed his eyes to study her better. "Have you seen the illustrations in our paper sent back from the front?" He pulled a sheet from his desk and pushed it toward her. She glanced down long enough to see a burning landscape and fire consuming both earth and sky. "Mr. Winslow Homer painted that. He can show you what you don't want to see," he said, pulling the sheet back and turning it as if out of concern for her feminine sensibilities.

Emily squared her shoulders and lifted her chin. "I think any human being can imagine the horrors on the battlefield. And if you listen to Mr. Brahms's work, you understand any heart can be broken by the thought of the suffering, just as surely as it would be by the fact of it." She turned and started to walk away from the desk, then stopped and came back to the angry clerk one last time.

"Music teaches one that when tension is very high and dissonance overwhelming, resolution can't be far off. I'm sure the war is almost over." The clerk looked as if he were sorry he'd let the crazy young woman take up so much of his precious time. He shook his head, sighed, and went back to reading the book, with the subtitle *Being*

Events Which Have Actually Transpired During the Present Rebellion,
second edition. She dropped her head to bring an end to the conversation. Whether it was the discussion with her tormentor at the desk or the war itself she'd already had enough of, the thought carried her out the door to a carriage in the street and the continuing search for the elusive Johnny Dunne.

Half an hour later, Emily found herself standing in the middle of the *New York Times'* newsroom. "Well, I'll be. If it isn't the stunning girl from St. Stephen's Square!" Johnny Dunne looked up from his desk, wearing only a vest over his shirt with the sleeves rolled up. His thick hair was roiled with repeated passes by his hands through its waves, and his ragged dark beard and mustache needed trimming. He looked more like a tormented mad scientist than the dashing rogue she remembered. "Sorry, Miss . . . I can't remember your name." His grin assured her his lapse of memory was more of an amusement to him than a discomfort. Not the greeting she'd imagined when she'd pictured being reunited with her savior from Vienna. But then, nothing about this day was what she'd expected, least of all the home of the famous *New York Times* newspaper.

This was clearly a very big, powerful business, evidenced by the fact that the impressive five-story structure at 41 Park Row was the first of its kind in the city built for the sole purpose of housing a paper, as all New Yorkers had been informed repeatedly in print. Blatantly self-promotional, this impressive architecture had dominated the paper's front pages for years before its completion—the articles decorated the hallway. Directly across from City Hall and dwarfing the offices of Horace Greeley's *New-York Tribune,* the *Times* building made a statement that the paper was a powerhouse of politics. No one standing on the steps of City Hall could miss the newspaper's message, including Emily. She had a fleeting doubt she tried to ignore that some of the world's citizens might not be important enough for this paper, including her.

Moving quickly across the street to keep from losing her nerve, she'd passed through arches carved from Maine granite and Indiana limestone. The paper's readers had all been assured in print they should be proud of this reliance on native raw materials. Polished marble and old-growth wood moldings inside the hallway led to a frightening contraption called an "elevator," used apparently for passengers as well as supplies, but Emily started up the staircase after referring to the index of offices on the lobby wall. She was already feeling out of her depth and had no intention of plunging to her death in an "elevator." The three flights to the newsroom would be a challenge she could easily handle after her conditioning in the Alps. It had been easier than meeting Johnny Dunne again.

"Emily Alden, Mr. Dunne. I took the liberty of looking you up from the calling card you gave me in Austria. I hope I'm not inter-rupting anything." She tried to steady her breathing after her climb and make her smile relax to show she had no expectations. She wanted him to know she'd gone to some trouble to find him, though, so she lightly dropped his card with the erroneous information on his desk. The gesture disguised a slight tremor in her hand.

"So you found me in my new home." He laughed, looking at the card and then back up at her. "What can I do for you, Emily Alden?" He still hadn't stood to greet her, and his smile seemed more mechanical than genial. She couldn't help thinking he'd prefer she weren't there. It seemed an odd welcome from someone who'd once gone out of his way to catch her, unsolicited.

"Is this an intrusion, Mr. Dunne? Perhaps we could talk another time when you're not so . . . busy." She kept her voice strong enough to be heard, noticing that the young men from the other desks scattered around the floor were looking over with interest. They made a sea of dark suits flecked with white shirts and broad silk ties. A few beards were in evidence, and everyone had a mustache of serious consequence. Gentlemen, apparently, one and all—but not quite.

Emily was surprised to see a young woman at one of the mahogany desks. Also dressed in dark clothes, with the addition of a bonnet, she looked as if she had just returned from somewhere. A sign on her desk identified her as MARY A. TAFT, REPORTER. Emily had never considered the fact that a woman might work at the paper. She glanced around the rows of desks but found no others. Each name plaque spelled out the function of its owner as far back as she could see. EDWARD CARY, ASSOCIATE EDITOR; TRACY BRONSON, STAR REPORTER; CHARLES LORD, SPORTS EDITOR; HENRY P. DU BOIS, ART EDITOR; JACOB HALE THOMPSON, EXCHANGE EDITOR; and JONATHAN R. DUNNE, ASST. MANAGING EDITOR. She suddenly realized they must all be wondering who she was and why she'd decided to come here today.

"No disturbance," Johnny Dunne, the assistant managing editor, assured her, pushing up from his chair at last. "Let's go over to the conference room and catch up on old times." He came around to her side of the desk, taming his hair with his right hand and placing his left on her waist. A slight pressure in the direction of the hall she'd just left was enough to start her moving, and she noticed how gracious his manner had become now that they'd taken center stage for his audience of young writers. She struggled not to let the transformation unnerve her. It was not, after all, any different from the way most relationships were displayed publicly between men and women, but she'd hoped for better, and it changed her mind.

"That won't be necessary." She stopped abruptly, offering firm resistance to the force of his hand. He stepped on her skirt and stumbled. The surprise on his face turned to annoyance. He shook his head, forcing his shaggy hair back over his eyes where he left it in defiance. "This is a busy office. It's impossible to talk privately out here." The disdain in his tone suggested she was used to the rarified air of discreet conversation, and the push that followed was definitive.

Emily suddenly wondered what she'd ever found appealing about Mr. Dunne. Different time and place, different circumstances, all made a different impression. His easy, free spirit had become casual and callous. Why? She didn't have time to figure it out. She wished she hadn't come, even more so because she'd made the choice herself. Apparently her judgment was impaired. She knew if her father or Robert had heard her plan they'd have advised against it. She'd have been angry with them but they'd have been right. Yet now, she was here at the *Times* headquarters. Oak paneling and desks closed in around her, and pendulum wall clocks reminded her of opportunity slipping away, so she decided to make the most of her visit, no matter how outrageous her request was beginning to seem, even to her. "I hoped you might be able to give me some information, Mr. Dunne."

He moved past her through the door to the conference room and shut it behind them. His restless energy made her feel as if she was locked in a cage with an impatient mountain lion. She struggled to push away the impression that he was trying to decide when to spring, but she forced herself to focus on her mission. She hadn't known what she'd say until her disenchantment over him somehow cleared her head.

"I need information on a prominent New York family that disappeared after the war began. I thought, with your connections, you might be able to find out something about them, if you didn't know their whereabouts already." She was sure the tone of her voice and steadiness of her eye would convince him this had been the intention of her visit all along, as it had been, in part. She prayed he'd not guess her initial attraction to him.

"I'll help if I can, Miss Alden. Who are you looking for?" He leaned on the edge of the conference table, one leg slung over the corner, the other keeping him propped against its gleaming mahogany surface. Emily stayed standing, preferring to be at his eye level since he'd decided not to sit in one of the matched chairs around the room.

"I'm looking for the de Koningh family," she said, aware of a sudden knot in her chest.

"De Koningh . . . as in the textile fortune with the mansion on upper Fifth Avenue?"

"Precisely," she said. "The shopkeepers tell me their home has been closed and boarded up for a month, and no one seems to know where they are. When I saw them last, it was probably no more than six months ago, and there was no mention of them leaving the city."

"Then how should I know?" Johnny leaned on his bent leg and cocked his head to one side. "Though I could probably find out. How important is it to you?"

"Very," she said. "I'm worried about Mr. de Koningh's Southern connections and the pressures they may have brought to bear on other members of the family. I'd consider it a great personal favor if you'd help me find them, or at least tell me something of their whereabouts. I'm afraid it's an imposition but I don't know who else to go to for help." She was taking the advice of the clerk to ask for what she wanted, but she wasn't going to beg.

Johnny was watching her with an appraising stare as sharp as a diamond cutter's. That could mean almost anything, little of it complimentary. The informality of his attitude, to say nothing of the smile that played at the corners of his mouth, all made her feel she was flawed in some way and the brunt of a joke. This was not a message from a comrade or a rescuer. "What do you offer me in exchange for this 'great personal favor'?" Johnny asked. "I've already saved you once, so the debits are mounting."

"How could I forget? That's why I'm here. But is a favor not an act of kindness granted out of goodwill? I thought it specifically precluded repayment." She reached inside her purse and took out another card without allowing him to answer. "Here's my calling card, Mr. Dunne. If you find out anything about the de Koninghs, I hope you'll contact me. I won't take up any more of your time." She handed him the card, and snapping her reticule shut, turned to go. Opening the conference room door, which would not have been closed in the first place by a gentleman, she walked out to the newsroom floor, suddenly stopping so abruptly she could feel Johnny stumble behind her. Emily gasped in surprise. "What now?" she heard the editor mutter.

A man of medium height and build was talking with Tracy Bronson, the star reporter. Dressed much like the other men in the room, in a dark suit and vest and white shirt, he had the popular styling of a full beard and mustache, but his hair was a distinctive and unusual rust color, and his air of thoughtful reserve seemed at odds with the nervous electricity of the newsroom. This was no reporter. This was Robert Haussmann. She wasn't sure which was greater: the shock of seeing him in this place or the pleasure of connecting with a valued old friend in an alien environment.

"There must be records; real estate, relatives, charities, business dealings, obituaries," he was saying quietly, though Emily knew him well enough to detect anxiety.

"Robert!" she called, as she moved across the room toward him. "What are you doing here?" He spun around to face her. "How amazing to see you," she said, holding back the urge to reach for his hand.

She was sorry they hadn't parted well. She'd brought that on herself. She could feel and hear Johnny breathing just behind her. Sandwiched between friend and foe, she wondered at the irony of finally reaching her majority only to find she didn't like herself. She'd have to change that. It wasn't too late. She'd gone in all the wrong directions, making an enemy of an old comrade with a rich shared history, while all but embracing a new acquaintance with no provenance of worth whatsoever. She'd alienated her only real family, her father, just because he'd tried to secure her future for her with his not insignificant power and prestige. She was doing much the same thing now, using her connections and position to get her own way. The uncomfortable reality of who she was becoming suddenly overwhelmed her, making her feel ill.

"I'm trying to find the de Koninghs," Robert said. "I thought the paper would be a good place to start. Why are you here? Are you alone, Emily?" His voice gained strength as he noticed the handsome Johnny Dunne lurking behind her. The professor of the pianoforte and assistant managing editor of the newspaper looked each other up and down, each understanding nothing and everything, all at once.

"Who's this? Have you brought your whole family with you?" Johnny quipped. Emily turned slightly to give him a cold stare.

"Professor Haussmann is not my family," she shot back at him, disdain for his derogatory comment coloring her voice.

"Does he work for you, then?" The tilt of his head gave him a condescending air. Emily found herself wondering what she'd ever found attractive about the editor.

"Certainly not," she spat out, turning away from Johnny again and back toward Robert. She couldn't seem to get herself off dead center between the two men who had her all but trapped without a clear way out. She froze in the clear amber light of the oak-paneled chamber, while the sounds of the busy newsroom went on like an orchestra vibrating with the nervous energy of anticipation. She heard her own violin in her head, as if she was poised to step up to play her solo part. She knew the others were waiting for her to speak. She lifted her head and took a deep breath. These moments were what she'd rehearsed for all her life.

"I, too, came here looking for the de Koninghs," she said to Robert. "But it was a mistake. Let's go talk somewhere. There's nothing else to be learned here." She saw Robert looking over her shoulder questioningly at Johnny Dunne. "I am alone, Robert," she said, without following his gaze.

BOOK THREE

The War

CHAPTER TWENTY

COREY HAD never felt so alone in his life. He'd never lived anywhere south of New York City before, and so Virginia seemed alien from every point of view. But he also realized he'd never been without family, friends, and a sense of his own history, either. Now he felt lost, with no one to notice that he'd disappeared and no reason to expect a rescue of any kind.

An early fall chill had crept in overnight, suggesting that the South was mourning its once-unspoiled landscape. Predawn fog clung to the edge of the woods like bales of cotton strategically placed to protect trees and bushes. Fretful eddies of wind whirled dry leaves anxiously around his ankles, each squall attacking as if to trip him up as he walked the brick path to the college.

He stopped to watch the leaves twist across the path and come to rest on still bright-green grass; a strange and jarring union of living and dead beyond the Old School building. Pushing a handful of his unruly hair back off his forehead, he grabbed the thick blond waves in his fist to tame them with force. In the middle of this strange cyclone of sad, deciduous spirits he was possessed by an irresistible urge to anchor himself. Agreeing to gather information for his father and the Northern cause had seemed simple when he was sitting in the de Koningh library in New York, but waking up on the campus of the University of Virginia had produced a sense of anxious unreality in him that couldn't be shaken.

Two rows of uniformly spaced hybrid oaks accented the north–south axis of the quadrangle courtyard. Only minutes after Corey's arrival at the college, a helpful gardener had explained, "The oaks were planted following the ten-step method: plant a tree, walk ten long steps, plant another, and so on . . ." Anyone could tell the truth of it looking at their sentinel stand. But oaks were the last to leaf out in summer and last to drop leaves in the fall, at least at home. So why were their leaves already swirling on the ground in September in the South, where life was presumed to be slower and therefore longer? Maybe the trauma of war was enough of a shock to force everything to stand barren. His eyes moved to the graceful college building, reminding him of Harvard's brick-and-limestone buildings guaranteeing permanence.

Horrified when Corey suggested that this edifice might have been copied from the venerable institution he'd only recently left, one of this university's professors had declared, "We came first!" It disrupted Corey's grasp of history. He was trying to adjust still to the demolition of so many of his cherished beliefs about the originality of life in the North. Much of the culture in the South was, in fact, just as old. But it was all so . . . British. He could find no hint of his Dutch ancestors here. He'd taken the influence of the Netherlands on New York for granted just because the Dutch had always been a part of his family's stories, the base of what he believed without question. Although, he realized he'd paid more attention to it when Emily Alden came to live with them because she'd forced him to.

He missed the city, missed his friends, and, most of all, missed his family and Emily. He hadn't heard from his father in weeks. He was unprepared for this kind of work. Why had he ever agreed to do it in the first place? Because he'd have agreed to anything his father suggested on that evening just a few short months ago, now seeming a lifetime away. He'd wanted to keep his father close. He'd wanted to drown out Emily's betrayal with Robert Haussmann. He'd wanted to run from himself. A college campus was meant to be a home of sorts, but no matter how beautiful it was, this place could never be home to a Yankee. It was Southern, graceful, warm, and languorous. Even with the battlefields so close that he could hear the fighting, there was a slow environmental elegance completely void of the energy and drive he'd been born to.

His longing reminded him of how small his circle of family was, how cloistered and monochromatic, and how inexperienced he was: a credulous child learning new things, yet worn to the bone, like an ancient ancestor who's seen too much. Grow up, Corey de Koningh. There was no longer any choice. The horror of war still seemed far away even though it wasn't, while the pain of losing Emily was immediate and very real, even though it wasn't. He'd become a man burning with her loss, and he still agonized over it even with so many other reasons to hurt. He'd welcomed the numbness that finally enveloped his exhausted nerves yet realized there was a different kind of pain in the deadness in his chest.

Corey turned up his collar and shoved his hands in his pockets. Bending his fair head into the wind, he changed direction down the path to the college chapel. He tried to look purposeful. His hope for recovery lay with the chamber organ he'd noticed on his first day on campus during a tour. A test of the acoustics in the little chapel, whose paneling of native pine and walnut over plaster should make any music within lively and bright, was his goal today. It would be perfect for the student a cappella chorus Corey hoped to start. He felt the pull from the sanctuary as if it needed him as much as he did it.

He'd been assured this collegiate chapel looked like many in Great Britain. The royal arms of Kings George I and II were on display in the chapel gallery, a reminder of the close connection between church and state at its founding. He was quite aware of the inappropriateness of that European linkage as stated by his own country's forefathers, but he'd not intended to say it out loud and received a cold stare from the headmaster when he did, reminding him to be more in awe of the university's "unique" history in the future. He bit his lip. There was his old childish habit again.

Pushing the wooden door open on huge iron hinges, Corey looked down the aisle at the empty rows of dark-stained pine pews. Notable southerners were buried in the crypt under the chapel, including several distinguished Virginia families, an Anglican bishop, and a beloved colonial governor whose statue greeted students in front of the college. Corey had never heard of any of them, but he hadn't come here for the proximity of greatness. He'd come to find comfort in the music. That alone might tell him who he was and give him some sense of belonging. He was used to evaluating churches as performance spaces rather than places of worship.

He'd supposedly been hired to teach music to incoming freshmen students—mostly women, he'd been told—because the men were all dying on the battlefields. There were no women in his glee club up north because there were none in the college. But women had been singing together publicly for years—encouraged to do so as parlor entertainment—so he was sure he could make a success of this endeavor meant to cover his real purpose at the university. He had to listen for information that might help his father and the Union cause, but focusing on his teaching would help steady him and keep him sane. He started to close the door, noting he'd been followed by a rush of fiery fall foliage he felt too aimless to brush out. He moved down the narrow aisle past the first rows of gleaming pews, clapping his palms together to test the acoustics and listening to the percussion dance around the chapel.

Finally he turned slowly in place, appreciating the beauty of the walnut paneling and the balcony's high molded ceilings. His eyes were drawn to the lovely little chamber organ above him, gleaming golden pipes clearly visible from where he stood. He was just about to move to the gallery stairs when he heard the iron door handle behind him start to turn. Still wrapped in the peace of isolation, he watched the handle rotate. A full head of curly white hair belonging to one of the college servants, a former slave from one of the nearby plantations, peered around the door. This kind, well-educated, elderly black man had befriended Corey on his second day at the school. Henry reminded Corey of an older version of Tom, the young black sharecropper who'd come back with Klaas from Virginia to escape the impending ravages in the South and gain an education; and now, Corey thought, they had exchanged places in an odd way. More pleased than surprised at Henry's interruption, Corey's smile lit up his face as he called, "Henry!" He was delighted to see one of the few people he knew on campus. "Have you come to sing with me? Come in and shut the door. The wind and leaves are wreaking havoc with what was a clean-swept floor."

Dressed in a formal dark suit and white gloves, Henry did as he was told, moving forward with a smile and small bow. "Master de Koningh . . . forgive me. Or should it be Professor de Koningh now?"

"I have no idea, Henry. I don't think it matters. Whatever you're comfortable with."

"Thank you." Henry's warm, dark eyes reflected Corey's smile. "I didn't mean to disturb your work, but I came to tell you . . ." Henry paused and widened his eyes, as if expecting his news to surprise Corey. ". . . you have a visitor. He's waiting in the headmaster's office."

"My father!" Corey leapt down the aisle in two strides and grabbed Henry's arms as if to shake more good news free. His eyes glowed in his pale face. "I've been thinking of him, Henry. I knew he must be close by."

"I doubt it, Master de Koningh. This young man's your age, and he's quite dark in coloring, unlike you." Henry's modulated southern drawl resonated with the upbringing in his master's house instead of a harsh life of thrashings in the fields. He smiled gently, intuiting that his news was an initial disappointment, but might eventually be welcome.

Corey let his hands slip from Henry's arms and hang lifelessly at his own sides. "Oh," he said. "I see." The expectant spark had gone out.

Henry waited, but when nothing was forthcoming, he spoke again. "I believe he said he was a dear friend of yours from your school days. He's in uniform, Master de Koningh, a Confederate uniform. He seems most eager to talk with you. He gave me his name right off, but I don't remember anything well these days. I'm sorry."

"It doesn't matter, Henry, if it's not my father." Corey sighed and took a long, last look at the chamber organ in the balcony before turning back. "Let's go. I'll come back here later."

He knew Henry was watching him keenly. Their talk the night after his arrival had revealed that Henry's own father was sold when Henry was three years old, so he had no clear picture of the man he'd forgotten. But as a child so favored by the master and mistress of the plantation, he'd been made to feel part of their family. Always separated from the slaves in the fields except at night, his own people had ostracized him and had little in common with him. Eventually, he'd had to leave them all behind anyway when he was freed at the age of twenty-three. He knew how many of them would have willingly traded places with him when his master and mistress died within weeks of each other, bequeathing him his freedom in their wills.

Set free in an alien white man's world, Henry had finally understood his connection to his black ancestors, which was no doubt why he now felt Corey's ache for his own father and family so deeply. Nothing could fill that hole in the heart. "It must have been hard to leave your home to come here," he'd told Corey the first evening. The look on Corey's face had confirmed how close Henry had come to the bone. "You must ask me for anything you need to make you more comfortable," Henry had said, and might have added, "to ease your pain." Watching Corey now was like reprising his own young misery, Corey could tell.

Pushing across the quadrangle courtyard together against the wind, Henry and Corey entered the college building through the arches to the front hall. A corridor at the left of the entrance led to the headmaster's office. Corey made the turn on his own. He'd had plenty of time to get his bearings since his arrival a few weeks ago—plenty of time and nothing to do with it. He paused in the doorway, looking into the headmaster's office and feeling like an intruder in another man's home, an uneasiness he'd experienced ever since leaving New York. A stocky boy standing behind the desk lifted his head when he saw Corey, the light from the window on his unshaven face showing he was not a boy at all. Staring at him in disbelief, Corey suddenly cried out, "Bill! Bill Henry, what are you doing here?" He closed the distance between them with two long strides and grabbed his friend's hand. "What in God's name are you doing here?" He spun around for a minute to catch Henry's reaction but found only the empty space he'd left when they'd separated on the way into the building. He hadn't noticed when Henry slipped off—but then, he wasn't noticing much these days.

Corey closed the door after hesitating a moment, as it wasn't his door to close. "Billy! Am I ever glad to see you. After that last letter you sent me I had no idea when we'd get together again." Grabbing Bill's hand he pulled his friend toward him and wrapped him in an awkward hug. No one could fail to note the physical difference. Bill disappeared beneath Corey's six-foot frame. "And what the hell are you doing in that uniform? Why are you fighting for the South?" Corey pushed Bill away from him again to look at him better, and let him go with a little pat on his shoulder. "As a matter of fact, why are you fighting at all?"

Bill spread his hands in a kind of supplication. "Before Gettysburg, almost everyone in Philadelphia was on the side of the South. I know that's hard for a New Yorker to believe, but Philadelphia has always lived on the cusp of North and South when it comes to its identity," Bill said, shrugging. "Families are split right down the middle by this war. I know people now who've been imprisoned in Philadelphia for their Southern sympathies. But after Gettysburg, opinion went the other way. I'd left for the fighting already and by the time I came back for my first leave, I wasn't welcome anymore." He looked down at the cap he'd started twisting in his hands, then shyly back up at Corey. "That's a bad thing, Corey. Almost nothing could make you feel worse than knowing people hate you for what you're doing when you think you're doing it for them."

"But why did you leave school, Bill? You never had any burning desire to go to war."

"I was following you."

"Me?" Stunned into silence, Corey's breath caught before he could go on.

Bill nodded. "You, Corey. You took off without even saying goodbye and I was afraid you'd get killed and I'd never have a chance to tell you . . . anything."

"But you had to know I would never fight for the South, even with my father's friendships and business connections down here."

Corey slid down onto one of the visitors' chairs in front of the headmaster's desk and stared at Bill. He knew he should form his questions carefully to get as much information about the Confederate forces as possible, but he couldn't do it. He looked like a scarecrow missing most of its stuffing. "The only letter you sent never mentioned anything like that, Bill. You talked of fighting, and oppressive heat, and noise and . . . dying. You even talked at the end about how the wounded were left behind and neither side buried the dead. You see? I was paying attention. You said it was an 'awful affair' but you never talked about looking for me."

"Strangers read private letters during wartime, Corey. I didn't say it, but I was looking. When Jock wrote me that you were teaching here I couldn't believe it. I was so close. I got permission to come see you for the afternoon. Since I never go home anymore, they could hardly deny me. But why are you here? I thought you were enlisting when you left school."

"They wouldn't take me. My height's a liability—makes me impossible to house and clothe, and to miss as a target. Father agreed I could stay out of school but wanted me to . . . work. Knowing how I hate the textile business, he got me this teaching job through his contacts in the South. I'm just trying to adjust to all the changes like everybody else. It's been so sudden . . . for all of us."

Bill stopped rolling his cap into a tight twist and stood still, watching Corey's eyes. "You didn't leave school because you wanted to fight, not any more than I did," he said in a hushed voice. "You left because of that girl you knew who went to London with your music professor. True, Corey?"

Corey lowered his eyes, and then lifted them without moving his head. He took a deep breath. "True, Bill. I was running away."

"Doesn't work, does it, Corey?"

"No. You carry the cage right along with you."

"You've changed, maestro," Bill said. You're not as . . . young anymore."

"I think you mean naïve, Bill. It's impossible to stay innocent with the war. My world had already collapsed around me, but now it seems everybody's going down, and it's almost worse watching from a distance and not being able to help. You've changed too, Bill."

"I came here to apologize and ask for your forgiveness," Bill said, quietly.

"Why? You've never done anything to apologize for."

"I have, and I can't die on one of those stinking battlefields without knowing you understand and forgive me." Bill still didn't move. He squeezed his hat tighter and turned away toward the window, walking slowly to the edge of the desk and then turning back to face Corey; the solid mahogany surface gleamed between them like a shield.

"I planted that article in the paper about your friends where you'd see it," he said.

"Why?" Corey asked, with a shrug. He hardly seemed interested in the answer.

"Because I hated the way you felt about that girl. I wanted you for myself. I can't say it was out of love for you, because you don't treat people you love that way." Bill looked down at the mangled felt hat in his hands. "I need to tell the truth and hope you'll understand."

"I do," Corey answered. "I did then, and I do now."

"And you don't detest me for it?"

"For what? Your feelings, or your actions?"

"Either or both."

"Nothing you did altered the outcome," Corey said, staring over Bill's shoulder to the window. "Emily and the professor would have been engaged and gone to Europe whether you told me or not. And the way you feel about what you did is your own torment."

Bill flinched and leaned against the desktop. "I should have known you'd understand," he said, almost under his breath. Corey refocused his gaze on him slowly and narrowed his eyes.

"We're all our own jailers, Bill. Don't add to your punishment with a lot of crimes no one would hold you responsible for. I've known you had feelings for me that were, well, not what they should have been, but assumed you'd get over them when you realized they'd come to nothing. If you didn't, it's not your fault. We can't love someone we don't care about, or stop loving someone we do. We don't learn those things in school, and we don't earn them with majority. Those feelings can't be legislated. I wish they could."

Both young men looked at each other, their gaze meeting over the gleaming desk. "What are we fighting for, Corey? Life, liberty, and the pursuit of happiness? We'll never get any of it, no matter who wins this war." Bill looked down at his tortured hat and sighed.

"I refuse to worry about all the things I can't do anything about." Corey laid his hand over the other one resting in his lap; a resolution or prayer or both. He sat up straighter, still holding Bill's eyes. "I've been terribly depressed here these last few weeks; missing the people I care about; worrying about friends like you; and in agony about my father's location."

"Is your father missing?"

"Yes. Maybe; I don't know, but I'm frightened for him, and there's only one way I can handle the fear." Bill cocked his head to one side and watched Corey, but said nothing. "You too, Billy. There's a way for you to deal with what you're facing right now."

Corey pushed himself out of the visitor's chair, unfolding to his full height and stretching his back. "It's my secret weapon, Bill. Always has been. You're more familiar with it than most. I was about to use it when Henry announced you were here. There's a pretty little chapel with fabulous acoustics across the courtyard. It made me think of our glee club the minute I saw it. Let's go sing together and test it out." He took a step toward the door. "Come on, Billy. It's the best medicine in the world. Maybe if you get a taste of it you'll use it when you go back to your infantry. If I were you, I'd sing every chance I got, for your own sake as well as your fellow soldiers'."

Bill started to unwind his crumpled infantry cap, a smile playing at the corners of his mouth. "What'll we sing, Corey?" The gray felt army hat looked like it had been crushed under the wheels of a carriage, though they all looked crumpled, even without an assault like Bill's. "How about that duet we worked on from Bizet's new opera, *The Pearl Fishers*?"

Corey nodded. "The friendship duet," he said, pulling the door open. "It's just made for your tenor and my baritone."

"Yes, but I wish we were made for each other," Bill said under his breath. "The duet says, 'Let us swear to remain friends!'" he called out, fitting his cap back on his head with a look of resignation, and following Corey through the door.

"It also says, 'I will cherish you like a brother.'" Corey grinned back at him. "And I will."

CHAPTER TWENTY-ONE

EMILY LOOKED around her bedroom as she packed a small trunk to take with her to college. She'd spent so little time in this room she felt more like a visitor packing to go home; although of course, she had no home to go to. Her most cherished belongings, her violin, and its case and bow, already waited for her on a window seat. But except for a few music scores and books, there was little to remind her of a past. Her wardrobe would be considered minimal by most aristocratic young ladies' standards, and it was always packed in its entirety when she traveled, leaving nothing behind, and the closet and bureau bare. She'd purposely left her mother's jewelry locked in the safe in England, even though it was technically hers now, and she always kept all pictures of importance in her violin case. There were none sitting out around the room. Scanning her space methodically was giving her a new appreciation for how few things she owned.

Her father had rented this house in New York a few years ago. It wasn't impressive, nor was her room up on the third floor under the eaves. Part of the original servants' quarters, it had since been renovated to give the house more guest rooms. She smiled, remembering the fight she'd had with her father when he found her settling in up here. She'd told him it was warmer in the winter (which wasn't true, so far from the fireplaces) and had a friendlier feel (which was true). Besides, she liked dormers. They reminded her always of her time as a child with Corey, climbing foolishly over the de Koningh roof dormers just because it was so much fun to do such a daring thing. They added personality to this strange room now, and gave her a chance to daydream or read scores on the window seats where the light was best.

Her violin practice was private and less disturbing for the household up here under the eaves. She'd always wondered if the servants or occasional guests from England were annoyed by her practicing. Having heard so many pejorative comments about it when she was a child, it never occurred to her now that it might actually give people pleasure to hear her violin sing, even just exploring the scales and modulations she toyed with every day. There were times when the extra stairs to the top floor annoyed her, but that was only when she was in a hurry before she'd changed the size and weight of her skirts. Usually she enjoyed the extra exercise. After her trip to Europe, the repetitive up-and-down reminded her of mountain climbing in Switzerland. It was a nice memory and exercise that could only do her good. And of course, the isolation and privacy at the top of the house was the biggest benefit of all.

The house was not what one might expect of a diplomat, but as he filled no official role for the Crown, there were no set requirements for entertaining. A large house would also have attracted attention he didn't seem to want in America. He'd lived in it virtually alone, except for the servants or Emily when she visited from finishing school. Even so, she thought of this small, clapboard-sided house as home now because there was no other, and looked down at its exterior from her dormer window with affection. It was only a few blocks from the de Koningh mansion on Fifth Avenue, but farther over toward the East River, and with the feel of a country residence because its side-street location offered less traffic. Only a lone horse or small cart or carriage rattled past, occasionally.

Outside Emily's window, a Bradford pear tree reached for the morning sun, a supplicant glorifying nature. The home's owner planted it just before she and her father moved in. It grew quickly, but she questioned what that meant for its longevity. Trees of slow growth were most enduring, like friendships. Trees and relationships had to withstand the shocks of hardship before they could develop into something sure and strong. She let her mind wander through the difficult associations in her life, wondering if they'd end up better for the challenges. Her father, Klaas de Koningh, Robert Haussmann, Johnny Dunne, even Corey de Koningh, would they all be with her in the future? She thought not. Still, it was a big world, and anything was possible.

Her father and Klaas de Koningh should have filled the same comfortable place together, father and surrogate, respectively. But Lord William Alden had dumped her on Klaas's doorstep when it became difficult to care for her after her mother's death, and although she knew there were probably mitigating factors surrounding that seemingly heartless act, none of them were her fault. Even now, she felt that she might be little more than a responsibility for him, and not a very urgent one at that. Klaas, on the other hand, had always offered her a steady and supportive welcome, making her feel from the start she could count on him.

She'd never forget their first "picnic" lunch together in his study a few months after her arrival. Corey was with his Latin tutor and Klaas had asked her to join him to find out how she was doing. He wanted to report back to her father, he said, and although all accounts from the household were good, he felt she'd give him the "most accurate" report. She'd been proud of that attention, but also nervous about their first meeting alone, until he agreed to camouflage her passion for the violin and public performance in his report to her father with tales of the many instruments she was studying with Professor Haussmann. Even more reassuring, he'd followed his promise in the most amazing way: with a wink!

She'd never experienced the power of secret alliance with an adult male before and felt her heart soar. She'd attempted to return the gesture, but felt so awkward about it, she asked Klaas, "Did I do that correctly?"

"Do what?" Klaas responded with a puzzled look.

Emily lowered her eyes. "Wink."

Klaas broke into a smile, quickly covering his mouth with two fingers. "More than correctly," he'd assured her. "Your wink was a butterfly's kiss!" He'd always treated her as an equal even though she was female and still a child. Was that his Dutch heritage? Europeans always talked of how unusually attached adults from the Netherlands were to their children. She thought it was more his nature and inherent wisdom and kindness. He'd made sure the de Koningh mansion was her home right from the start. Occasionally she'd wondered if her own father might have been aware of Klaas's unusually responsive connection to children and chosen him for her specifically, but she'd never allowed that thought to lessen the hurt she felt over being abandoned in an unfamiliar country and dumped on a strange family at the time she'd most needed her own. Turning out as well as it had was not to her father's credit, she believed.

Robert Haussmann was another matter. He could have taken on a mentoring, parental role when Emily first arrived, as he certainly had for Corey. But in truth, all she'd wanted was a good teacher, and that he'd surely been. However, Corey was younger than Emily and, like all boys, immature for his age. For Corey's sake, she'd hoped music would offer the tie to bind all three of them, but wondered initially if the professor was maybe a little jealous of her all-consuming relationship with Corey. Over the years, she'd slowly had to accept that she was tuned to Robert's personal interest in her long before he was, and it had embarrassed and angered her. She knew that was not his fault as much as her own newly developing womanhood, but the extra pressure of dealing with his feelings as well as her own was unfair when she had so much else to handle.

Still, his commitment to her career in music, his acceptance of her desire to perform, his assistance in furthering that goal with never a hint of criticism, made her rejection of him particularly unkind. Now that he'd finally expressed his personal feelings for her, she felt less angry and almost maternal in her concern for his unrequited love. They would always share an appreciation for the power of music and for the violin. She'd try to make up for her cruel treatment of him on their European tour someday. She wasn't sure what embarrassed her more about those memories, Robert's unwelcome feelings or her own treatment of them.

Johnny Dunne was truly a work in progress, and one she didn't fully understand yet. He was unlike anyone she'd ever met before and offered a completely fresh challenge. She could neither assume anything about him nor expect anything from him. He was his own person, seemingly without a history or background anchoring him and closing off possibilities. He was beyond conformity, and she was inexorably drawn to him for that reason above any other. Thinking of his rakishly handsome, slightly dangerous façade, she realized how few relationships of that kind she'd been allowed in her life, and that was another reason she wanted to be educated in a new environment, without the aid or influence of anyone in her current social circle.

Corey, too, had seemed to be made from a completely new design she'd never seen before, his soul and body infused with confidence born of something elemental without need of anyone or anything to give it strength. Her spirited, intelligent, energetic, and sensitive friend had been her partner since the day they'd met in the hall of the de Koningh mansion. But that had been when they were children. He'd seemed different at each of their infrequent meetings since then, and although transformation was understandable as he moved into manhood, it was also unnerving. She couldn't tell if he'd guide her into the future the way he'd led her across the de Koninghs' roof in the past, almost a lifetime ago.

In a way, the changes in Corey wrought by adulthood made him even more interesting, while he still offered the solid safety of friendship. They were much alike, she and Corey, and their differences only served to give them answers to life rather than questions. They were a good team. It had been years since they'd shared the kind of intimacy that created their friendship in the first place, and she missed most of all the sharing of everything, important or trivial. The war had separated and decimated so many families that she was frightened for Corey's life and said another small prayer that he was safe. More than that she dared not ask for. No one ever expected to be on the losing side in life, but someone always had to be.

She sighed, putting the score for Robert Schumann's newly discovered violin concerto into her briefcase to finish packing, but stopped to peer out the window again, distracted by a huge carriage working its way down the street. It would have been unusual in any setting. It reminded her of the papal coach she'd seen in Vienna on her visit to St. Stephen's Cathedral. The enclosed front half of the cab doubled the usual seating capacity, and only the half behind the door was open enough to see inside. All four wheels were covered with rubber, making their impact on the road negligible, and the front wheels were even bigger than the back ones, which was also unusual. She could see an elaborate suspension system, providing both a great deal of support to the passengers and the ability to transport many of them. Both the front and back top were finished with seating for drivers and footmen, or extra passengers who preferred to ride in the fresh air. It looked more like a public stagecoach than a private carriage.

She was trying to make out the gold crest on the black side panels when she realized it was slowing down in front of her house. Someone inside gestured to the driver, and then it turned slowly into the Aldens' U-shaped cobblestone courtyard, designed for single riders and very small carriages only. She was afraid it would get stuck between the lampposts.

Jumping up from her window seat, she ran downstairs. Whoever was inside the coach was going to be disappointed to find they'd come to the wrong house. The third floor seemed suddenly too far from the courtyard, so she took the stairs two at a time, skipping the last and jumping onto the parlor-floor landing. Spinning around the newel post like laundry in a stiff wind, she skidded through the back parlor and out onto the side porch to the courtyard, slightly out of breath, but still too slow. Her father's manservant was already opening the carriage door. Much to her surprise, the black leather boot and dark flannel trouser leg stretching out to the carriage step was followed by the body of Mr. Gerrit Smith. She hadn't seen Mr. Smith since that night on stage at Miss Carter's over a year ago, but even though he was buried beneath the full beard and long hair of a New England minister, there was no way to mistake him. An hour of watching him talk of new freedoms for women had been more than enough to fix him in her memory for good.

"Mr. Smith!" she cried out so suddenly that even the horses looked up at her with a start. Both he and his recruiter, Mr. Barnes, who had just begun his descent from the carriage as well, froze in place and stared at her. Surprised by the shrillness of her own voice, she shrank back for a moment to one of the porch columns to collect herself. She had a feeling of uneasiness, very much like what she'd felt at the newspaper office with Johnny Dunne. Sometimes she felt like a disapproving parent watching herself be a naughty child. Growing up was a good deal more complicated now that she'd passed her legal majority. Shaking off her self-doubts, she moved from the porch to the carriage and reached out her hand.

"Welcome, Mr. Smith. What a surprise to see you here. And you, Mr. Barnes. What brings you gentlemen to the woods of upper Manhattan?" She stepped sideways after Mr. Smith's handshake to put her other hand on the rump of one of the horses, with a reassuring pat. She owed the horses an apology, too. It was easy to ask their forgiveness with a touch of her palm, and perhaps her guests would note the offering and accept it as well.

"We're here to see your father, Miss Alden. And you, of course.

We're just returning from a trip to deliver a group of students and thought it best to find out if you needed anything before we take you and the last young women down south." Mr. Smith held his hat in his hand and spoke in an unusually soft voice, making Emily feel her boisterous arrival in the courtyard was even more outrageous. He moved with the controlled precision of his New England ecclesiastical roots, a Ralph Waldo Emerson out of his familiar transcendentalist Concord.

"We also thought you and your father might have last-minute questions for us," Mr. Barnes said, moving toward Emily with the same open, relaxed movement she remembered from her first meeting with him in Switzerland. The difference in body language of the two men was marked, and she wondered if one could feel the restriction and the other the freedom the way it showed. Did a body ever lie? Possibly, if its owner was practiced enough.

"How thoughtful of you . . ." She smiled her warmest greeting, the one she could feel showed in her eyes as well, fully aware that her next announcement would disappoint. ". . . but I'm afraid you've missed my father again. He's in Washington this week working with the president." She could see both men shift uncomfortably. So she'd been right about the purpose of their visit. "However, I do have some questions, and would appreciate any last-minute answers you could give me." Both men recovered quickly and nodded, as if nothing would please them more. "Can we stable your horses?" Emily asked.

"No need for that, thank you, Miss Alden. Perhaps a bit of water, but they were well fed this morning before we left, and it looks like they're still being spoiled now." Mr. Barnes smiled and winked at her, and she realized she was still rubbing the horse's rump. She smiled back and pulled her hand away quickly, knowing it must smell strongly of horseflesh already. She controlled the urge to wipe it on her skirt and turned to her father's manservant.

"Tate, please see to their water if the groom is out already." Tate bowed slightly, but the tiny curve at each end of his mouth said he was not used to accepting Emily's authority when her father was away any more than when he was at home. The interplay had gone on since she was fifteen. She led her two visitors up the side porch steps to the back parlor, suddenly sorry the approach to it wasn't a bit more impressive. That feeling, too, was a new sensation, increasing her discomfort with her inner life. "I hope this will do," she said, motioning to the settee and chairs grouped near the windows facing the courtyard. "We don't entertain often, and the house is surprisingly informal."

"How so?" Mr. Barnes asked. "Why 'surprisingly,' I mean."

"If you knew my father you'd expect to find less comfort and more elegance." She laughed a little, immediately embarrassed by her description of Lord Alden. He wasn't there to defend himself and it wasn't a totally accurate picture, either. What was she becoming? "Actually, that's not entirely true." She moved to one of the chairs to sit down so the men could take their own seats after her. "My father is really very fond of physical comfort in a home, as he's an active athlete, but . . . he's a bachelor. His choice to rent this house was made purely based on convenience I think, rather than appropriateness."

"Often the soundest reason for choosing anything," Mr. Smith agreed. "Have you finished what you needed to do before leaving, Miss Alden? Is there anything we can help with?"

"I fear the campus of the University of Virginia won't offer the kind of charm it would if the country were not at war," Mr. Barnes continued, looking more worried than Emily remembered seeing him before. "You'll need to take the things you feel most essential to your well-being, as there won't be opportunities to return home anytime soon, and supplies cannot be sent from New York once you're living down there." Emily noted the change in the rosy view of the school presented in Europe at their first discussion. Obviously, the advancing hostilities since then had greatly affected the South. What Mr. Barnes was really describing was a complete isolation caused by the inability to cross enemy lines. Her growing nostalgia for the safe home and family, often elusive no matter what her age or circumstance, sharpened.

"There are still a few loose ends," she answered, hearing the wistfulness in her voice and looking quickly out the window behind the men. Watching Tate watering the horses would keep her eyes clear of the tears always ready to spring up these days when she thought of the changes in her life. "Most chores are done," she continued, "but I've tried to see some old family friends since I got back from Europe to say goodbye, and they've disappeared so completely it's been impossible." The crack in her voice couldn't be covered with a glance out the window, so she cleared her throat and sat up straighter on the edge of her seat.

"How sad, Miss Alden. You have no idea where your friends have gone? No one who might know?" Mr. Barnes looked as worried as Emily felt.

"I've tried, Mr. Barnes. I even have a contact at the *New York Times*, but he was unable to find any information about them. Or so he said," she added with a shrug. "I assume his silence since that day at the *Times* was an admission that he's found nothing," she added.

"What's the family's name, Miss Alden?" Mr. Smith looked at her with the intensity she was coming to expect.

"De Koningh, Mr. Smith." She caught a glance slip from one man to the other in the silence that followed, a strange interlude filled with something she couldn't recognize. She continued, "Their house is about a mile from here. I walk to it and back every day in the vain hope of finding some clue to their whereabouts." She was gripping her hands in her lap to keep them still, but assumed the men would think her ladylike rather than desperate. Yet she was uncomfortable giving Mr. Smith, her champion of women's rights, an impression she might be one of those acquiescent females hiding her individuality behind false mannerisms. Finally, Mr. Smith took a breath.

"I know Klaas de Koningh well, Miss Alden. How are you connected to the family?"

"I lived with them many years before my father moved here. Mr. de Koningh was more a father to me than my own; the whole family was closer to me than any relatives in England."

Both men were silent again, and she caught another glance go between them, just a glimmer of eye contact, and then Mr. Smith spoke. "I believe Klaas has moved down south for the duration of the war. He's protecting his textile manufacturing sites in person."

"And his family?"

"Moved upstate to be with Dutch relatives in . . . Albany or Schenectady, I believe. He was uncomfortable leaving them alone after the race riots broke out in New York."

"The whole family went?" Emily whispered.

"His wife and the household staff, most certainly," Mr. Smith answered.

Emily wasn't sure why it was so important to hide the crushing weight of her visitor's news. She shifted on her seat and looked down at her hands again, still gripped tightly in her lap. Her fingers were turning white, so she let go and deliberately smoothed out her skirt. "And . . . his son?" she asked, trying very hard to steady her hands as they slipped over the folds of fabric running from her waist to her knee. "I suppose his son went with Mrs. de Koningh." She looked up calmly, but couldn't control the tremor in her voice.

"That's another story," Mr. Barnes said, pushing forward in his chair in preparation to stand. "And I shall tell it to you once we're on our way."

CHAPTER TWENTY-TWO

There was something worse than fear; it was hopelessness. Corey tried to control both with work, but when he tried to sleep, floating anxiety filled all his dreams. This night, he didn't know exactly how he realized something was terribly wrong, but he'd wondered both awake and asleep about his coming to the University of Virginia. The latter state always signaled a nightmare, as it was now. Nothing felt right to him the more he thought about how his father had suddenly come up with a mysterious connection to the music department. He felt suspicion seeping through his body like an infection. It spilled into his bloodstream with increasing intensity as he passed one unfamiliar, empty room after another. But his dream wouldn't calm down long enough for him to figure out where he was. He was lost.

At first Corey thought he'd been looking for someone familiar, but now he'd be happy to find anyone at all. He never called out, but pressure spread up to his chest, radiating surges of panic. He finally threw open the last door. His terror exploded in greedy, bright white-orange flames leaping from wooden pews and licking hungrily at the base of the chapel balcony. He knew in an instant they'd consume the support structure and the beautiful little chamber organ with it. He gasped to call for help. He tried to scream above the roaring firestorm, pushing his voice. Again and again, his cry barely moved through the air thickened with smoke, and no one came. With one last effort, he shrieked with all his strength. No sound came out, but the force pushed him upright in bed, drowning in enough sweat to put out any fire. Still panting in the hell of his nightmare, he stared out his dormer window at the university, searching for a telltale glow in the sky across the courtyard signaling destruction of the college chapel. But the sky was a deep, cool, predawn blue. There were no flames scorching the horizon. He lay back exhausted on his drenched sheets, wondering about the illusion, if it had truly been one.

Staring at the ceiling, he relived the horror of finding he was alone—entirely alone. Then he remembered the shock of watching the organ threatened, and with it his connection to . . . everything. Why had he wasted so much time before calling for help? The organ sat there, even now, patiently waiting for him to come. What a fool he'd been.

He swung his legs off the bed and stood up in his drenched nightshirt. Stripping the bed linens off in one sweep like a matador passing a bull, he draped them over the reading chair by the open window, hoping they'd dry there faster. It made him feel better to move. He undid his nightshirt and let it drop to the floor in a cloud of damp linen around his feet. Stepping out of it, he gathered it up like a tangled sail and shook it out. The cool night air had dropped a few degrees as it neared dawn and he shivered, lifting his light wool robe off the hook at the back of his door and tying the robe's sash around his hips. He couldn't help noticing how thin he'd gotten, more a brittle scarecrow than a man, he thought.

A freak of nature, his friends had teased when his height pushed past the six-foot mark. So what? Everyone was an anomaly of some kind. It was just that some were more different than others; Henry and his people, and Bill and his. And he, Corey de Koningh, had always been different, too, so he'd never been affected by the strangeness of others. A black man was a man. Love was love, no matter who was involved. He looked down at his body. There wasn't a thing he could do about the long, stretched-out form he'd been given to go through life with. He'd just try to make sense of whatever he was. That's all anyone could do.

Corey moved over to his cramped desk, sitting down sideways on the straight wooden chair so he wouldn't have to stuff his legs underneath. He pulled a piece of clean paper out of his leather briefcase and started to draw with a ruler straight lines that would end up holding the notes of a new musical piece. He knew once he got started that last night's dream would disappear miraculously into early dawn, bypassing another nightmare. Emotional extremes often opened his imagination. They added so much to his compositions but got in the way of his performances. After breakfast, he'd head straight to the chapel for the first time since he'd arrived on campus and put in a few hours of work on his new arrangement. He continued drawing the lines carefully across the page with his pen, already feeling a steadier hand. A fresh predawn breeze whispered through the window, lifting the edge of the curtains and his spirits with them. The change in his outlook reminded him he was getting hungry. It was a reassurance of his return to everyday life, and Corey found himself looking forward to breakfast with a cheerful anticipation he hadn't felt for months. He dressed quickly and clattered down the stairs and out to the main building.

After a satisfying breakfast of freshly gathered produce from the campus farm, he was on his way out of the college dining room when he heard, "Hold up there, de Koningh! I want a word with you, young sir!" Corey stopped and turned, already knowing from the German accent to expect the elderly professor he'd nicknamed "the little mushroom." They'd collided near the beginning of his arrival at college when he'd been walking with the only three students on campus, all female. Chuckling "Schwämmerl," as he'd watched Professor Meyer retreat after introductions, Corey had explained to the young ladies that "schwämmerl" meant "mushroom" in Austrian dialect, and an umlaut over the "a" made it diminutive (just like the little professor), or so he'd been told by his own Austrian music teacher years ago.

Seeing derisive grins hiding behind the ladies' gloved hands, he'd quickly added it was the name Franz Schubert's friends had given him, since he'd been barely five feet tall. "Professor Meyer's in good company," Corey added to relieve his guilt for what might have appeared a personal slight. It felt odd to be on the side of the adult authority on campus, and so more comfortable to jump in with the students at first, his own childhood so proximate he was often more at ease with it than with his new adult persona. He resolved to be that person, however, as he turned toward the professor.

"Professor Meyer, what can I do for you?" he asked, watching the little man in a formal black waistcoat bump his way through the seats in the dining room. Noticing the music teacher was barely past Corey's own waist, he sat down on the stairs along the entrance to be at the teacher's eye level.

"My goodness, you move fast, de Koningh," Professor Meyer huffed. "It only takes you two steps to cover the entire dining room from one side to the other."

Corey laughed. "Only without a seated audience, Professor. That's when the exit route can be more direct—as the crow flies, so to speak."

"Haven't been enough audiences of late," the professor grumbled. "Looks like you and I are almost the only people on campus."

"Everyone else is fighting a war," Corey said, stretching his legs out past the bottom step to release the cramping from his jackknife position. Leaning back on his elbows, he propped his upper body on the top step. "And I'm only here because they wouldn't have me in the army." He explained the limitations of his height, noting to himself the irony of doing it with someone who suffered from the opposite extreme. "I'm just a freak of nature," he added.

"Wouldn't have me, either, even though I'm an American citizen. Too old. But I guess you and I are both rarities, now. And any man on campus is uncommon these days."

"Do you mind that, Professor?"

"Not at all. I've seen too much to mind anything. Do you mind the women on campus, young sir?"

"No. I like women," Corey said with a smile.

"That's good! A healthy sign at your age, or any age, for that matter." Professor Meyer straightened up, sucking in his breath and holding it to flatten the weight of his stomach.

"But I'd like a few more students," Corey added.

"They're coming, de Koningh, or so I've heard from our recruiter, Mr. Barnes. Just a few more days and there'll be a dozen or so new young ladies for you to teach, which is what I want to talk with you about. Was that you I heard singing in the chapel the other day?"

"Most likely. I had a friend visiting. We used to be in a glee club together in New England, so we sang a bit before he left campus to help me test the acoustics in the chapel."

"Most impressive, de Koningh, a lovely pairing. And the organ music afterwards—that was you, I suppose?" Corey nodded. "What were you playing? It was a stunning piece, the harmonies soaring— so romantic."

"Oh, that was something I composed a long time ago. I play it occasionally. It's like returning to a member of the family." Corey looked past the professor to some unseen memory.

"You! You composed it? What a gift you have." The music teacher stared at Corey as if he'd just discovered buried treasure. "But you haven't played much since you've been here. Why is that?"

"I've been too upset, I guess—anxious all the time. This is a painful period." He noticed the music teacher had taken a step closer and suddenly felt a hand on his shoulder.

"Chin up, young sir. There couldn't be a better time for your compositions." Corey looked into the older man's face and saw what he meant in his eyes. "Every composer of our century was a great pianist first. Most of them have had terrible lives and known great tragedy—starvation, illness, and often early death. Mendelssohn, Mozart, Schubert, Schumann—they all composed to stay sane and relieve the stress of their challenges."

"All except Franz Liszt, eh, Professor? He's still alive and making enormous sums of money with his recitals."

"And giving most of his earnings to charity! He works to live what he loves, not to make money. If the outside forces in this world sicken you, turn to your inner resources." Professor Meyer squeezed Corey's shoulder. "Trust me when I tell you everything in this world will resolve itself eventually. Like a diminished chord with a major one, yes, young man?"

"Your philosophy gives away your European background, Professor Meyer. Wait long enough, and yes, everything will be resolved because we'll all be dead." He instantly felt guilty for returning the teacher's optimism with cynical contempt. "But you're too kind. I doubt my gift, as you call it, can be compared to the composers you mentioned." Corey looked into the teacher's eyes, feeling his own need for support like a weight on his back.

"I'm not flattering you," Professor Meyer said, shaking his head. "I was so impressed with what I heard that I went straight to the headmaster to find out who was playing. He was unsure, and you were gone by the time I returned to see for myself. Now that I know . . ." He dropped his hand from Corey's shoulder. "Come! Walk with me on the way to the chapel now. I have an idea for you." He held his hand out as if to pull Corey up, but quickly thought better of it and laughed. "You can stand better without my help!"

Corey pushed himself up with a grin. "Lead the way, Professor. I'm all ears."

"Indeed, you are not, young man. You're all legs!" Corey lifted his chin and laughed, which admittedly felt very good. He gestured for the professor to go first, thereby setting the pace that would be most comfortable for his short legs, while Corey moved slowly behind him.

"Where were you trained?" Professor Meyer asked, turning his head to talk over his shoulder. "What conservatory did you attend? I ask only because your style is so distinctively that of the modern Romantics."

"Really? I hadn't thought about that. In what way?"

"It's very . . . liquid . . . expressive . . . what I hear in all the European composers of today. I assume you trained in Vienna or Salzburg. Am I right?" Corey moved up beside his new friend to continue the conversation. He realized the professor was already slightly out of breath and didn't want to cut their talk short because of it.

"No. But I was lucky enough to have a wonderful teacher in New York by the name of Robert Haussmann. Perhaps you've heard of him?" Professor Meyer shook his head and Corey continued. "He's Austrian, but also the foremost proponent of the pianoforte in the city. I think that's why you hear a tone in my work that's less . . . dry." It felt good to be talking about intonation with someone who understood, helping Corey feel he belonged.

"Really? Now I'm the one who hadn't thought of that. You believe the pianoforte is responsible for the evolution of piano composition?"

"Absolutely! Professor Haussmann used to say that so much more is possible, and imaginable, with its capacity to modulate volume. I was fortunate he was prepared to teach me using the piano my father purchased when I was born." Corey felt a lightness as he moved down the path. He couldn't tell if it was the pleasure of having someone to talk music with, or the relief of discussing Robert Haussmann with a stranger who knew nothing of their connection. Either way, he felt freer than he had in weeks.

The professor pointed to a bench near the walkway. "Stop with me here for a minute. I want to enjoy this early fall sunlight before going inside to work without it all day." Corey noticed the shortness of breath again in the little round man. Perhaps he'd not adjusted his pace quite as well as he'd planned.

"Of course, sir. A little sun would be nice." He glanced past a bronze statue of two college founders near the chapel entrance, trying not to show his frustration at prolonging the wait before going inside. He noticed the professor was already sitting on one end of the bench, so he slid down lightly on the other, feeling like a praying mantis alighting momentarily on a pile of sticks, legs folded neatly beneath him but ready to spring off at any moment.

"This is my thought, de Koningh." The professor leaned in closer, as if to keep their talk private from the bright fall leaves exploding on all the trees behind them. "I don't know if you've been told about our opening the campus to Confederate soldiers now and then." He watched for a sign of recognition from Corey but got a shake of his head instead.

"I thought not. Well, the headmaster has long felt we owe the fighting men some respite from the hardships of war if the campus is still open. He has friends who command many of the brigades fighting throughout the state, and he's offered to open the college grounds to them for an occasional day off from their war duties. We give them a decent meal and have different faculty members tour them around to teach them of the history of the old place. I've always thought it a wonderful idea, the beauty and peace of the campus being just what these poor boys lack most."

Corey sat up very straight. He knew important information when he heard it. "You're comfortable aiding the Southern soldiers then, Professor?" He realized he might appear to be paying unusual attention to the professor's words, well beyond their importance. He tried to relax and seem more casual, while aware this was the first information he'd heard that might be of value to his father, though he didn't know why. And to be honest, he had no idea how he'd reach his father if it did turn out to be crucial in some way.

Professor Meyer shook his head. "I'm a truly neutral observer," the little man announced, almost cheerfully. "We're used to wars in Europe. I never got involved there, either. But I certainly sympathize with the suffering. So my thought is that this time when the soldiers come through, we give them a piano or organ recital . . . perhaps showcasing that lovely piece of yours!" He beamed like a devoted family doctor who'd just come up with a cure for his patients' sufferings.

"Interesting idea, Professor, but when is this infantry battalion coming through? Do you know which one it is?"

"Does that matter? Oh yes, I remember, you have a friend in one nearby. I can find out of course, but would you be willing to work on something to perform for them? I think what I heard you playing in the chapel the other day would lift their spirits mightily."

"Of course, Professor. I'm honored you asked me. If you could find out exactly when they're coming, I'll know how long I can prepare. And how many of them—how many we'll be entertaining, I mean. All that would be helpful. And yes, I'd like to know if my friend would be among them, so which battalion, too." He realized he'd deposited a string of specifics in the professor's lap like a shopping list. Wanting to blunt the directness, he stretched his long, stiff legs out in front of him and smiled, intending to change the subject. "What's your instrument, Professor? Do you practice often? Would you be joining me in this proposed recital?" More questions, but surely a deflection from his earlier inquisition about the movement of Confederate troops.

"The human voice, my young friend," Professor Meyer said, with a sparkle in his eye. "I'm a musicologist who trained opera singers in Europe, but here I teach—taught—history of music and organized the chorus for choir. None of that happens anymore, though. I'm just hopeful our new feminine students will have some interest in musical origins, and have some lovely soprano voices to fill the chapel." He straightened up again at the suggestion of the female students.

"As do I, Professor! I'd love to work and sing with you and the 'lovely sopranos.' I need to go do some practicing now while I can, though. Would you excuse me, and we can continue our talk later?" Corey unwound himself from the low bench, stretched, and watched as the professor pushed himself up with more forearm pressure than would have been necessary if his legs had been better able to support his girth. The little man beamed at Corey.

"Thank you. It's been a real pleasure sharing breakfast and our walk this morning, de Koningh. I'll talk with the headmaster and get back to you today. He may have more specifics about the students' arrival from Mr. Barnes, and perhaps you could do a little welcome recital for them as a rehearsal for the performance for the troops. There would most likely be at least a week in between for rehearsal. Enjoy your practice!"

Corey watched his new friend bob down the path toward the main college building. He felt awkward about his secret agenda and the fact that he was using his elderly colleague to get information. He had no wish to jeopardize what might be a new bond, and no idea if the information was of any value at all. Moving slowly toward the chapel with his hands shoved deep in his pockets, he wondered if his father ever had moments of doubt about his commitments. War was certainly doing strange things to them all. He sighed under the weight of his doubts, trying not to focus again on the ones revolving around Emily.

Stopping just outside the chapel, he looked up at the discreet old building. The organ was a beauty, and practicing on it was going to change many of the bad feelings he'd had over the last few weeks. He reached for the iron door handle and turned it, but it wouldn't budge. He tested the point of resistance several times to see if he'd jammed it. He pushed, but nothing happened. He stared at it, unable to absorb the truth that the door must be locked.

He wondered if Henry had the keys. What if there was an emergency—a fire? Corey realized his nightmare seemed to be coming alive in broad daylight. He needed his father to talk with and feared he might be dead. He missed his friends and knew they might never be together again. He wanted Emily back, but couldn't have her. He was afraid he'd never get the picture of her and Robert Haussmann out of his head, and that would be the worst nightmare of all.

CHAPTER TWENTY-THREE

THE HUGE, shiny coach bucked clumsily along the dirt road at high speed, but the ride was surprisingly comfortable thanks to the carriage's rubber wheels. Emily leaned against the smooth, padded leather upholstery next to the door, with the rhythm of the big wheels rocking her someplace between waking and sleeping. Her thoughts got muddled and clearer, as if the important ones were collected and centered by the motion of the carriage while the peripheral ones flew off in unseen directions.

No matter where she'd been, in Europe, at home, or in school, she'd found ways to read about the war and keep up with its developing chaos, though she was finding it hard to remember which general oversaw what and who'd been replaced by whom and where. Even with her confusion, she was acutely aware that her carriage was now careening toward the fiercest fighting yet seen in the East, and she thanked providence that she and her chaperone were clearly non-combatants, and therefore unlikely to see any horrors unfolding on the battlefields of North Virginia. Still, it could not be denied they were headed right for the heart of it all at this very moment, a truth she'd not considered when yearning for the adventures so far from home. She was beginning to realize she might also find herself adrift in the male world of war, and that was not something she wanted any part of.

And what of Corey? She thought perhaps he was with his father traveling around the South to protect his cotton exports. But Corey was just as ill-prepared for combat as she was, and in fact, she didn't even know if the de Koningh men were still alive. As the carriage rocked front to back with the occasional dip to one side or the other, she felt her bravery born of naivete shaken into a fearful, disordered mess, to such an extent that her breathing was having trouble staying even. She seemed to have been running alongside the carriage instead of sitting within it. Will you be staying with us at the university? She wanted to ask Mr. Barnes questions she'd not considered before and realized how frightened she sounded as she listened to her voice in her head. Will you be keeping me safe? was what she really wanted to say, and obviously that was not something anyone could guarantee her anymore.

She was willing to accept the fact that there were forces beyond her control, because something had brought her to the de Koninghs a long time ago, and something was bringing her back to them now. Was there some connection with her father again, perhaps having to do with the de Koningh link to cotton exports? She thought not, as her father had mentioned nothing of consequence about his friend Klaas for a long time. Corey's father had gone south as always, to check on his cotton business, and she assumed Corey followed to be near his father. He'd never traveled with him during peacetime, but this war was changing a lot of things. Learning Corey had taken a job to teach music at the very college she was headed for, an opportunity provided by the same man who'd offered her a scholarship, had left her with more questions than answers. But as she'd so often felt she and Corey were tied together, Emily also accepted this coincidence as if it had been planned by a greater power.

She smiled, and noticing Mr. Barnes smile back, yawned and closed her eyes to suggest drowsiness, but in fact to help her see inside her head better without distraction. She felt safe enough with

Mr. Barnes to know he'd take no offense where none was intended. She could feel her smile deepen into the dimples she'd almost forgotten she had, as the face of Klaas de Koningh floated up behind her lids. It had been many years since she'd sat with him for any length of time. Klaas had looked then every inch the refined gentleman he was: a gentle man. She could still see the fine lines of his face under his delicate skin pulled taut over high cheekbones and forehead. The soft waves of white hair brushed back from his temples and pale blue eyes looked out at the world with curiosity. His neatly trimmed white beard and mustache framed his expressive mouth, a precursor, she was sure, of Corey's still beautiful lips.

But she realized Klaas's features had faded to a weaker outline as he'd aged over the past few years. She had little doubt that Corey would look much like his father someday. And she felt the father had looked much like his son once. Why do your bones stand out above your eyebrows? Corey used to ask his father, while he hung over his chair as he read. Because my head is so full, Klaas would answer, laughing, and hugging Corey around his neck. Emily was often a little jealous of their affection for each other, this beautiful boy and his handsome father, but she'd learned a lot from them about sharing and showing. Nothing was lost, and everything gained from their displays of affection.

For all Klaas de Koningh's look of purpose, he was an open man, available to new thoughts and ideas, and fair in his judgments. His help had made it easier for her to enjoy her music and her growing up, just knowing he was there if she needed him. Her father had been more of a challenge for her: how to approach him, how much to tell him, what to ask for. But Corey's father was more straightforward. How kind it had been of Corey to share him with her. Maybe that hadn't been easy. She'd never thought about it before. And now, she didn't really know where in the world they were. Mr. Smith's news of the de Koningh move down south had distressed her more than she liked to admit. Surely Northerners were no longer welcome under any circumstances in the South, and it didn't escape her that even she, a British subject, might well be mistaken for a hated Yankee once she arrived to live alone at the college.

"Hold up there!" a deep Southern drawl bellowed as the coach jolted to a severe stop, lurching forward on its fancy suspension and throwing Emily off the leather seat to her knees at the feet of Mr. Barnes. He frowned and clutched the window curtain to pull forward, as she struggled up and back onto her seat again.

"We need to see what you're carrying in there, sir," the deep voice drawled again, derisively emphasizing the normally polite form of address.

"We carry only passengers and their luggage," one of their drivers answered.

"Confederate soldiers," Mr. Barnes muttered under his breath. "Bad timing! I wonder why they're stopping us." He looked much more disturbed than Emily thought the situation warranted.

"Would they not be required to check all traffic on this road, Mr. Barnes? I can't see that it's any cause for alarm." She noted her own control of her breathing, the trick she'd learned to slow her heart rate down when performing, which meant she was scared herself, or perhaps just excited rather than afraid.

"Maybe . . . which would be fine under different circumstances." Mr. Barnes looked grim as he pressed himself farther back in his seat, so the soldiers couldn't see him from their horses.

"I'm not sure I know what you mean, Mr. Barnes. A young British woman being delivered to school by her chaperone would seem an innocent enough situation. Why would that be of interest to Confederate soldiers?" Emily dropped her voice to barely a whisper at the end, intuiting something that wasn't appropriate for sharing with the armed pair outside the carriage.

"We have . . . supplies for the school hidden with all our other things. They'll certainly find them if they search the carriage," he whispered. His eyes shifted down to the seemingly bare carriage floor. "They'll confiscate them. What we need is a diversion so I can hide them more securely." He scanned the view out the window. "There's nothing in sight," he muttered. Emily had never seen him look so tense.

"Are we carrying valuables?" she asked, noticing his eyes move to the floor of the coach, as if looking through it instead of at it.

"To the people who need them," he answered. "And frankly, I don't want to put anything helpful in the hands of the Confederates if I don't have to."

"Who rides inside? Open the carriage!" the anonymous voice bellowed.

Emily knew it was time to act. Without pausing to consider, she reached for the handle and turned it, pushing open the door and stepping down into the afternoon sunlight. It glinted off the barrel of one of the soldiers' muskets, reminding her she was getting into something very unpleasant and altogether alien. She'd never seen a weapon like it before and knew instinctively it could wreak a nasty kind of havoc. She put her hand up to shade her eyes from the sun so she could lift her gaze to the horse and rider in front.

The instinct to cover her eyes bought her the time to assess her challenge. The nervous pacing of the horses, side to side and back and forth in a narrow range around her, was making her more anxious. One of the men had stripes sewn on his shoulder but she had no idea what they meant, except that he might be an officer. The two of them wore dirty, disheveled outfits that seemed cobbled together by hand. Their odd costumes made them look even more threatening and desperate, as if they were rogue troublemakers beyond the control of their units. She wondered in a flash of insight why a clean uniform meant law and order to her.

Her throat was so dry her voice seemed to stick in it, but the insistent circling of one of the soldiers as he attempted to peer inside the carriage demanded she shake it loose somehow. The big horse stamping so close to her made her more desperate to find a way to move the soldiers off. "I'm riding down to the University of Virginia, gentlemen," she said, working hard to sidestep the horse who couldn't settle down, and trying to radiate charm at the same time. "My elderly teacher is also with me, and we have nothing else but our personal effects."

"Really," the officer drawled, clearly dubious. "You're a Yankee, aren't you," he stated flatly. "Accent gives you away." At least the huge horse had finally stopped moving. It helped her gather her thoughts as she didn't need to dodge the big hooves anymore. She noticed it had a wild look in its eye that kept her always in view. It seemed a different kind of animal than the horses pulling carriages in the cities she'd visited or lived in all her life.

"Oh indeed, no, I'm no Yankee," she laughed, fluttering her eyes at the soldier as she lifted them to his. She was surprised to note they were a soft blue with light brown lashes, nowhere near as threatening as his horse's. His dirty brown hair stuck out from his cap as if he'd missed a haircut for a long time, and his beard was spreading under his chin and partway down his neck to disappear in his collar. She forced herself to stay focused on him alone, paying special attention to the angle of her raised arm and the grace of her extended fingers over her brow. If there was anything she knew how to do, it was hold that left violin-support-ing arm and hand with style.

"I'm from England," she told him, emphasizing the British accent she'd worked so hard to leave behind in her youth. "So, yes, north on the map, but not in America." She lowered the hand from her eyes, paying a great deal of attention now to the wrinkles in her skirt, brushing and batting at them as she turned from side to side in hopes of finally attracting the attention of the other soldier as well, which she did. He pulled his horse up next to his comrade's and grinned down at her. "That's a British accent you're hearing," she assured him with a pride she didn't feel, instantly becoming a more avid propo-nent of the King's English than she'd ever been.

"Wouldn't be too proud of that!" the officer with the stripes chuckled. "Those Britishers didn't do too good when we ran them off our lands." He pulled his horse up short, almost on top of her.

"It's those 'personal effects' we're interested in, princess," the other soldier laughed, drawing out her new title and looking over at the luggage strapped to the back of the coach.

"Now, why would two strong men like you care about a lady's travel case?" she asked, putting her hand back up to her eyes and looking from one to the other. She felt desperate to keep the second soldier away from the coach, though his horse seemed drawn to it no matter what she did. She'd begun to feel like the half-dead mouse a cat tosses around before finishing it off.

"Because it might have treasure in it, princess," he drawled.

"Heavens, no!" she laughed, tightly. "Just a few changes of clothes, a light coat, and . . . some undergarments." She dropped her eyes to the ground as if that last admission had slipped out by mistake and embarrassed her. She worried she was possibly overdoing the flirtation, but as the carriage was silent inside and Mr. Barnes had chosen to remain behind the curtain rather than help her with the soldiers, she assumed he was doing something important. He hadn't jumped to her defense either, so he must not believe her to be in any immediate danger.

"One case you say? No lady I know could get all those skirts and undergarments into one case!" the officer snickered, as if his expertise in women's dress was unassailable.

"Times have changed, Sergeant," she cried out, raising her voice merrily and hoping her wild guess at his rank would be more of a compliment than a slight. She'd still heard nothing from inside the carriage and judged Mr. Barnes to need more time and distractions before he could join her. "Will you help me with my case, Sergeant? I'll show you how different an English lady's clothing is today."

Gesturing up to the driver, she indicated he should untie her case and hand it down to the man on horseback. The soldier laughed and, putting his rifle in the same hand as his reins, took the case and rode off a little ways with it. As if the suitcase had rehearsed its part all week it sprang open, ejecting the contents with what appeared to be an explosion of petticoats. The soldier roared with delight while Emily feigned great distress.

"Gentlemen," she cried out, "gentlemen, please, have a care. Those clothes have to last me for all the time I'm at school!"

"Oh, come now, lady." The second soldier pulled out his vowels like taffy. "Are you telling us you have nothing else in there with you?" He rode his horse up next to Emily, and again she felt very small and threatened by the jumpy animal who seemed to take cues from his jittery master.

"That's right, nothing but an old fiddle. I'm a musician, so I brought it with me." Suddenly her blood pressure plummeted, and she could feel her face drain of color. She thought she might faint as cold sweat broke out on her palms and forehead. The thought of these two louts mauling her beautiful Guarneri sickened her. She prayed Mr. Barnes had secured it somehow.

As if responding to her desperate, silent plea, his face appeared in the open window over the carriage door. "Emily, my dear. What's going on here? I just woke to find we aren't moving." He opened the door and descended from the carriage with the withered movements of a much older man. Emily regained her composure, trying to force her thoughts away from her cherished violin.

"These soldiers want to know what we're carrying. I tried to tell them we have nothing of interest or value, but the lock on my case broke and now, as you can see, all my personal belongings are scattered in the dirt." She looked as if she was about to cry, although in truth the sight of her petticoats decorating the horse's neck made her want to laugh instead.

"Oh, for heaven's sake, young men, was that necessary? Come, have a look inside the coach if that will satisfy you. You've put my young student through quite enough for one day. I can't imagine that

picking on defenseless young ladies is the best way to fight a war." He
shook his head and opened the carriage door wide, so the soldier
could ride up beside it to look in. He didn't bother to get off his
horse, and Emily prayed both soldiers were tiring of the incident at
last.

"Is that the old fiddle?" the sergeant asked when he leaned his
head inside the door. "It's a pretty fancy piece of packaging for an old
piece of junk. I'll just have a look at it; give it here," he ordered Mr.
Barnes, clutching his gun as if readying it for immediate use.

Grasping the violin case under his other arm as Mr. Barnes
handed it out the door, the sergeant backed his horse up and
returned to his comrade's side. Shoving it at his companion, he
ordered his friend to look inside. Emily thought she might faint for
the first time, trying to steady herself by leaning against the side of
the carriage. "No," she whispered, meaning to yell at them but
unable to make a sound. She saw the case flip open with the fasteners
hastily unlocked without the usual reverence she paid them. The
rich red velvet lining glowed in the sunlight and her mementos of
inspirational musicians dislodged unceremoniously as the soldier
struggled with the case between himself and his horse's neck.
"What's this all about?" the annoyed soldier muttered.

"Pictures of the musicians I admire most and postcards of the
places I've traveled where the composers I play have lived and
worked. That's Mr. Paganini!" she exclaimed, reaching down for a
card shaken loose and drifting to the ground with the horse's angry
prancing.

"Don't know him," the young man jeered, "but hello, who's this?"
He pushed the case around so his colleague could see inside better.
"Feel like we've met this one somewhere." He raised an eyebrow,
waiting for his friend's reaction as he tapped the portrait of Corey
and Klaas de Koningh together that had long been a staple of Emily's
collection.

"Oh no, not possible," Emily exclaimed, trying to grab the card held just beyond her reach. "That's a pianist I've worked with, and my teacher," she added, hoping her concentration on the card looked natural enough to hide her lie. "They live in Europe. That's why I keep the pictures, so I can remember all these people who are either gone or live far away. And please, could you close the violin up now. It's all I have left from my childhood in England."

She didn't have to pretend to be close to tears. She could feel her desperation pushing her over the emotional edge between control and chaos just as the soldier snapped the violin's case closed without fastening the buckles and flipped it onto the grass. "Oh God," she cried, fear and pain strangling her voice. The case opened when it hit the ground, pictures and postcards scattering all over, but the Guarneri still seemed nestled safely in its velvet bed. She dropped to her knees, running her hands over the violin as if to check for breaks or sprains, and then crawling around to gather the cards together. She shoved them back into the case and quickly closed the top and secured the locks, pushing it back into the carriage to save it from the horses' stamping hooves. "It's all I have," she kept moaning, pushing it farther in than she could reach at first try.

"Sorry for the accident." The sergeant gestured at the clothing bag lying open on the grass. "You'll have to go without any undergarments for a while, I guess." He chuckled, grinning at his colleague. "That should be mighty interesting." Emily took a step behind Mr. Barnes. "But if that's the worst to happen on this trip, you'll be getting off easy. You're lucky we took to you. Just a few miles down the road you'll see a greeting we Southerners give people we don't like."

"Come on," the sergeant's comrade urged. "It's late and there's nothing here." Both men turned their horses and cantered off across the field, laughing and glancing back once or twice at Emily as they went. She was frozen in place, afraid to move for fear they'd come back, until Mr. Barnes took her by the arm and started toward the carriage. She could see the driver jump down to collect her soiled clothes and stuff them as best he could into the bag. She left him to it and climbed up into the carriage with Mr. Barnes's help. Seated next to the window with her violin case clutched in her lap, she felt the drivers preparing to leave and realized she was starting to shake. She rocked slightly back and forth as if to soothe the violated violin, calming her own nerves just as a mother might deal with the after-shock of an assault on her now safe child.

"My god, that was well done," Mr. Barnes said. "You should be a spy, not a musician."

"Where did all the valuable supplies go?" she asked, through chattering teeth.

"Still hidden in the false bottom of the carriage covered with that heavy lap robe," he said, with a grin. "This coach is designed to carry people and supplies of all kinds entirely out of sight." He banged on the carriage floor with his walking stick, and she could hear the muffled echo she'd misjudged as a thud before. The carriage's unusual size and seemingly elaborate suspension, as well as the large wheels up front, all began to make sense to her. It was prepared for any burden, visible or concealed.

"And the supplies? Were they always with us?"

"Indeed. Money and gold," he said. "We pay legal tender of these United States to escaping slaves." Emily's eyes grew wide as the impact of what Mr. Barnes had said hit her fully. "We're part of the Underground Railroad moving people and information from the North to the South. It seemed an impossible task at first, but where there's a will, there's a way." Emily was already in shock, and so the knowledge that they were aiding slaves to escape, something she was sure they could be arrested for, didn't knock her down in the way it might have before starting on this strange trip down south. "Once we'd started to move people to safety and to give them hope, it was habit-forming," Barnes continued. "We couldn't stop. They deserve a future, and a new way forward in America."

"Why are you telling me this now?" she asked, her breathing and pulse still labored. "It seems to me both I and my father should have been told before I came on this trip to begin with." Mr. Barnes looked at her without changing his expression or moving his eyes from hers.

"You've wanted to come to the university for months now. Mr. Smith's abolitionist connections are well known to everyone, but no one seems to suspect that he might be involved in espionage of any kind, which is why he's so valuable. You never questioned his involvement with a Southern university, either. And having made many trips like this one, all of them successful, we had no reason to believe you needed to know any more than the other students."

"And you told them all eventually?" He shook his head. "Then why me?" Emily asked, still watching him as if she wasn't sure she could trust him anymore.

"Because your handling of those soldiers earned you the right to know," he answered.

Emily felt as if the carriage was starting to slow down again but she assumed she might still be somewhat numb from her encounter with the soldiers. "I would think the fear of getting caught, or worse, would cure one of the habit quite successfully," she said, craning her neck to see if and why they'd changed speed. "Mr. Barnes, have you any idea why the carriage is stopping now?"

"None at all, but I'll find out. You rest here and try not to worry anymore. I'll be right back as soon as I learn something." He opened the door and hopped out, climbing up to talk with the drivers to keep Emily from hearing the conversation. She felt he was trying to make up for the harrowing meeting with the Confederate soldiers, but she clasped her violin tighter, as if afraid someone would pry it from her as she sat still in the coach. In a few minutes, her companion returned, climbing back into the carriage and closing the door. He pulled the brown velvet curtain across the window so they could no longer see out. "You should rest," he said. "We'll be starting up again soon. There's a small gathering in the road ahead and our drivers have to wait until it clears."

"A gathering? You mean a crowd of people blocking our way?" Emily put the violin carefully behind her feet on the floor where it seemed to disappear in the darkness of the footwell. Then she yanked the curtain back and leaned forward on the edge of her seat again to see out for herself. "Can't we just go around the trouble or use another road?" She feared the return of the violin's tormentors if the coach didn't put more distance between them. Mr. Barnes watched her carefully as if assessing her state of mind.

"There's no other route this big coach can take safely," he said. Settling back against his seat purposefully, sending a message that it was time to relax, he took a small cigar from his breast pocket and lit it. He pulled a few puffs on it, resting his hand on the edge of the open window to keep the smoke from bothering Emily. Watching his face begin to soften, she realized he might not have enjoyed the "excitement" any more than she had. She put her head back against the seat and closed her eyes for a minute. She knew waiting was a skill she had to master if she hoped to deal with the challenges of a life on the road as a performer.

A picture of Corey as she'd first seen him almost a decade ago came swimming into view. Blond hair falling across his forehead and light blue eyes shining with intrigue, his little body vibrated with that energy of the free spirit and exhilaration she'd been so surprised by and taken with. So many people in America had that confidence. They all seemed committed to the future and the promise of change, something she'd been unaware of in her early life in England.

She'd spent hours that first morning in the de Koningh mansion before coming downstairs to meet the young heir, brushing her hair around her fingers into the ringlets her nurse in England had required. She'd felt so lost that day, not her usual obstinate self, and knew she had to start on some even footing before finding her way. After her mother's death and her father's departure from England, she'd needed a place to live and, more than anything, a friend. She could never have imagined Corey would end up being more than that. She'd fallen instantly in love with the New World and its freedom; and with feisty, sensitive little Corey de Koningh as well. Then, in only a few years, she and Corey went separate ways, and when she'd seen him again he was a stranger in adult skin, and a foot taller than she. He'd had new friends, new interests, and a new life, each of which was normal and understandable; but why their early ties had unraveled and not been repaired before she'd left for Europe was incomprehensible.

She noticed a flutter in her chest, but nothing like the panic that gripped her after the soldiers had left when she'd allowed herself to consider the mayhem they'd been capable of. This quiver was different from fear. It whispered to her of possibilities, like those attendant to her first days in the de Koningh home on upper Fifth Avenue; reminiscent of the silence between Mozart's notes, or the opening strains of a Bach violin concerto, this feeling was more than the relief of fear. It was the excitement of anticipation.

"Perhaps you'd like to join us in our work," Mr. Barnes was saying. She opened her eyes and saw he'd been watching her just as closely as she'd watched him. Her expression must have given away her thoughts behind her eyelids. "There's no doubt you have the courage for it," he continued. "I'm going to tell you a little story about some people you know."

"What kind of story?" she asked quietly. She was reluctant to lose her peace to conversation.

"A story of two de Koninghs, father and son, and the work they're doing for freedom." Emily held her breath. Mr. Barnes waited, silent and still as he watched her. They waited together, much like the audience in a concert hall, trusting the moment to react would become self-evident.

"Klaas de Koningh is a spy for the Union and his son is gathering information for us while teaching at the college." Mr. Barnes looked neither grim nor dramatic. There could be no doubt he'd reached the end of his speech, but his quiet delivery underplayed its significance. "Klaas is currently being held," Barnes continued in the same voice, "behind enemy lines. I can think of no one in a better position to break that news to his son than a trusted friend like you." He watched Emily steadily as she took in this information. "Do you understand what I'm saying?" Emily avoided his eyes, staring out at the now seemingly sinister purple mountains, thinking a trick of light had somehow transformed them. She wondered how her new freedom of choice had brought her to such a strange place and time, in search of once-familiar people she no longer knew.

"This is ridiculous," she spat out. "We have to get going." Without waiting for a reaction from her companion in the coach, she pushed the door open and hung partway out calling up to the drivers, "What's wrong? Let's get moving!"

"In a minute, miss. They've blocked the road over the trestle bridge but they're leaving now. There's no way across the river but here." The driver's voice sounded half asleep, as if the delay had been more a bore than frustration. Emily pulled back into the carriage and shut the door, but she left the curtain open for better visibility. She'd started to feel impossibly closed in and needed some connection with the outside world.

"What river is he speaking of?" she asked Mr. Barnes, needing more support inside this world of her transport, too.

"It's some tributary or branch of the Potomac," he answered, inhaling a short puff of his cigar, "but I'll be damned if I can remember which one. That river jumps in and out of three or four states at once."

"Why would there be a crowd at the road?" Emily asked. "Surely they have to keep such an important artery open for travel."

"Yes, normally they would, but these are not normal times, Miss Alden. You'll become more aware of that the farther south we go."

"So, what was so important they blocked the only road for travel over a major river crossing?" Emily realized she was sounding more and more irritable. But the thought of her Confederate tormentors returning to brutalize her violin was more than she could bear. Mr. Barnes looked at her steadily before he finally spoke.

"There was a lynching down there," he said, putting what was left of his cigar out on the bottom of his boot and tossing it out the window. "Ah, you see? We're starting to move again, Miss Alden. Time to get some rest before we get to the university."

The coach was indeed starting to roll slowly but steadily ahead, and Emily found herself praying it wouldn't stop. She saw small groups of people moving off on foot and by wagon, and purposely kept her thoughts only on reaching the other side of the bridge, which had become the main goal of her life now. Needing to encourage that result, she leaned a little out the window as if to assist their passage. A trestle spanning the river was coming into view as the road approaching the crossing curved toward it. She watched the bridge looming larger and larger, and her breath caught in her throat. Her hand flew to cover her mouth to stifle a cry. She clapped her other hand over the first to keep her horror in, so it wouldn't be shared with her companion. Mr. Barnes had told her it was a lynching that blocked the road, but she was completely unprepared for the sight of it. She could feel the coach's suspension absorbing the shocks of the uneven boards of the trestle bridge, but nothing could cushion the tremors now running through her body. She grabbed her violin from the floor where it vibrated with the uneven boards of the bridge, clutching it to protect it and to stop her stomach from turning upside down again, as it had at the sight of the trestle bridge hanging.

"I told you not to look," Mr. Barnes was saying as he reached forward to steady her by the shoulders. He placed her gently and carefully back against the seat. She didn't move immediately, but finally looked down at her small, white hands gripping the violin's case. Mr. Barnes sat quietly, allowing her the space to recover. Finally, she felt the silence was too empty to be borne any longer.

"I've never seen a hanging before," she said, softly.

"I'm sure," he answered, just as quietly. She didn't respond as her thoughts raced. Then she stirred a little on the seat to check if she was still whole. She kept staring at her hands.

"Why would they do that . . . in such a public place?" she whispered, desperately clutching the violin.

"To make an example of them. It's a warning to other slaves who might want to escape. I'm afraid it's been going on a long time in the South."

"But one of them was white!" Emily exclaimed, staring again at her own white hands. "Why would they hang a white man, too?"

"Same reason: to make an example of him. They don't spare anyone they find helping runaway slaves. If anything, their rage over those whites who think differently than they do knows no bounds. They can be even more cruel in meting out punishment for collaborators."

"And women?" she asked. "Do they ever hang women who are suspected of spying?"

"Of course," he answered levelly. "War makes all enemies equal."

Emily stared at Mr. Barnes, allowing his words to sink in slowly enough to begin to make sense. The two men she'd caught sight of hanging above the water from the trestle had appeared to be standing at attention, as good soldiers might; except there was no ground beneath their feet. The African still had a cap on to protect him from the sun, which she noted was relentlessly beating down from a cloudless cerulean sky and glinting off the metal bridge as if to highlight its sharp purpose. Their arms and legs were straight, and feet pointed forward. Only the quizzical position of their heads gave away that something was wrong. Ringed by roped nooses, the bend in their necks made them look surprised with their predicament, puzzled by what fate had delivered against their will on such a clear day. Two grotesque carcasses on display like chickens in the butcher shop. That humans could do that to each other would have been unbelievable if she hadn't witnessed it with her own eyes.

She pulled the violin in its sturdy black case tighter to her rib cage, suddenly aware of her deeper responsibility for its welfare as a part of her own life. "Why can't we let each other alone?" she whispered, shuddering. "The world might be a better place if it had only artists living in it."

CHAPTER TWENTY-FOUR

HIGHLIGHTING AN undulating brick wall overhung by rusty old oaks, the late-day sun stretched long, tarnished fingers of gold and red across the green lawns leading to the university's chapel. It was a warmly romantic scene, or would have been had the two men standing in the middle of it mirrored the pastoral peace, but they did not. Their stiff backs and rigid, defiant expressions embodied a stubborn purpose. Corey stamped his foot, eyes flashing with a temper he hadn't exposed in a long time. He recognized himself in his early childhood and the recollection made him squirm. "Henry!" he hissed. "Give me the key!"

The servant bent his white head. "No," he said, barely loud enough to hear. "I can't give it to you now, Master de Koningh." A smooth, clear blue sky arched above the combatants, never suggesting there could be any disturbance in the world, either atmospheric or human.

"I've told you not to bolt the chapel anymore. I need to get in to practice whenever I like. Now it's locked again." Corey clenched both fists at his side and his mop of blond hair slipped into his eyes as he glowered in Henry's face. He hadn't cut his mane in a long time, so it defied control, like his rage.

Henry nodded his neat, regal head slowly. "We are friends, Master de Koningh." The old man slowly lifted his eyes to meet Corey's glare. They both looked at each other. Corey's breathing slowed a little, and he barely nodded. "Just so," Henry continued, with an exaggerated calm. "Then we must trust each other." He held Corey's pale eyes fast with his own clear, dark gaze.

"But you . . . you promised me!" Corey sputtered. "How could you go back on your word?"

The old man never flinched. He spoke deliberately, clearly trying to slow the pace of the rhetoric. "As soon as I'm able, I'll let you into the chapel," he went on. "You must remember I told you it would be at my discretion. I have many responsibilities to others who count on me, too. Have faith, Master de Koningh." The calm resolve in his expression reminded Corey of another look some other time. His eyes shut, wet lashes glistening. "What's wrong?" Henry asked. "I've not seen you so frantic since you arrived here."

"It's my father, Henry." Corey's voice sank along with his shoulders. "You reminded me of him. Everything reminds me of him. I haven't heard from him for over a fortnight. I'm afraid he's in danger, maybe even been captured . . . or killed." His voice dropped almost to a whisper, and he sank down on the stone bench next to the guardian oak tree at the chapel's entrance. "I see him in my head at night, carry him in my heart all day. And all I can picture is his seizure in a land not his own in the middle of a bloody war."

"Imagination, my young friend, is not real. Something you can't know or see should not get the better of you." Henry looked at Corey sadly. "I understand the ache of an unnamed fear for someone you love. A man in a black skin knows what it's like to be powerless to stop bad things," he said, nodding his head. "There is no fear as deep as the one we have for our family's safety." He put his hand on Corey's shoulder with a gentle pressure.

"Do you have any family, Henry?" Corey asked, looking down at his own long fingers knotted in his lap.

"I do. Children and a grandchild."

Corey started a little and sat up straighter, looking back up at the elderly porter. "Where are they now, Henry?" he asked. "Isn't it hard to be here without them?"

"We haven't been together since my children were very young," Henry said, in a quiet voice propelled by a sigh. "Most slave families are separated at some point."

"Good Lord, I thought you said you were freed, Henry. Weren't they also?"

"No. They're the physical assets of the master who owns them. I was a part of an estate specifically divested of its human property because of my master's special attachment to me over the years. My family had long been sold elsewhere."

"Horrible!" Corey muttered. "It's one thing to read of such things but another entirely to meet someone who's lived the atrocious truth of them."

"But that's what this war is about, among other things. There's much we can't affect at certain times, but we can do something when our chance comes. Until then, it does no good to exhaust ourselves with worry about unknown terrors."

"I try not to let my imagination take over," Corey whispered, in a tight voice. "My music has helped, and I guess that's why I feel so desperate when I can't get to the organ. I'm afraid the terror will swallow me up, pull me down in a nightmare spiral with no way out."

"Music . . . ," Henry murmured. "That is true. My people have sung for strength and solace for a very long time."

Corey dropped his forehead on the black man's arm as it rested on his shoulder. "I'm so sorry, Henry. You were never my target. I was mad at everything but you," he said.

"I know, Master de Koningh."

"Forgive me, please?"

"I already have, and I'll give you the key to the chapel this after-noon, though I must ask you to lock the door and return the key to me by dinnertime. Can we agree on that?" He kept his hand on Corey's shoulder and added a little to the steady pressure.

"Do you think my father is well?" Corey asked.

"Probably," Henry said slowly, letting his hand slip from Corey's shoulder and looking out over the chapel courtyard. "But until you know, you must engage yourself with the things that make you feel strong and good about yourself."

"Is that what you'd do? Truly, Henry, if you were in my place?"

"Yes, I've had much practice," Henry answered, returning his focus to Corey. "I would take action only when there was a clear choice. Until then, I'd stay busy." He stepped around and put both hands on Corey's shoulders, smiling a little and looking him directly in his light blue eyes. "Don't lose faith." Henry lowered his head, so their faces were only inches apart. He squeezed Corey's shoulders gently, and saw his young friend close his eyes as if to deflect some of the images he feared. He watched the afternoon sun warm the pale, young skin so near his.

⊱⋆≼❈≽⋆⊰

The motion of Emily's carriage rolling along a few miles from the university campus gave her time to explore the phantoms in her head and the flutter in her chest. She didn't like to put off dealing with things that frightened her. There was a new world waiting for her and she wanted to understand who she was in this one before taking on the challenges of that one. Frayed nerves were predictable, a lasting fright perhaps from her first encounter with Confederate soldiers. But her feelings seemed unrelated to that close call. She felt anticipation rather than residual fear. She'd already discounted her run-in with the men in gray uniforms. They were gone, and their threat went with them. No need to think about what might have been. The sight of the lynching of a slave and white man later had disgusted her, but leaving it behind had already relegated it to another time. She was good at pushing away useless, debilitating fear. That skill, she had to admit, had possibly been enhanced by the unfailing care and support of a young Corey de Koningh when she came to live with him right after her mother died.

I'm going to Corey, I'll soon be with Corey, was the reprise in her head in time with the relentless swaying of the coach. Her spirits rose with the thought of being with Corey again. It seemed so long since they'd met by chance at the Artists' Club in New York. She knew she had changed, and remembering how her old friend seldom stood still she imagined he'd have changed, too. She tried to imagine stepping down from the carriage at the university and seeing Corey's lean silhouette in the distance. Their last time together had etched his new height in her memory. The boy she'd known first was shorter than she, though always a spiritual giant. She remembered his little blond head and feminine features lecturing her on the politics of the adult world as they sat side by side on the roof of the de Koningh mansion. Heads above everyone else now, his blond waves still swept over his brow and brushed the collar of his coat. And those light blue eyes had reflected her own dark brown ones ever since they'd first met. She wondered if that would still happen when they'd been so far apart for so long.

"Worried?" Mr. Barnes asked, making Emily start with the surprise of his voice. She shook her head, realizing with some guilt that she'd forgotten he was in the coach, and even that he existed. "It's a courageous thing you're doing, Miss Alden, and you wouldn't be human if it didn't give you pause. But we'll soon be there," he added, stretching a little to look out at the graceful countryside, "and then the fear of what you don't know will disappear in the firm reality of finally being at the university and reuniting with your friend." Emily was reminded that her travel companion didn't really understand her if he thought she'd be worried about what she didn't know. It was the movement of the real world that worried her most. She looked at Mr. Barnes's solid, strong face as he took in the scenery they passed through, wondering at the assumptions people make about others without asking or truly hearing their replies.

As they drove toward the beautiful old campus, Emily felt the coach slowing down and heard the horses' hooves echoing on a stone surface, likely heralding the entrance to the university. She drew a long breath to steady her nerves, grateful she knew how to calm her heartbeat when necessary, before stepping out from the carriage into Corey's welcoming arms. She was grateful also for the extra time to gather herself as Mr. Barnes opened the carriage door and alighted first before turning to assist her. But as she leaned out the door and looked up, she could see that Corey hadn't come to meet the coach after all. No one was there waiting for them.

Mr. Barnes pointed out a man he identified as the headmaster sitting alone on the porch of a graceful brick building. She put her disappointment aside to complete the final circle from home to her new environment, mindful of the importance of the men who could help her go where she wanted to. Mr. Barnes introduced the headmaster and Emily presented herself with the poise and enthusiasm she'd learned to show her father's friends and the audience members who spoke with her after her performances. Coming south to get an education had been her primary purpose for leaving home, and though it had taken second place to her determination to find Corey and his father, she knew focusing on the first reason single-mindedly would most likely enable the second to be realized. She said goodbye to Mr. Barnes with the assurance that she could carry her own cause better on her own than with his help.

Emily committed herself to the task of settling into her rooms. She'd be living in one of the old faculty homes just at the edge of the campus with a few of the other women who hadn't arrived yet. The house was very gracious, or must have been at one time. Standing empty for a while now, it had a slightly unsettled air, apparently unsure of its reason for being. A house needs people for purpose. The living room was filled with European furniture and soft fabrics, and Emily spotted a piano, now closed and abandoned in a corner near a window. A tall case clock stood in the hallway, dignified and quiet, its rosy wood gleaming under a yellow brass face ringed by black numbers. She wondered if a clock still stood in the dark de Koningh mansion, shuttered against light and intrusion while half the family escaped to the North and the other to the South. Maybe the clock was gone, too. This wounded southern timepiece didn't make a sound, but a look inside at the chain and pendulum bandaged in protective cloth convinced Emily she could resuscitate it quite easily, so this house would regain its pulse, too. She rather liked the feeling that she was the first here and could make it her own in some way. Her first night in her new home felt comfortable and hopeful, and thus she slept well after a meal delivered to her rooms by a soft-spoken, elderly Negro servant with a head of healthy snow-white hair.

In the morning, hoping to see Corey for breakfast in the main building's dining hall, Emily imagined he'd look up surprised, smiling a greeting that would make his eyes light. Emily Alden, he'd say, is it really you! She dressed carefully, discarding the tailored skirt and jacket she'd traveled in and choosing a lighter cream-colored dress, only three-quarters in length and without any hoops or extra petticoats. A simple cashmere shawl of the same color would ward off the morning chill. Heaping her dark hair on top of her head in a slightly disheveled pile as she knew Corey used to prefer it, she pulled a few flagrant wisps loose at her forehead and ears, curling softly in any direction they chose. He'd often told her how impressed he'd been by her early defiance of the hair fashions of the day.

She wondered if he'd even been told of her arrival. She sought out Mr. Barnes immediately before breakfast, knowing he'd planned to leave early, and found him at the headmaster's office and heading for his coach that waited at the bottom of the steps. "Ah, Miss Alden," he said, seeming delighted to see her. "How good of you to see me off. You're looking lovely today and none the worse for wear after the hard journey we made. Have you settled in comfortably?" he asked, taking off his right glove and clasping her bare hand in his and bowing slightly.

"Indeed, I have," she answered with a smile, fixing him with a direct gaze he couldn't look away from. "But there is something important I need to ask you, or perhaps that you forgot to tell me." His smile faded a little and he let her hand slip from his. "I've been wondering, Mr. Barnes, if perhaps Corey de Koningh hasn't been informed of my arrival, or perhaps that I was coming at all." She arched one of her dark brows over her steady gaze, making her expression more pointed than it had been. Mr. Barnes drew himself up. "And if that is so," she went on, "why was that determination made? If I'm to help you and Mr. Smith in the future, it would seem essential that I understand all the reasoning behind the decisions, and in fact am included in them from the start. Being excluded makes me wonder about your true purpose in involving me in the first place."

Mr. Barnes's eyes softened, and she thought she saw something like a small smile pull at the corners of his mouth. "To put it more directly, Miss Alden, you want to know if we can trust each other. Is that so?" He nodded without waiting for her reaction. "To be honest, I couldn't understand why you didn't ask me sooner, knowing how close you've been to the family and particularly to the young Master de Koningh." Her expression never changed, so he continued immediately. "We didn't want to run the risk of major disappointment for the young man if you decided not to come. Which, frankly, we both thought was the likely outcome of our proposal. He's in a somewhat fragile emotional state and we didn't want to aggravate it."

Emily stared at him. "You certainly don't know me," she said. "Goodbye, Mr. Barnes. I hope you have an uneventful trip, unlike my wish for my stay here at the university." She curtsied slightly but never dropped her head or her gaze and left her travel companion holding on to the door of his carriage without entering, as if he'd lost all direction for his simplest thoughts. She reentered the building to see if anyone was in the dining room at this early hour.

Her walk to the main building from her house at the edge of the campus had set her appetite not only for breakfast, but also for the countryside around her. The early morning air was cool and gray, in sharp contrast to the heated vibrancy of the fall leaves on unruly green lawns whose lushness sang of autumnal nourishment. Ancient rounded mountaintops in the distance flowed in contiguous layers across the horizon through a blue-gray velveteen mist. Seating herself alone by one of the windows where the outline of mountains in the distance was clear, Emily held a teacup poised in her hand after satisfying her hunger with a true Southern breakfast of eggs and ham, corn muffins, and fresh country peaches. She forgot herself in the beauty and peace of the view. A good night's sleep and hearty breakfast, a lungful of pure mountain air, and the vibrancy of nature as far as she could see started a flow of tranquility through her whole body.

It reminded her of the Schubertian stream in his "Trout" Quintet, and she realized the view was as therapeutic as any music. How could there be a war just beyond those hills, or even nearer, perhaps? She could see graceful streamers of sunlight reach out across the wet grass and light the old oak trees with halos of warmth. Soon the scenery would have a whole new effect as the morning grew stronger. Would young men be dying this beautiful day? Of course they would. Their blood would soak the ground where the morning fog had baptized the dawn only moments before, and fires from exploding weapons of war would ignite the landscape in pyres of molten foliage.

"My, you look grim, young lady. What unpleasant thoughts have taken the place of our lovely view?" A small, elderly man in dark trousers and a light gray vest trundled toward her and stopped beside her table. She hadn't noticed him, lost as she was in the lush scenery outside the dining room window. The little man seemed to have been standing there a long time. She wasn't sure where he'd come from. "Professor Meyer," he said in a thick German accent, bowing slightly with both hands behind his back, and tapping his heels together. "You must be Lady Emily Alden." Emily stared at him, her teacup still poised midair.

"I am," she said. "How long have you been standing there while I daydreamed?" She blushed a little, finding she was yet again uncomfortable with her slips in etiquette. "My exhaustion from yesterday's trip has finally caught up with me," she offered, to explain her rudeness. "My movements seem slower than they ought to be . . . than I expect them to be." She smiled with the only peripheral energy she could summon.

"I understand. No need to apologize. It is we who must be forgiven for the paucity of your welcome. Please allow me to be your guide today and assist you to regain your comfort after such a long, arduous trip." Professor Meyer smiled a warm, cheering beam that made him shine. "I assume you know nothing of the college and its inhabitants, Miss Alden," he said, as Emily put her cup down and reached out toward him to take his hand. He looked surprised.

"Nothing other than what my travel companion, Mr. Barnes, has told me," she said, shaking the professor's hand with her usual firm grip. "Please sit down, Professor." She nodded to the seat directly across from her. He thanked her wordlessly with a quick incline of his head and sat down on the mahogany dining chair. An errant ray of sun slipped across the table, igniting the high luster of its mahogany sheen and bouncing off the silver tea caddy with a blinding flash of light. How oddly like her father's table at home this was: English bone china and fine furniture. She was momentarily disoriented by the similarities.

"Mr. Barnes also told me a young friend of mine is teaching music here now. I expected to see him last night when I arrived, or perhaps this morning, but I haven't found him yet." Emily picked her cup up with care not to let it rattle.

"Master de Koningh!" the professor exclaimed. "Is that who you mean? What a small world. I have no idea where he might be now. We often meet here for breakfast." The professor twisted in his chair to survey the dining hall behind him. "He's a lovely young man. A little troubled of late, but then, aren't we all?" he muttered, as he turned back to face Emily.

"Troubled? How so?" she asked.

"Oh, I believe he's suffering from little more than homesickness, but he's a sensitive soul, as I'm sure you know, and the difficulty of getting information about his family down here takes a toll. . . ."

"Poor Corey," Emily whispered under her breath. The professor didn't seem to notice.

"I learned he'd stopped practicing and cut himself off from his music, as well as other people, when he got here, so I suggested he return to the little organ we have in the chapel on campus for daily practice."

"Yes!" Emily exclaimed, sitting up a little taller and straighter. "His music will help. It's the only friend we carry with us wherever we go." She noticed how much better she felt talking with the professor. "Are you a music teacher yourself, Professor Meyer?" she asked, looking at him with a more discerning eye.

"Yes indeed, how did you know? I'm the choral master, Miss Alden, and head of the music department at the college when we're in matriculating mode. But right now, I'm anything they need me to be!" His little body rocked with silent laughter and his ruddy cheeks grew rounder under his shining dark eyes. "I sense you may be interested in music yourself, Miss Alden. Am I right?"

"You are, Professor," Emily said, finally relaxed enough to hold her cup steady. "I play the violin." She couldn't help noting the way his dark, bushy brows shot up to the creases in his forehead, but he said nothing, so she continued as if there'd been no reaction at all. "I've spent much of the past year studying in Europe with a childhood teacher of mine, visiting the great performance halls and walking in the footsteps of famous composers. There's been an explosion of work coming from Europe right now, including European women, at last," she added with a smile, unable to resist the small provocation.

"True!" the little professor agreed, looking as if he might pop out of his chair with pleasure. "What a wonderful experience that must have been, Miss Alden, and how lucky we are to have you here. Would you satisfy an old choirmaster's craving and tell me if you heard any new choral works while you were there?"

"I did indeed, sir." Emily's spirits rose continuously as she watched the professor's excitement increase. "I was most impressed with the works of Mr. Brahms and Mr. Liszt. Both men have written beautiful requiems for civil strife. The whole world seems weighed down by our suffering in this war, and that's produced gorgeous, expansive works to express the grief. As a matter of fact, I brought the music for Brahms's Human Requiem with me here. Perhaps you'd like to see it." She couldn't help noticing the little professor was rocking back and forth ever so slightly as she spoke, as if keeping time to some private rhythmic line.

"I would be so, so grateful," he said. She had no doubt of his sincerity. Shaking himself a little and bouncing to his feet, he cried out, "Miss Alden, would you like to learn more about our beautiful campus? I'd be honored to be your guide." He held out his hand with a little formal bow, and Emily couldn't get over feeling she'd become the seated partner in Carl Maria von Weber's romantic musical prelude "Invitation to the Dance." If ever there had been a human manifestation of the formal request for a dancing partner made by von Weber's cello part, Professor Meyer was now it. And if ever there had been a feminine response, it would now be hers.

"Delighted, Professor Meyer, and thank you." She stood up, noting again how tiny and round he was. She would have to work hard to be graceful enough to deflect the discrepancy between them. He held out his arm, indicating she should move to the door first. She knew it was more than politeness. Usually a woman's voluminous skirts would fill all the space between the dining room furniture, leaving no room for anyone else to walk. She supposed perhaps Southern women might still be attached to the formal fashions, so the professor was moving out of the way with his own safety in mind. She tried to hide her smile by dropping her gaze demurely as she passed him, knowing he would no doubt be stunned to find she had no layers of hoops and petticoats expanding her circumference, nor floor-length skirts brushing his shoes as she moved past. She allowed him time to recover behind her back as she moved to the door, and then slowly turned to face him.

"Where to first, sir?" she asked.

"Have you seen this main building?"

Emily nodded eagerly, feeling less of a newcomer than she was. "I've seen the theater," she said, a formal curtsy suggesting an imagined curtain call, "the headmaster's office, and where the other professors' offices are." She pulled herself up to show the required respect for the men of letters. "Mr. Barnes thought I should see those few essentials before he left me last night. I must say this building is very impressive even at night," she said, moving forward and out of the dining room slowly as she talked. "Walking in from the carriage through the arches at the front," she waved her arm to take in the hall ahead of her, "all lit with a glow from the tall windows behind them, I felt like an honored guest arriving at a ball instead of an exhausted student disembarking from a long, dusty trip."

Professor Meyer glowed with pleasure listening to her animated description of the building he'd come to take almost for granted. "Well then, perhaps the wing to the left where we have most of the classrooms," he suggested. "Although I must admit they're not more than square boxes with desks and tend to get quite hot by midmorning. They're all on one hall, and I think we could skip them without jeopardizing your orientation."

"I had hoped some classes could be held outside while the weather is nice," Emily said, with a sigh. "Yes, let's skip the classrooms, this morning, anyway," she added in afterthought, not wanting her host to find her ungrateful and worry that she might not be academically inclined. "Perhaps a tour of some of the outer buildings would be nice while the air is so fresh."

"Let's start with the chapel then, and the beautiful organ," he said, gesturing outward to someplace she knew nothing of yet. Emily nodded and passed through the door and down the steps.

"You're in charge, Professor," she said, with a lilt in her voice. "Lead the way." She was feeling much better and ready for adventure, especially if it included the discovery of Corey's whereabouts at the end of it. A big breakfast and talk of music and the beauty of the outdoors in the morning air were working wonders already. In truth, she loved to travel. Never having been rooted to a home of her own, she hadn't really missed one as some might have. She knew how lucky she was. She might have grown up always aware of the hole that omission had left, yet instead she was born to appreciate the fullness of the possibilities outside. They left her excited about her performance career, always on the move to a new place, instead of sad about leaving something behind. Though she didn't have much to leave behind yet.

"I suppose if we're lucky, we might even find Master de Koningh in the chapel at his morning practice. Shall we go?" the professor said. Emily turned to look at him as if she'd finally heard what she'd been waiting for. Suddenly all the other aspects of the university, her education, and her new life disappeared. It was time to find Corey. Her eyes danced with light.

"Yes, please," she agreed, quickening her steps down the brick path toward the other side of the quadrangle where the professor was pointing. She realized she'd started off almost at a run, and the little man had to push to keep up after her. Logic slowed her down again, because she had no idea where they were headed, and the professor finally passed her with a smile.

"Follow me." He moved on toward a building formally introduced by a row of old oaks and stone benches at the end of the path. He was obviously eager now to lead her, but apparently didn't see what she saw on one of the benches nearest the building. While the professor pushed on, Emily came up short, recognizing the long slope of shoulders brushed with waves of blond hair on the youth slumped on the last bench in the distance.

An elderly man in a dark servant's coat stood with the youth. The servant's thick head of curly white hair bent and almost touched his companion's. It was a scene of such poignant gentleness she couldn't imagine interrupting. All the time she'd spent envisioning her reunion with Corey had been wasted energy. While she'd pictured them meeting again, his thoughts had been elsewhere. Keep your mind here, Robert Haussmann had often said to her, gently tapping the music on her stand as she practiced. Don't imagine some future performance or applause from an audience that doesn't exist. Stay right here.

Perhaps if she'd spent more time asking questions of Mr. Barnes right there on the trip in the coach, she'd have realized Corey didn't know of her arrival so he couldn't be looking forward to it. He had a painful present to deal with. If she hadn't been dreaming of the future, she'd have known Corey had moved on in his life to handle some aching realities she'd never had to face. Mr. Barnes had made that clear. Instead of waiting now for Corey to look up and notice her, she should take this pause to think of how best to help him. She saw Professor Meyer walk up to him and his companion, and knew her time to think was vanishing, just as Corey's head snapped up to look her way. She couldn't see his face well enough to know what was on it, but his body was rigid.

"Ach, do come this way, Miss Alden," the professor called to her as he waved her over. She knew it was time to meet her old friend, and the closeness they'd had as children would surely fill in the gaps between then and now. She moved along the path, noticing that Corey hadn't stirred. He was staring as if he didn't recognize her. His white-haired companion, whom she now recognized as the servant who brought her dinner to the room when she arrived, straightened up and stepped away slightly.

"Miss Alden," Professor Meyer called out. "Over here. We've found him! I knew he'd be near the chapel and his beloved organ." The little professor kept waving her on.

Emily started forward through the arched row of grand old oak trees lining the pathway. She remembered her first long walk down the de Koningh hall to meet her new young host in his mansion when she'd arrived from England after her mother's death. A thirteen-year-old child scared and defiant in her new role as a guest in a foreign country, she'd done everything in her power to fit into the surroundings while still holding on to herself. She'd wanted to be accepted on her own terms and not absorbed into someone else's household.

Don't do that; stay right here. Robert's warning came to mind again. How different her feelings were right here as she approached Corey on his bench at the end of the long corridor of oak trees. In a way, she was part of his family, and she wanted to take up all his loneliness and pain to give him her strength. At this moment, for the first time in her life, she feared more for him than for herself.

The servant introduced by the professor as Henry faded off somewhere with a polite nod and smile. Professor Meyer also disappeared after a few cheerful comments about turning her over to "Master de Koningh's good care," and Emily found herself alone with Corey on the bench under the oaks at the end of the brick path.

"Is it really you, Emily?" he asked, not moving or reaching out to take her hand as he stared almost through her. She dropped quickly to the bench beside him, bringing herself closer to him without moving forward. She felt as if she must be careful not to frighten him with any quick movements for fear he'd run away like a frightened wild animal. She moved imperceptibly closer and he kept staring at her but stayed as he was, collapsed on the bench. Some sadness in his eyes warned her to stay where she was. She dared not move to his side and he made no move to hers. A wall of something—time, loss, or something unknowable—stood between them preventing the pull that had always brought them together.

CHAPTER TWENTY-FIVE

"LET'S GO," she said gently to Corey, unable to bear his look of numbed shock and hoping that movement would help him recover. "I have to get back to my lodgings and it's a ten-minute walk at best. Would you come with me?" She was careful not to touch him or suggest he hold her hand, fearing that would upset whatever stability he was struggling for. She knew Mr. Barnes's news about his father would unsettle him even more than her arrival had, and worried that he was already aware of the consummate dangers posed by supporting the Underground Railroad. Had he not already made an obvious friend of the gentle servant with the white crown of hair she'd seen him so close to when she'd arrived unnoticed?

But he didn't move, just stood looking at her as if he was translating slowly from a foreign language. "Come with me," she said again, more firmly this time. "Please, Corey. We can talk while we walk. I'd like to know more about this unusual pattern of parks and pavilions. The house I'm staying in is beyond the public buildings. I had to come down through all these gardens on the way to breakfast this morning and was amazed to see such variety. Do you know what these trees are?" She kept talking, her voice light but firm, and took a step back, inviting him to follow.

Finally, pulled by an invisible thread joining them together, he rose. "That's an umbrella magnolia you've been standing under," he said weakly, "and the old pecan trees at the edge were both planted by some science professor . . ."

"How do you know? I don't think you were here when they were planted, were you?" She looked up at him through her lashes, a distinct tease sparking her smile. She kept walking backward so she could hold Corey's eyes, moving closer to the small garden gate in a brick wall leading to the path between the next garden, and then the next. He followed her, quickening his pace a little to catch up.

"Because," he said in a stronger tone, "when I first arrived the groundskeeper took me on a three-hour tour of every specimen tree on the campus. I think he was starving for a new head to fill. If you came down this way you must have woven through the crabapples along the wall and those four plum trees. The walnut grove is up by the house you're in."

"So, that's what they are: walnuts!" Emily stopped, ostensibly to marvel at his knowledge, but actually to let him catch up to her. "I noticed the yellow leaves before I even left the house, and when I got to them and crushed them in my hand they smelled sweet, but I couldn't tell what the big seed was. I also saw neglected herb and vegetable gardens along the way. Was there a plan of some kind to make the college self-sustaining?"

"Precisely!" His voice and the spark in his eye made her heart jump with hope. Corey stopped in front of her, tossing his long blond hair back off his face so he could see her more clearly. "You've got it. The ten gardens provide a mix of ornamental trees and shrubs, combined with many ways to feed people. Unfortunately, the herbs and vegetables have almost all died off in the desolation of this war. Seems odd . . ." He paused, looking at her still.

"Odd? Why?"

"Oh, that some things have to die to make new things." Emily turned on the path to watch him intently, wondering if he meant only the war and its consequences. "Why are you here, Emi?" he asked, jerking his head away so she couldn't see his eyes anymore. The abruptness of his movement and question returned the knot to her stomach. "Doesn't your husband mind?"

The knot pulled so tight it took her breath away. "Husband! I have no husband," she gasped. "Whatever gave you that idea?"

"I saw your engagement photograph in the newspaper, yours and Professor Haussmann's. In the 'Arrivals and Departures' section, before you left for Europe in the spring." The cold accusation in his tone couldn't be missed.

"It was not an engagement photograph." Emily's voice was low with the weight of her new understanding. She took a deep breath and looked up at her friend, seeing his painful expression for what it was at last. "Come, Corey. I have some explaining to do and still need to get back to my rooms. Let's put those long legs of yours to good use, and we can also cover a lot of personal ground at the same time." She held his eyes with hers again for a few seconds, and then took off through the garden without glancing over her shoulder. She wasn't sure enough of her own feelings or whether to claim him as something more than a beloved brother in the face of his assumptions about her and Robert Haussmann. But she said a prayer he'd follow, nonetheless.

Together the small, intense young woman with dark hair tied back off her face and shoulders, and the tall young man with a loose cascade of blond waves tumbling in his eyes and around his neck wove their way over the brick paths, through the gardens and pavilions, to the far end of the campus. Emily stopped on the steps of the old Rotunda to catch her breath. The Roman architecture added to a sense of grace and balance with a lush landscape, a carefully executed plan she had begun to appreciate. Corey explained that the domed building was the heart of what was called the Academical Village, designed to create a community where culture and ideas are shared between the learned and learner.

Emily seized on that to explain how her father had chosen Robert to act as her tutor on a grand tour of Europe's concert halls. "I didn't want to go," she admitted, "but knew I was unusually entitled to experience something only young men enjoy, and so I was enticed by the opportunity. But eventually I found it was just another way to take me off my father's hands."

A rueful smile flickered across her face as she started off again, threading her way through the rhododendron and mountain laurel bushes leading to the next garden. She kept talking, always leading on, so Corey could only listen and follow. The story came out like a relentless piano roll that couldn't be stopped: the snide remarks and glances on board ship, her father's attempts to toss young beaux in her path, her disappointment with the suffragettes in London, the rock climbing in Switzerland, concerts everywhere they'd stopped, all ending in Vienna at Mozart's home. It tumbled out and Corey could do nothing but try to keep up and listen, which was the only way Emily felt she could handle the tension around the trip to Europe and the roles some of the most important men in her life had played.

The recitation of her itinerary stopped abruptly as they climbed some steps up to another bedraggled garden. She pulled her skirt to free it from the grapevines now intertwined with blueberry for lack of care. She pushed her way through a low boxwood hedge to reach an intimate flower garden, no longer blooming and looking doubtful about its appearance at any time in recent history. Emily felt more comfortable blaming the turn to cool autumn days than the neglect of war. "That's a crape myrtle," she said tightly, pointing to one of the smaller trees. She didn't wait for a response from Corey, unused to the constrained silence when she and Corey were together. "And there's a rose of Sharon. Too bad it's so late in the year. These bushes must be beautiful when they're blooming."

"Too bad and too late," Corey said, seeming to slip off into his depression again.

"That hedge of golden rain trees on the bank up there reminds me of the ones in England," Emily went on, as if he hadn't spoken. "In fact, there's a lot of England on this campus. I'm not sure I like that."

"Buildings and furniture, too," Corey said. "I would have assumed it would make you feel at home."

"Assume nothing, Corey de Koningh," Emily scolded, finally daring to look directly at him again. "I like new things and people, and I love America. That's why I'm here for the education I couldn't get any other way, and to be in my chosen homeland in its hour of need." How was it that Corey hadn't questioned the coincidence of her arrival at the college with Mr. Barnes and his own father's disappearance? She couldn't tell yet where his mind was going to settle as she watched it touch down in so many different directions.

"You must be crazy, Em. You've already had a better education at home than you could ever get in one of these places." He waved his hand to take in the expanse of the campus and buildings. The beauty, both natural and man-made of the environs, made it obvious to Emily that there were few, if any, other places like this one.

"Easy for you to say, Corey." Emily turned to fix him with one of her stern looks. "You've always known you'd have a formal education. Perhaps I need to be exposed to it to decide for myself." Again, he seemed to take her quest for a formal education as the prime reason for her arrival. He watched her steadily, considering carefully. "And I think the exchange of ideas among people with no prior connection is important. You can't do that at home."

Emily reached up, pulling a couple of small twigs out of her hair. The bushes they'd been pushing through at times had lots of dead wood in them, signaling a few years of disregard even with a groundskeeper struggling to keep them healthy. Emily turned to look back at the old Rotunda, which they could see in the distance through the boxwood hedges surrounding the last garden. She was not at all sure she wanted to end her narrative with the change in Robert Haussmann's relationship to her, or even hers to her father, but there wasn't much of anything else to tell. All the twisting and turning through the brush and buildings of the campus still brought her back to the fact that she was totally estranged from two of the most important people in her life. She wanted to stop talking and let Corey pick up with his story from here on. She needed to know if he was already aware of the Underground Railroad, or perhaps even involved with it. She took a deep breath. "Corey, how did you end up here? Did you finish college? Mr. Barnes told me you got this job through your father, but I don't understand why you needed it. Were you intent on aiding the Union cause in some way?"

They started walking again. Helping Emily over one of the raised turf parterres, Corey explained his desire to fight for the North, but Emily wondered if his yearning to distract himself by going to war also had something to do with his mistaken assumption about her and Robert Haussmann. Passing over the last terrace together, and then out to the lawn in front of a gazebo, he told Emily of Bill's enlistment, and Bill's personal attachment to him, careful not to give her the impression that he had either encouraged or condemned it. She looked shocked, stating her amazement at how supportive Corey was when others wouldn't have been. "Did you know or suspect that of Bill before?" she asked. "I assume even the best of friends are kept in the dark about some things." She looked both sad and a little lost. It was the last thing she'd expected to hear from him.

"It's still not a world that permits people like Bill to live freely and talk openly," Corey told her, as they passed under two Biltmore ash trees shading the haphazard path through the oval flower beds. Their crimson fall foliage reminded her of the flames consuming so much of the country now, but remembering how sturdy the ash was, resilient and particularly resistant to shock, she marveled at the way nature reminded her of the basic truths of life. She felt it was not random, remembering how many composers had chosen to represent the powers of transformation in their work. "Things are changing all over the world," she told him. "New life will grow out of the ashes of this war. Maybe soon there will be acceptance of every-one's differences."

"Not in our lifetimes." Corey shook his head. "Bill would be tried as a criminal in England, where they're so committed to abolishing slavery. Humans don't accept others easily who look or act differ-ently, Em. Belonging and fitting in still seems the goal of life."

They passed a small thicket of shrubs in oval raised beds that included a carpet of snowy ground cover and left the last garden under the great silver bell tree that marked its entrance. Stopping to look out over the lawns stretching beneath more oak trees, Corey told Emily of Bill's last visit and his own slide into depression after seeing the reality of war on his friend's face. Suddenly he grabbed her by the shoulder and spun her around to face him. His eyes had a look of desperation she hadn't ever seen before.

"Why did your father send you down here, Em? After all, you'd just finished up your tour of Europe, so why did he think it necessary to expose you to the danger here just for more education?" His voice rose to match the haunted look on his face.

"First of all, he didn't send me," Emily answered, with quiet assurance. "I wanted to be here myself for more than just the educa-tion. I left his European tour and Robert on my own to come back to my chosen homeland to help . . . help the Union cause and get a chance for more education while the young Southern men have left the classrooms empty. And secondly, I'm not on speaking terms with my father anymore, so he doesn't know I'm here." She could feel Corey's shock, so she sped up again past the side of the little gazebo and on toward the campus outskirts and the house she'd barely moved into yet. Though she was almost running across the open lawn, Corey had no trouble keeping up with her just by opening his stride.

"Don't be crazy, Em," he shouted at her back. "You only have one father. There's no reason to lose him when you don't have to. I'd give anything to know I still have a father, and you go and deny yours just because he cared a little too much about you." She stopped and spun around to look at him, causing an inevitable crash that almost knocked her down.

"You have a father, Corey," she yelled in his face. "He's just being held for his own protection. And how can you compare the two in the same breath? I'd give anything to have a father like yours, but I don't."

"What? What do you know about my father?" He stared at her.

She lowered her voice as if to keep the whispering trees from hearing her. "Only what Mr. Barnes told me. He asked me to help you, and your father."

"Being held? What does that mean? My father's a spy, Emily. No other word for it. They hang spies; they don't hold them. But what do you know about all this? Do you understand why my father got me this job?" He looked at her with such disgust she thought her heart would stop.

"No, Corey, according to Mr. Barnes your father would not be treated like the average Northern espionage agent. He has so many friends in the South through his lifetime of business dealings that it's believed someone has literally removed him from circulation rather than turning him over as a prisoner of war."

"He's a hostage, then," Corey said just above a whisper.

She grabbed both his hands and held them tightly. "Of course he's still not free to move around, but they feel he's alive and well and will be spending the rest of the war in relative safety. I'm sure they'll continue to get information out about him, but he's alive, Corey. They have no doubt about that, and asked me to tell you myself," she finished, staring up in his pale blue eyes as if to sear the message onto his brain.

"Why?" Corey asked.

"Because I helped Mr. Barnes with some Confederate soldiers on our way down here, and I suppose because I told them a while ago what good friends you and I are . . . were. They know I tried to find you and your family when I got back to New York. I made no secret of it, quite the opposite."

Corey stared at her, either not really following her explanation or perhaps not really listening. There were too many other anxious voices competing in his head for attention. "But a prisoner of war, Emily! What if they're starving my father? Or he's been injured and can't get help? He's not a young man . . ." his voice trailed off.

"Stop that right now, Corey de Koningh," Emily ordered, squeezing his hands again. "You can't worry about what the future will bring or what happened in the past or even what's happening right now if you're not there."

"Ah, I get that advice a lot these days, but always from people who don't share my fears. So, what can I do for my father?" he asked, challenging her to propose something to take the place of his apprehension.

"Nothing. Not directly, I mean. But you know what he wanted you to do while you were here, and we can both still work for him that way to the best of our abilities."

"What? You know what he asked me to do? Oh, Mr. Barnes again. But Emily, you can't," Corey said, as she let go of his hands and turned to cover the last bit of lawn between them and the house. "There are no women spies; for good reason," he called after her.

"Which is . . . ?" she asked over her shoulder, a small smile starting to play at the corner of her mouth. If Corey had half the intelligence she gave him credit for, he wouldn't continue that argument. "And besides," Emily went on as she always did, "there are women spies, plenty of them, according to Mr. Barnes." Her dark eyes snapped a warning not to challenge her. "Mr. Barnes says women make better spies than men! And besides, I love your father too, Corey. I owe him a great deal, and I want to help." Emily turned to enter the house, and Corey followed her, as he so often did. She was glad now that her classes wouldn't start for a few more days. With the serendipitous connection to her dearest friend in this new place, she needed more time to adjust to her surroundings, and to him.

They toured the house she was staying in, both learning all they could about its nooks and crannies in case they needed hiding places of their own one day. They were good at uncovering a building's idiosyncrasies. They'd both perfected the skill at the de Koningh mansion long ago. Emily showed Corey the piano in the living room, and asked if he could tune it himself. He sat and stroked the ivory keys softly, testing the tone and pitch of the neglected keyboard.

"This will work so much better for you than the chapel organ." She smiled, feeling as if the sun had just broken through a cloud of biblical proportions, igniting two small sparks at each end of her mouth—the magical smile he'd always claimed was a kind of blessing.

"I've been happy with the organ and the chapel," he said, still not sure he could let go of his fears.

She placed her hand on his arm instinctively. "Yes, but now it's best not to go there." He looked at her with a question in his glance. "Because of Henry," she answered, nodding at him as if they understood each other.

"What about Henry? You know him?" Corey asked, holding his breath. Emily stepped very close to him and spoke quietly.

"We met when I arrived on campus. He brought my dinner and he told me Mr. Barnes had explained my arrival and my role here. Then I saw him knocking on the chapel door when I was on my way to breakfast. Two slow knocks, and one fast one, repeated three times. A code, Corey. Don't you see? Morse code for 'M' and 'E'—me!" He spun around on the piano bench to stare at her. "Mr. Smith comes south to find slaves seeking freedom. I figure that your father has apparently been doing the same thing," she said, watching Corey to be sure of his awareness. When she saw he was calm and attentive, she continued. Obviously she'd described his father's involvement just as he understood it. There were no real surprises revealed in his expression.

"They're called 'pilots' on the Underground Railroad." She stopped talking to watch him again, unsure of how much Klaas had told him about the method of helping slaves escape. Mr. Barnes had explained the vocabulary of the Underground Railroad, but how it worked remained a mystery to her. "Those who guide slaves to safety and freedom, like Mr. Barnes, are 'conductors.' The slaves, like Henry's family members, are 'passengers.' The places along the line to Canada where fugitive passengers can safely hide are 'stations,' I think." She hoped Corey wouldn't question her further or her flimsy grasp of the facts would be all too clear, possibly making him doubt her information about his father.

Corey narrowed his eyes, looking down at the ground, and then back up at her. She could see he'd followed her logic and felt a quickening pulse as he caught his lower lip in a short breath. How long it had been since she'd seen that small familiar habit! How close the recognition of it made her feel to him now. They'd been friends for a lifetime, so she decided to tell him everything she knew.

"This college is a station, according to Mr. Barnes," she said, just above a whisper. "Did you know that? And there can be no question that the chapel with your organ is currently serving as a substation . . . of the Underground Railroad," she finished. Corey shut his eyes for a moment, and then opened them to look at her with such a deep, penetrating look that she thought she saw the trust and connection built from the beginning of their friendship, as well as something more she wasn't sure of. Yet she was surprised to find that unlike her confusion over Robert Haussmann's feelings for her, Corey's seemed as natural and welcome as the affection from his father always had. She wasn't sure what it was, but she didn't need to be. She reached for his hand.

CHAPTER TWENTY-SIX

"TENTACLES OF TREASON," BY J. R. DUNNE. Johnny stroked his hand across the newspaper article's title, as if connecting with a beloved possession. He liked the alliteration. It played on the public's horror of poisonous sea creatures, like the jellyfish reported to be invading New York's harbors, supposedly because of the pollution of war. His reporter's skepticism told him that was unlikely, but if everyone was in a panic about the ugly medusozoans, why not use it to sell papers? Most of all, he enjoyed the references he'd made to the illegitimacy of the Confederate cause. The point of view was clear, but it took reading through a lot of supposedly opposing opinions to determine that. He liked toying with people's prejudices in hopes of exposing them to the readers themselves. It was his first editorial piece at the *Times*, and since he oversaw the department, he could choose to make it the first of many more.

The *New York Times* office still had its late-night pallor with daylight more than an hour away. The sun was coming up later and later as fall progressed. Johnny had expected these predawn Sunday vigils to wear thin quickly on his new job. The temptation of fame won out over the disadvantages, however, and he'd been surprised by how much he'd enjoyed the peace and quiet of the office at quarter-staffing, to say nothing of the moment of private communion with his literary baby. Like the gestation of an unborn child, one can only imagine its existence in advance of its arrival. Of course, he wasn't the only one responsible for this creation. In many ways, he had that pretty Alden woman to thank. He couldn't help smiling at the irony of his own metaphor, recognizing he'd carried the creation and produced it, while she had planted the seed.

Johnny picked up his coffee cup, taking his first sip and noting the piping hot contents had been reduced to room temperature while he read. Had he not felt so pleased with his creativity he'd have been repulsed by the cold, tasteless brew in his cup. His eyes jumped to his final paragraph. In it, he'd laid out the premise that there were many different forms of treason, committed by everyone from politicians to common citizens. As the springboard for his broad definition of betrayal, he'd used the disappearance of Klaas de Koningh and the supposition that "treasonous acts" might have had something to do with it, a complete fabrication on his part. He'd used the same irony and sarcasm Shakespeare put into Mark Antony's mouth at Julius Caesar's funeral, making the case for the fallacy behind the accusations.

The public might well jump to the wrong conclusions about Klaas de Koningh, given his lifetime involvement with the South and its produce, yet his reputation as a New York businessman of honor with any who knew him well was unassailable. His family history of involvement with and dedication to New York ran deep and strong from the earliest days of the port of New Amsterdam. But none of that was news. Yes, he'd just fit his premise into Shakespeare's structure, picking up the Alden woman's lead and running with it. One might be tempted to call this manufactured facts, but fake or real, the news could be almost anything anyone needed it to be to sell papers.

Why hadn't he paid more attention to Emily Alden when she was in the office? He supposed it was still so unusual to have a woman there he hadn't taken her seriously, or hadn't taken what she thought seriously, at the very least. Why should that be so when he had a female reporter working for him now, but only one after all, whom he never spoke with because she handled the home and fashion pages. Horace Greeley had hired Margaret Fuller at the *Tribune* decades ago to report on the revolution in Italy, as well as all the seamier subjects this city had to offer in her later career. But she was unique, with a strikingly unfeminine brain, and she'd been the only woman after all so not a good example of what to expect of others of her gender.

It was becoming obvious to him that he didn't need to be in the field anymore to describe the action. There was something important going on everywhere, all the time. He'd stay with the opinion pieces from now on and let the other reporters run around like ants. He wished he could thank Miss Alden in person for freeing him up to see the possibilities, but he couldn't. His own stubborn pride had blocked his way with her.

"Nice piece, Johnny, very provocative!" a female voice said. He hadn't heard the rustle of her black skirts as she approached.

"Thanks, Mary." He smiled up at his colleague, who was already poised for flight. Wondering suddenly if she objected to her arts and society assignments, he looked directly at her. She had a stern, self-protective manner and a totally unremarkable face, but who knew what lay inside? "Still having trouble with the angle for your article?" he asked. He vaguely remembered her objection to being assigned the piece on the new restaurant near Bowling Green Park. "Why don't we have a look at it? I'm sure we can come up with something good if we put our heads together." He tried to ignore the look of disbelief on her face as he motioned to the chair in front of his desk.

⁂

Robert Haussmann sat by his window in his music room's wing chair, holding the newspaper open like a sail drying in the wind. He enjoyed the feel and look of it on a quiet Sunday morning as much as he liked reading it. Usually he fed the last pages from his right hand into his left, scanning the lines with only partial attention. But this day, his eyes froze on the opinion piece on the front page and the name of his graceful, discreet former employer. He glanced up to the title to see who had been responsible for this piece of manufactured news, instantly recognizing the name of the reporter he'd met at the newspaper's headquarters the day he went searching for information. He had a photographic memory, sharpened to a fine point by the memorization throughout his life of many scores of music. This indeed was the same Johnny Dunne Emily had been with, the same J. R. Dunne the clerk at the paper had referred him to. Finishing the entire article with careful precision, Robert lingered over the closing lines: *If it be so, there is no such thing as honesty and loyalty. If it be not, the laws of the United States are wastepaper and its Government moonshine, with only the laws of every man for himself in play.*

Robert let the paper rest in his lap and looked out the window. It had the ring of Shakespeare: The noble Brutus hath told you Caesar was ambitious. If it were so . . . if it were not . . . very clever. The inference about Klaas de Koningh's commitment to the Union cause was implicit. But was that healthy for Klaas? What did "being held" mean if they thought him a spy, as Johnny had so surreptitiously offered up as a possibility? Robert's mind slipped back to the sight of the handsome Dutch merchant sitting by his fire while he discussed the direction his only son's music career should take. He could almost hear the fire crackling as they talked, just as his housekeeper Margaret was rattling the pocket door to his back parlor now to announce a visitor. His reverie was snapped into the present with the sight of his uninvited guest at his parlor door.

"Lord Alden, what a surprise!" Lord William Alden marched into the room before Margaret could announce him. Robert rose slowly from his chair, stunned by the suddenness of the arrival. Lord Alden stopped and stood staring at Robert like a hunted stag stumbling out of the forest. Robert braced himself, realizing he always felt Lord Alden's arrival as an intrusion. No matter which one of them entered the other's space, there was an adversarial air Robert couldn't ignore.

"There have been many surprises this morning, Professor. Did you see the paper?"

"I did. I assume you refer to the piece on Klaas de Koningh."

"Bloody hell, right!" Robert couldn't escape the feeling that Lord Alden was somehow blaming him personally for the suggestive opinion piece. "What in God's name was this man trying to say, this J. R. Dunne? The idea that a citizen such as Klaas de Koningh should take it upon himself to serve an enemy of the United States must fill readers with outrage." Lord Alden gaped at the paper spread out in Robert's chair where he'd let it slide. His hand seemed to shake slightly as he reached to remove his hat.

"Please, Margaret, will you help Lord Alden with his hat and coat? And then be seated, sir. You look tired. Would you like a cup of tea? Margaret, please bring us a cup for Lord Alden." Robert noticed an unusual disconnected glassiness to his guest's eyes. "Are you not feeling well, Lord Alden?" he asked, motioning to one of his side chairs. His guest looked vaguely at the seat being offered and backed into it to sit.

"I'm exhausted from the trip to Washington. It was never easy, but now, in wartime, the trains are few to nonexistent, and travel by coach in the fall is a nightmare of mud, to say nothing of the tensions caused by Confederate troops at the beginning of the journey home."

"Must you expose yourself to so much turmoil in a time of war, sir?" Robert didn't exactly feel sympathy for his guest, but he recognized the man seemed torn in many directions, and it was a time when empathy could not be overrated.

"The trip was necessary," Lord Alden offered in a calmer voice, "only because I have a duty to report back to England on the state of the Union. If the Crown is going to lend money to the US government to support the president, then it has to be assured this president will be around to do something with it. I am none too sure the Union cause will prevail."

Margaret reentered the room with a cup of tea on a small tray, and Robert's guest looked at her as if he was unable to figure out a use for it. She put the cup beside him as Lord Alden was about to speak again, but Robert shook his head slightly while watching Margaret, alerting his guest to the fact that their conversation was most likely being monitored by the housekeeper. Robert asked her to pull the pocket doors shut as she left, nodding to his guest to continue talking. He noticed again how agitated and strained the ordinarily calm and debonair man appeared. "Are you sure you're feeling well?" Robert repeated, a bit more insistently this time.

"I've had tension in my chest, in my whole body for that matter, for many weeks, and this news about my old friend's possible capture and confinement as a spy is tightening the tourniquet even more. I wonder, is it safe to print such conjecture about Klaas?" He picked up the teacup beside him, holding it distractedly. "Will it only enrage his captors and force them to commit some heretofore delayed atrocity?" he continued, still holding the cup in midair. "I wonder if this is why the house on Ninety-Second Street at Fifth Avenue has been boarded up for so long." Robert could hardly keep up with his guest's torrent of anxiety as it poured out. The tension in his own body built to a point where he gripped both arms of his chair, pushing himself back into the wings as if seeking shelter. Without meaning to, he unwittingly braced himself for Lord Alden's onslaught but was unprepared for the strike that came next.

"And is the de Koningh involvement in the war why my own daughter has disappeared? Good God, that must be so!" William Alden exploded, his cup crashing down to balance precariously on the edge of its saucer. He flung himself out of his chair in an explosive leap, staring at Robert as if they were separated by a great deep chasm that neither could cross. "Professor, I have no family to call on and no intimate friend now to lean on for advice. There is only one man to turn to for help where Emily is concerned."

Stunned by his guest's unusual familiarity and the poignancy of his appeal for help, Robert tried to clear the mass of worry over his own role in Emily's discomfort from his mind long enough to be of some support to her obviously disturbed father. "There's no way of knowing where the truth lies," Robert said, pulling himself up from his chair to face his visitor. It seemed Lord Alden was already assuming the worst.

"Of course there is," Lord Alden said. "I find it very hard to believe all Klaas de Koningh's friends in the South would abandon him, and just as hard to believe my daughter has vanished leaving no trail behind." His tone was more straightforward now. "I am not so worried about Klaas, as I witnessed his popularity down there myself when we traveled together, and I often used his contacts and introductions to speed my own work in the South."

"Then your true upset is about—"

"Emily!" Lord Alden hissed at Robert. The strain was apparent in his stance and movement. "I'm afraid she's gone off in search of the de Koninghs. You know she's always had that unnatural connection to the son."

"From my perspective, Lord Alden, it's the most natural relationship in the world. They've been the very best of friends since childhood." Robert moved slowly toward his uninvited guest, careful not to startle or upset him further. "I know where Emily is, Lord Alden," Robert said, quietly. "She's in search of an education, not the de Koninghs' son."

"What?" Lord Alden looked like he'd had a severe blow to the head. "How could you know anything? She abandoned you just as she did me. Has she been in touch with you?"

"I ran into her at the newspaper when I went to find out myself if there was word of the de Koningh family. She was already there.

She'd beaten me to it, as usual," Robert said, ruefully. "We met the man who wrote this piece in the *Times*, but he told Emily he had no information whatsoever. We left none the wiser about the de Koninghs' whereabouts."

"And Emily?"

"She left with me. We went to a café to talk about her plans for the future. You know from your interrogation of me when I returned from Europe that she had not fully explained her desire for autonomy before terminating my employment." Obviously, this was not the time to bring up how shocked, hurt, mystified, and tormented Robert had been over the abrupt ending to his and Emily's tour through Europe. He'd kept his proposal of marriage to himself, since Emily had never taken it seriously. She'd found it humorous while he was humiliated, so she'd clearly been pursuing some plan of her own rather than simply running away from him. Her father must only understand her desire for freedom to have a better feeling for what made Emily move in unpredictable directions.

"She told me that a New England philanthropist is financing her year at a Southern university. He's supporting the institution while the male students have all gone to fight. Emily saw it as an unusual opportunity to get the advanced education she's always wanted. And so it is. Did she hint at none of this?" Robert noticed Lord Alden seemed to shrink, as his shoulders sagged, and his back took on a deepening curve. He was beginning to feel sympathy for the nobleman, who was slowly disintegrating before his eyes.

"We're not on speaking terms," Lord Alden said. "She thinks I betrayed her trust when I hired you to watch out for her. May I . . . ?" he asked, gesturing to the chair Robert had just left.

"Of course, forgive me, Lord Alden. Let me assist you," he said, slipping one arm under his guest's elbow and lowering him gently into the wing chair. "Can I get you some water?"

"No, no, nothing. Thank you. Just tell me you don't think she was right." Lord Alden sank into the chair as if he never intended to leave. He looked at Robert in the most beseeching way, as if pleading for a kind of help Robert hadn't yet offered.

"I can't do that. I do think she was right . . . but you are not the only one to blame. We both betrayed her," Robert said in a low voice. "I should not have allowed myself to get involved."

"But that was my idea, Professor. How could you possibly be at fault?"

Robert took a deep breath and watched Emily's father. If he was ever going to rid his conscience of its burden, this would be the time. Lord Alden might be more impartial than his daughter. Practice on him and be better prepared to deal with her again in the future. He feared Emily had understood his warped motivation before he had himself. Perhaps her father had, too.

"I should not have agreed to take Emily to Europe as her tutor because I had a . . . preoccupation, a romantic fixation with her that I was aware of on some level. I'm deeply embarrassed by my foolishness, but there's the whole of it. I should never have gone to Europe with her under those circumstances."

Lord Alden's face went rigid. "Well, what exactly did you do to my daughter on that trip, Professor? I heard from friends in England and others onboard ship that you were the soul of propriety in public. Is there something more I should know about what went on behind closed doors?" He shook his head as if to clear it of the secrets he was learning. "My daughter mentioned nothing, and I'll have to depend on your rendition of the facts as she's not here to defend herself. Although I doubt she would offer anything conclusive if she thought either your or her privacy was at stake."

"I would never have compromised your trust in me or Emily's, knowingly. I hadn't dealt honestly with my own feeling. That's all I meant, Lord Alden. It was very unprofessional of me."

"Oh, good heavens, Professor. There's nothing wrong with an older man enjoying a fantasy about a pretty young woman now and then. I hardly think you need prepare yourself for the gallows over that!"

Robert sank back down onto the chair his guest had occupied at first. "But don't you see that neither one of us dealt with her honestly? We both lied to her to serve our own ends, no matter how lofty we convinced ourselves they were." He looked down at his long pianist's fingers, wound together in his lap in a tortuous tangle. He was now the tenser participant in the discussion; they had each moved to fill the other's place.

"I disagree, Professor." Lord Alden looked at Robert more levelly than he had since his arrival. "Women need guidance and control," he said, leaning forward toward his host and resting on his knees as he found Robert's eyes and held them with his. Robert realized he was holding his breath in anticipation, but of what, he didn't know.

Lord Alden jumped to his feet in a display of manic energy that had remained hidden until then. "That's why we must go after her now. I'm sure she's in more trouble than she can handle. Where did you say she is?"

Robert's eyes grew suddenly wide under his red brows. "Please calm yourself and listen for a minute, sir," he said, as quietly as he could while still being heard. He stood and took a step toward his guest, laying his hand gently on his shoulder. It was not meant as a restraint, but more as reassurance. Emily's father slipped slowly back into the wing chair, watching to see what was coming next. He didn't have to wait long.

As soon as Robert saw Emily's father seated again, he walked to the piano bench and sat on it backward to face his guest. He felt in charge at the piano, no matter which way he faced. "Lord Alden, I urge you not to follow Emily," he began, knowing full well what he had to say would be most unwelcome. It was time to unravel his own mistakes, spooling them out as if they were lessons he'd already learned and practiced. "She's of age now and quite capable of handling her own decisions," Robert continued. He found it getting easier as he described Emily's strengths. "She's resourceful and bright, and she has enough courage to tame any challenge. If she needs help, she will get it. She doesn't need anyone else to get it for her." He wondered if other teachers were better at handling their own advice than he was.

"How do you know?" her father asked, momentarily breaking into Robert's sermon. But by now, Robert believed in his mission completely. He realized he had known Emily better and longer than her own father, thanks to the widower's early abandonment of her on the de Koningh doorstep. Robert knew he was the man between Emily and all the others. His unique position gave him a new confidence that was much more comfortable than his self-loathing and pity had been. He took a deep breath and faced Lord Alden fully. Even seated, Robert felt larger than his guest for the first time.

"I've watched her since she was thirteen," he said. "She's gifted and determined. If any female can change the way the world works, it will be Emily. Her battles have shown me my own shortcomings. In her quest for personal freedom, she helps to set others free, too—and I don't mean just other women. You should be very proud of her. Let her set her own course."

Robert had never felt as sorry for any man before as he did for Lord William Alden now. He'd only pointed out what the nobleman already knew himself, but acknowledging the truth out loud seemed to have sapped the father's last ounce of strength. Robert was suddenly glad not to be a parent himself. "How can I let her go that way? She's my daughter. She's all I have," Emily's father moaned.

"She'll always be your daughter, Lord Alden," Robert said. "But you have your own life. Emily's giving us all the right to take care of ourselves instead of her. What a great gift that is." He knew it was easy to say when one had no children of one's own, but leaning toward his guest as if to reach out and touch him, Robert looked Lord Alden in the eye. "And that gift is freely given." He paused for a moment to look at his hands in his lap. They were resting calmly, one on top of the other, as they did when he prepared to play the piano.

Then he looked back up at his guest again. "I suggest we both accept it with the grace with which it's offered."

"Don't be ridiculous, Professor," Lord Alden muttered. Straightening up and squaring his shoulders, he looked at his host now with the assurance of a man who's found his way. "Emily knows nothing of the world, other than what we tell her. She's a musician because you made her one. She's an accomplished, well-brought-up young lady because her mother and I saw to it at an early age. She will be what we've made her, and not what she makes of herself. And for that she should be forever grateful to her circumstances."

Robert Haussmann watched Lord William Alden move toward the pocket doors, clearly indicating the visit was over without saying so. Robert knew his view of Emily was the right one, although it didn't appear to her father to be, and knew just as surely that her father's wasn't, although he and the world might consider it the fuller truth.

CHAPTER TWENTY-SEVEN

SEATED ON one of the low benches in the garden next to Emily's college residence, Corey hoped he was at just the right height for the task: cutting his almost shoulder-length blond mane. Everything seemed aligned to produce the desired outcome. The sun had warmed the day already, and no autumn breeze threatened to send Emily's clippings into a whirl. "Don't move, Corey. This isn't going to be easy." Emily stood over him, scissors in hand, staring at his long blond hair through narrowed eyes.

"Why not? Surely just a straight cut." He tossed his hair back with a snap of his head, a young colt in defiance of containment. He squirmed again, knowing he was more uncomfortable because of Emily's intense scrutiny. The hard-stone bench was not the problem.

"You've let it go too long for that. It will expand like parchment in water if I don't shape it. You'll look like one of those characters in *The Magic Flute*!" Emily circled Corey, sizing up her challenge with scissors balancing in her hand as if to weigh their efficacy. "It needs to be cut in layers," she reflected, mostly to herself.

Corey tipped his head a little and looked at her out of the side of his eye. "You always did take a special interest in hair, didn't you, Em? I remember the first time we met; you were outraged at being forced to wear those bouncing ringlets. I thought they were very pretty, mind you." A tiny twitch at the corner of his mouth was the closest thing to a smile he'd made in weeks.

Emily saw it, but pretended she hadn't, possibly to avoid any reference to the original mood she'd found him in when she'd arrived at the university. "I took exception to the outrageous maneuvering to produce those ringlets. I'll bet you thought they were pretty. They were designed to satisfy the male aesthetic, or so women thought, but they had nothing to do with comfort or pleasing the female who wore them, as usual." Her eyes flashed with the spark he'd come to know so well, but had missed too long. The scissors waved with each gesture, punctuating her soliloquy, and Corey pulled back involuntarily to avoid their dangerous trajectory.

"Calm down," he begged, with a little laugh. "I agree. I only meant you're an expert on hairstyles. But how did you learn to cut hair?"

"You sound nervous," Emily teased. "Don't be. I learned in school from some of the servants. Not a skill I was expected to acquire but useful nonetheless, and now I even do my own."

"Your own! How?" Corey twisted around on the bench to look back up at her. "It's so long!" She grinned down at him and started to run her hands through his hair, combing it in place with her fingers.

"It's a secret, but I'll let you in on it since you shared your greatest secret with me."

"I did? What was that?" Corey's questioning eyebrows shot up under his wavy forelock.

"The roof outlook at your home in New York," she answered, smoothing his hair back at his temples. "So, Corey the masterful, my secret is that I've started cutting the front of my hair myself. First just at the top, and then around the sides of my face. As you can see, it curls there when it's short, and no one has really noticed what I'm doing. I've worked it off a bit more every few months, so there's less length to deal with. I just pile the back part up on my head anyway, and no one's any the wiser!"

He turned again, tipping sideways so he could stare up at her. Yes, there were soft wisps of brown curling around her face and her neck, framing her deep, dark eyes and softening what could have been too sharp an outline for her jaw. "Why, you little hussy! You're a clever girl, you are. Cut away, Lady Alden," he added, tossing his own long hair off his face. "I'm in your hands."

"Indeed, you are!" she laughed, turning his shoulders so he had to face forward again. "And now, if you don't uncross your legs you'll have a slant to your haircut, a rakish look suggesting to your concert audiences you've been drinking before performances." His shoulders shook with merriment, imagining the tilting haircut weaving a path toward the piano. Emily slapped him lightly on the back of his head. "Stop that immediately! You risk the loss of an ear if you unsettle your posture all the time." He could tell from her voice above him she was struggling not to laugh. How long had it been since he'd had fun? But she snapped the sharp blades of the scissors together a few times as a threat and a warning, so he sat up straight and still, never sure just how far her teasing might go.

Separating the top and front of his hair from the back with her hands, she started to section off portions at his neck and behind his ears with her smooth, deft fingers, snipping the ends of the hair held in her left hand before taking up a new section. The scissors cut in an even rhythm, with intermittent pauses for Emily to comb through with her fingers what she'd cut to judge the results. The sound of the shears and feel of her hands lulled Corey into a sitting meditation.

The way Emily felt every lock of hair before she cut it reminded him of a blind person reading a text. Her hands were useful; graceful and skilled. They had always astonished him with their child-like delicacy, yet they were surprisingly sure and strong. He sat very still so as not to arouse the wrath of his benign jailor, but also to enjoy this space they both shared. He was reminded of the times they'd lain on the roof in New York, soaking up the heat of the tiles and talking about the latest books and music while she combed his hair with his head in her lap. He stirred a little with recognition.

"Getting tired?" Emily asked, mistaking his movement for discomfort.

"No, but I was thinking of your father. Have you heard from him since you got here?" He saw he was not the only one trapped in place with the haircutting. What better time to try some questions on Emily?

"No," she replied, the sharp emphasis leaving no doubt she expected the questions to end.

"How could that be, Em?" he asked, knowing he was the only one in her life who could get away with pushing her where she didn't want to go.

"We haven't been on speaking terms since I returned from Europe," she said, with a flatness to her voice expressing too much emotion rather than too little.

"Why?" Corey was trying to stay even in both his posture and his tone, but sensed the disapproval he felt showed in both. No matter. She was used to him prodding her on.

"Because he deceived me when he hired someone to take me out of the country without my agreement. Making poor Robert Hauss-mann a party to his plan was also unthinkable. I cannot forgive him." Layer by layer, Emily worked through the narrative of how her father had tried to regain her trust, a move she truly welcomed without question, until he informed her she was being sent abroad to study and travel with Robert Haussmann as her mentor and guide. "We'd been having a nice discussion in the carriage and suddenly he told me he'd decided to send me to Europe with Robert, of all people, whom apparently he hadn't consulted, either. Even if it had been the thing I'd wanted most in life, which it was not just at the time tensions were surfacing over the possibility of war, I'd still have felt the same level of betrayal when I understood I had no say in my own life. I had the horrible feeling he'd planned to put me off guard with charming pleasantries and a tone of inclusion. That made it all the worse."

Knowing every care and emotion forming Emily's character, Corey could easily imagine the desperation she must have felt as she watched her chance at self-determination slip through her fingers. But there was nothing unusual about the control her father tried to hold over her, and the fact that he'd offered her so much of what she'd wanted in the form of a real education was more than laudable. Still, he knew of Emily's fierce pride, honed on the grief of losing her mother and then her father, leaving only herself to count on.

"Oh, Emily," Corey sighed, "your father is the only one you've got. Think of how he's worked to keep you near him. Most single men of his position would have left you off with that maiden aunt and a governess and never thought twice about it. He must have loved you very much to go to the trouble he did. And without your father, you and I would never have met."

"So, I suppose you think he should get away with robbing me of myself, just because he aided, unwittingly I might point out, our meeting as children?" The scissors made a particularly loud snap and Corey jumped. "Sorry," she said. "You have one piece shorter than the rest now, but it's in back so it won't show. Lucky your hair is so wavy and thick. There's nothing worse than fine, straight hair for showing the barber's mistakes."

Corey was silent for a few minutes. Then he took a slow breath. "Em, do you remember me telling you that grown-ups need all the help they can get? We were on the roof together and you were just as mad then as you are now." He didn't wait for her answer. "If I were you, I'd be grateful to have a father I knew was safe, and I'd help him any way I could. You have one, I don't. I want one, you don't. Sounds like a Dickensian predicament if ever there was one."

"Yes, I remember," Emily answered, barely above a whisper. "We were on your roof discussing Mr. Dickens's arrival in New York . . ." Her voice trailed off, so Corey waited to find out where it had gone. "But we're the adults now, Corey," she said with a new firmness. "And I think it's our turn to do the things that matter to us."

"I don't deny that, but you still need to accept compromise, Em. You haven't improved much in that department."

The rhythm of the scissors slowed for a moment, but then picked up again. Emily whispered under her breath, *"Think that he may never have known a mother's love or the comfort of a home."*

". . . that something taught my heart to love so dearly from the first!" Corey echoed back. Emily seemed to drift off silently in thought while still concentrating on her job at hand.

Finally, she stepped out in front to face him. "Not bad." She nodded approval, reaching over to run her fingers through his hair at the top and sides again. "You must feel about five pounds lighter, not that you can afford to lose much weight," she chuckled. "Look at the grass around you. Anyone would think a giant mastodon was groomed here!"

"Thanks a lot. How do I look?" Corey started to pull his shirt out of his trousers.

"Very handsome," she said, uncomfortably. "What are you doing?"

"Even mastodons have to clean up. I'm going to shake this hair out on the lawn."

Emily watched as the man she'd known as a boy pulled his linen shirt off over his head. "Lord, I'm glad I don't have to make your shirts, Corey. How did you get so tall?" She tried not to stare at his shoulders, broader than she'd expected, though awfully thin. "Corey de Koningh, I do believe you're malnourished. Don't they feed you anything here?" She brushed off her dress with more force than necessary, concentrating on the folds of her skirt instead of the smoothness of his skin. Wrapping her scissors up in the cloth she'd brought out, she started back toward the house, but suddenly stopped dead in her tracks.

"Corey, I have a great idea," she said.

"Ye-e-s?" His tone held a wary familiarity.

"You know that problem in the chapel?"

Corey tucked in his shirt and tried to fasten the collar. "Yes. I spoke with Henry yesterday. The problem is his daughter, her husband, and their little girl." He finally got the button done, but the collar was twisted. Emily came back to straighten it for him.

"It's good Henry trusts you, Corey. How long have they been hiding there?"

"A couple of days. He says his granddaughter's had a bad fever and they need to let her recover from their journey, so the time has helped."

"I'm sure; but time can also hurt. The longer they're there, the more likely it is they'll be caught. They need to keep moving, Corey."

"Obviously. But they can't go anywhere now with Confederate soldiers all over the state of Virginia, and civilians all over the countryside, an even worse threat. Henry was quite frantic when he saw Bill with me that day, and now I know why. His family was just about to be smuggled in right under our noses."

"Yes, and that's exactly how they should be smuggled out again!" Emily looked up at Corey, the dimples at each corner of her mouth deepening as the two friends stood with her idea between them. "Do you think you could get dressed now?" she asked with an exasperated shake of her head. "It's hard to focus on Henry's predicament with you half naked in front of me."

"Too distracting," he asked, with a mischievous grin.

"Indeed," she said. "I need all my calmest wits about me. Put your shirt on and let's talk about the next piece of the journey for Henry's family on the Railroad." She worked hard to look at anything other than Corey's engaging grin, trying her best to appear to be thinking very hard on the problem of movement for the slaves in the chapel out of the university campus. Suddenly, her eyes gave a little flash as Corey was tucking his shirt back into his trousers. "Does the headmaster approve of soldiers coming to campus?" she asked.

"I told you, he invites them himself. He thinks music, a good meal, and a beautiful setting will feed their souls as well as their stomachs." He reattached the button closure on his waistband.

"And of course, he's right. Good! I hope he can get every soldier within a few miles of here. We'd need to do it soon—before any more troops are garrisoned in the area, as they surely will be before long."

"Emi, what is this all about?" Corey asked, shrugging his jacket on and running his fingers through his hair again, feeling its unfamiliar length and weight.

"We need to create a diversion, something that holds the attention of as many soldiers and officers as possible. I think a concert could do it. I guess we'd need the Rotunda. There's a stage and plenty of seating. I didn't see a piano, though. We'd have to get them to take this one at the house over for us. Could you work up enough offerings on a musical menu to tempt and satisfy the appetites of the lonely war-wearies with only a short time to do it in? We do need to get the 'travelers' moving as soon as possible."

"I suppose," Corey said hesitantly, "if we all worked night and day. But there are only three of us you could call musicians. Who would perform?" Corey sank back down on the garden bench, the weight of his imagination too much for his legs.

"You, me, the little professor I met at breakfast, and there may be others we don't know about. But if not, then everyone can sing. I mean everyone—gardeners, Henry, cooks, teachers, staff of any and all kinds, children if there are any around, students, and us. The only ones exempt would be Henry's stable boys who'd need to prepare the coach for the escape."

"Escape? Right then? When they're all here?" Corey stared at Emily, his eyes wide with the dawning recognition that her bold plan made a perverse kind of sense.

"When better?" she asked. "The soldiers will be where the escapees aren't. The only people who would stop them from leaving will be a captive audience, so to speak. There's more than one way to hold someone hostage," she said, her dark eyes flashing with a light Corey hadn't seen in too long to remember. How often the challenges that had come from those flashing eyes of hers had put him in the direct path of trouble with the de Koningh house staff, his teachers, even Robert Haussmann. He would have to hold the thought of Emily's eyes on fire all the way to the headmaster's office, in hopes that their heat would revive his resolve when it slipped slowly away under scrutiny.

"On your way then, Corey de Koningh," she said with a grin, reminding him of being sent off to request a special favor of his father for her, a new book from the library or valuable score to be read at night, that he feared would be an outrageous demand. He watched the afternoon sun warm the brick steps and path outside the headmaster's window with soft yellow light, raising the terra-cotta of the patio to a rich burnt umber glow. He felt calm and warm as he reviewed his speech in his head. The commitment he'd made to Emily's plan was complete. Now it was a matter of convincing some collaborators to join them.

It would not be the first time Corey had gotten what he wanted from an unwilling administrator. The teachers in college had not been as eager to cater to his fancies as those he'd grown up with in his home in New York, and he'd learned not to expect automatic capitulation when a request was made. He had to be more convincing and less charming, even when the appeal was for some greater good. He looked out across the beautiful Virginia countryside he could see beyond the campus, and narrowed his eyes as if to glimpse the battlefields in the distance. He felt like the little boy waiting to spring one of Emily's schemes on Professor Haussmann, using all his wiles and influence to get what they both wanted without regard for the risks. Why was he always bargaining for someone else's freedom? Maybe because he had so much of his own. Or maybe he was under Emily's spell. The hammered brass knob started to turn, and the huge polished mahogany door opened, making it impossible to change his mind.

"Master de Koningh!" the headmaster exclaimed, surprised to see an unexpected young faculty member arriving unannounced in his office. "What can I do for you?"

"It's more what I can do for you, headmaster," Corey said, moving smoothly into the room with a radiant smile. He ran his hand through his newly cut hair, mindful of his greater-than-average height making him suddenly awkward with the man who alone could authorize putting his and Emily's plan into action. "I was wondering, sir, if it wouldn't help the poor soldiers garrisoned near here to have a concert given in their honor."

"A concert, Master de Koningh? What kind of concert?" He motioned for Corey to step in closer and close the door.

"Oh, something to lift their spirits and remind them of home and what they're fighting for. Shared music is the best way to motivate people. And there are so many young ones who should be right here in school instead of on the battlefields. Music could help them reorient and feel surer of themselves. Between Professor Meyer, Miss Alden, and me, I'm absolutely sure we could give them the hope they may be sorely missing right now." He seemed to glow with the desire to give these soldiers just these specific gifts. The headmaster smiled broadly, soaking up the optimism and enthusiasm Corey brought with him. "It would be wonderful to help every one of them in the audience. No one should be left out or it wouldn't be . . . fair." Corey watched the headmaster with as much innocent concern as he could show through his guilt at using the soldiers' distress for his own ends.

"Officers and enlisted alike?" the headmaster muttered, and then he smiled and looked up at Corey. "Yes indeed. I like the idea. And I think the commanding officers will, too. But we'd have some work to do getting the word out. Still, I know enough of the officers from the old families, and I could probably count on them to help. It pays to be connected," he said with a wink.

"I felt sure you would be, headmaster," Corey exclaimed, and he continued outlining his plan even as the dinner bell called them both away. "It would start with a gorgeous piano and violin duo with Miss Alden and me—she's performed all over Europe," Corey said as he held the door, "then possibly on to some choral work to make the air vibrate with Professor Meyer, and if you like, I could even lead them all in some southern folk tunes!" he added with growing excitement as they walked down the hall together. "Miss Alden tells me combining popular music with classical is all the rage in Europe these days. It keeps everyone connected, and if they seem very involved," Corey continued as they entered the dining room, "singing all together would be a wonderful way to end it." His blue eyes shone, and the headmaster nodded vigorously.

CHAPTER TWENTY-EIGHT

COREY SAT still at the borrowed piano in the Rotunda, listening carefully. He could hear Emily practicing on her violin somewhere in one of the small oval rooms ringing the circular structure on the second floor. The main domed room he sat in was unlike anything he'd ever been in before. White columns circled the open space rising to Corinthian capitals topping the pillars and supporting the wooden vaulted ceiling. The dome spanned a diameter exactly half that of the Pantheon, he'd been told. Full-story windows circled the entire first floor behind the columns, with one of them serving as the door for an entrance from the lawn outside.

Emily was practicing scales. He'd heard her play them daily as he lay on the couch in the library in New York when they were both children. The notes were soothing in their predictability, floating down in this strange, unfamiliar place designed by Thomas Jefferson to represent, Corey knew, the authority of nature and power of reason, both of which seemed in short supply now. "O judgment! thou art fled to brutish beasts, and men have lost their reason," he chanted softly.

It wasn't the architecture wrapping itself around him that inspired him. As lovely as the building was in its neoclassical order, the irony of the Rotunda's construction had not escaped Corey as he prepared for his concert with Emily to aid the Underground Railroad. Every brick of this spherical building with its ocular skylight in the middle had been laid by the hand of a slave. He hoped they knew, wherever they were, that the concert here would be for them. He put his own hands back on the piano and tried to start one of his own compositions. He hadn't played any of them since he'd performed with his friends at the Artists' Club over a year ago, but the notes and harmonies still lived in their special place in his head.

Encouraged by the strength of these musical connections he remembered so well, he started to run through a few of his part-songs, finding that each one suggested another. Just as he was finishing and about to pull out a score to practice for the freedom concert, as he and Emily had surreptitiously named it, she appeared at his elbow, violin and bow in hand. From the angle of the sun he realized they'd practiced away a few hours and it must be nearing midday. "Is it going well?" she asked. He felt a familiar anticipation that reminded him of the past when he'd led Emily out onto the roof of the mansion.

"It's going beautifully," he answered, realizing he meant it. "It could be the music, or . . . it could be you standing there beside me with your violin, just as you used to." It had been quite a while since he'd been comfortable with that level of honesty. He'd been finding pretexts for his reactions to life lately. Emily's dark eyes held his light ones steadily, and the small dimples in each of her cheeks told him she was as comfortable as he was.

"Or it could be everything," he added. "You . . . me . . . and the music. That's an unbeatable combination." The smile in her dimples spread to her eyes, making him feel whole and sure. How could he have thought she'd ever leave him to marry Robert? He and Emily had lived in each other's heads and hearts since they were children. He knew her too well to have doubted her. "You know, you almost killed me when you ran off to Europe without telling me why," he said, his smile fading. "At least you could have explained why Robert was going with you."

Emily's hand tightened on the neck of her violin at her side. "It's still hard to think about how I tried to hide from Robert's feelings for me, and how I was unable to unwind them on my own. They reminded me of the mess of knitting yarn in my lap at finishing school. I always ended up cutting the string to extricate the knot. I had no patience for a task I wasn't committed to in the first place." She pursed her lips and narrowed her eyes as if to focus better. Corey noticed the violin strings were cutting into Emily's hand, but she didn't seem to mind. He wanted to reach out to touch her fingers and soften her grip; but he held his breath as he saw her about to speak again.

"The abrupt ending to my European tour with Robert came to much the same conclusion, but my shame at not dealing with the confusion better from start to finish made me want to hide the mess." She looked at Corey for a moment and then quickly away again. "It didn't occur to me that sharing it with you might have pointed out . . . the unfairness . . . of both Robert and my father. You often helped me around my worst predicaments when we were children," she added, never making eye contact, but snatching small glances at him and then back to the piano keys. Corey didn't move or make a sound, just watched her, allowing her all the space she needed to work out her tangle. She squirmed as if she needed even more room.

"I should have written you as soon as my father came up with his idea," Emily said softly. "But I was knocked off balance by it, and it had been quite a while since you and I shared every private thought with each other." Now it seemed the floodgates had opened, and she couldn't stop talking. "I wanted to think my father had my best interests at heart, but that fairy tale wasn't real. I guess I've been the one to fantasize, after all. Frankly, I was embarrassed by what he planned for me and wanted to pretend it was as normal as possible. I wish you and I had talked it out before I went." She looked down at her stranglehold on the neck of her violin and softened her grip to balance it in her fingers, letting the blood flow back to their whitened tips. She took a deep breath and smiled a little, forcing herself back to Corey's eyes.

"You used to be the one to fantasize, Corey de Koningh," she said, studying him with her head cocked to one side. "Maybe that's because you're younger than I am."

"Only six months," he reminded her, with a quick wink. "And my emotional maturity makes up for those. While you, Lady Liberty, have never taken enough time to practice the art of empathy for yourself." He'd heard and accepted her explanation of her father's plans for her future, but felt uncomfortable with her acquiescence and failure to reach out to him for help, to trust him, so he couldn't resist a small critique. "It's not where you end up that matters, it's just how you get there and who you've hurt along the way. You ought to consider how your actions affect you and others before moving so fast." Corey looked at her quite sternly, just as he had when delivering his "life lessons" on the roof tiles of the de Koningh mansion.

Emily stared at him without moving. "I don't disagree," she said, quietly, and then she looked off at the view of the soft, green southern landscape. "I've been thinking . . . I don't like the way I've treated a lot of people. I've had trouble letting go of the make-believe of what a 'real' father should be. You were right that I never thought about what he had to deal with when my mother died. I must stop seeing the adults in my life as idealized people I've only dreamed about. But I think something had to die before a new start could be made with my father. I probably owe him an apology, and Robert as well. I know they were both trying to secure the future for me. I'm sure there are many women who would appreciate the support of the older men in their lives, but I've always wanted to do things for myself, including make mistakes. That's not easy to understand." Corey had grown silent sitting on the bench so near her. They were almost at eye level now even though he was seated, and she was standing.

"I understand," he said.

"And I owe you the biggest apology of all, Corey," she continued, resting the violin and bow on the top of the piano and her hand on his shoulder. "I should have known it would matter to you what I did, and that you'd misread Robert's accompanying me to Europe. I should have told you myself. But then again, you should have trusted me, and you were always free to ask me, too. Why did I never hear from you after you went away to school?" She turned her gaze to him with full focus, holding his eyes now. Her face grew solemn. "You seemed to forget me as if I'd never existed." She took a breath, making it clear she wasn't waiting for his explanation.

"You always used to make me feel as if I was fully heard and seen by you when we first met. We used to trust each other completely, Corey, and talked over anything we worried about. Let's not ever forget that again. You see the trouble we can get into without each other!" Her expression had softened again, and she seemed to have regained her comfort now that she'd explained her own hurt.

Corey looked away for a moment, then back at her. "You think we can live in the future the way we did when we first met?" he asked. She nodded and continued holding his eyes with hers. Now he couldn't look away, but let out a deep sigh. It was something he'd not dared to hope for in a long while. "I wonder if there's enough time for us with so many other problems to solve in this world." His focus had changed, and he seemed to be looking right through her to some-place she couldn't see. Was it folly to pretend they were the only people who mattered, with all the pain of the war and his own father still missing? She squeezed his shoulder to bring him back.

"Well, we don't have forever to get this concert ready, Corey," she said, matching her voice to her hand, breaking into his thoughts. "Sometimes you have to act and not think so much." Her smile deepened, telling him she understood his struggle over his father's safety and whereabouts and that the thread of conversation could be picked up again in the future. "I'd like to rehearse our duet together," she said. "I'm worried about the acoustics in this place." Picking up her bow, she waved it in an arc taking in the whole Rotunda and its dome. "We have to test the sound to see how we're going to handle the echo." She placed the bow on the piano again with a finality that made Corey wonder if she was giving up before they'd started.

"The room will be packed with soldiers," he said, weakly. "That will probably help to soften the sound . . ."

Emily shook her head. "Not only are we going to be unable to hear ourselves unless we stand right on top of each other, but our music will never project out to the audience," she added, punctuating the negative with a stab of her bow in her right hand. "We're supposed to keep everyone riveted . . ." she went on with another stab in the air, ". . . so there's no straying around or ducking out for a smoke while we're playing. But I don't see how we're going to hold them if they can't hear us. It's going to get lost up there," she moaned, rolling her eyes up to the dome and clasping the bow and violin together at her side. It seemed a gesture of submission.

A look of grim determination clouded her face and Corey reached out and grasped her free hand, offering reassurance he didn't feel. He'd lain awake worrying about how two young musicians with no experience at espionage were going to assist in a daring escape without getting anyone killed. His resolve was slipping with an ever-increasing momentum, a landslide of doubt and fear taking over where only happiness over finding Emily again had been just a few days ago.

"Corey, what will they do to us if they discover we've helped slaves to escape?"

There it was. The question they'd both pretended would never be asked. But now that she had, Corey steeled himself. For Emily, he could do it. He noticed for the first time that Emily was afraid. He couldn't remember when he'd ever seen that before. There was no one else but him now who could pull her back from that cold threat of panic seeping out to get them both.

"We'll tell them a story they can't resist," he said, squeezing her hand again. "You and I have never had a problem pulling people into our narratives, Em. We're good talkers."

But truly, he had no idea how they'd fare at the hands of angry Confederates. If they weren't spies themselves, they could certainly be called collaborators. Emily seemed to discount his assurances by shaking her head. They were both aware of the consequences for Northern sympathizers who actively undermined the Confederate cause. The evils men were capable of could not be avoided by Emily's and Corey's ages or connections. They were in real danger.

"Corey, the windows in this building encircle the whole circumference and the door is part of that. Anyone looking out can see the whole of the grounds. When is Henry going to take his family from the chapel?" Always practical, Emily tried to move on to the particulars.

"He'll wait until we've just started the second movement of the Brahms," Corey said, dropping his voice, even though there was no one in the Rotunda with them. "All that unrequited love makes the scherzo more than stirring . . . the emotion and passion . . . no wonder audiences can't resist. It's been in constant demand since Brahms composed it." She looked at him as if he was quite mad, the weight of a performance so riveting it blotted out the escape happening right outside the windows seeming too great for either one of them to bear.

"I know, but I wish we had a cello to join us. It is a trio, after all."

"Oh certainly, why not bring one more person into our plot, Emily?" He shook his head as if he thought her the lunatic now. "Good God, no, it's better this way. After all, a piano trio is really three soloists playing their own sound together, as opposed to a chamber music quartet of four people blending so no one stands out. We'll do fine without the cello. It will just be you and me, making something beautiful," he said, smiling at her as he pushed his thick hair back.

Emily returned his smile as if she couldn't resist him any longer. "I have a feeling those poor men will be ripe for a little romance," she said, nudging him with her hip. Corey took the hint. It was time to rehearse, not dream. "But I'm still worried about the acoustics," she said, taking her violin and bow up off the piano again.

"Wait a minute," Corey cried, springing up from the bench suddenly and running to the center of the room. Emily watched as he slowly turned in place and then stopped to face her.

"How do you dampen sound, Em? With fabric!" he exclaimed, unable to wait for her to answer. "And how do you cover windows to block the view? With fabric!" he crowed again, refusing to let her speak. "We can kill two birds at once, Em, by hanging something in the windows to dampen the sound in here and make it impossible to see out as well." Emily's eyes started to widen as she caught up with Corey's thought.

"Unfortunate choice of words, Corey. All that hanging and killing of birds does little to reassure me!" Her shining dark eyes had the same snap in them Corey had admired when she'd come dancing into his life at the age of thirteen. "Where will we get that much cloth, and how will we cut it to order in a few hours?" she asked. Corey ran to her and spun her around twice in place like a toy top, with her violin and bow still clutched in her hands.

"There are literally tons of cloth just the right size around here," he grinned down at her.

"Where?"

"All over the campus," he said, obviously delighted with himself.

"I haven't seen any," Emily said, looking at him now with something more like suspicion than admiration.

"Yes, you have," Corey contradicted. "See over there on the wall? There are flags of the Confederate states hanging everywhere in this place."

"Good heavens," Emily said, rising a little to see better. "It looks a lot like the Austrian flags I saw in Vienna," she exclaimed. "That must have been chosen while I was away. I've not seen it before."

"You're right." Corey nodded. "And not so strange it should look familiar, because an Austrian woman who lives in the South designed it and the Confederate uniforms! Europe keeps injecting itself in our affairs," he grumbled, moving off toward one of the flags for a closer look. "How many stars does that one have? Looks from here like nine. I think there are thirteen in total now, so they haven't had time to update these with all the secessionist states."

"So, if they're an older version they won't mind if we take them all down to enhance our own décor, right?" The look of fear was finally gone from her eyes. It made Corey feel as if he'd fulfilled his responsibility to lift Emily's mood, perhaps more important to him even than the pending escape. In truth, Emily was almost all he'd been thinking about for the past week.

"I can get the staff to collect enough of the Stars and Bars to get our job done," he reassured her. "And no one will question our need to control the sound in a bare room with a ceiling this high while we 'decorate' to welcome the Confederate soldiers. We can give them a song and dance about the light coming through the flags to make them seem more ethereal." His eyes danced in a way Emily hadn't seen since he'd led her on merry chases through the de Koningh mansion when they were young. She remembered the way his jacket had flapped around him then as he'd pranced into her room, his fine, blond hair, longer than it should have been, bouncing around his little velvet collar.

"Not bad, Corey de Koningh," she said, slowly nodding her head. "And I think I've just solved another problem." She turned around to face the door. "You know those damask screens in the dining room with birds on them?" Corey watched her inquisitively for a moment, and then suddenly started to smile again. "Yes, I see you're with me. If we arrange the 'stage' where we want it, the screens can be placed behind us like a fan, ostensibly to focus our own playing more narrowly so we can hear each other and send the sound out directly to the audience . . ." Corey's smile grew broader. "But in fact, the screens can be placed so they block the door. Since the room is round there's no problem arranging the chairs to face that way, and when the entire audience of soldiers is seated, we can put the screens up. The door will be blocked and covered just the way the windows are. We're brilliant, Corey!" she exclaimed, running to him and gesturing for him to lower his head to hers so she could throw her arms around his neck. He slipped his arms around her waist and lifted her gently off the ground. The tall, blond pianist and small, dark violinist clung to each other in the middle of the Rotunda, aware of nothing else.

He liked how strong his arms felt as he held her and how petite, almost doll-like, her waist still was, just as when they'd first met when she was only thirteen. But he could feel a softness and round-ness to her he'd never experienced before holding the pretty young socialites of his Harvard college days. He realized there were none of the usual rigid underpinnings, no corset forcing the waist into a smaller-than-natural circumference, and the thought that his hands were very nearly on her skin, instead of layers of whale bones and petticoats, made his heart pound uncontrollably. How happy he was with his arms holding her easily against him in the air, and how thrilling it was to find her returning his embrace just as firmly.

A long, slow kiss seemed to come from nowhere and everywhere at once, as if they'd been doing it all their lives. But he was aware that it was unlike anything he'd ever felt before with either the daughters he knew of the New England elite or the prostitutes of Boston's best brothels. He'd always known there must be more, something much deeper and more affecting, as he'd felt it vicariously in the music he loved to play so much. This kiss with Emily seemed to gather its energy from the core of a deep, caring, and vulnerable connection neither one of them had ever been able to duplicate, but had never questioned, either. It was entirely about trust and sharing and love. Finally, they parted, neither one looking as if they had any intention of separating for long.

"Good heavens!" Emily breathed into his neck. "And that was certainly brilliant. Why did we wait so long? Had I known a kiss could bring that much feeling I'd have done better with the little ones we started on the roof of your home all those years ago." Her eyes held a warm promise of closeness to come. "But perhaps we weren't ready then. Everything in its time!"

"I'd say we're both brilliant," Corey laughed, a bit dazed as he lowered Emily gently to the floor and she finally let him go. "There's an awful lot going on suddenly, and no time to sit back and think about it as you know I prefer to do." He smiled at her, knowing she understood him perfectly. He need say no more now about their unexpected physical connection.

"It's a good plan we've come up with," he said, knowing again she'd understand and appreciate the shift back to work they must do together. "I hope the soldiers will be as cooperative as the students and staff," he muttered, slowly backing up to the piano and lowering himself onto the bench. "Everyone needs to stay here at least through those first two movements of the Brahms. Once Henry's family has fled in the carriage, he'll come back and give us the all clear, but I want the audience to stay longer," Corey added. "I'd like a margin of safety to give our travelers a head start."

"The soldiers won't leave before the chorus at the end." Emily looked as sure as if she'd already heard the concert's finale. "We can explain at the beginning how we're going to have the choir of faculty and students sing Mozart's 'Lacrimosa.' I spoke to Professor Meyer about it. He says there are some local singers who work with the choir coming, too. It's going to be irresistible!"

"A crushing requiem, Em? Do you think that's appropriate when we're trying to lift the soldiers' spirits?"

Emily sat on the bench beside him. She put her hand on his knee and looked into his eyes. "I've never heard a piece of music more uplifting in my life," she said, without looking away or letting go of his gaze. "Mozart found a way to let people weep to be healed."

"How?" he asked, very quietly.

"I'd rather let the requiem tell you. It's so hard to explain a piece of music or describe a painting to someone else. They're better experienced in person."

"But why a requiem, or why this one? Why Mozart's?"

"Because this movement seems so uniquely right for these soldiers. Hearing it in St. Stephen's sent me almost into a faint." She grabbed her arm and started to rub it, as if to bring herself back from someplace else. "It starts with a low, distant swell of music and voices," she began. "They rise and fall, come into view and disappear again in a trough between the waves of sound, moved entirely by the ebb and flow." She started to rock silently to the music in her head. "It just takes you over." Corey watched her listening to something in her head as if she was in a trance. She was always so present, so fully and energetically engaged in whatever place she inhabited unless she was listening to music. Then she went somewhere else.

"I know exactly what you mean," Corey said, sitting up straighter. "Often, I have no idea where I'm going when I compose something. I worry that I'll drift too far if I don't take control, but just letting go is most important, like not fighting a current. It's why I love composition more than anything. You must let your feelings do the writing and then you have something worthwhile at the end, and you've learned something about yourself, too."

"But there are some feelings you shouldn't think about too hard after all," Emily said, with a soft smile. She moved closer to him on the bench until they touched. "I've missed our talks, Corey. How would you write music to describe the sensation of sharing feelings with someone?"

"Now you're making fun of me," he laughed, nudging her shoulder a little with his elbow. "That's all music ever does."

"How good it will be to work with you again," Emily said, "and I hope, good for Henry's family, too. Though I admit I'm scared to death about this whole plan. I don't think I'm cut out to be a spy after all. Being in this room with all those soldiers will be like being caged with the very thing I want to escape. I felt brave when I was desperately searching for you, but now that we've found each other I don't want to risk anything at all. And we won't get a second chance to free Henry's family, either. I don't want to lose you, or us, or them. I don't think I can do this, Corey." She gripped her skirt to stop her hands from shaking.

"Stop talking a minute," he said, to slow the momentum of the fear that was taking her over. "We can escape the cage with our music," he added, without hesitation. "I don't mind telling you I'm scared, too. I haven't slept for days just worrying about it." He shifted on the bench uncomfortably. "And I understand how much harder it is to take chances when there's so much to be lost. But I guess that's the true test of courage, Em. And that's something you've always had."

He bent and kissed the top of her shining dark head. "I think there are lots of people like us in this war. People who've never fought anything or prepared to be brave who've been forced into it." She tipped her head back for another kiss, pulling his head down to hers unexpectedly. He offered no resistance even though he was caught off guard. He decided he could enjoy this one a little longer, as the last had only left him wishing it hadn't been over so soon. It was important to get lost this time, becoming entirely wrapped up in the strange feeling of being outside himself while exclusively with Emily. Some of their long talks had given him much the same joy, but they'd never shared a physical pleasure of this magnitude.

"Remember what you used to tell me on your roof, Corey?" she asked, finally pulling back to look into his eyes. She sat with her shoulders square, chin level, her gaze holding his with the intention of assurance. "You'd make me sing from *The Marriage of Figaro* and tell me not to look down until I got to the other side of the steep, slippery slate roof tiles," she prompted. "Fill your mind with the music, you'd say. So now I say the same thing. Don't look down and before you know it, Henry's family will be free, and we'll be planning our own future at last."

"Well, not really." He looked away, out the window to the rolling, still-green lawn. "I don't think we should stay here after this."

"Why?"

"Don't look down, Em. We'll talk it over later, after the concert," Corey said, sounding very tired. "Let's just get through this first."

⁂

Water, lemonade, sandwiches, and fruit arrived for their lunch soon after courtesy of Henry, who looked far cooler and more collected than they felt. Assuring Emily and Corey that his family was well and poised for flight, he omitted the fact that Mr. Smith's carriage had not yet arrived on campus. It was an extra strain these young people didn't need, there being no possible way they could control its arrival.

Corey described their idea to cover the windows and door with the flags and screens, and after reviewing the timing on the start of the second movement of the Brahms piano trio, Henry explained that he'd slip away from the audience down the back hall used for deliveries. He smiled a little as he assured them he'd learned long ago to leave and enter a room silently and without being noticed. He parted from them to help collect the Stars and Bars around the campus and bring the screens from the dining room.

Young appetites always at the ready, they consumed the picnic lunch Henry had thoughtfully prepared for them. They spent the rest of the afternoon playing the piano trio with special attention to the second movement that would need to bring the composer's heart-stopping passion to every person in the Rotunda. "A little less pounding there, please," Emily begged, more than once. Corey knew he got carried away with the music from time to time, and he'd forgotten what it was like to play with a violin needing support, not subjugation.

Finally, they had to admit there was no more to do; they'd both have to change clothes and try to find that stillness inside their heads for a little while before the performance. They prepared to separate, with a worried look and a kiss, taking the same path they'd return on in less than an hour, just as Professor Meyer came trundling down it toward them.

"Oh my, our two young performers!" the professor exclaimed eagerly, reaching out both of his hands to them. "I was hoping to see you before the concert. How did rehearsal go? What do you think of all this craziness on campus?" he continued without waiting to hear what they had to say. "I started noticing the noise of the soldiers coming a few hours ago. And you see how they ride across the lawns and trample the flower beds? The campus will never be the same." He shook his head, looking utterly discouraged. Emily couldn't resist thinking that much more than just the flower beds would never be the same, but said nothing.

Still, now that they were outside the Rotunda, it was impossible to ignore the horses, wagons, and messily uniformed foot soldiers beginning to stream across the grounds. Some were dressed in gray coats with blue trousers, while others were in a scruffy beige getup that looked more like potato sacking than cloth. Emily stared at the worn-looking troops, wondering how they'd last if the war took longer than expected. Some men clutched guns or swords, others packs of who knew what—food or ammunition, with blankets twisted around their upper bodies, traveling with their essentials attached to their chests. They reminded her of the pictures of nomads roaming the desert, more like the persecuted than the pursuers.

Combatants of a different sort, Corey hugged his big book of sheet music and Emily clutched her violin case in a desperate embrace. "They make me very nervous, Professor," Emily admitted.

"It's the first time I've worried about the safety of my violin since I arrived on campus. You don't think they'd hurt it, do you?" It was not a question she sought an answer to.

The three musicians parted to go their separate ways, all engaged in thoughts they preferred not to acknowledge. Emily lost herself in the routine of dressing. She had only three costumes with her, and this was the only one in a silk fabric with the reflective sheen she wanted for the stage. The top she'd chosen, also of silk, had a low-cut neckline with gathered fabric that just skimmed the tops of her shoulders to leave her arms free. Corey whistled his approval of her plunging neckline and bare arms when he saw her, assuring her southern men were well used to and appreciative of feminine charms displayed that way—but perhaps just not on a public stage, she feared.

She could hardly account for the minutes that sped by before she found herself back in the Rotunda again. Once there, she and Corey stood off to the side of the room together, trying not to look too hard at the soldiers packed into the space, many standing in what had become the back of the room due to the unusual placement of the chairs to face the door. Ten semicircular rows with forty chairs in each and an aisle down the middle created a theater in the round that felt surprisingly intimate. Later, neither Corey nor Emily could account for a single impression of the faces before them, just the sea of gray, framed by Confederate flags with the low-angled afternoon light shining a ring around each one where they didn't completely cover the windows. They were relieved that nothing could be seen of the outside through the small spaces left around the Stars and Bars.

Corey purposely avoided searching for Bill in the crowd, and Emily recited Robert Haussmann's mantra under her breath: Don't lose focus. Nothing and no one else matters but you and the composer. She knew nothing of spies other than that she didn't want to be one. She was a violinist, and she and Corey were a duo who were going to have the first professional performance together in their lives. Neither one of them could ever have guessed when they were children that it would be here in front of a room full of enemy soldiers. The remarkably tall, blond, graceful young man and small, dark, intense young woman made a curious sight together, but they felt instinctively that would identify them as special. It would be a good way to ensure audiences would remember them in the future. They were noticeably unusual, as much for the audacity of Emily's solo position as for their appearances.

There was still no real acceptance of ladies standing at center stage and lifting their arms to play a violin in public. Audiences were only just beginning to welcome female pianists and singers performing for pay. Somehow a determination had been made that women playing instruments usually handled by men were unwomanly, and doing so for remuneration was demeaning and unseemly. Corey had told her he enjoyed the special attraction of her exceptional skill and beauty, both of which made it impossible for the audience to deny her its full attention. She drew an extra interest he might not be able to get on his own, and he provided her legitimacy, she knew. They each got what they needed from the other, which felt wholly natural.

Emily investigated the dome of the Rotunda as the headmaster announced the concert, welcoming the soldiers and everyone else. He described the program, naturally making much of the Virginia chorus that would assist Professor Meyer with Mozart at the end of the performance. For once, Emily was grateful not to be the center of attention. Watching the headmaster's mouth move as he spoke, she couldn't grasp what he was saying about the history of the campus; something about the third president of the United States and the room they were in, but it was all a muffled blur in her head. Then she felt Corey tap her hard on her leg buried in folds of the cream-colored skirt she'd chosen for the performance.

". . . this is your home in more ways than one now," the headmaster was saying. "Your officers have decided to billet here indefinitely. The school will currently have to cease operating as an academical institution . . ." And as a safe house for the Underground Railroad, Corey and Emily were thinking when they glanced at each other.

"Oh, Corey," Emily whispered. "There goes my college education again. Just as I thought I had it within reach." She leaned against him, his long torso supporting her.

"See Henry over at the back of the room?" he muttered into the top of her head. "Remember to look for him at the end of the first movement, and then again by the end of the second." Emily straightened up and searched for Henry's white head and starched black suit against the rows of disheveled gray cloth, and there he was. Looking placid, and engaged in the speech, he never let his eyes stray from the headmaster and the front of the room. His calmness helped Emily get back to her own quiet place.

Unexpectedly, she felt Corey put his hand at her waist, encouraging her with a gentle pressure in her back as if to lead her politely in a dance. She stepped forward instinctively and they both kept moving to the front of the room. The piano stood at the apex of the triangle made by the pale silk screens with birds embroidered on them, a lovely backdrop framing the musicians and instruments. Emily was pleased now with her choice of the cream silk dress, which mirrored the screen's background. She could feel the welcome relief of a long-practiced routine take over as she and Corey bowed, smiling first to the audience and then to each other. There was a confident, almost carefree expression on Corey's face that gave her all the comfort she needed as they stood side by side, center stage in front of the piano, with Corey just slightly behind her. She returned his smile to him and the audience again, thanking them silently for their applause of welcome and him for his backing.

Corey seated himself at the piano, his long, thin torso slipping effortlessly into place as if a magnet drew him there. He rested his hands in his lap as Emily tightened the hairs of her bow and prepared to test her strings. She remembered it was important to quiet the audience and ground them to her and Corey, so she tried to make her tuning a part of the overall performance, as Robert Haussmann had taught her to do. She knew her strings were undoubtedly still per- fectly pitched—she'd checked them before entering the room—but tuning again would be a good opportunity to let the soldiers look her over and decide she was worth spending time with, at least visually. There were so many deficits women were considered to have and rebuffs they had to endure in practicing an art form publicly, she might as well fully use the natural advantage of her figure and looks. The stir in the audience, evidence of their surprise that a woman was playing for them, drove her to work harder to attain their approval. The appreciation for her music might have to come later.

She turned sideways so she could hear the piano better, and the men could see her better, too. Corey pressed the middle C key gently twice, and then the A. She played the A string continuously with a long stroke, satisfied with the sound, and moving on to the D, G, and then the E strings. She worked always from below the note up, adjusting the corresponding peg from low to high, and then eventu- ally played the A and D strings together, listening for the perfect fifth interval to ring in tune. Then she played the D and G strings together, followed finally by the A and E. Wanting to be sure she heard the true pitch of the notes, she closed her eyes and tilted her left ear toward the F holes. She knew she made a pleasing picture because she'd seen her reflection in the mirror when she practiced, and understood it was even more important to her performance than usual for this strange audience of mostly men traumatized by war. The role of an appealing, accomplished performer was one she had to step into now that she was an adult. You're not just a charming little girl who can play the violin anymore, Robert told her before she'd left for finishing school. He was right, but she hadn't been ready to admit it then. It was time to become that woman who could play the violin better than most men.

She took a deep, calming breath and nodded at Corey. She intended to travel with him from the first soaring notes to the final awe-inspiring ones. She stopped thinking and started feeling. Before she knew it, she and Corey were finishing the first movement, the Allegro con Brio, with all the liveliness it demanded. It was a great crowd-pleaser always, and she could tell the men were fully carried along with it. Some of them even clapped. Without meaning to, Emily looked out over the room and saw Henry slip away at the back. With his disappearance, she knew they were under pressure to delay and drag out the performance. She glanced at Corey with a nod, tucked her violin under her arm, and gestured for the soldiers to quiet down. It took the better part of a minute for them to believe she truly expected them to be silent.

"The breaks between movements are like chapters in a book," she said, smiling out over their heads as if they were all music students. "If you applaud between movements it breaks up the feeling of the whole piece, as if someone started talking to you just when you want to go on with the next chapter in your book."

Many of them nodded and laughed. "Never read a book like this one," someone called out. "Nor heard music with a fiddle that sounds like singing," another voice joined in. "Never saw a lady like you playing like an angel on stage, neither," a third yelled over the others, while the whole audience laughed, and sporadic bursts of applause started up again.

Seemingly unruffled by the outbursts, Emily smiled apprecia- tively and continued. "So please, if you don't mind, there are three more movements in this piece and we and Mr. Brahms, the com- poser, would be so grateful if you could hold your applause until we've finished his whole story." Smiling most attractively as she singled out one or two men in the first row for eye contact, she lifted the violin again and put it under her chin while the bow was poised to join its partner.

The second movement could not have been played better than it was by the two of them together. Corey held back his sound a bit even though the notes read forte, and Emily played as energetically as was required, with the nuanced intonation that gave color and warmth to the light scherzo movement. Both were visibly aware of and in touch with the other's presence. For all of Emily and Corey's consciousness of their looks before the audience, they were unconscious of the power of their personal attraction and what that chemistry did to enhance their performance. It was hard for those who didn't know them to tell if the vibrations came from the music or the two young musicians playing it. But before they knew it, the second movement was ended, and the performers had to take a few quieting breaths. Emily touched her forehead with the handkerchief she always kept between her chin and violin. She could tell Corey understood she needed to catch her breath and quiet her pulse before starting up again. Finally, she looked at Corey and nodded to show she was ready to begin the third slow, adagio part.

But the expression on his face made her freeze. He wasn't looking at her, but out over the audience in the direction of Henry's pre-chosen position. She opened her stance a little to follow his eyes, and saw that Henry wasn't back. She calmed herself, carefully and deliberately, as if her playing partner wasn't ready to begin, which in truth, he wasn't. She didn't let her mind go to all the things that might have kept Henry away, because they were out of her control. She prepared herself with slow breaths and watched only Corey, finally turning her back almost fully to the audience. At last Corey lifted his head to indicate it was time to begin, although she could see he was not happy. They played through the rest of the third and fourth movements with all the passion, love, and optimism the composer had written into his piece, finishing as they'd begun, with their hearts in full view. No two performers could have made a more passionate, convincing portrait of Johannes Brahms's romantic soul.

Thundering applause greeted the ending, and as Corey stood to join Emily for their bows, she took his hand and they lowered their heads in unison, linked together. When they raised their eyes to the room, they saw caps flying in the air and heard the men stamping their feet in approval. Much of the scene seemed far away and mixed-up in their senses, but the feelings were all good. They tried to leave the stage but were called back twice by the soldiers' ovation. Finally, they walked down the side of the room. Professor Meyer passed them with wet eyes, on his way to assemble his chorus on stage for Mozart's gorgeous "Lacrimosa." "Lovely, you two. Just perfect," he sniffed. Squeezing Emily's bare shoulder and kissing her on both cheeks, he then continued to the stage muttering, "Lovely, lovely . . ."

"What happened?" whispered Emily, seeing Corey's attention was still directed to the empty spot Henry was meant to be filling at that moment.

"No idea," he said, grimly, "but I'm going to find out. Stay here. Don't join the chorus, in case I need you." He quickly left the room by a small side door Emily hadn't noticed before, nodding and thanking a few soldiers who reached for his hand as he passed. No one tried to delay him. But there was no sign of Henry during the "Lacrimosa," and Emily's legs had started to feel weak. She leaned against the wall for a while until a flood of relief washed over her with such intensity she felt dizzy when she spotted Henry returning behind Corey. She looked up at her partner with a question in her eyes as he left Henry to come stand with her.

"The carriage broke a wheel," he whispered. "It was a half-hour late. They're just off. We need more time."

"But the chorus is finished," she cried out, a little more forcefully than she'd intended. "What shall we do?" She turned away to look at Henry, then turned back, but Corey was suddenly gone, bounding to the stage in front of the audience alone. The singers and their delighted chorus master looked at him in surprise, wondering what was going on, as did everyone else in the room.

"There are so many different ways to use song for support," Corey said to the crowd, bowing to the chorus as he did so. Emily thought his tall, elegant form seemed as pleasing to everyone now as it had at the Artists' Club so long ago, when she was in the audience with her father and Robert Haussmann.

"Singing, especially together, makes people happy, brings them peace, and soothes their souls. I've always felt the human voice is the most beautiful instrument of all. And so now, I'd like to sing one of the South's favorite melodies and would be delighted if you'd join me," he added, reaching out to the audience as if to hold everybody's hand at once. Then he dropped his head and raised it again, starting the familiar lyrics a cappella, "Oh, I wish I was in Dixie . . ." His clear, energetic voice slowed the chorus to the popular song in a mournful, nostalgic call to the life Southerners held dear. Verse after verse continued, most of them unknown to Emily, and it took a few before the men would slow down to match Corey's romantic rendition instead of the hearty jingle they were used to.

She noticed there were soldiers who'd stopped singing quietly along, so probably they didn't know the verses either, but they swayed in place to the haunting melody she'd taken scant notice of in its up-tempo form. Suddenly she saw a few of them at the end of their rows moving to the Confederate flags in the windows as they sang, and to her horror, they started to take the flags down and hold them above their heads as they sang. She almost choked from fear but glancing to the back of the room in clear panic—luckily unnoticed by the chorusing soldiers—she saw Henry was smiling calmly and nodding at her, a sign that his family was well enough away to be unseen through the windows. She looked at Corey on stage and saw he'd crumpled against the piano, undoubtedly at the same moment her own panic took hold when the flags came down.

Finally, the last verse, a repeat of the first, led to the last chorus, and Emily looked around the room, finding many were in tears after the final "look away, Dixie Land." No one moved, which was exactly what she knew Corey wanted. Turning to find Henry in the back of the room, she spotted his glorious head of hair like a cloud of white cotton and saw a small smile on his face. He caught her watching him, dipping his head again in confirmation. She started for the front of the room to collect Corey from Professor Meyer's rapturous grasp, and to ensure that he, too, had seen Henry's affirmative nod. The three of them clung happily together, the professor enveloped in the ecstasy of beautiful music and Emily and Corey in the headiness of relief. None of them had the strength to hide their feelings any longer.

CHAPTER TWENTY-NINE

EVENINGS WERE coming faster now in late November, sneaking up on afternoons, with long shadows stretching across the porch and down the brick path to Emily's lodging at the edge of the old Virginia campus. Each day seemed to rush forward leaving the autumnal equinox well behind, and only three days after Emily and Corey's concert, the chill morning air had turned to cold afternoons and night air with a bite. No longer supported by the buoyancy of their performance and praise from soldiers and college staff moving around the campus, Corey and Emily were happy to collapse on the veranda, unable even to dump themselves in the white rocking chairs arranged along the front like watchful grandparents.

Sitting on the top step with her knees tucked up under her chin, Emily wrapped her skirts around her shins and closed her eyes, reliving the moment at the end of the concert when Corey had started to sing "Dixie." He'd been in complete command of the stage, gathering all sense and emotion from the audience around him. At that moment her fatigue from performing, combined with fear for Henry's family, made her feel she'd passed beyond some barrier that usually protected her from total collapse. She was sinking fast. Then Corey's strong, clear tenor voice had picked her up with such power she knew it was the thrilling sustenance she wanted to count on for the rest of her life. They'd accomplished so much together, each there for the other when needed, and it had been performing in the

Rotunda that had made her realize what it was to work with a collaborator rather than an accompanist. There was much more between them than just the music. They had full trust in each other. They were a great team.

Her eyes still shut, the sweetness of remembering that moment allowed her to let go of her last remaining tension, slowly becoming aware of the fullness of the southern evening air. "What's that glorious fragrance?" she asked. "It's surprisingly sweet for this time of year." She rocked back and forth almost imperceptibly to soothe her weariness. Sitting two steps above Corey, she could feel his presence even without looking at him. She knew he was as drained as she was, sitting against a bottom step as if he wanted to melt into it. One of his long legs was stretched out on the ground for ballast, the other bent for support. His eyes were shut.

"That's the sweet olive," he sighed. "It blooms all year long down here, I'm told."

"Where is it?" Emily asked, not opening her eyes to see. "It smells like it's everywhere."

Corey squinted so he could peer across the lawn, then shut his eyes again and let his cheek rest against the column. "It's tucked away in the far corner of the garden, and it's just one," he told her. "You can smell it from over a hundred feet away, but it doesn't look like much of anything—just shiny, tough green leaves and little nondescript white flowers."

"Looks can be deceiving," Emily laughed, "as you and I know from that performance we gave the other day. We both seemed like two musicians with nothing on our minds but our concert. I'm sure even what little nervousness we showed was believed to be about our professional debut. Talk about deception!" Emily was silent again, taking a deep breath that seemed to travel the length of her compact feminine body.

"That tree could certainly mark the entrance to paradise with such a heavenly fragrance," she said, looking down on Corey's blond head from her perch on the top step. "You've certainly lived up to your name this week, Maestro de Koningh." She smiled at his peaceful expression, running her fingers through his unruly hair, curving it across his forehead and out of his eyes. It wasn't necessary, since his eyes were closed, but she wanted him to know she was there as much as she wanted to touch him herself.

"How so?" Corey asked, without opening his eyes. His half-smile said the trust they shared on stage still permeated him, body and soul.

"Your performance the other night, and all week for that matter, has been fit for a king," she assured him. "I know how hard it was to concentrate on Henry and his family when you were afraid for your own father, and me, and yourself, but you did it. You had to present the plan to the headmaster and then implement it, coordinating all the rest of the faculty as well as your panicked partner on stage. And through all that, you kept your sights on Henry and the escape, always working on the safest way to make it happen."

Corey opened his eyes, sitting up straight and turning to reach back for her hand. He kissed her palm inside its curve. Pulling it down to his chest and holding it there, he said to her, "The escape plan was as much yours as mine, and you've lived up to your name this week as well," he assured her in a firm voice.

"How?" she asked.

"Alden. It means *old friend*, does it not?"

"I don't know." She gave him a tired smile. "I never thought about it."

"Well, I made it my business to find out, just as I promised I would when we first met. And I can assure you, Alden means *old friend*, though I never had the chance to tell you. If there was ever a week that showed me what you are, this was the one." He held on to her hand and watched the two dimples at either end of her mouth deepen as her eyes began to shine. "Actually, the plan was entirely your idea, and whenever I lost heart, no matter the reason, you were there propping me up."

"I've never known such a challenge to keep men's attention," Emily chuckled.

Corey laughed to himself, remembering how Emily had continuously moved and changed her position on stage so all the men could appreciate her beauty. "By the way, where did you learn to show yourself off that way, my friend? It was a new Emily I don't think I've met before. I fell in love with you out there, just as all those men did." His eyes flashed as he nudged her knee with his shoulder to make sure he had her full attention. "Had I met her on the roof of our house in New York all those years ago I probably would have fallen to my death!"

"There's the romantic in you, Corey," Emily teased. "Just like Schubert, you find the balance in every relationship, tie up the loose ends, and bring everything back to its beginning again. I'd forgotten your promise to find out the meaning of my name when we met."

He half-closed his eyes looking up at her through his lashes. "But did we ever guess back then that we could be so much more than friends? I think we knew. It's been many years, and there's certainly been some excitement along the way with you, Em." Corey frowned dramatically and shook his finger at her. "I've almost drowned more than once in the riptide of changing keys and tempos of your emotions." Then he relaxed his face and smiled.

"Here we are," Emily said, returning his smile, "back to almost the same shore we started from. We're good together, Corey," she added. "We speak the same language in so many ways. When we go back up north, let's start to work together! I've always had such a craving to perform, but it's still so hard for a woman alone to do that in any publicly acceptable way. Playing for private audiences isn't enough for me. I want to be a professional violinist and you and I could break that barrier together where I might never do it alone."

"You and Herr Mozart," he laughed, shaking his head. "It's not good enough to conquer an instrument or compose the best music on earth, you still have to perform. I'm truly not all that sure it's my help you need to get where you want to go, Em," he said, looking worried. "It's too bad you're not on good terms with Professor Haussmann anymore. You could use his support getting your career launched." He was surprised by how easy it was now to say Robert's name without the painful rebound of jealousy that had kicked him in the past few months. "But Em, it may be nearly impossible for you to perform in public with the acceptance and respect you want and deserve."

"I refuse to think that way, Corey," Emily said, the old fire he was so familiar with flashing in her eyes. "Anyway, Robert and I are on good terms," she insisted, reclaiming her hand to push some loose dark curls in her eyes away from her face as the November wind picked up. "We met after our return to New York and talked out most of our misunderstandings. I always felt it was my father's fault Robert was involved in what amounted to my abduction, but in many ways, I only made things worse."

"How do you figure that?" Corey tilted his head back to look at her, surprise in his eyes.

"Oh, I suspect I was feeling the power of my newfound woman-hood rather strongly, and I used it to taunt and tantalize him, knowing full well I was making him miserable." Corey stiffened noticeably against the pillar, but watched Emily in silence. "I wish you'd seen him scrambling after me in the Alps, fully appreciative of the looks of my new climbing britches but unable to keep up with my newfound freedom of movement. I suppose handicapping young women with outrageous hobbling clothing is the only way older men could catch them in the past," she giggled.

Corey laughed as well, having no trouble picturing Emily leading Robert on to danger, just as she had a young Corey at the de

Koningh mansion. "I doubt the Alps could offer you anything in the way of challenges after the steep pitches of the mansion roof at the age of thirteen," he said admiringly.

"Oh, no! The mountains were breathtakingly difficult. I'd certainly never experienced anything in the natural world like those peaks or that weather moving so fast around them. But I'll see Robert always," Emily went on, clearly enjoying herself, "clinging to a rock ledge in panic, but unwilling to go back to the hotel without me. He was crippled with soreness the next day, completely unable to leave his room. That was when I met Mr. Barnes by chance at breakfast in the hotel lobby and learned of the plan to send women to the University of Virginia. I knew instinctively to grab at that opportunity while I was on my own without Robert."

"That doesn't sound like a friend," Corey scolded. Robert had no chance against Emily's will and creativity. Her father, too, had seriously underestimated her, something Corey felt he'd never done and was unlikely ever to do.

"I told Robert he just got in the way of my rage over what I saw as the unfairness of my life." She seemed too uncomfortable now to look at Corey. He noticed her change of mood and asked her what she meant. "Robert has so many of the old-world inhibitions," she explained, quietly. "He seems to provoke me without even trying. Still, I think we parted friends in New York after all. I think he wants what's best for us. We can count on him to help, I'm sure."

Now Corey looked doubtful, a frown giving away his unintentional discomfort over Robert's connection to both of them. "Perhaps . . . with our music careers. I don't doubt he'd be polite to me when we see each other again, but we'll need a lot more support planning our working life together than he can give. And you must accept that people feel slighted by your treatment of them sometimes, Lady Liberty. Robert may not be so quick to rally to our cause. It's one thing to help you, and quite another to help us." His warning was followed by silence from them both, the precariousness of their situation slowly clarifying itself in the chill evening air.

"We don't really know where Robert would stand if given the choice, but your father may also have reached a point of no return, Em," Corey continued when she didn't respond. "You threw all his plans into a cocked hat and stirred them up until they bore no resemblance to what he wanted for you. How do you know he won't take you at your petulant word and push you completely out of his home and heart?" Emily stared at him and he held her eyes. Clearly she had never faced the possibility that she might have lost her father as well as her mentor for good. Both of them watched each other as if unsure how to move on past the possibilities. Corey finally broke the stillness.

"You're not the only one who'll be adrift. I don't even know where I'll stay when I get home," he said. "I'm not returning to college and I'll need to let a room when we go back. I don't want to open the mansion unless . . . until Father comes home."

"You'll do no such thing, letting a room, Corey. You'll stay at my house with me. There's plenty of space, and a Steinway piano I never touch anymore. We can work together full-time . . . until we're ready to go out to the big concert halls." She wouldn't say out loud that her life was just as unsettled as his. She needed to feel everything was possible. But he had to face the fact that his father might not come home again, and then everything would change forever. She felt that somehow both of their futures depended on getting everything back in order again. Maybe that was the Schubert in her, too. Or maybe she truly couldn't accept that there was nothing she could do to make that happen.

"Do you think your father might help find mine?" Corey asked, almost breathlessly. "I was thinking he could move more freely down here with his diplomatic immunity." He looked at Emily with a desperation he didn't try to hide. She stared back at him, clearly weighing his need for help against her own for autonomy. She shifted her seat on the step with a sigh.

"I'm sure my father would certainly help if he could. But I doubt that will be possible." Her jaw took on a harder edge. "Father's on his way back to England, so I'm told. I got a letter from him two days ago. Robert told him where to find me, apparently." Corey's eyes grew wide, hearing about this communication from Robert Hauss-mann for the first time. "Two Confederate officials heading for Britain on the high seas were picked up and returned here to jail. It's caused an awful ruckus in London, and Father is going back to confer with the queen. It's always something . . ." she muttered under her breath. "Just when we need him . . ." her voice trailed off.

"Would you ask him anyway, Lady Liberty? If this trouble at sea needs negotiating he'll be back here at some point." There was a long silence. Corey looked up at Emily's face through his lashes again. He could see a cloud lift and her expression ease.

"For you and your wonderful father, I'd ask for almost anything, Corey. Anyway, I'm not so brave. It's easier to ask for you than for me," she said. "What a long, tiring week this has been," she added, putting her head back and shutting her eyes as if the subject of her father was closed for the moment. Corey understood her need to move on, and loved looking at her resting again. The vulnerable place under her chin just above the pulse in her throat where the violin left its mark in a light blue bruise was exposed now.

"Long and hard," he nodded. "Transposing, practicing, rehears-ing, more practicing, more rehearsing . . . to say nothing of planning a daring escape for freedom and—"

"And now we're almost done," Emily interrupted quietly, "just as I said we'd be. Someday this very first and hardest performance of our lives will all be a distant memory."

"Right!" Corey tipped his head back, stretching the sharp line of his own chin up toward Emily. He was aware that they probably made a handsome couple sitting on the steps together. "We'll be waiting together in the wings, stage right, to go on at one of the major concert halls of the world . . ."

"The Vienna State Opera or Musikverein, or maybe the Hungarian State Opera House in Budapest . . ." Emily chimed in, her eyes gleaming.

"You're so much better traveled now than I . . . but why only Europe? Can't we perform in America?"

"Certainly we can! But there aren't any great concert halls here yet."

"I'm sure one of our wealthy robber barons will step up to that challenge soon," Corey chuckled.

There was another silence. "The only thing I regret is missing out on my chance for an education, like the ones all you men are guaranteed," Emily murmured, deep in thought.

"Maybe there are more important things, Em. You've mostly educated yourself all your life, and that's the best way. You've battled for your place, your freedom, and your music." Corey looked unbearably sad, a dark cloud suddenly scudding across his face. Emily knew what was hurting him and couldn't let him slip back into the black hole.

"Yes, and you must remember all you have, too, when you're worrying about your father," she said, gently. "I care about him, Corey. He's always been so good to me and made me feel as if I was a full member of your family. At the same time, he treated me as if I had something to offer—I wasn't just a silly, thoughtless girl to him. I think he'll be found unharmed, as Mr. Smith does. We'll get Mr. Smith and Mr. Barnes to help us find your father, if he hasn't been found already. I feel as if that may be so." She reached down to stroke his forehead.

"Possibly . . . but I'll believe that when I see him with my own eyes, when we can all be together again." He pulled her hand from his forehead and, holding it, turned partway around to face her. "I've been wondering," he said, pausing to see if she was paying attention,

". . . if it wouldn't be a good idea for us to get married when we're back home. There'd be no better way to be a family again than to start one of our own." He held his breath, knowing how delicate the balance was between Emily's desire to belong to someone and to be free. He watched her carefully, preparing himself for any move that would show how she might respond. There was no physical change he could discern, but the ease with which she sat looking at him suggested she was not, at the very least, upset by what he'd said.

"Certainly," she answered, smoothly and seemingly without the need to breathe. He let his own breath out at last. Bending to kiss the top of his head, she added, "Even a king needs an old friend now and then, and we two friends need and love each other. But would you understand that this old friend would need to do things a little differently? I would want to live not quite as most other wives do. This lady needs space of her own, Corey."

"Of course," he said without a pause. "Even a king knows a lady needs her liberty."

ACKNOWLEDGMENTS

There can be no doubt that many souls are involved in the successful completion of a novel. I'm delighted to have had the help of so many generous and skilled collaborators for *Certain Liberties*. I see my teammates as inhabiting two distinctly separate categories. One contains the helpmates with very specific skills and roles. This one included my editor, Walter Bode, who somehow summoned up the patience to guide me through the tortuous labyrinth of historical data he's uniquely qualified to navigate. It was an unexpected added benefit to an author as enamored of historical fiction as I am. My proofreader/line editor Dan Janeck also adopted the kind and persevering demeanor of a delighted teacher, suggesting I knew more than I did when he asked my opinion and then leading me where I needed to end up. Katie Holeman, my always cheerful and deeply creative graphic designer, donned many hats, as usual, ensuring that the book looked as good as its narrative promised it would be. And my permanent writing partner, Paul Pitcoff, played all of these roles at once, never losing interest in the characters inhabiting *Certain Liberties*, and thus securing my belief that I had an irrevocable responsibility to bring them to life, no matter how often I lost faith in my ability to do so.

The other category of supporters is made up of all the artists and friends who read, commented, and faithfully followed the progress of the book and its characters over the many years of its creation.

The sustenance these reader/writer/friends offered freely was the nourishment that kept me going. It's why the book is dedicated to The Writers' Table, my motivation in the round that puts King Arthur's group to shame. There's also an unusual collection of spectral contributors from the past who are very much responsible for igniting my fascination in the women of an earlier generation who worked so hard to follow their own rhythms in times that would have had them do otherwise. The lives of my great-aunt, opera singer Louise Homer, Civil War survivor/grandmother Sarah Hardwick Stires, and her sister Mary Hardwick Wood, and my Dutch grand-mother Glover Van Cott of a slightly later era, all of whom taught me much about the definition of liberty.

Thank you, one and all, forever.

Sidney S. Park

BOOK CLUB QUESTIONS

1. How does the nineteenth-century New York setting shape the story? Does the de Koningh mansion seem like another character in the novel, and if so, why?

2. Discuss the series of events that led to Emily's arrival at the mansion. Who abandoned her, and who was there for her? How did her circumstances affect her view of her world throughout the book?

3. Give examples of how Emily's decisions were influenced by her life with Corey. Does she understand what a family is?

4. How did you feel about Emily's decision not to marry Robert Haussmann? How different would her life have been if she'd stayed in Europe with him?

5. Did the men in her life owe anything to Emily? What did it mean for her to be "different" from other women of her time, and how does it affect her life and choices?

6. How is music used in the book? What does it mean to Corey and to Emily?

7. Compare Emily's relationships with her father and Corey's. What does each of them offer her, and what does she represent to them? How about her connections to Professor Haussmann, Johnny Dunne, and Corey?

8. What does Emily learn by watching women of her day and how they're treated? How is her idea of womanhood influenced by her observations and by her life in music? Does her lack of a mother affect her view?

9. Is Emily a victim? Did your opinion of her change over the course of the book?

10. How did you feel about Corey and Emily's participation in the Underground Railroad? And about the ending of the book? Were there still some unanswered questions? What were they?

ABOUT THE AUTHOR

Sidney S. Stark is currently working on a sequel to *Certain Liberties*, her second novel of historical fiction about the life of a professional female violinist at the turn of the twentieth century. She writes personal essays published on her popular blog, **The Unblocked! Writer**, and is the founder of MOMENTUM INK PRESS, a micro-press cooperative printing the books of writers whose work deserves to be shared with discerning readers. Follow her on Facebook, Instagram, Twitter, and on her blog http://theunblockedwriter.com.

Momentum Ink Press is a private micro-press cooperative advancing the work of writers unavailable through traditional commercial publishers. Each book is carefully reviewed by a collection of authors and designers, ensuring an authentic artistic version of the writer's best work. By selecting and reading a Momentum Ink Press book, you are joining and supporting a community of readers and writers dedicated to giving voice to talented authors purposely avoiding the commercialization of art.

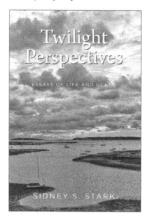

CPSIA information can be obtained
at www.ICGtesting.com
Printed in the USA
BVHW041814210519
548924BV00018B/207/P

9 780997 523959